Wild Young Bohemians

Kate Saunders is a journalist and writer. She has written for the *Sunday Times*, the *Sunday Express*, the *Daily Telegraph* and *Cosmopolitan*, and has contributed to Radio 4's *Woman's Hour*, *Start the Week* and *Kaleidoscope*. She lives in London with her son.

OTHER BOOKS BY KATE SAUNDERS

Night Shall Overtake Us
Lily Josephine
Bachelor Boys
The Marrying Game

KATE SAUNDERS
Wild Young Bohemians

arrow books

Reissued by Arrow Books in 2011

2 4 6 8 10 9 7 5 3 1

First published in Great Britain in 1995 by Century
First published by Arrow Books in 1996

Arrow Books
Random House, 20 Vauxhall Bridge Road,
London SW1V 2SA

www.randomhouse.co.uk

Addresses for companies within The Random House Group Limited can be
found at: www.randomhouse.co.uk/offices.htm

The Random House Group Limited Reg. No. 954009

A CIP catalogue record for this book
is available from the British Library

ISBN 9780099564195

The Random House Group Limited supports the Forest Stewardship
Council® (FSC®), the leading international forest certification organisation.
All our titles that are printed on Greenpeace approved FSC® certified paper
carry the FSC® logo. Our paper procurement policy can be found at:
www.randomhouse.co.uk/environment

MIX
Paper from
responsible sources
FSC® C016897

Typeset in Ehrhardt by SX Composing DTP Rayleigh, Essex
Printed and bound in Great Britain by
CPI Bookmarque, Croydon

*To Bill, Louisa, Etta, Eddie
and Charlotte*

Prologue

1865

The hem of her black silk gown swept up a miniature storm of dust in the lane. She had thrown back her veil, and her close straw bonnet hung by its watered-silk ribbons between her shoulder blades. She had lost one of her tortoiseshell hairpins, and one side of her grey-streaked brown hair straggled loose, but there was nobody to see her here.

In front of her lay the flat Norfolk fields, between high hedgerows and deep ditches. Behind her, an eternal weight on her back, was the solid, unforgiving bulk of Quenville – her house and her prison. The thought of her dead father's wealth, and the elaborate, boastful monument he had built to it, was enough to crush the blood out of her heart. She could walk away to the ends of the earth, and still the vengeful eyes of the stone angel above the porch would follow her, to drag her back.

The princess, for whom so much had been hoped, was old, barren and despised. She inched through her days in the magnificent, empty rooms of her father's castle; struggling with the dreary knowledge that the husband she had once loved had gone through dislike and hatred and had now reached the stage of refusing to notice her. Even the servants, who tormented her with the sound of their laughter below stairs, no longer looked her in the eye.

She was frozen to the point of invisibility. Somewhere, buried fathoms deep inside her, were the slumbering ghosts of her passions – the loves that might have been lavished on a man or a child, if her spirit had not begun its long, pining descent into loveless middle age.

Walking in the lanes around Quenville was her only solace. The country people avoided her, thinking she was crazy. That suited her perfectly. She liked to wander undisturbed, gathering the wild flowers and emptying her mind to the companion she did not have.

'He used to love me,' she muttered to the red cows who blinked at her over the fence, 'but he turned against me.' She giggled, and began to sing in her tinny voice:

> 'My little old man and I fell out,
> I'll tell you what 'twas all about,
> I had money and he had none,
> And that's the way the noise begun.'

Her nurse had sung it to her, years ago, before Quenville, when they had lived above the brewery, and the great dray horses had snorted and stamped under her window. 'But it was better,' she said. 'Now I'm Mariana in the moated grange. I'm aweary, aweary, I would that I were dead. It couldn't be worse than this. Nobody knows how cold he is, how cruel to me. The money was all he wanted.'

A branch of wild briar roses snaked through the hedgerow. She plucked a spray of the hot red blooms and a vicious thorn pierced her ungloved palm. The blood welled up, and she was marvelling over how red it was when she saw him – a man, lying beside the hedge in the flower-studded meadow. A common labouring man.

The cry of alarm died in her throat as she realized he was fast asleep. She was still at first, not daring to move. But as she stared she had the strangest sensation of something melting or thawing in her chest. A great wave of tenderness loosened her fingers and she dropped her roses and stalks of columbine on the grass.

He lay with his curly head in the harebells, his face flushed and childish. His hardy limbs were powerful in their stillness. His chest rose and fell softly. Sometimes, she thought, God liked to show that He could fashion something

viii

perfectly beautiful out of the commonest clay. The man was Endymion, in labourer's boots and homespuns.

And she was the moon goddess, so lonely in the cold night sky, who looked down and saw the shepherd boy asleep on Mount Latmos.

She longed for his lashes to stir, for his hidden eyes to stare into her face. But she dreaded shattering the spell.

You are perfect as you are, she wanted to say. I wish you could rest your head among the flowers for all time.

PART ONE

1987

One

The stone angel reared across the porch of Quenville like a great crucified swan, its mouldering, moss-blinded eyes fixed on the still figure of the handsome gypsy, sleeping below.

In the field on the other side of the dense tangle of weeds and shrubs, not a hundred yards away, the two girls glowed golden in the drowsy afternoon sunlight.

Deep in the earth, the memories sighed and stirred. The first note had sounded; the dance was beginning again.

'Oh, I meant to ask you,' Melissa said, leaning from the bank to snap the ear off a stalk of wheat. 'Are you fixed up for the ball yet?'

Ernestine was wrapping the remains of their picnic in tin-foil, and packing the parcels into the large wicker basket. 'I told you ages ago, I'm going with Cecily. We split the ticket.'

'I meant, have you got a man?'

'Come on, Mel. You know perfectly well I haven't. Where would I find one? They don't grow on trees – well, maybe they do for you.' Ernestine grinned resignedly at her cousin. At school, they had been known as Morecambe and Wise, because she was Little Ern with the short-fat-hairy-legs; the least interesting half of the double act. The faint similarities between them only served to emphasize the fact that Melissa was a beauty and Ernestine was merely pretty. They were variations on the same family theme; one in poetry and one in prose, or two layers in a box of chocolates; one dark, one milk. 'The only offer I got was from Craig Lennox.'

Spread-eagled on her back on the baked earth, Melissa snorted at the sky. 'Craig! He's such a – '

'Well, I know. Feet like canoes, and breath that would take the enamel off a bath. I'm not that desperate.'

'All the same,' Melissa said airily, 'you can't possibly spend the whole evening at a Commem Ball with another girl. Oxford is paved with available men.'

'No it isn't. That's just another dreaming spires myth, like white flannels and plovers' eggs.' Ernestine stood up, to shake the crumbs from the tartan rug. 'Once you've discounted the gays, the nerds and the ones with steady girl-friends, a decent available man at Oxford is so rare, he's practically a tourist attraction.'

'I know one.'

'I dare say.'

'I mean, I know one for you.'

Long experience had attuned Ernestine's ears to the fine gear changes in Melissa's languid, casual voice. She was instantly suspicious. 'What are you after?'

'Oh darling, come on! I'm only trying to put a nice man your way.'

'Bollocks.' Ernestine began, with much grunting, to pull the big garden umbrella out of the hard bank where she had planted it. 'I know that look. You're up to something – and whatever it is, you can forget it. I'm not going to desert Cecily.'

Watching her struggles with the umbrella with mild, detached interest, Melissa began to rub the ear of wheat between her hands. 'Suppose you got a man to take you to the ball. Cecily wouldn't be mean enough to spoil it.'

'I've made the arrangement, and I can't just kiss her off at a day's notice. You think any date with another woman is automatically cancelled by a penis.'

'You could always set her up with Craig.'

'Why should she want him any more than I do?'

'She can hardly afford to be fussy. Not with that face.'

Ernestine yelped with indignation. 'God, you're a bitch.'

'Let's be realistic.' Melissa spoke in tones of kindly regret. 'Cecily's a very nice girl, and we all love her, but she's the most utter dog. If you hang around with her, you'll never pull anyone. And you could, Ernie. That's the point. Don't you want to know who it is?'

'No. You're always trying to palm your rejects off on me.'

Melissa smiled her heartbreaking smile. 'It's Frank Darcy.'

Ernestine stared at her cousin, stunned. 'Frank? But he's yours. I mean, he's going with you. He's been telling everyone for weeks.'

Melissa was suddenly up on her knees. 'I can't go with him. If you keep him out of my face, I'll be eternally grateful.'

'I don't understand.' Ernestine was still gaping. 'How could anyone not want Frank? He's gorgeous. And why on earth would he take me instead of you? The minute word gets out he's free, there'll be a queue around the block.'

'The thing is, I'd rather word didn't get out – that's why I wanted to fix it this weekend, while we're both at home. I've arranged to meet him outside the main lodge tomorrow night, at half-past nine.' She hurried on, over Ernestine's clucks of disapproval. 'I thought you could simply go instead. And make sure he doesn't come looking for me.' Very sweetly, she added: 'You can snog him, if you like. I shan't mind.'

'You're outrageous, that's all. You want poor Frank to find me, when he's expecting you – '

'You're not so bad.'

'Thanks a lot. What about his feelings? You don't give a toss, do you?'

'You fancy him,' Melissa pointed out.

Ernestine's cheeks reddened. 'Who doesn't? That's not the point. Standing him up is rude, and – and cruel.'

'He likes you, you know.'

'Does he? Oh God – '

'You're tempted.'

Ernestine sighed, exasperated. 'I just wish I understood why you're trying to get rid of the sexiest man in Oxford. You never tell me anything.'

Melissa seized her hand and caressed it urgently. 'Please,

darling. It's incredibly complicated – I can't afford to let Frank ruin it all.'

'Ruin what? Oh, look –' She shook her hand away. 'This is the last time, okay? I suppose I'd be better than nobody, wouldn't I?'

'Miles better.'

'He's not the type to cry, that's a comfort.'

'God, no.'

'Simon Reynolds cried, that time after the pink gin party,' Ernestine said accusingly. 'It was the most harrowing evening I've ever spent in my life.' But Melissa had carried the day, as usual. 'You are going to explain to Frank afterwards, aren't you?'

'Absolutely.' Melissa stood up, stretched, and began to amble off through the wheat. 'So glad it's settled. You'll have a wonderful time.'

'Wait!' Ernestine grabbed the picnic basket. 'You haven't told me anything! Are you meeting someone else? Who is he? Wait for me –'

'I must see Quenville, before we drive back.'

'Melissa, we can't – it's not safe! Wait –'

Johnny woke, moaning with hunger, and painfully dragged his bruised limbs into a sitting position on the grass-tufted flagstones.

The heat, which had charred his bones while he escaped through the narrow green lanes, had lifted. The intense blue sky was bleaching to twilight, and the breeze made him shiver. For a second, he was giddy with hopelessness. He had gone three days without food, and God knew where he was. The faded, blistered sign saying 'Quenville. Danger. Keep Out' meant nothing to him. This was the middle of nowhere. If he lay down again, he would die.

But survival was more than a habit. After twenty-three years of clinging to life by his fingernails, it was an addiction. Hugging himself fiercely, as if trying to stoke up the embers of his strength, he leaned against a pillar of the great, crumbling stone porch.

Look on the bright side, he thought, Mick would never find him here. The fat bastard had returned unexpectedly early from lifting handbags at Newmarket, and found Johnny in his trailer, with Karen. Mick was big, and he had beaten Johnny until the stars rained down around him, but Johnny had managed to limp away before the rest of Mick's family could kill him. The clan spread its tentacles across the countryside. They would be out looking for him now, Johnny knew, in every hedge, ditch and caravan site. He cursed his own stupidity – risking life and testicles for half a tab of E and a roll with an ugly old slag like Karen. This was what boredom drove you to.

You're slipping, Johnny. Just when you had a nice thing going.

No, not a particularly nice thing. The familiar heat of rage warmed his starving limbs. A sleeping bag under a caravan propped up with bricks, on the kind of waste ground nobody wanted until the travellers moved in. It had been better than nothing, and Johnny was familiar with nothing. But being used to shit did not mean you had to like it.

He was certainly back to nothing now. All he had in the world were the jeans, boots and leather jacket he stood up in, one cigarette, one box of matches and a knife he had providentially nicked from one of the blokes on the site the previous week. Where to now? Half the biggest, meanest tinkers in East Anglia were after his carcase, and even if he could get anything out of the wankers at the DSS, any tangle with officialdom was risky. The police of several counties were warmly interested in the whereabouts of John Joseph Ferrars (aged twenty-three, long black hair, grey eyes, no fixed address) and captivity was the only thing in the world he feared.

He would have to get to a town where he could build a new client-base. Maybe back Plymouth way – he had grown up there, and still spoke with a strong West Country inflection. If that didn't pan out, he could always turn a few tricks round the dockyard. A fine family tradition, he thought wryly. His mother, before she had scuttled off with a new boyfriend, had worked the docks.

The first thing he had to do was get his bearings, since he had lost his sense of direction while losing himself in the flat Norfolk fields. Johnny looked around him, curiosity stirring. He was sitting under the vaulted roof of a massive stone porch, open on three sides. Behind him was a crazy old wreck of a house, the bones of the roof visible through three collapsed floors.

It was lashed together by thick, spiked stems of wild rose, which strangled the walls like living barbed wire. The black briars were spattered with blooms of intense, bloody scarlet, with a choking perfume that turned his empty stomach. Lumps of striped masonry lay in the tall jungle of weeds that lapped at the house like a leafy sea.

Even in his exhausted state, Johnny had been impressed by the huge stone angel carved above the porch. He had dreamed about it while he lay sleeping. When he could scrape up enough energy to battle through the thorns, he would enjoy examining the carvings in detail.

But food – he had to get food. Wincing as he shifted his aching bones, his survivor's eye roved round in search of anything edible. A brown pigeon fluttered down from the roof, and began pecking at the grass between the sunken flagstones, not six feet from where Johnny lay. It was an elderly, sordid-looking bird, its scaly claws twisted and dis-coloured, but Johnny could not afford to be critical. He became as still and silent as a stone. Over the years, he had learned to silence himself almost to invisibility.

Crawling towards the pigeon, he clamped a hand across its wings and snapped its neck. One convulsion rang through it, and a warm spray of bird-shit squirted up his sleeve. He began tearing the feathers from its meagre breast, too impatient to work out the toughest quills – this bugger had led a rich, full life, by the feel of him. With his stolen knife, he sliced off the bird's head and scooped out its guts.

He made a spit from sticks and a rusty scrap of wire, and built a fire with more sticks and two of his matches. The wood was green, but Johnny could make anything burn – he had once set fire to his school gym with very little more than this. Watery pink blood started to drop, sizzling, into the flames. Johnny watched intently, protecting the fragile blaze with his arms.

Then he froze, sensing the intrusion before he heard rustling in the tall weeds. Rooks and starlings reeled skywards, their wings beating like a round of applause.

Distantly, a female voice called: 'Melissa!'

The grove of weeds trembled.

'Mel, come back.'

The voice, high and strong in the sweet summer evening, came from the unknown continent of Posh. It was an accent as heavily fortified against the likes of Johnny as a stone bunker. He swept his boot through the fire and fled up the back of the ruined porch, easily finding footholds in the ridges of elaborate brickwork. Safely hidden behind the leprous, crumbling head of the stone angel, he watched the weeds below part.

A vision stepped out into long shafts of sunlight filtered through leaves – a tall, slender girl, tenderly fleshed over bones of exquisite delicacy. Her head seemed to droop forward under the weight and gloss of the long brown hair that hung down to her waist. She wore white shorts, plimsolls and a tight white T-shirt which showed the outline of her nipples. Her taut bare skin, toasted golden, made Johnny's teeth ache with the desire to bite it.

Her beauty pierced him with actual physical pain. She was beyond his imagination, worlds removed from the weazen-faced strumpets he used for sex. Pushing back her heavy hair, she raised her face. He saw her long eyes, of a blue unnaturally clean and bright against her tan. Her mouth was grave and childish, and the hollows beneath her cheekbones had a poignant perfection which filled Johnny with desperate, frustrated anger. She was gazing up at the house with calm satisfaction. He crouched behind the angel while her eyes swept over it like searchlights.

'Mel!' the voice called again, nearer now, and breathless, 'Where are you?'

'Here,' Melissa said quietly.

The screen of weeds shivered, and another girl stepped out into the clearing. She was nearly a head shorter than Melissa; compact and gently rounded. Johnny's ravenous senses took in beautiful skin, of a soft, clear whiteness that looked as if it would melt on the tongue. She wore a blue cotton dress, which showed creamy arms and shoulders, and fitted closely round a slender waist and generous breasts. With the attention he had left over from Melissa, Johnny noted that she was not wearing a bra, but that the breasts were firm enough not to need one.

She was carrying a large basket and a calico garden umbrella, which she set down on the grass-tufted flagstones. Her hair, though cut into a halo of glossy curls, was the same colour as the vision's. Her eyes, which were large and round, were of the same improbable pure blue. Fleetingly, Johnny wondered if the two of them were sisters.

'You must be mad. You know how dangerous it is. Mum will have a stroke – she begged us not to come here.'

'Go back and wait for me then,' Melissa said.

Yes, fuck off, Johnny thought. He wanted Melissa alone. He wanted to jump down into the clearing and take what he would never be given. He wanted to punish her for stopping his heart.

The little one, however, showed no sign of leaving. 'You might get hurt. Something could fall on your head – I'm sure there are more bits on the ground since last time.'

'It's still standing. That's all I care about.'

'I'll never understand why you don't sell it.' She folded her arms stubbornly. 'It gives me the creeps.'

Melissa stepped forward, and touched one of the arches of the porch. Johnny imagined her hand sending an electrical impulse up through the stone.

'No!' she cried, with sudden violence. 'God, how disgusting! Someone's been here. Ernie, look –' Her voice became damp and echoing as she moved inside the porch. 'They've made a fire, it's still smoking. Of all the bloody nerve! They must still be here – how dare they?' She sounded furious, near tears.

'I expect we scared them off,' Ernestine said reasonably. 'Though if there is some homicidal pervert hanging around, it's all the more reason to go home and leave him to it.'

'It's disgusting, it makes me sick. I don't care what it costs – Tess has got to do something about the fence. I won't have tramps sneaking into my house.'

Ernestine, still standing doggedly beside her basket, said: 'They haven't done any harm.'

'It's defiling, degrading –' Melissa stepped back into the light. 'There's a ghastly dead bird, and flies everywhere.'

Johnny watched her kneading her fingers together angrily while Ernestine went into the porch to investigate.

Disgusting. Defiling. She made him feel like a speck of shit. His empty stomach burned with fury.

'Pigeon,' Ernestine's voice floated back. 'He's tried to pluck it and cook it, poor thing.'

'Fuck,' Melissa said petulantly. 'It's only a bird.'

Ernestine emerged, wiping her hands on her dress. 'Not the bird. I meant the person who killed it. He must have been starving.'

'Oh, spare me the bleeding heart. If people are hungry, they should get proper work, or sign on the dole. There's always something they can do.'

'Not always,' Ernestine said. 'The welfare net is full of holes.'

Johnny nearly laughed aloud at this. Silly mare, he thought. The concerned type. Reckoned she knew it all.

'This isn't Victorian times,' Melissa said. 'You and Tess are always making up reasons to be depressed.' She began to move away. 'This time she's got to mend that fence. Could I get an electric one, do you think, like the ones they have for cows?'

Into the wall of vegetation she slipped, like a mermaid vanishing into a lagoon. Johnny watched Ernestine gathering her luggage to follow. She walked a few steps, then halted and put the basket down.

Shit, he thought, she's spotted me.

She glanced around speculatively, frowning slightly, then

took a package wrapped in tinfoil out of her basket and placed it in the hollow of a flagstone. She added a red apple, and a half-full bottle of Evian water.

'Ernie!' called Melissa.

'Just coming.' She hurried after her, and the rustlings among the weeds gradually died into silence.

Food. She had left food.

Johnny did not know how long he stayed crouching in his hiding place, staring down at it. She was bringing people to get him. It was a trap. He waited, but the silence and the twilight deepened. He was alone.

The sandwiches inside the foil were weird. The bread was nearly black, and had the texture of a doormat. The ham was all right, but the cheese had a chalk rind and smelled of socks. Johnny wolfishly devoured it all, down to the last drop of water in the bottle.

The night was coming on fast. He scraped together the embers of his fire and lit his last cigarette, savouring each drag – he knew how to concentrate on any brief interval of physical comfort. Only when the cigarette was gone did he begin to think.

He had forgotten Ernestine, and did not care why she had left him food. His mind was saturated with Melissa, and the picture she made among the decaying stones. He imagined her sleeping in some sheltered posh house, as far beyond the reach of the likes of him as the sliver of moon above.

The sky had darkened from lilac to purple. Out in the fields, a fox barked. It suddenly mattered acutely to him that he was out here, utterly alone, with such a great gulf fixed between himself and all the good things lucky people took for granted. Down in the gutter, there was an unspoken law that you survived by accepting what you could get – filthy food, ugly women, inferior drugs, alleys, squats and door-ways. The minute you wanted more, the things you could get turned sour and you were left with absolutely nothing.

Johnny realized now how long he had avoided sights that would make him too angry. He had always lived with the awareness that there was something more – glimpses of the esoteric, the costly, the purely beautiful. Everything symbolized by Melissa. The rage boiled inside him until he felt his head would burst like a volcano.

What had he ever had? He saw the squalor of his past set out as harshly as a court report. Born to a mother who had left when he was a baby – 'She give you a kiss, she give me a fiver, and off she fucked,' as Nan had once told him. Nan was no relation, simply the old woman who had, for some reason, brought him up in her dented trailer, and taken him out begging with her in Plymouth when he was a pretty little boy.

After Nan died, Johnny took to the streets. He had dealt in soft drugs, he had gone on the game, he had stolen pathetic amounts from shops. By the time he was fourteen, he had been a hardened old lag, with a spell in care, a stretch in Borstal and a year in a Catholic institution for delinquent boys.

End of story. He had learned enough to stop getting locked up. He was part of the rabble outside the law, falling in with others like himself, falling out with them and moving on. He would have been more successful if he had been able to bring himself to play in a team, but he had always despised his associates. He knew he was made of better stuff.

For one thing, he was beautiful, though this could be a mixed blessing. The kind of people he lived with saw the sexual act as something to be sold, bartered or simply stolen. He had learned that men who would have killed anyone who called them poofs were perfectly capable of fucking anything – man, woman, child or dog – because it took their fancy. Johnny had become adept at sniffing out when someone wanted him, and calculating his power over them to the last penny. As for women, he had any who wanted him, though he knew they were beneath him and loathed them from his soul. Karen had said admiringly, 'I bet you're a right wicked bastard. You've got such evil eyes.'

The evil eyes were dark grey with spiked black lashes, gleaming through a dirty shock of long, black curly hair, and able to reflect whatever people wanted to read in them. Johnny was tall and bony, with whipcord muscles which seemed ready to start through his thin, pale skin. His stubbled face was thin too, and its fine bones had a delicacy and refinement wholly at odds with its expression of watchful scorn. He wore an imitation gold ring in his left ear. He was the dark stranger of a thousand moist female nightmares; a sexy gypsy with an enslaving, lethal smile.

If this had been all, he would not have stood a chance. But Johny was clever, too. It marked him apart from his illiterate associates like a plague spot. He had taught himself to read and write – without help from his teachers, who had written him off as a no-hoper. The difference between Johnny and the others was that he knew there was more, and he wanted it. He had devoured the meagre school shelves. He had warmed himself beside the radiators of public libraries. He had lifted books from trays outside second-hand bookshops, and sold them to other bookshops when he had finished them.

This was the greatest difference of all, that he had sneaked into a world known to none of his companions; the preserve of the rich. He had loved being clever enough to startle posh people with quotations – hit them between the eyes with Swinburne or Keats, and they twitched as if suddenly gripped by a Masonic handshake. It was as good as saying out loud: you're no better than me, you smug bastard.

But they were, of course.

The question that had been gnawing at his subconscious for months hit him now – If I'm so fucking clever, why am I living like this?

He was handsome, he was smart, he could talk the pattern off wallpaper. And there was something else. In stories, people sold their souls to the devil and riches poured into their laps. Johnny laughed to himself and felt a mighty surge of exhilaration. His most priceless asset was that he did not care. He was already damned – a monster, miles above the tacky sentimentality that held back other people. All right, devil, he thought, you've got my soul. Now give me what I want.

Money, of course. And power. But, above all, a woman good enough to be his missing half, his physical counterpart.

Now he had found her.

Two

'For the last time,' Ernestine said patiently, 'you can borrow my red. You'll look lovely.'

Cecily honked damply into a wad of sodden Kleenex. 'But what about you?'

'I told you. Mum's given me her old coming-out dress.' She bent to open the oven door, and the room filled with the smell of warm chocolate. 'Coming-out is the word, too. I can't believe she ever wore anything that revealing.'

'Well, you've got such a gorgeous figure.' Cecily glanced forlornly from her own bony, galumphing outlines to Ernestine's china-shepherdess curves.

'Stop crying and take my red taffeta, okay? It's the least I can do after involving you in Mel's machinations, and landing you with Craig Lennox.'

They were in the students' kitchen; a claustrophobic tank at the end of the corridor, intended for the brewing of nocturnal tea and cocoa. It was furnished with a dented steel sink, a shelf of crusted pans and a howling fridge. The walls were plastered with faded notices, imploring the young women in the hall of residence not to use the mini-oven for reheating takeaways, but there was a historic tang of curry. The most recent notice was in Ernestine's writing: 'PLEASE do not alter the setting of this oven without asking me. Anyone who ruins one of my recipes will be KILLED. Ernie B.'

Kitchens, even squalid ones, were automatically Ernestine's domain. She had colonized this one with her jars of spices, bags of flour and notebooks full of recipes. She had managed to bash open the little frosted window, and they could now glimpse the college garden outside. It was a rather penitential garden, of seared lawns and gravelled walks, not to be compared with the lush delights of the men's colleges in the heart of Oxford. It looked better than usual, however, on a hot June afternoon. A sluggish breeze moved the sweet-scented fug hovering over Ernestine's tray of chocolate biscuits.

Cecily crammed one into her mouth, and grabbed another before she had finished the first. 'Mmmm. These are fantastic.'

'Go easy, Cec. There's a ton of hash in those.'

'Hash? Oh God!' Illegal substances were a terrifying mystery to Cecily. Dropping the second biscuit, she whispered: 'What will it do to me?'

A dimple appeared in Ernestine's right cheek, as she pursed her lips in an effort not to laugh. 'Nothing, honestly. Don't panic.'

'Suppose I get smelled by a police dog, or something?'

This time, Ernestine could not help laughing. 'I don't think they can smell the contents of people's stomachs.' Cecily's thin lips were peppered with crumbs, which she spat off as if they were radioactive. She was a slouching, defeated person, with wispy dark hair, and small, anxious greenish eyes. She adored Ernestine, and this made her more critical of what she considered to be flaws in her idol's perfection. She frowned censoriously. 'I'm sorry you feel you need this stuff, Ernie.'

'They're for Frank, actually.'

'Oh, I see. Something to sweeten his disappointment when he finds out you're not Melissa.' The other Wild Young Bohemians used to say Cecily had failed A level tact.

Ernestine, however, looked chastened. 'Serves me right if he throws them at me. I never should have agreed to do it.'

'It's obvious why you did,' Cecily said. 'You fancy him. And you know he likes you. What shall I do if this Craig doesn't like me when he sees me?'

Ernestine sighed. 'He's disposed to like anything in a skirt, I'm afraid. He's so far from being an oil painting himself, he'll be thrilled to get a date that walks on its hind legs. I'm sorry I couldn't fix you up with something a bit sexier.'

Perversely, this seemed to cheer Cecily. She giggled through the last of her tears. 'If he's really terrible, I'll ditch him and join you and Frank.'

Ernestine was deftly lining a plastic box with greaseproof paper. 'Don't you bloody dare. This is probably the last time in my life I'll get a date like Frank Darcy, and I intend to keep him to myself.'

'What is Melissa up to, exactly?'

'You can search me. You can turn me upside down and shake me. I haven't a clue. In the fullness of time, her purpose will be revealed.'

Accusingly, Cecily said: 'You always do everything she tells you.'

'No, I don't.'

'I suppose, if you look like she does, your problems seem more important.'

'Well, I can't help getting involved. She's always in some drama or other.'

'Yes, and you're always there to bail her out. She doesn't even have to buy Tampax because she knows you'll get enough for her.'

'We're practically sisters, for God's sake. If we really were sisters, you wouldn't think it at all odd.'

'You should leave her to sort out her own dramas, for once. I bet she'd cope if she had to.'

Ernestine was looking mulish, and preparing to launch into a defensive speech, when Melissa herself breezed in. 'Darling – I might have known I'd find you here.'

Cecily shrank against the wall, as if she had no right to any space in the aura cast by such loveliness. Melissa wore a long tube of slithery, midnight-blue crepe, hanging in one perfect, serpentine line from her bare shoulders to her bare ankles. It was patterned with curlicues of glass beads, which glinted in the tired overhead light like a shifting web of silver. 'Well, what do you think?' She displayed the dress, keeping her exultant, excited eyes pinned to Ernestine.

'It's fabulous.'

'Fabulous,' Cecily echoed miserably.

'I found it in the market. Vintage 1920s, and it doesn't even pong of armpits.'

'Why are you wearing it now? The ball doesn't start for hours.'

'Oh, I've one or two things to do first.' Melissa shook out her long, shining hair, and a gust of her musky perfume blew through the room. 'And I'm afraid I need to borrow thirty quid. Giles says he won't give me anything this time, unless he gets cash.'

'Sure. Save me a lump – I used all my stash in the biscuits.' Ernestine reached for her purse austerely, maddened by Cecily's Cassandra-like expression – the sorrowful prophetess who piously wishes she had been wrong.

Melissa suddenly smiled upon the prophetess; one of her rare, full smiles, which showed a dimple like Ernestine's in her right cheek. For a second, the cousins were, visibly, branches of the same tree. 'Cecily, thanks so much for helping me out tonight. Please don't say anything – you won't, will you?'

'No, no,' Cecily stammered eagerly. Whatever she said about Melissa behind her back, her actual presence reduced her to slavery.

'You're such a pal. What are you wearing?'

Cecily's lower lip buckled. Ernestine said quickly: 'There was a bit of a disaster, but it's fine now. I'm lending her the red Laura Ashley. Why don't you go and try it on, Cec?'

Cecily hurried off towards Ernestine's room.

Melissa asked: 'What disaster?'

Ernestine, with her mouth full of biscuit, was in paroxysms of silent laughter.

'Ernie, you're stoned. Deary me, I've never met anyone who giggles so much under the influence.'

Ernestine mopped her steaming eyes. 'She asked her mother to send her evening dress, and the silly cow sent the wrong bag. And when Cec opened it, she found this utterly unbelievable Crimplene suit – '

By now Melissa was hysterical too – they had always set one another off.

'Oh, how typical,' she sighed in ecstasy, wiping her eyes. 'Why are unlucky people so funny?'

'She let out this great scream, and we all rushed in to see what had happened, and there she was lying on the bed in floods. Thank God I had the other frock – though Cec was in such a state, I'd have given her anything and gone to the ball in a binbag. I just felt so mean.' Still giggling guiltily, she clapped a lid on the biscuit box to shield herself from temptation.

'I feel a bit of a fool, not knowing what's going on – why I've got to take care of your reject, and palm poor old Cecily off with mine.'

'She'll like him. They're admirably suited.'

'Oh, why? Because they're both – well, a bit – '

'Ugly,' Melissa supplied airily. 'On the scale of sexiness, they occupy exactly the same notch.'

'People don't want someone from the same notch,' Ernestine said wistfully. Frank Darcy was so high on the sexy scale, he flew right off the top. Why should he cast his famous blue eyes down to her level? She was not bad. The point was – the point always was – that she was not Melissa. 'Can't you tell me what you're up to?'

'Ernie, it's poised on a knife edge. It's just got to work.'

'What has?'

'Oh darling, I'm so happy. I think I'm about to meet my destiny.'

Ernestine snorted. 'You always say that.'

'No, this time it's different. I had an incredible dream last night. I was going towards Quenville, and it was all restored, with every window full of light. I can't describe the colours, the gorgeousness – '

'Phooey,' said Ernestine.

'No, you don't understand. It rode on the fields like a galleon at anchor, and I belonged there. I was coming home, to a missing part of myself. And I'll tell you something really amazing –' she lowered her voice – 'when I woke up, I was wet. You know. I was on the point of coming. I actually had an erotic dream about a house.'

Ernestine was laughing again. 'Good thing you woke up, before you found yourself being poked by a chimney or something.'

'Seriously.' Melissa took her hand. She liked to squeeze and caress her cousin, as if moulding Plasticine, when she was working out one of her plans. 'It was a revelation, telling me something about tonight. I suddenly saw what I had to do. And with whom.'

'Are you in love, then?'

Melissa considered this. 'Let's say I might be. After tonight.'

Frank Darcy ran his index finger around the inside of his wing collar, and looked again at the watch under his immaculate cuff. He was ridiculously early. He hoped the syrupy June heat would lift a little. The tuxedo looked great, but he was already sweating out the starch in his shirt, and he did not want Melissa to write him off as some red-faced meatbrain. Elegance and poetry were called for. Melissa, shimmering in the magical robe of the dreams he had woven around her, was about to drift down to earth into his waiting arms. Queen rose of the rosebud garden of girls.

With the light of anticipation glowing in him, he watched the noisy groups charging into the college through the porter's lodge behind him. Funny, he thought, how posh Brits looked so alike. They all seemed to have pink faces, bony noses and large, luminous, pale eyes. The boys had locks of light brown hair flopping coltishly over their foreheads. The girls wore their light brown hair long, swept back from their fresh, pleased faces without partings. Nearly all had a habit of raking their fingers through it and tossing their heads. Several of them smiled at Frank as they passed, and their callow escorts called out, 'Way to go!' or 'Yo!'

Frank smiled back, thinking it sweet. It had once annoyed him when British people thought they knew how Americans should behave. Now he had his Wild Young Bohemians, and if they understood him, who else mattered?

He also thought it sweet that the dinner jackets of the

boys were so limp and ill-fitting, bearing ghostly witness to corpulent paters who spilled soup on their lapels. You would have had to chloroform Frank before you got him into his old man's tux. His was made to measure, breathing money from its every silk-lined fold. His mother had provided it, so he could escort her to a-thousand-dollar-a-plate charity dinners, while the old man was otherwise engaged. The Rolex had been provided too, when he graduated from Yale. Frank would far rather have had the money, and considered the watch an insult – one of their dreadful, unsubtle hints about the kind of person he ought to become. Still, such things had their uses. English people could mooch about like hoboes, but they expected Americans to look rich.

He surveyed the pleasure grounds in which he would spend the next nine enchanted hours. The ancient college had been turned over to youth and festivity, and made him think of a faded tapestry swarming with live butterflies. Silver balloons floated on the entrance to the lodge. Beyond the cloisters, he could see a striped marquee, and strings of Japanese lanterns, pallid in the mellow sunshine. More silver balloons bobbed in the Main Quad. Half a dozen couples were leaping on a red and yellow bouncy castle; screaming with laughter because one of the boys was wearing a kilt. Frank had learned enough about British formal occasions to know there would always be at least one guy in a kilt, with a swinging sporran and a knife down one sock. The fact that he no longer found it bizarre was surely a sign that he was getting acclimatized.

A juggler, in a medieval jester's costume, was working his way across the grass, tossing three spangled clubs in hypnotizing rhythm. A single balloon had broken its moorings, and slowly soared heavenwards, a burning speck in the cloudless sky. A gang of girls brushed past Frank in a rustle of taffeta petticoats, momentarily embracing him in a cloud of clashing perfumes.

This was bliss; the essence of Oxford he had conjured up at his desk in New York, and strained to capture ever since. The streets of this Oxford were truly paved with gold, he thought – the golden lads and girls of the University, who milled around him, shrieking like birds of paradise.

Lovingly, he recalled the notes he had scribbled that afternoon, while reading Chaucer's *Romance of the Rose*: 'A young poet enters a garden, where he meets the figures of Gladness, Mirth and the God of Love himself, among dazzling flowers and flocks of dancers.'

> So faire they weren, alle and some;
> For they were lyk, as to my sighte,
> To angels that ben fethered brighte.

And now the God of Love was poised to make his longings flesh. The picture forged by his imagination melted into the scene around him – the amber light, the soft grey stone of the college buildings, the emerald lawns, the feathered angels who wore the glory of it all as lightly as the summer weather. His heart gave a great throb of delight that he was part of it. Where else, in all the world, could you step into a living poem?

Frank had often wondered what genetical quirk had plonked him in the midst of such a determinedly unpoetic family. The other Darcys were strangers to throbs of delight – to throbs of any nonphysical kind – and found Frank's passion for literature deeply perplexing.

His appearance was at odds with it, for one thing. He towered over six feet. His broad-shouldered, narrow-hipped body was hardened to granite by jogging, rowing and English football. He was an all-American beauty, of the most aggressively healthful kind. Health shone on his crisp dark hair, and gleamed on teeth which could have been shown in his orthodontist's front office as an advertisement. Rude animal health bloomed in his crinkled, humorous blue eyes. When he had worked in his senator uncle's Washington office the previous year, he had been nicknamed 'Clark Kent'; Superman imperfectly disguised in a suit and tie.

The Oxford girls he had to beat off with a stick could see

no further than his exotic muscles. Melissa alone seemed to sense, inside the spectacular body, the dauntless romantic on fire with the sweets of literature. Melissa was also reading English, and she was the only woman he had ever met who could discuss his beloved Tennyson, Arnold and Browning – especially Tennyson – with perfect knowledge and empathy.

Frank's parents thought poetry should be taken in very small doses. It was the province of unwashed and impoverished intellectuals, not the business for a scion of the most respected Catholic clan in New York. The Darcy money was old enough to have obliterated the shamrock and potato from their coat of arms. Frank's mother, Patricia Conway Darcy, lunched and dined for liberal but socially irreproachable causes, and entertained formidably at her Fifth Avenue apartment and house in East Hampton. His father, Francis senior, ran the city's richest and oldest law firm. There were many male Darcys, and they were all lawyers, politicians or both. Their sons were groomed for mahogany desks and Gucci briefcases before they could walk. With this in mind, the most delicate care had been lavished upon Frank's education.

But Frank would not fit the mould. He dreaded turning into his parents. Their marriage had been dead for years, and existed in a cryogenic state of nullity, like Walt Disney's corpse. Patricia was a fanatic and a snob – she would go down on the Pope to be photographed beside him in her diamonds – and Francis senior was an old letch who kept a string of executive blonde mistresses. Francis Xavier Darcy Junior had other aims and yearnings.

Poetry and puberty hit him together. He paced the lawns of East Hampton reciting Tennyson aloud. He jogged in Central Park with his blood racing to the rhythms of English verse. To his father's annoyance, he insisted on studying literature at Yale, and would not hear of law school. Frank's soul belonged, he felt, in England. Before he applied for his Rhodes Scholarship, he had started his life's work – a novel about an American student who is transformed by the love

24

of an English rose. A real Tennysonian heroine; beautiful, ethereal, enigmatic.

'It's a pose,' his sister, Breda, had told him scornfully, when she found the manuscript in his sock drawer. 'It's not an English woman you want – you won't find her over there. Or anywhere on this planet. Your Great American novel is the Great American wet dream.'

'Oh, you're a critic for the *Times* now, are you, to add to your other talents? Crawl off and die, bitch.'

'Excuse me, Mr Hemingway. You know nothing about women. Try writing with both hands on the keyboard, for a change.'

Frank grinned to himself whenever he remembered this exchange. His big sister had always been a thorn in his side, held up by their parents as Ms Perfect – great grades, neat clothes, suitable Catholic boyfriends. She had matured, without a second's friction, into a star Harvard graduate and thoroughly deserving occupant of a desk in the family firm. She had done everything they wanted. She had not thrown all her prospects after an immature fantasy about Oxford. Yet it had been perfect, uncomplicated Breda who raised the family storm that blew Frank to his heart's desire.

They had been staying with Aunt Geraldine, at her weathered clapboard house in Martha's Vineyard. The morning had begun with yet another argument about going to Oxford. Dad had lost it, of course. 'Don't expect any money from me, pal. I don't pay for you to waste your time.'

Frank had paced the beach, gazing out at the Atlantic rollers, brooding angrily on his vision of dreaming spires.

Later that day, at the grim institution of brunch – at which they all sat fuming while supposed to be relaxing – Breda had swept the far-off dreaming spires into his lap. Frank treasured the memory. The sea winds had been blowing grey sand into the hammocks on the porch, and tugging at the rough grass in the dunes. Watery sunlight had struck the glass jug of orange juice. They were gathered around coffee and muffins, the perfect Ralph Lauren family.

Then the bombshell. Breda had said: 'Mother, Daddy, I want you to celebrate with me. I'm gay.'

They had reacted with eerie predictability, as if reading from a script. Mother, in her pressed jeans and polished deck shoes, had croaked: 'Oh my God.'

Dad had stared, guppy-mouthed, his eyes bulging in his ruddy face.

Frank had used the pause before the storm to say, savouring the exquisite pleasure of it, 'Breda, I want you to know that if this makes you happy, I'm happy too.'

'Thanks, Frank.' She had looked startled but slightly misty about the eyes, like a person in a mini-series.

Dad had found his voice, and the blustering began. Frank watched, eating muffins. Seeing the bluster directed at someone besides himself had been an interesting novelty.

'What are you talking about? Jesus Christ, why am I paying that damn analyst?'

'Nancy,' Breda had supplied, in a voice dripping with meaning.

Another lull, followed by a mighty bellow that raised seagulls for miles, and caused Scooter, the dog, to hide under the porch until nightfall. The revelation that Breda was having a lesbian affair with her analyst instantly pushed every other Darcy drama out of the headlines, and Frank had known there would be no more objections to Oxford.

He was free.

But Oxford itself, so long wished for, had been a grievous disappointment at first. He had landed at Heathrow airport, and found a small, dirty, meagre country, pressed against the damp countryside by a heavy grey sky, and populated by mute people with suspicious stares. The sweet city of dreaming spires squatted drearily in grey vegetation, a place of bicycles, rain and exclusion. Frank walked in dank cloisters with uneven stone floors, constantly battered by the bass clang of bells. He was unpleasantly reminded of churches, and the legendary architecture of the colleges was cancelled out by the overwhelming smell of boiled cabbage, lingering sourly over the dining rooms.

Christ Church, his own college, could not fail to impress him. Frank had simply stood and gaped at the honey-coloured expanse of the Great Quadrangle, dominated by Tom Tower. His room, on the other hand, was a dump. He could not believe it. Wooden panelling defaced by pock-marks and scratches, dilapidated furniture, and the bathroom – a third world bathroom, plastered with coy notices about gentlemen please lifting the seat – three floors away.

And the food! He sat in Hall (not dining room, Yankees were to note) on his first night, listening to a Latin grace with half an ear while staring in stunned disbelief at a lump of cow-shit bathed in brown gloop.

'Excuse me,' Frank had said, to the black-gowned young man sitting next to him at the long refectory table. 'What the hell do you call these?'

The young man had replied: 'Rissoles,' and not addressed another word to Frank for the rest of the meal.

Rissoles. Following by a 'pudding' of similarly turdy aspect, awfully veiled in canary-coloured custard.

'Oh God,' the boy opposite had groaned cheerfully, 'prunes again.' And eaten them with noisy relish.

The Hall vibrated with a deafening din of cutlery, crockery and baying male voices. Where these came from was a mystery, since Frank could not see anyone actually talking. They certainly did not talk to him.

It had taken weeks to break through that famous British reserve. When he did, however, he found his fellow students far more in awe of him than he was of them, and disarmingly anxious to admire him. He had begun to enjoy the idiosyncratic style of Oxford tutorials and lectures, once he grasped that their air of austere indifference actually covered a love of literature as consuming as his own. They treated the language of Shakespeare and Milton like old money – securely possessed and taken for granted.

He also enjoyed the mild eccentricities of the more flamboyant undergraduates – such as Paul Dashwood, star of the Dramatic Society, who called everyone 'my dearest old darling' and wore blue mascara, but was, mysteriously, not a faggot. There was Giles Ross, too, an Old Etonian of great glamour and charm, deferred to by everyone.

Frank deferred with the rest, until Giles made a 'professional' call as the university's leading drug dealer, and kindly offered a welcoming free sample of hash. 'I don't do smack, because it's dangerous and too common for words. But if you want anything that can be sniffed, smoked or snorted, up to and including Harpic, I'm your man.' God, even the drug scene was refined over here. Frank, who disapproved of hard drugs, tried not to be impressed that Giles numbered an earl and two viscounts among his customers.

Giles was not to be avoided, however. Frank liked him too much, and he was – oddly enough – Will Ivery's best friend.

Will, the young man who had said 'Rissoles' on his first evening, had become Frank's closest friend at Oxford. He had been at Eton with Giles. He had inherited a large fortune of several million pounds, which he could not mention without turning brick-red and stammering. He was shy, kindly and faintly goofy, with the air of being splendid in a crisis, should one occur. Frank found the blushing and the stammer extremely endearing. Conversations with this male English rose made him feel like Robert Taylor in *A Yank at Oxford*.

And it was because of Will that the Wild Young Bohemians had been founded, adding the grace note to Frank's Oxford experience. Little by little, the place had been working under his skin. He fell in with the rowing set, easily won an oar in the college eight, and learned to drink immense glasses of warm brown beer. He founded and coached a college baseball team – the Christ Church Prunes – which practised every Sunday in the Meadow. He was on friendly terms with the other men on his stair, and absolutely bombarded by nice girls who wanted to feel his biceps.

She, the English Rose, was not among them. But when love struck, it came suddenly, like a bolt from the blue Oxford sky – love for a city, a group of friends and a woman, in perfect chemical fusion.

It came together on a brilliant spring day, at an impromtu picnic in Christ Church Meadow. The occasion was a case of champagne, which Giles had been given for a bad drugs debt. He had invited Dashwood and his leading lady, Bella Fogarty. Bella had brought three girls from her college – a plain and rather tiresome creature named Cecily Wilton, and a pair of cousins who plucked out Frank's romantic heart before he knew it had gone.

Ernestine and Melissa. Ernie was the little one, pretty as a peach and sweet as marzipan, who had arrived with a hamper full of food. Melissa was one of the reigning belles of the university; of a miraculous loveliness, seeming to exist in an invisible bell jar, to be looked at but not touched.

Frank, as he lay on the damp grass, performing his party trick of cracking walnuts with his bare hands, was high on the sheer, ridiculous beauty of it all. Sunlight lay upon the trees and made the venerable stones appear soft to the touch. He was reeling and giddy with gratitude that he belonged here. He wanted to own Oxford, to eat it, to inhale it. This was the moment when he realized he was never, never going to leave.

Ernestine unpacked her hamper, and he burst out Tennysonianly:

> '– a dusky loaf that smelt of home,
> And, half cut-down, a pasty costly made,
> Where quail and pigeon, lark and leveret lay – '

The others laughed at his accent, and Ernestine said: 'Veal and ham, actually. They were out of larks.'

Melissa's gentle voice murmured: '"Like fossils of the rock, with golden yolks/Imbedded and injellied."'

Dear God, this was the sign. He had found her. His Pre-Raphaelite princess, distant, virginal yet sensuous. It made him itch to get back to his novel.

He groaned afterwards, to think of the daftness of his behaviour. Fortunately, everyone else except Melissa had been as tipsy as he was.

Giles sang his own version of the 'Eton Boating Song':

> 'Jolly boating weather, and a hay-harvest breeze,

Take me behind the chapel, give my bottom a
squeeze.
Oh, oh, great heavens, I've never seen balls like
these!'

'Don't l-listen to him, Frank,' Will said. 'You'll get completely the wrong idea.'

'No you won't,' shouted Dash. 'They're all poofs at Eton.
I'm profoundly sorry for their wives.'

'This has been the best afternoon of my life,' Ernestine
announced. 'We ought to do it once a week.'

'Absolutely – why not?' Giles demanded. 'Who better
than us? Are we not the most brilliant, the most beautiful,
among the most brilliant and beautiful in the world? Are we
not poised to take that waiting world by storm?'

'You'll be doing it from a prison cell,' Will said, 'if you're
not careful.'

'Will, what a terrible worrier you are, to be sure. I hereby
found the most exclusive dining club in Oxford. The – what
are we called?'

'The Wild Young Bohemians,' Frank said. 'Dedicated to
hedonism and high living.'

Dash, very unsteadily, stood up. 'Fellow Wild Young
Bohemians, let me propose a toast. To youth, hedonism,
brilliance and beauty. May they never fade.'

The Bohemians held their inaugural dinner the following
week, in the poky house in Jericho which Dash shared with a
gloomy pair of Marxists who were always out on Tuesdays.
Their disapproval of the goings-on lent a spice of decadence
to the proceedings. Ernestine provided a feast of watercress
soup, roast duck and chocolate trifle. Dash gave his toast
again, and began the club's tradition of smashing their wine
glasses against the Marxist posters on the walls. The Wild
Young Bohemians were born.

Frank had never been happier in his life. The club were
close-knit, but he began to suspect that Melissa was paying
him special attention. It was, admittedly, difficult to tell. She
treated all three of them – Frank, Will and Giles – as her

special adorers. Giles played along humorously, Will with extreme diffidence, and Frank with naïve delight.

'You're the three knights of the Grail,' Melissa said one evening, when Dash and Bella had retired upstairs and Cecily and Ernestine were washing up the kitchen. 'Sir Bors, Sir Percival and Sir Galahad.'

'Which is which?' Giles asked. He was rolling her a fat joint.

'Well, you're Sir Percival, I think. The Holy Fool.'

'Thanks a lot.'

'Will is Sir Bors, conscientious and great-hearted. And Frank is Sir Galahad. His strength is as the strength of ten, because his heart is pure.'

This was what gave Frank the courage to ask Melissa to the Commem Ball in one of the other colleges at the end of term. All the Bohemians had agreed to meet there informally, but the fact that the tickets – a hundred pounds each – were sold in pairs made some coupling necessary.

She had agreed. He had jogged round Addison's Walk at twice his normal speed, with the 'Hallelujah Chorus' belting out on his Walkman. Though it was too early to be in love with a woman he did not really know, he was madly in love with the woman he imagined Melissa to be.

Sir Galahad was unfashionably early at the ball. If he was not careful, he would start to look like what Will and Giles quaintly called an 'ah-sole'. He studied the printed programme, to see what they would get for his money.

Champagne reception in the large marquee.
Jazz orchestra in the Buttery.
String quartet in the Rose Garden.
Medieval Chansons D'Amour in the Senior Common Room.
Midnight supper in the Cloisters.
Bryan Ferry in the large marquee.
Perry Wooston-Granger's All-Nite Disco.
Breakfast in the Long Room.

Survivor's Photograph in the Main Quad.

Frank would certainly do his best to make the photo. He liked the idea of himself as a gilded youth in the summer dawn, with Melissa on his arm.

Meanwhile, he watched the other loiterers round the lodge. Here was Cecily, poor haddock, wearing burgundy taffeta too tight at the waist and too baggy at the bust, trooping off to the marquee with a boyfriend who looked like Pinocchio with zits. Frank waved to her kindly – she irritated him, but God, that face – and was glad to see that she was beaming with happiness.

'My dearest Frank, what a toothsome suit. You look as if you were about to accept an Oscar.'

It was Dash, not arriving so much as making an entrance. He was a small, slight creature, with untidy dark hair, and the face of an intelligent monkey. His voice was deep and mellifluous, with rolling Shakespearian flourishes.

'Shit,' Frank said, laughing. 'What have you come as?'

Dash was wearing a purple velvet smoking jacket with a matching tasselled cap. He struck attitudes with the slightly wearing air of one who knows he must submit to admiration. His *Hamlet*, in which he had directed and starred, had closed at the Playhouse the previous night; the sensation of the term.

He was a star, a genius; pointed out by other undergrads as he sauntered along the Corn, or held loud, darlingy conversations with his friends in Blackwells. Bella, almost as sensational as his Gertrude, clutched his hand proprietorially. She was a head taller than the genius, and had a bronzed, haughty face, like an old Roman coin.

'Frank. Do join us, when Melissa comes.'

'Sure,' Frank said, intending to do nothing of the kind.

They strolled away through the parting crowd, their eyes glazed with the modest pretence of anonymity.

Frank, tired of standing around, was relieved to see Will. He had his hands in his pockets, and he was weaving in and out of the cloisters, blinking rapidly – a sign that he was anxious. Will was tall and gangling, with pinkish blonde hair, heavily freckled fair skin, and very pale blue eyes with startling yellow lashes. When he caught sight of Frank, the freckles were submerged in a swift, painful blush. His transparent complexion telegraphed his emotions in sudden, damson rushes of blood.

'William, old bean.'

He staggered slightly as Frank slapped him on the back. 'Hello – you are waiting for someone, then?'

'Sure am. Didn't I tell you?'

'Is she l-l-late?'

'Just a trifle.'

'Well, I'm awfully glad. I mean, that you found someone. I didn't think you'd have any trouble. You're being pretty good about it, I must say.'

'Oh, waiting won't kill me.'

'She swore you wouldn't m-mind. Are you sure you don't? I wanted to square it with you first, but there wasn't time.'

'What? Sorry, I don't quite follow your –'

'Glad you got the fifty quid back, anyway.' He shot back his cuff to check his watch. 'God, she'll go mad if I keep her waiting. Thanks, Frank. See you later.' He hared off through the cloisters, as if the police were after him.

Before Frank could work out what on earth he was talking about, he felt a hand on his arm.

The hour had come. He turned to claim Melissa – and found himself looking down into the sympathetic, slightly defiant face of her cousin Ernestine.

'Hello.'

'Ernie. Hi.'

He was deeply confused, not only because she was not Melissa. Ernestine was laced into a strapless ballgown of delphinium silk that made her eyes miraculously blue. A full skirt ballooned from the narrow waist. The fitted bodice displayed her bare shoulders and breasts like alabaster. He thought he had digested the fact that Ernestine – the lesser cousin – was extremely pretty in her way. And he had some-how assumed that her way was rather harmless and childish. There was nothing childish, however, about this deliciously sculpted little siren. In fact, for a second or two, he had not recognized her.

They stared at one another. She kept her hand on his sleeve.

'I'm awfully sorry about this, Frank.'

'Why is everybody sorry? Where's Melissa?'

Ernestine was carrying a plastic box under one arm. She offered it with a smile more sparkling and zesty than any-thing he had seen on the face of her cousin. 'Have a biscuit.'

Johnny froze with the dart poised in his hand.

He had found her. Not a vision. Really her.

Insubstantial behind the thick veil of smoke, she stood in the doorway of the pub, arching her long neck like a swan.

A wild laugh bubbled in the pit of his stomach. You had to hand it to the devil – he was efficient. She had magically appeared, in the last place he had expected to find her. The Railway Inn was a loud, dirty pub, on the least select fringe of Jericho, full of loud, dirty and – probably – dangerous people. Johnny had recognized his own sort, and cased the joint for friends or relations of Mick before daring to order his pint.

And here was Melissa, elegant beyond imagination, buy-ing cigarettes from a machine on the wall.

Early that morning he had woken in the ruined house with his head full of her. In the village, he had learned that she was to be found in Oxford. Switching on his charm, which was considerable when he put his mind to it, he had hitched lifts cross-country in a van and two lorries. He had arrived at the Oxford Sainsbury's at lunchtime, and lifted a purse from a handbag hanging on a trolley. The baby sitting on the trol-ley had started to squeal, but Johnny was well out of the door by then.

This was his first visit to Oxford, and the weather was so pleasant that he spent the afternoon as a tourist, wandering around the colleges and parks, leaving a trail of takeaway cartons behind him. The place made him angry because it was beautiful and he was an outsider. He stared at the groups of young men and women, blocking up the pavements as if they owned the place, and felt weighed down by the knowledge of a thousand things never guessed at by these innocents.

Eventually, he had ended up in The Railway, drinking lager and playing darts, wondering where to go next. And here she was.

She left, and Johnny dropped his dart to hurry after her. In the still summer twilight, her tall figure was a shadowy column of blue, flitting across the shabby streets with languid grace.

He followed her to a seedy café, with clumsy toadstools painted on its steamed-up windows. Inside, he was hit by an overpowering smell of hash. The woman behind the counter, who had long grey hair straggling down the back of her Indian cotton dress, had a joint clamped between her lips. Flakes of ash dropped from the end, into the tub of red stew she was stirring on the gas. The menu was chalked on a blackboard behind her: 'Ratatouille. Carrot cake.'

The small tables were crammed with elderly hippies in peace bells and fringed jackets. In bizarre contrast, very clean young men in dinner jackets and bow ties came and went around a table in the corner.

'Giles,' Melissa said. 'Thank God you're still here.'

A boy in evening dress, with a magnificent waistcoat of crimson brocade, was smoking hash in a ten-inch clay pipe, and playing dominoes with a group who looked like the cast of *Hair*. He had light brown curls, worn romantically long around the face of a six-year-old choirboy – sticking-out ears, a smile that showed pink gums, wide blue eyes and a turned-up nose.

'Darling,' he said. 'Wait till I've finished the game.'

The 'darling' put Johnny on hot thorns of jealousy and curiosity. Was this Melissa's boyfriend?

It was not.

35

She asked: 'Did you save me some?'

'Of course, of course. But I really can't take sex this time, darling – even with you. I have more blow jobs than I know what to do with, and only one willy. So I'm afraid it'll have to be cash. Do not ask for credit as a refusal often offends.'

Melissa dug down the front of her dress, and pulled out a wad of notes. She carried no handbag. 'Here.'

'God, they're warm. Forgive me if I count them.' He flicked through the notes, as practised as a bank teller. 'Honestly. You're a hundred short.'

'Don't be mean. The rest is coming.'

'All right, all right.' From his breast pocket, he drew a lump of rocky wrapped in clingfilm. He added the money to a huge roll in his waistcoat pocket. 'I can afford to be generous. Business is absolutely booming tonight.'

'Shut up shop and come with me.'

'Yes, O Queen. No need to drag me by the scruff of the neck.'

Melissa waited, serene and scornful, while Giles handed his pipe to the woman at the counter and said his farewells. Finally, he took Melissa's elbow, and steered her out into the street.

Johnny slipped after them, staying close enough to hear their conversation.

'God, Giles, you hang out in some horrible places.'

'Oh, it's not so bad. All the same, you shouldn't be hanging about round here – not on your own, and certainly not with a bra-full of cash. It isn't really safe.'

She laughed. 'Nothing ever happens to me.'

'No, it doesn't seem to, does it? Perhaps sticking to you will bring me luck. I've had another row with the Bastard. He's cut off my allowance again. And for all he knows, it's my only source of income.'

'I'll never understand what you and your father find to quarrel about,' Melissa said, smiling.

'You think he's the perfect liberal and all-round cool dude, because you only see him on television. In real life, I promise you, he's a thoroughly conservative paternal shit-bag.'

'He's rather sexy, your dad,' she teased.

'If you like old sixties farties in corduroy suits.'

The streets leading out of Jericho towards the centre of Oxford were narrow and gentrified. Johnny fell a little way behind Melissa and Giles, keeping to the shadows cast by front hedges.

On the wide thoroughfare of St Giles, he dared to get closer. The pavements were crowded with tolerant locals, curious tourists and braying young things in evening dress. The ancient stonework glowed golden in the last of the balmy June sunlight. Johnny took a step nearer his quarry, and almost cannoned into them when Melissa suddenly halted, to contemplate a Gothic tower in the middle of the road.

'The Martyr's Memorial,' she murmured. 'Scott – such a genius. I can never get over the way it refers so seamlessly to everything around it, yet manages to be so much of its own time.'

'Of course, it's your period, isn't it?' Giles said indulgently.

'Some of his work is awfully like Seddon's – the man who designed my house. You must come down and see it some day.'

Johnny, hovering just in earshot behind them, was instantly alert at the mention of the house.

Giles, kind but not much interested, searched his pockets until he unearthed a large joint. He lit it. 'I thought the place was a ruin.'

'Yes, but you can still see the details.' She took the joint from Giles, dragged heavily, and handed it back. 'The spirit survives.'

'Melissa, you are so sweet about that house of yours. Your holy reverence for Victorian Gothic whatnots reminds me you're not such a nasty, superficial girl after all.'

'You mark my words, I'll restore it one day, and you'll know the meaning of poetry in bricks and mortar. It might happen sooner than you think.'

Giles grinned, taking her arm. 'Why, have you found the famous buried treasure?'

'You can laugh. Ernie doesn't believe in it either – but I know it's there.'

'I'll come to Quenville and find it, darling. Then you can cut me in for a percentage.'

They were moving again, sauntering arm in arm towards the insistent throb of disco music, which was grinding out behind a high college wall. Johnny dodged after them, straining for another reference to buried treasure. This hint of mystery, bound up with Melissa and the ruin she was so possessive about, gave an edge of wild urgency to his desire for her. He would not lose her again.

The porter's lodge was blocked by two burly security guards, one of whom had an Alsatian growling beside him. Melissa and Giles walked past them without hesitation, glorious in their assumption that they belonged.

Through the vaulted tunnel of the lodge, Johnny had a tantalizing glimpse of lights, balloons, and blithe revellers in evening dress.

Shut out. He could have roared and stamped, revealing his devilish nature in a frustrated tantrum.

Wrestling down his anger, he ducked out of sight of the guards and skirted round the wall, looking for a gap. The bricks were built high and smooth, and a wave of barbed wire rolled along the top. Climbing in meant risking capture, and he had to be invisible. If he could only melt into the scene, and walk through the lodge, as Giles and Melissa had done . . .

A single figure in a dinner jacket trotted out of the gate and along the deserted street. He was a tall, stooping youth, neverously fingering the spots on his chin and plucking at his bow tie.

Humming to himself, the youth ducked down a narrow alley in the shadow of the high, blind wall. Johnny idly watched him going to a bicycle chained to the iron railings, and rummaging for something in the saddlebag. In the light of a single, feeble streetlamp, he examined the object he had been looking for – a packet of condoms. He appeared to be reading the instructions.

Johnny was suddenly gripped by an idea so brilliant and so wildly hilarious that he nearly howled aloud at the moon.

'Whims and caprices,' Frank said, striding along the cloister with his mouth full. 'I never met a woman who had those before. Shit. I hate to look like a fool.'

The couples flitting across the quad shimmered in the grey twilight. Muffled by the furred hush of historic peace, which no amount of revelry could entirely destroy, music hammered at them from several directions – the bass thud of the disco in the large marquee, the effete carolling of the medieval singers in the Senior Common Room and the sweet drone of the string quartet in the Rose Garden.

Ernestine had to canter to keep up with Frank's long strides.

'I don't think you look like a fool,' she ventured.

He halted abruptly, bending his handsome head towards her. 'I tell you what, Ernie, it has to be a game. Can you honestly tell me she didn't want to sleep with me?'

They had been going over the same piece of ground for half an hour, and Ernestine was getting bored. She sometimes felt as if she spent half her life listening to the outraged monologues of Melissa's rejected swains.

'I assumed she did.'

'And am I supposed to believe, after all those lingering looks and stuff about Sir Galahad, that her blatant hots for me just suddenly chilled out?'

'Look, I just don't know. I don't even know who she's gone off with.'

'Oh, I do,' Frank said, frowning. 'That's why I won't believe it. She's skipped off with Will.'

'What!' Ernestine exclaimed, 'Will Ivery? You're not serious!'

She was so genuinely surprised that the mist of annoyance lifted from Frank's hot blue eyes, and he smiled down at her. 'I know. Nice guy, and all that – but did you think Melissa had designs on him? Truly?'

'Never for a second. She thinks his Adam's apple sticks out, and she doesn't even like his car.'

Frank laughed richly, and helped himself to another biscuit. 'Well, Cupid's a fast worker, isn't he? And your cousin's a cool customer, making you do her dirty work for her.'

'Oh, I don't mind.' This was absolutely true. Ernestine had been nursing a monstrous crush on Frank for months. It had started when she first glimpsed his glorious head brushing the low rafters of The Bear, the tiny pub into which Christ Church men perversely squeezed their giant, cavalry-twilled bodies. She had a rather childish weakness for good looks of the showy sort, and it was an acknowledged thing that Frank was gorgeous. She was by no means the only girl in Oxford who loitered in the Meadow to watch Frank's muscles rippling under his Yale sweater as he directed an illegal game of baseball. In his lustrous dinner jacket, he looked good enough to eat.

Crunching one of Ernestine's biscuits, Frank gave her a long, thoughtful look, then his face suddenly lifted in a warm, intimate smile.

'These cookies are stupendous, you know that? You should open a restaurant.'

'Yes. The hash does make them rather moreish.'

'Your cookies don't need hash.'

His appreciation of her biscuits made Ernestine's heart expand with euphoria. The next Wild Young Bohemian dinner would be for him – a meal so tender and romantic that it would amount to an edible love letter. A salad of quail's eggs to start with, she fantasized mistily, followed by slices of duck in a fruity sauce, and possibly a terrine of striped red and yellow peppers.

He was still surveying her with flattering concentration.

'I didn't tell you how great you look in that dress.'

'Thank you.' She suddenly felt glamorous and intriguing. Frank, when you got him on his own, had a wonderful way of wrapping you in his total attention.

'I'm sorry if I've been a boring fart,' he said. 'I was mad at Melissa, but that's no reason to take it out on you.'

Ernestine glowed. 'You haven't at all.'

'It's nice of you to look after me. Did she make you break a date? Some poor guy must be furious.'

'No, not really.'

'Well, let's enjoy ourselves. I never went to an Oxford Ball before, and I might as well soak up the atmosphere. Where do you want to go first?'

It was like stepping into one of her own daydreams. Beneath her soaring joy, however, Ernestine noted how quickly Frank had snapped out of his disappointment. Perhaps he doesn't care, she told herself hopefully. But she knew this was not true. He was cheerful because he had refused to accept defeat. Well, he would learn. When Melissa did not want to be found, she vanished. He would discover he was pursuing a vapour.

Dazzled as she was, Ernestine was still baffled by Melissa's current plot. She could have sworn in court that her cousin was making a play for Frank. What was she up to? When had she conceived this urgent passion for Will Ivery? A dear, but hardly Mel's type. She made a mental note to worry about this later. The present was too beautiful to spoil with doubt, and the magic of the setting almost lulled her into believing the enchantment would last for ever.

'Shall we go and listen to the quartet?'

'Sure. Why not?'

In companionable silence, with just an edge of tension, they strolled to the low iron gate that opened into the college's famous Rose Garden.

'Chaucer's garden of love,' Frank said.

Between groves of variegated shrubs and weeping willows, the clipped grass was blue in the fading light. The rose trees, heavy with blooms of cream and carmine, were dying away into bleached ghosts of themselves. As the moon burned brighter above the trees, thousands of rose petals poured their dizzying scent into the still evening air. The string quartet, surrounded by a shadowy audience, played Mozart by candlelight.

They wandered across the lawn. Ernestine gripped

Frank's arm. This was so perfect, it almost hurt. She drank in the sense of his body, so pulsing and vital, beside hers.

'This would have been the place,' he said regretfully.

Of course, he was thinking of Melissa again. Even this did not bring Ernestine back to earth. She may have been the wrong woman, but she was The Woman tonight. Nothing could spoil it.

Presently, he said: 'I guess you know her better than anyone. Is there a trick to working her out?'

'Not really. People get distracted by the way she looks, that's all. It makes them chase her.'

'Who chases her?'

'Everyone,' Ernestine said patiently. 'Male and female. I hear them hammering on her door at all hours. They stick begging notes to it.'

'Why? Where does she go?'

'The point is, it's more than her not being available. They seem to want acknowledgement from her – possession. They chase her, so she has to run.'

'I see.' His voice, in the semi-darkness, was thoughtful.

'I think she disturbs people, because she's beautiful,' Ernestine said. 'Plotinus says that beauty induces wonderment, and a delicious trouble.'

Beside her, Frank chuckled. The spell of Melissa, cast even by the mention of her name, faded. 'Do you read Plotinus for fun?'

'No, don't be silly. It's just something I remember from school. Mel's the one for fancy quotations. I'm only reading PPE, which suits a more ordinary cast of mind.'

'Do you have an ordinary mind?'

'Yes. If Mum and Dad weren't so obsessed with going to university, I'd probably have gone off to some polytechnic and studied Home Economics.'

'You're a great cook. You're touched with genius in a kitchen.'

She laughed. 'Thanks.'

'No,' he persisted, 'really. It's a gift as precious as Melissa's beauty. And it'll last longer.'

'I wish you'd tell her. She thinks my cooking is rather pathetic and dowdy. She's above mere eating.'

There was a short silence. Frank asked, in an unexpectedly tender voice: 'Are you – have you ever been – jealous of her?'

Ernestine considered this seriously. 'I don't think so. Once or twice, I've wished I knew how it felt to be as beautiful as that. I'd love to be tall and skinny, instead of small. But if I had the chance to swap with her, I wouldn't take it. We're different, and I like being me.'

'I like you being you. You're great to be with, Ernie. I wouldn't let you change either. Don't you ever do it.'

It was not a particularly handsome tribute, but it was delivered with such kindness and sincerity that her throat was suddenly prickling with tears. She smiled up into his shadowed face. 'I never do. I'm like my mother – she's looked exactly the same since she was fifteen. You can always rely on us.'

He stepped back into the circle of candlelight. His luxuriant eyelashes cast fan-shaped shadows on his cheeks. He looked vulnerable; almost delicate.

'You should have something to remember this evening by,' he said. 'A tribute to your loveliness.' There was a scarlet rosebud level with his eyes; fat, tight and perfect. He reached up for it, and as he snapped off the stem, a thorn ran into the pad of his thumb. 'Ouch – you little bastard!'

Rendered giddy by such a courtly attention, Ernestine stared at the bead of blood forming on his thumb. When it dropped, it seemed to hang suspended in the air for a moment, flashing like a ruby, before it vanished into the darkness.

Frank sucked his wound. 'Poetry comes to life,' he said. 'Chaucer's lover is pricked by a perfect rose, and the God of Love fires a shaft that pierces him through the eye, right down to his heart.'

Ernestine knew exactly the blend of delight and misery Chaucer had meant to convey. Her own heart, struggling under her tight bodice, bled exquisitely.

43

'"The takel smot, and depe it wente,"' Frank quoted softly, '"And therwithall such cold me hente/That, under clothes warme and softe, Sithen that day I have chevered ofte."'

He placed the bud in her hand. Time slowed as he bent forward. He kissed her lightly but firmly on the lips, and whispered: 'I don't know why I did that. Yes, I do. Of course I do.' He did it again.

The moon rose. Couples darted like pale moths in and out of the light of the Japanese lanterns. A small crowd had gathered round the porter's lodge, where Cecily was weeping into one of the tissues she had stuffed into Ernestine's dress.

Craig Lennox sat whey-faced at the porter's desk, wearing nothing but a vest and a pair of turquoise underpants. A St John Ambulanceman held a bag of ice to the back of his head, while a policeman, his radio hissing and spitting on his shoulder, crouched in front of him.

'Let's get this clear, mate. Someone hit you and pinched your clothes?'

Johnny grinned to himself, hearing the subdued laughter of the crowd. Perfectly camouflaged in Craig's dinner jacket, pleated shirt and black tie, he was soaking up the atmosphere. Scanning the crowds boldly, he went into the marquee and helped himself to a glass of champagne. He had never tasted it before. His mouth and nose were instantly flooded with sour fizz, and he hiccupped loudly.

Not all it's cracked up to be, he thought. Then he felt a bubble of reckless glamour expanding in his chest, rushing up his neck and exploding between his ears in a shower of stars. He took another glass from the long trestle table, and knocked it back appreciatively.

The marquee was full of damp heat, and smelled like the inside of a plimsoll. A red-haired boy, with a Meat Loaf T-shirt under his dinner jacket, was presiding over a disco. The floor was crammed with pink-faced couples thrashing about to 'The Time Warp' from *The Rocky Horror Show*.

Johnny chortled to himself, thinking how stupid they looked, bumping and grinding in their fancy dress.

Melissa was not here. He pushed his way outside, where a limp breeze cooled his wet forehead. Night was falling fast, cloaking the pleasure grounds in mystery. Weaving and dodging through the canoodling pairs, he scanned each face boldly. Occasionally, a girl smiled at him, thinking she ought to recognize him, or wishing she did. He wanted to laugh and laugh. This was brilliant. If he had not been searching for Melissa, what an evening he could have had. It was like being an evil spirit in disguise.

He recognized Ernestine, and idly admired her – knock-out pair of tits she had. She had 'fuck me' written all over her, and was hanging on the arm of a flashy bastard who evidently fancied himself enough for both of them – exactly the type of man Johnny most envied and hated. They were deep in conversation with some dickhead in a velvet jacket and hat – thank God, Johnny thought, he had not had to nick that guy's clothes. He wanted to see the sights of the ball, not become one of them.

But he did not overlook his objective, and when he saw her, detaching herself from the main body of the crowd, firmly clutching the sleeve of her escort, every sense was sharpened to a fine point of readiness.

'How funny,' Melissa mused. 'Here I am, with a house and no money, and here you are, with money and no house.'

'I'll have a house one day, I suppose,' Will said. 'My father always meant to buy a big country place. But then he died. Of c-c -' He could not say the word, and finished miserably: 'Last year.'

'Poor you. My father's dead, too, and my mother. But it's different for me, because I don't remember them. And they had nothing to leave me, except Quenville.'

'It's ruined, though, isn't it?'

'A wreck. Has been, as long as I can remember.'

'Is the land worth anything?'

Melissa halted, with her hand on the latch of the door to

the Rose Garden. 'Oh God, I couldn't think of selling Quenville. I'm going to restore it one day. I'm going to live there.' She took possession of his hand, and tugged him into the indigo garden.

The string quartet had finished, and extinguished their candles. One other couple lay on the lawn, snogging ineptly. Melissa took off her flat blue pumps, and walked barefoot towards the inky shrubbery.

'Tess – that's my father's sister, who brought me up – thinks I'm crazy,' she said serenely, 'and so does Ernie. They can't see the point of art for art's sake. No wonder, when my Uncle George's paintings are so bad. He's a professional artist, but he hasn't a shred of talent. We've always lived on Tess's hand-thrown pots. They're hideous too, but at least they sell.' She skirted the large shrubbery, and threw herself down on a bald patch of earth around the trunk of a weeping willow. Its branches drooped around them like the walls of a room. 'Perfect. Nobody will disturb us here.'

Will hovered beside her, glancing round anxiously and looking as if he would rather like to be disturbed. 'Isn't it damp? Your dress is awfully thin.'

'Don't be silly,' Melissa said, with a barely perceptible edge of sharpness, 'it hasn't rained for weeks.'

Obediently, Will lowered himself down beside her.

She scrabbled inside the neck of her dress, and pulled out a fat, dented joint. 'A bra is invaluable when you don't carry a handbag. Want some spliff?'

In the darkness, Will blushed richly. 'No thanks.' She handed him a lighter, warmed by her breasts, and he lit the joint for her with a trembling hand.

She inhaled, blew out a fragrant plume of smoke, and settled her back against the tree with a sigh of contentment.

Will asked: 'What happened to your parents?'

'It was a car smash,' Melissa said, without emotion. 'They were on the way back from Glyndebourne, and I expect my father had been drinking.'

'How awful.'

'I suppose so. Rather distinguished of them, though, to die in evening dress.'

'And you grew up with Ernie.'

'Yes. Like sisters, in a way. They tried not to make differences between us, but of course there already was a difference.'

There was a silence. She seemed to be giving Will a cue.

'The h-house?' he hazarded.

'I was the one who inherited Quenville. I'm glad it was me, because Ernie doesn't understand. It's more than a house.' She leaned in closer to him, so that his vision was swamped by her large, glittering eyes. 'It's a superb example of Victorian Gothic, designed in 1853 by John Seddon. He was heavily influenced by Ruskin and Pugin.' Her voice was hushed and fervent. 'Tess and Ernie simply don't see how I can love a ruin so much – but Seddon wrote that a beautiful building is beautiful for all time, as long as one stone stands upon another.' She smiled, and touched his cheek with her cool palm. 'Listen to me droning on. Ernie's right – I'm obsessed.'

'It's interesting,' Will said, stiffening self-consciously.

'I'm glad you think so. Victorian Gothic is my passion and Quenville is my special mission. You see, the only other part of my inheritance was the folder of Seddon's original drawings for Quenville – down to every doorknob and bell pull. It's an incredible opportunity to recreate each detail. My thesis is going to be about the influence of Victorian literature on the Gothic Revival.'

'Gosh. I mean, I didn't have you down as the thesis type.'

She laughed. 'Why, what type am I?'

'Well – you never seem – you don't look like – I don't know.'

'You mean, I don't look the part.'

He was embarrassed, but smiled. 'No. You're so p-pretty.'

'Ernie would have you arrested for sexism, if she heard that.'

'Sorry.'

'It's all right. I won't tell her.' Melissa lightly, experimentally stroked his hair, and removed her hand. 'I wish you

47

could see my house. I'd love you to understand how important it is to me. The fact is, Quenville is in my blood. It's
printed on my DNA.'

Will had never heard her speak with such intensity. It was
dark under the tree, and all he could see was the subdued
sparkle of her eyes, but his other senses compensated for his
blindness. He could feel the heat of her body beside him,
and smell her musky, flowery scent under the cannabis
smoke. Like the roses, she released her perfume at night.
Her voice seemed to insinuate itself into a very secret, sensitive part of himself, and though he thought it was
pleasurable, it made him squirm, too. When she touched
him, his throat closed in something like fear.

'There's a legend, isn't there?' he asked.

'Oh, yes. The legend of the Lost Fortune, the buried
Treasure and the Fall of the House of Lamb. Every family
should have one.'

'Is there a ghost?'

'Not that I know of.' Her voice was caressing and teasing.
'Would you like one?'

'Well, if ever I get my own house, a ghost would be an
asset. But buried treasure sounds good enough.'

'It's like a haunting, in a way,' Melissa said thoughtfully.
'The ghost of the lost money has haunted our family for
generations. Tess gets very upset when I talk about it,
because she thinks it ruined her father's life, and my
father's. We were very rich once. Joshua Lamb, who made
the fortune, was a poor boy who married the boss's daughter
and inherited her father's brewery. He wanted to be a
gentleman, and the local gentry snubbed him, because his
money reeked of malt and hops. So he built himself a palace
fit for a prince, and called it Quenville, after a Norman
knight he found in an old book. I think he kidded himself
that they were related.'

'Why did it matter so much to him?'

'Class always matters', Melissa said, 'even now. Anyway,
Joshua had one child, a daughter whose name was Rose. It
was his dearest wish that Rose would marry a real gentleman, and found a dynasty of gentlemen. So he yoked her to

the tenth son of a Scottish peer – he hadn't a bean, and he was only too happy to change his name to Lamb, in exchange for the fortune. Thanks to him, Ernie and I have some rather fine tartan blood in our veins.'

'Did they live happily ever after?'

'I don't think so. When Joshua finally died, Rose had been married for nearly twenty years, and there was no sign of his genteel dynasty. Then the husband died too, and Rose found she was pregnant. She had a son.'

'And what happened to her money?'

'Well, there's the mystery. Before her son was born, it vanished.'

'Money doesn't just vanish,' Will protested.

'Ours did. It disappeared, almost overnight. She sold everything she owned, and lived on at Quenville as a poor woman.'

'But she must have done something with it.'

'Yes, but what? She was cracked, you know. She used to make wreaths of wild flowers, and wander around singing. The point is, when young Joshua grew up, he was naturally wild to know what had become of the fortune he should have inherited. And Rose started burbling about buried treasure. Finally, when she lay dying, she whispered the words: Matthew, 13:45.'

'Dramatic.'

'Isn't it? Young Joshua rushed to his Bible to look up the reference: "The kingdom of heaven is like unto a merchant man, seeking goodly pearls: Who, when he found one pearl of great price, went and sold all he had, and bought it."'

'Did he find anything?'

Melissa sighed. 'God, no. He tore Quenville apart, looking for Rose's hoard of goodly pearls. The last thing his mother heard on earth was her son yelling at her to tell him the secret.'

'Poor woman,' Will said warmly.

'Oh, I don't know. I think she was rather mean to keep him in the dark and leave him with nothing. Anyway, he searched for the rest of his life. And his son took up the search too, and his grandson. The house fell into ruins, because nobody could afford to live in it. But it was never sold – in case the treasure existed. Our grandfather had a good look, and I know my father did.'

'But surely,' Will said, 'by then they must have realized it was a wild-goose chase?'

'They had faith,' Melissa said, 'and so do I.'

'You believe in the buried treasure?'

'I think so. But that isn't why I love Quenville so much. It's partly its splendour, and partly because my family have invested so much hope in it. Do you see?'

'Yes,' Will said doubtfully.

'Tess has always hated the place. She thinks it looks like a mental hospital – she's the wrong generation to appreciate Victorian Gothic. And she blames it because she thinks it destroyed her brother's life. My father believed he had a birthright. Tess says he never did anything worthwhile – just hung around waiting to be rich. She doesn't like fantasies.'

'But you do?'

'It's not a fantasy. It's my inheritance. Not the money – the whole story. It needs an ending.'

'I see,' Will said. He did not, but he was mesmerized by Melissa's sublime conviction, and honoured by her confidence. At the Bohemian dinners, she rarely spoke to him directly.

Her velvet voice dropped to a whisper. 'I'm destined to liberate the sleeping beauty of those crumbling stones. So I wouldn't swap my inheritance for yours.'

'No, there's nothing m-mysterious about mine. I'll get the money next year, when I turn twenty-one.'

'What will you do with it?'

'Well, I don't know – '

'It doesn't matter.'

'Sometimes,' Will blurted out, 'I feel guilty about being so rich.'

Her hand found his thigh, and inched towards his groin. 'Why? There's nothing reprehensible about being rich.'

He could not speak. His tongue had swollen with nervous

dread. Melissa crushed out her joint, and he felt the fragility of her ribcage as she leaned against him. He was drowning in her perfume, unable to breathe under the pressure of her beauty. He tasted the powdery sweetness of her lips, and shuddered when she slid her tongue into his mouth. He clamped his arms around her. In his conscious mind, he wanted to possess her, but he was paralysed. She seemed to writhe against him like a huge snake. Waves of panic engulfed him. His heart hammered fit to burst out of his chest. His fear mounted as Melissa's fingers moved up his leg.

Desperately, he broke free. 'I'm sorry – ' he mumbled thickly, 'I c-c – '

Despising himself for his inadequacy, overpowered by a situation beyond his timid dreams, he wrenched away from her twining arms, scrambled to his feet and lurched away across the dark lawn towards the lights of the ball.

When Will's lips fastened on Melissa's, Johnny almost gasped aloud, pierced by a shaft of jealousy like the thrust of a dagger. The agony of witnessing someone else having her took him by surprise. He burned with the longing to obliterate this man from the face of the earth.

He had been watching them boldly, screened by the willow leaves, his desire mounting as he listened to Melissa's gentle voice describing the buried treasure of Quenville. When Will stumbled away in terror, Johnny's joy was savage.

This stuttering halfwit with a cock like a wet marshmallow couldn't even see that Melissa was after his money. She hadn't bothered to be subtle about it, dropping fucking great hints as heavy as anvils. This seemed perfectly reasonable to Johnny, and increased his admiration for her – under that cold refinement she was just another slut on the make. A woman who might have been designed with him in mind. Of course, the idiot's money was exactly what Melissa needed. But he still hated Will from his soul, and longed to rend him limb from limb, for daring to touch her.

She did not try to follow Will, but stayed leaning against the trunk of the tree, staring after him in a torpor of dreamy satisfaction. Johnny watched her taking another joint out of her bra and smoking it with concentrated relish. Far away, like music from another planet, he could hear the noises of the ball. They were alone together in the garden, cut loose from time and reality. The scent of the roses carried Johnny back to the briars of Quenveille.

She smoked the joint down to the roach, extinguished it and sighed to herself. Very slowly, she wriggled her long dress up over her slender legs and hips. She was wearing nothing underneath.

The shock pulsed through Johnny. Never in his life had he been so meshed, so helpless; propelled by sexual urgency as powerful as some supernatural force.

His mouth went dry. Melissa's legs fell open. He saw the dark triangle of her pubic hair, as she began to caress and stroke the pearl of her clitoris. Her lips were parted slightly, and her breathing became heavier.

Johnny was crashing through the willow screen before he properly knew what he was doing. His shadow fell across her, and Melissa saw him through her lowered lashes. She showed no surprise, she made no sound. The rhythm of her stroking did not falter. She stared up at Johnny as if she had been expecting him. Swept along by the mad intensity of his desire, Johnny dropped down astride her and pushed his erection into her with one violent, engulfing movement. In the second before he stopped her mouth with his tongue, she let out a great, trembling gasp.

She was tight and wet around him, and her mouth was hot. She gave back his kiss with unexpected strength, and suddenly threw her long legs across his back, grinding him into her. He had never felt anything as soft as her skin, or smelled anything as muskily fragrant.

His senses contracted to the awareness of his greedy thrusts. He could not have stopped if his life dpended on it. He pushed harder and faster, hurtling helplessly into his climax, and when his sperm exploded into her, he heard her guttural moan, deep in her throat.

He came in wild spasms, bellowing in ecstasy that was

almost unbearable, and plummeted back to earth like a singed Icarus.

While he lay on top of her, twitching and trying to collect his faculties, Melissa separated herself, as supple as an eel. Without one word or look, she glided away from him through the leaves. Johnny was left biting the soil, and marvelling at the force that drove him towards his destiny. It seemed incredible that he had only laid eyes on Melissa a few hours before.

Was this a dream? He sat up, brushing off crumbs of earth and straightening his stolen clothes. She had melted away from him, back into her golden realm, but he was not going to lose her again. He would haunt Melissa, entering her life as he had entered her body, until he knew her every thought.

Three

Come, let me read the oft-read tale again:
The story of that Oxford scholar poor,
Of pregnant parts and quick inventive brain,
Who, tired of knocking at Preferment's door,
One summer morn forsook
His friends, and went to learn the Gipsy lore,
And roam'd the world with that wild brotherhood,

Matthew Arnold, 'The Scholar-Gipsy'

'That bloody, bloody boy,' Dan Ross said morosely. 'That awful little shit of a boy. He hasn't given me a second's peace since he was five.'

His eyes were red and sore, and a film of silver stubble glittered on his cheeks. He raked his fingers angrily through his thick grey hair, and lit another cigarette with the stub of the old one still smouldering in the ashtray.

Will and Ernestine watched him, with embarrassed compassion, from the opposite sofa. It was the last day of term. Dan had summoned them for a crisis meeting about Giles, in the inappropriate, ersatz Victorian setting of afternoon tea at the Randolph Hotel. Giles had disappeared the day after the ball, leaving his room at Christ Church looking like the *Marie Celeste* after a poltergeist's tea-party. Dan claimed to be taking practical action to find his son, but it was becoming obvious that what he really wanted was an audience for his breast-beating and garment-rending.

'Yes, he's gone off before, but never like this. It's different this time – and the hell of it is, I know it's all my fault.' Smoking ferociously, Dan stabbed at his slice of fruit cake with a fork.

From the next table, two elderly matrons in hats watched him with naked curiosity. Will slopped his tea in his saucer, and his freckles were instantly drowned in a sizzling blush. Sitting with this agonized, grizzled King Lear was difficult enough. The fact that Dan was famous intensified the unwelcome naphthalene glare of publicity. For more than twenty years, he had presented a trendy television arts show, and was widely known as 'the intellectual woman's bit of crumpet'.

Ernestine noted that the bit of crumpet's thin, acne-bitten face was more ravaged and scored than it looked on screen, but that he still exuded an animal vitality which passed as handsome. Age had not withered Dan's sex appeal, nor custom staled his infinite capacity to cheat on his growing roll of wives. Beside him, Will, blinking his yellow lashes and struggling with his stammer, looked pink and tender.

Ernestine was sorry for him. He was hopelessly out of his depth with this man, and she wondered what strange chemical attraction had made the scapegrace Giles and the painstaking Will such devoted friends at school. Melissa should have been here to give him more confidence. Where on earth was she? The whole of Oxford seemed to know that she and Will were an item, but that did not mean he could find her when he needed her. Ernestine had left notes for her on a dozen doors, and finally come along with Will as a substitute. And this poor guy is supposed to be the great love of her life, she thought. It'll be a miracle if Mel turns up for her own wedding. If she ever has a baby, I'll probably end up going into labour on her behalf.

'You do your best,' Dan went on, 'and it's never enough. Oh, sharper than the serpent's tooth.' The soil of his Manchester roots still clung to his voice. When he had been at Oxford, in the early 1960s, regional accents had been fashionable. 'I expect Giles has filled you in on all my crimes, Ernestine. How I divorced his mother when he was only three, and used him to fulfil my own elitist ambitions. I bust my arse to send him to Eton, and what do I get? A bloody Etonian, pissing on me from a great height. But I've got to find him.'

55

'It might be n-nothing, you know,' Will offered, blinking distressfully. 'He was always bunking off at school.'

'Ha! Don't I remember! I was never off the phone to his housemaster. Then he gets expelled for drug-pushing just before his A levels, and I have to fork out a fortune for a crammer. Do I get a word of apology? Even acknowledgement? No. He wants me to pay for leaving his mother.'

'It's the end of term, anyway,' Ernestine pointed out, trying to keep to the agenda. 'He's probably gone to a friend's, or something.'

Dan groaned. 'Without any luggage? Without his dope tin? Where would Giles go without his stash?'

'We did wonder,' she admitted, suddenly feeling guilty because she had not been anxious enough. 'It's not like him.'

'And nearly two thousand quid, just left in his sock drawer. So what's he doing for money?' Dan poured tea, with a shaking, nicotine-stained hand. 'You probably think I'm a bastard, but Will knows how he treats me – like a cash-dispenser.' He laughed bitterly. 'A Nazi cash-dispenser.' He buried his face in his hands. 'I'm out of my mind. I'm going crazy. I've asked the police to drag the river.'

Ernestine drew in a sharp, shocked breath, but Will leaped in with unexpected firmness.

'Come on, Dan. Don't let's get this all out of proportion. Giles always turns up. I dare say he skipped to avoid paying his college battels.'

'I paid them this morning,' Dan said, pulling up his head with a genuinely brave smile which wrung Ernestine's heart. 'Come back, Giles, all is forgiven, eh?'

'He told my g-g – he told Melissa you'd had one of your spats,' Will said, 'but he seemed fine to us.'

'Did he say anything else?'

'No.'

Dan hungrily lit another cigarette. 'Well, the thing is, I spoke to him the day he vanished. And you'll say I drove him to it – but you know me, Will, you know how hard I've tried to do right by him. His mother got the Hampstead house when we split up, and immediately filled it with a lot of

Tarot-reading arseholes. Slept with anything that moved, never gave a toss about the child. It was down to me to give him stability. Yes, I know what you're thinking.' He glared defiantly at Ernestine, though she had not been thinking anything in particular. 'Funny notion of stability – four wives and umpteen girlfriends. But I provided for him. Prep school, Eton, two hefty drugs fines, vast allowance for loafing around at Oxford. He's bleeding me white, and he still hates me.'

'He doesn't hate you.' The surge of colour in Will's face had subsided. His soft, moist lips had firmed. Ernestine was surprised by how adult, how capable he suddenly looked. 'Talking like this won't solve anything.'

Dan let out another theatrical but heartfelt groan. 'The fact is, things came to a head. Nina – my wife – wants a baby. Nothing's happened, so we've been having fertility tests. Well, it turns out I'm the one who can't do it.' He sat back, to give this its full impact.

Will said: 'Oh God.'

'Precisely. All this time and effort, and he's probably not my son at all. It's never been an issue before, because none of my other consorts fancied babies. Giles was a mistake – not my mistake, as it turns out.'

'Poor Giles,' said Ernestine.

Dan rubbed his nose with his corduroy sleeve. 'I was angry. I gave him a lot of rubbish about disinheritance and disowning. Now I'd give anything to take it back.' He let out a deep, barking sob, which turned every head in the room. 'I love the bugger. You've got to help me find him.'

'I hope you realize you need four of those,' Melissa said, glancing up as Ernestine spooned trout pâté into individual dariole moulds for chilling.

'Us plus Will. Cec and the breath-monster aren't coming till tomorrow, and poor Giles obviously isn't coming at all. That makes three.'

'Oh, didn't I tell you? I asked Frank.'

Ernestine shrieked: 'What?'

'He's driving down here with Will this afternoon.'

'God, God! How could you've done it? Are you mad?'

Melissa was spread across two kitchen chairs, painting her toenails an opalescent pale pink. 'Supper will stretch. He can have my pâté, if it's a problem.'

Ernestine, surrounded by a battery of pots at the scarred pine kitchen table, hurled her spoon back into the bowl with a clatter. 'Mel Lamb, you're the utter limit. You know perfectly well, it's not just a matter of supper. I've spent the whole day sorting sheets and pillowcases – where on earth is Frank supposed to sleep? We haven't got enough bedrooms.'

'Yes we have. Think creatively.' Melissa began fanning her toes with the *Guardian*. 'I've bagged Tess and George's room for me and Will. Cecily and Craig can have the sofabed – I still can't imagine why you asked them – and that leaves our room for you and Frank.'

'But he's – we're not – '

'Well, if you're not sleeping together, don't you think it's about time you started? I thought you pulled him at the ball.'

'Of course I didn't.' Ernestine was on the edge of tears, sure she was about to face the worst humiliation of her life. 'I can't just order him to sleep with me.'

'Why not? He likes you.'

Ernestine flung open the cupboard to root out a fourth mould. 'That's not the point.'

'Darling,' Melissa exclaimed gently, with a misty look of concern, 'I thought you'd be pleased.'

'I am,' Ernestine said doubtfully. Since the ball, she had been living in a breathless, erotic, permanent dream of Frank. But she did not like the sensation of being pitch-forked straight into it, without a chance to prepare. Tonight's meal, for one thing, was not nearly good enough for him. And the thought of telling him about the sleeping arrangements made her want to lie down and die with embarrassment.

Melissa, however, did not know the meaning of the word. 'Lighten up, Ernie. It'll all fall into place. Dear me, you

58

look as if you're going to be burned at the stake – and there I was trying to do something nice for you.' She patted her toe-nails experimentally, and stood up, stretching like a contented cat.

Hazy late afternoon sunlight poured into the cottage kitchen, illuminating the stains on the tattered gingham curtains which framed a distant view of Quenville, far across the fields. Tess and George had a house in Islington – equally untidy – and only used the Norfolk cottage at weekends. They were spending the next two weeks in France, and had turned it over to the girls and their friends. This was the first time Melissa and Ernestine had entertained on their own, without the older generation.

Ernestine, checking the temperature of the Rayburn's oven, reflected on the great gulf between their standards. Her thoughts were full of cooking and linen, while Melissa only cared about getting her share of sex. Ernestine allowed herself a moment of pure annoyance – did Mel think meals cooked themselves? Did she believe house-guests were there for the amusement of the hosts? Did she really not care where they were all to sleep? And there was only one bathroom. And the lock was broken. Ernestine stuffed a homemade coconut biscuit into her mouth to stave off the horrible thought of Frank blundering in on her by mistake.

Melissa drifted to the window to stare at the ruins of Quenville, which drew her like a magnet. 'Perhaps it's just as well Giles isn't coming,' she mused, 'but I'm going to miss him dreadfully.'

'Me too. I can't stop worrying about him after his father made all that fuss about having the river dragged.'

'He was going to get me some dope.'

There was something about the exquisite way in which Melissa delivered her most spectacular pieces of selfishness that always made Ernestine laugh. 'You cow. You know you're worried about him too. And didn't you read Mum's list of instructions? No drugs.'

'No sex, no rock and roll,' quoted Melissa, 'in bed alone by ten, don't touch the wine bottles marked with red dots.'

They both began to giggle. 'I think she's exhumed the potatoes in the garden,' Ernestine said, 'to count them.'

'Well, I'm going to eat and drink and fuck and be merry, whatever Tess says.' Melissa went over to the wine rack beside the sink. 'While the cat's away, the mice will get plastered. What shall we have with our dinner? A bottle of Château WI parsnip cordial, or a red dot Bulgarian Cabernet?'

Tess's hospitable instincts vied with an incredible stinginess. Ernestine found her mother's compulsive cheeseparing touching, but also – particularly when she was with Melissa – hilarious.

'I'll open it, to let it breathe,' Melissa said, selecting one of the forbidden bottles, 'though this awful plonk really needs artificial respiration and an oxygen mask.'

'We shouldn't – '

'She'll know it was me. Remember what your report said at school.'

In unison, they chanted: '"Ernestine should not sit next to Melissa, because she is so easily led."'

The beam of the torch soared over the black vegetation and came to rest on the leprous, lichened face of the stone angel.

'Is it safe?' Will was whispering, awed by the jagged mass of Quenville's towers by moonlight.

'Of course,' Melissa said. 'I wouldn't lead you into danger, would I?'

'No . . .' He could not help sounding unconvinced.

An owl swooped out at them, so close that they could see the bright eyes of the mouse dying in its claws.

Will shivered. The ghostly, graceful bird reminded him of Melissa, palely glimmering in front of him in her white dress. For reassurance, he glanced over his shoulder at the distant light shed by the cottage window. So far away, its warm yellow glow could not compete with the ghastly, blue-veined intensity of the full moon. It seemed near enough to touch, as if the pitched roof of the tallest tower could pierce it.

He clutched at Melissa's cool, insubstantial hand. 'But Ernie told me one of the walls was unstable, and your aunt said not to go there.'

'That's nonsense,' Melissa said. 'She's superstitious because she thinks Quenville destroyed my father. It can't do me any harm. And I particularly wanted you to see it at night.' They halted on the patch of flagstones in front of the porch, and she flicked off the torch. 'Isn't it beautiful? I wanted you to see for yourself that the decay doesn't matter. It's still beautiful, still magical, and it will be as long as one stone is left standing. I sometimes think if I knocked it all down, and put the land under the plough, I couldn't wipe out the spirit.'

'It's extraordinary.'

Will had never seen anything like it. The inky rural darkness concentrated Quenville's chaotic dereliction into a mysterious looming bulk, which reached out and gripped him with its power.

Melissa, beside him, seemed almost luminous in the blackness, as if she carried a magic, phosphorescent light inside her. Will found that he could not look at the house without his eyes automatically swivelling back to her. This was how she had appeared to him at the ball, all hollowed cheeks and shadowed, velvet lashes. He smarted over the memory now. He remembered how he had run away from her, and could have done it again – but she was so lovely. Lovelier still in the wreck of her inheritance.

And she had been so sweet and gentle with him since that night. Amazingly, she had never mentioned his cowardice. She had even told people they were a couple. Love had been mentioned, though not by Will – he would never have dared. What could she possibly see in him? He found himself recalling the friendly group over supper half an hour before, as if watching himself, Melissa, Ernestine and Frank through the wrong end of a telescope. Why was he afraid? He decided to get it out of the way while he and the fair Melissa were alone.

'Sorry I was so dense earlier,' he blurted out. 'I must seem awfully thick, but I assumed I'd be sharing a room with Frank.'

Melissa laughed softly. 'He's with Ernie.'

'Oh. I didn't know.'

'It won't be so hideous, will it, sharing with me?'

'God, n-n-no – '

She squeezed his hand more firmly. 'I love the smell of the roses here.'

Will filled his lungs with the intoxicating, dizzying scent of the invisible flowers. It took him back to the dreadful débâcle in the college garden. Sickening plants, he thought. There was something indecent, faintly fleshy, about the heavy perfume.

'Come in.' Melissa switched on her torch again and led him through the damp chill of the porch, into the bottomless night of the massive, warped front door.

Before his eyes adjusted, Will stood in absolute blindness, clutching at Melissa's fingers. Her beam of light travelled slowly across a huge stone staircase, with gaping, cracked treads. The newel post at the foot was carved into the shape of a sort of medieval winged monster, and listing heavily to one side.

'All the original material is still there,' Melissa said. 'I don't see any reason why it can't be mended.' The light veered to a shattered wall, spewing out lathes and rubble through the remains of an elaborate plaster frieze. 'This sort of thing is the problem. The subsidence here has collapsed the upper floors like a house of cards. Luckily, I've got Seddon's drawings for the plasterwork so all that lovely moulding needn't be lost. The kitchens and cellars round the back are more or less standing, but the whole place is swarming with bats, and I can't bear them. So we won't go there.'

'Glad to hear it,' Will said, with a nervous, hollow laugh.

She led him back through the murky half-light of the porch, and he began to hope this meant they were returning to the cottage. It was a relief, in a way, to keep off the subject of romance, but the rank atmosphere of Quenville was beginning to make his skin creep.

She asked him, with her lips close to his ear: 'What do you think?'

'I'm b-bowled over. Truly.'

'Now you understand why it means everything to me.'

'I think so. It's incredible.'

He sensed her delight. 'Yes. Less dramatic by daylight, but you can see more. I'll show you the folder of Seddon's plans – then you really will understand.'

'You're quite different when you talk about your house,' he said impulsively. 'More – I don't know – idealistic.'

'That's because Quenville is the best of me. Every good thought and ambition I've ever had has been tied up in it.' Her grip on his hand tightened. 'You must understand. This house looks like the end of something – but it's really the beginning.'

She was begging him, almost with desperation. For the first time, Will seemed to hear a yearning vulnerability in her voice, which brought his protective instincts rushing to the surface. She was bound up in this mass of decay and needed to be saved. She was Quenville, and if it sank, her hopes and dreams would sink with it.

'Will,' she whispered, 'I wish you'd kiss me. Is there something wrong with me?'

'Oh my G-god, is that what you think?'

'I don't normally go out with men like you. I was scared you – I don't know – disapproved of me, somehow. Because I'm quite bad, and you're so good.'

Will groaned softly. 'This is ridiculous. If you must know, I couldn't do anything at the ball, because I didn't really believe it.'

Her voice was wrenchingly sad. 'You didn't trust me.'

'No, nothing like that. To be honest, I just could not see what a girl like you could possibly want with a boring stick like me.'

'Truly? Truly?' She laughed softly, leaning towards him. '"Said good Sir Bors, 'beyond all hopes of mine,/ Who scarce had pray'd or ask'd it for myself -/ Across the seven clear stars – O grace to me – "'

'That's it, exactly. Why "grace to me"?'

'I told you, you're Tennyson's good Sir Bors. Not as flashy as Galahad or Percival, but made of such decent, hardwearing material.'

He drew her into his arms, and was overwhelmed by a new sense of her fragility. 'Say some more.'

'"A square-set man and honest;"' she quoted, her breath hot on his neck, '"And his eyes/ An out-door sign of all the warmth within."'

'Warm for you,' he said.

The moonlit romance of the whole situation, and the knowledge of Melissa's wondrous beauty, flooded Will's veins like a drug. Quenville was a haunted wreck, with a snow-white pearl at its core. He was Sir Bors, granted a grace he had not dared to ask for. His heart hammering, he pressed his lips on hers, and sank drowning into the spell.

'Weird place,' Frank said, pressing his face against the kitchen window to stare at Quenville. 'I keep expecting to see a werewolf, or something.'

He was still eating. He had a mug of coffee in one hand, and a slab of moist ginger cake in the other. Behind him, the kitchen table was a litter of crumpled napkins, bleared wine glasses and melted candles. Ernestine, wrapped in her stout father's enormous butcher's apron, was stacking plates beside the dented stainless-steel sink.

Since Frank's arrival, his physical presence had swamped her senses. He was so big – a free-range giant from the land of the prairies, whose power could not be contained in a cramped English cottage. His dark head had been cracking against the low beams all evening and knocking the fly-speckled lampshades. The genteel supper she had cooked had not been nearly enough for him. He had attacked her dainty trout pâté in a single gulp, and the leg of lamb, which she had meant to last at least three meals, had been picked to the marrow. At their Wild Young Bohemian dinners, she had wondered how they got through such vast quantities of food when nobody appeared to be eating, and now she knew.

While the others crash'd the glass and beat the floor, Frank ate.

One entire wholemeal loaf had gone, along with half a pound of butter and a hefty lump of Stilton. He had inhaled his pudding in a breath, and vacuumed out her cake tins. Tomorrow morning, she would have to take Will's car straight to the supermarket. Feeding Frank was the most exquisite honour, but his appetite was alarming, too – she couldn't help remembering *The Tiger Who Came to Tea*, her favourite book as a child. Running the juddering hot tap, she muttered it to herself: "'He ate ALL the food, and drunk ALL the drink.'"

Oh, tomorrow, she thought. Was she ever going to get through tonight? He had frowned so blackly when Melissa announced she would be sleeping with Will that Ernestine's courage had failed her. She would have to make up the sofabed in the sitting room, and tell Melissa they must, must change the arrangements when Cecily and Craig joined them. Her mouth simply refused to form the words: 'Oh Frank, I'll show you our room.' He had only kissed her once, for God's sake.

And he had spent the entire meal – apart from demanding second and third helpings – monopolizing Melissa. Or had it been the other way round? She and Will had hardly said a word, while the two of them quoted Victorian poetry at each other. In any other circumstances, Ernestine would have sworn that Melissa was making a play for Frank. She knew that dewy, legs-gaping look of hers so well. But then Mel had whisked Will off for a romantic tryst in the moonlight, and Frank's black brows had knitted into a sulky frown. He couldn't fathom the situation, and neither could she. When he tore himself away from the window, he looked moody, wrapped up in himself.

And never in her life had Ernestine desired a man so consumingly. She had not known the meaning of the word until now – the trembling, numb fingers, the breathless constriction of the chest, the dry mouth, the urgent heat between the legs. He was wearing blue jeans, faded but supernaturally clean, and a red plaid shirt. Its sleeves were rolled back over his brawny rower's forearms, and the movement of his sinews closed Ernestine's throat with longing.

'I haven't thanked you for dinner,' he said, solemn and depressingly polite. 'It was really great, Ernie. I don't want you to think I didn't appreciate it – but I'm kind of off food at the moment.'

Ernestine gaped at him in astonishment for a moment, then let out an undignified snort of laughter. Frank clearly did not like being laughed at, and his peeved expression filled her with dismay, but she could not stop. Against her own best interests, she leaned against the sink and howled.

'What? What's the joke?'

'Oh Frank, I'm sorry, but I've never seen anyone eat so much in all my life. What are you like when you're not off your food?'

'Okay.' His face was puzzled, then hurt, then suddenly melted into a charming smile, which showed his dazzling teeth. 'Okay. I guess I do take a lot of feeding. My mother's always complaining about it, and the last time I stayed with my sister, she threatened to impose rationing.' With radiant good humour, he joined in the laugh at himself and, as if an invisible net around him had suddenly broken, reached out to grab a tea towel. 'Here, I'll wipe the dishes.'

'You don't have to.'

He was standing at her shoulder, a warm pillar of muscle and bone. 'I owe you. I just ate you out of house and home.' He began drying and stacking the plates, with admirable neatness. 'Do you do all the cooking here?'

'Yes,' Ernestine said, plunging her hands back into the soapy water. 'I like it, and Mel hasn't got a clue.'

'No, I can't imagine her working in a kitchen.' Frank was scrutinizing Ernestine thoughtfully. 'She wouldn't look right, somehow – my mother's just the same. The kind of woman who looks like an oppressed amateur when she prepares food. As if she expected someone to rescue her before she broke a nail.'

'Oh, Mel tries, but she's so incompetent. And I honestly do love cooking, you know.'

'You wear it like a string of pearls. You're a provider, a horn of plenty.'

Ernestine laughed. 'A French horn of plenty, with my figure?'

'No,' Frank said, shaking his head and smiling, 'you're not going to get me into one of those conversations about weight. Your shape, if you need to be told, is just about perfect.'

Smiling, he cupped a hand round one of her breasts, as if plucking a ripe fruit. 'You look incredibly sexy in that apron.'

Through the layers of fabric, he found the bud of her nipple and squeezed it. Sparks of pleasure charged through Ernestine's body and erupted in a firework display in her vagina when he slid his tongue between her lips. He kissed her with slow deliberation, savouring her. Wrapping his arms around her waist, he hoisted her up until her face was level with his own. Her feet swinging in mid-air, Ernestine felt as if the bottom had dropped right out of reality. She was floating with the angels.

He set her down, still swimming in his blue eyes, and said: 'Well?'

This was not the elaborate dance of courtship Ernestine had imagined. But they both wanted the same thing, and might as well be direct about it.

'Upstairs,' she said. And she led him up the narrow staircase, her pulse thrashing in her parched mouth.

They were to sleep in the room Ernestine and Melissa had shared since childhood; a cramped pink box around which George had painted a frieze of teddy bears. Ernestine was suddenly embarrassed about the bears. The two single beds, with their two identical limp duvets, seemed ludicrously small and babyish.

The sight of Frank stripping, however, blew all self-consciousness out of her mind. She had a delirious impression of lean, hairy shanks, a symmetrical torso, and a sublimely perfect penis leaping up towards his navel. Her few previous sexual experiences had been hurried, fumbling affairs. This was her first encounter with passion – consuming, animalistic, physical passion, as insistent and urgent as hunger.

67

They collapsed on one of the beds, and Ernestine folded his hard body into her soft flesh. He plunged his face into her breasts. His movements inside her drove out sobs of pleasure. The orgasm of her life crashed over her like a tidal wave.

Frank's face was gentle, almost businesslike, until – without warning – he lost control. Bunching the pillow into his mouth, he bucked and floundered on top of her, and finally came with a long, shuddering groan.

For a few minutes, he lay panting in her arms, twitching like a corpse. Ernestine clasped his head, aching with tenderness. Tears were streaming from her eyes and trickling down into her ears.

Frank raised his head. 'Jesus.' He smiled down at her in a friendly way, as if they had only just met. 'Is there anything else to eat?'

She laughed shakily. 'Biscuits. Home-made.'

'Wow – no, stay there, honey. I'll get them.'

'In the Mickey Mouse tin, first cupboard, top shelf.' Bathed in contentment, she watched him pull on his jeans over his naked buttocks, and listened to him blundering around downstairs.

Sex had never been like this before. This was more exalted and beautiful than sex. This was a whole new world. There was no turning back now – Ernestine had made the simple and astounding discovery that she was in love.

Frank returned with the open tin. 'Breathe in,' he said with his mouth full. 'I'm not lying in single beds, like the fucking *Dick Van Dyke Show*.' Shrugging off his jeans, he squeezed his warm body against hers. They wrestled briefly, laughing as their limbs clashed and twined. 'Have a cookie. Excuse me – a biscuit. They're unbelievable.'

'Peanut and toffee.'

'Ernie, you are touched with the rays of the sublime.'

They crunched companionably, scattering crumbs.

The front door slammed downstairs. Frank and Ernestine were still, listening to muffled voices and creaking footsteps on the stairs. Across the landing, the door of the other bedroom clicked behind Will and Melissa. This was a magic night, Ernie thought, her soul expanding with happiness. Love had blessed them all. The cottage was enchanted.

Frank's richly lashed eyes were meditative. 'This is your room? Yours and Melissa's?'

'Yes.'

'Which bed is hers?'

'This one.'

Frank murmured: 'It smells of her.'

Poppies and wild celandine nodded around the fringes of the ripe fields. In the cottage garden, the hard silver shafts of early morning sunlight made diamond necklaces of the dew-spangled flowers. Ernestine, unable to sleep for happiness, had gone out to gather a great bunch of pinks, larkspur and mignonette. She had put them in an old washstand jug, and placed them on the kitchen counter, where they dripped dew and bees in the rays that slanted through the open lattice.

Cleaning up last night's feast and making breakfast had given her intense physical pleasure, intimately connected with the afterglow of sex with Frank. As she worked, she marvelled over the change in herself. She had woken up on another planet, every sense sharpened and transformed by the new state of being in love.

Humming contentedly, she ran a damp cloth through the dazzling pools of light on the kitchen surfaces. Over the eternal pong of her father's oil paints and her mother's unfiltered cigarettes wafted the scents of warm bread and the bacon and egg pie baking in the oven. A glass bowl of freckled brown eggs lay waiting to become an omelette, beside a bunch of chives.

She had laid the breakfast table as if dressing an altar. Was it her imagination, or was the whole house filled with the grassy smell of semen? Frank had made love to her three times last night, and his lightest touch had been enough to make her come.

'Well, you have been a busy girl. Judging by that bloody great smirk.' Melissa stumbled into the room, yawning noisily.

'Mel. You're up early.'

'Oh God, seven fifteen. Is that really the time?' Melissa was wearing a small, pale blue T-shirt, which rode up half her buttocks and showed the edge of her nut-brown triangle of pubic hair. There were creases underneath her heavy eyes, and a disagreeable expression on her face, but she still looked as lovely as the summer morning.

'It's so gorgeous,' Ernestine said, spooning coffee into the pot. 'I couldn't go on sleeping.'

'Huh, neither could I – Will snores.' She lit a cigarette, blowing an acrid plume of smoke across the fragrances of fruit and flowers.

Ernestine made them both cups of coffee. 'I heard your bed creaking practically all night.'

'Yes, success – such as it is – perches on my banners.' Melissa's mood was as jarring as the smell of her cigarette. 'Will's not such a disaster when you get him cranked up.' She flicked ash into her saucer. 'He takes a lot of starting, but then he's away. Judder-judder-judder, like that crappy old generator they run at the farm next door.'

Ernestine handed her an ashtray, trying not to let her cousin take the bloom off her exultation. 'Has it started, then?'

'Has what started?'

'We've had the great love of your life. Now we're obviously into the next stage – the I-can't-stand-him stage. Next, we'll have the Ernie-get-him-out-of-my-face stage.'

'Look, piss off. You don't know anything about it.'

'I've seen it enough times.' Annoyed to find herself returning to earth, Ernestine began sawing slices of bread. 'But I wish you'd give poor Will a proper chance. He's easily the nicest lover you've ever had. Actually, he's really sweet.'

'Thank you, I don't need you to run an ad campaign,' Melissa snapped. 'I know all about Will's sweetness, and I've got no intention of letting him go. When I do, you'll be the first to know.'

'I don't doubt it.'

'Smug cow. One fuck with Dynamite Darcy, and she's the world expert.'

'Look, you got what you wanted. Why are you in such a foul mood?'

Melissa shrugged. 'It's too early to be madly in love. And I couldn't get into the bathroom.'

'I think Frank's in there.'

'Shit. I bet he uses all the hot water. Americans always think it appears by magic – they never understand about boilers. Isn't there any brown bread?'

'No,' Ernestine said shortly.

'You'd better get some, then. Bloody Cecily and Craig are coming today.'

'I haven't forgotten.'

'They're your responsibility, since you're the one who invited them.' Melissa spooned more sugar into her coffee, scattering it across the table. 'And this is more or less your house, as you never lose a chance to remind me.'

Ernestine's pulse had begun to flutter uncomfortably. She hated it when Melissa went for her like this. It did not happen often, but always made her feel slightly sick, and frighteningly helpless. All she could do was remain as neutral and tactful as possible, and wait for the storm to pass.

'My house?' she echoed carefully. 'Don't be silly.'

'It will be one day, when Tess and George are dead. I got Quenville, and you'll get this. Don't tell me it hasn't occurred to you.'

'Mel!'

'Grandpa left this cottage to Tess because he didn't like my father. If I'd been a boy, it would have come to me. So count yourself lucky.'

'Please – ' Ernestine was on the edge of tears. The hardness of her cousin's tone slashed at her beloved parents, causing her actual physical pain.

'Sorry. Oh darling, I'm sorry.' Melissa relented, as she always did eventually. 'You shouldn't listen to me – though if you don't I can't imagine who will. I got out of the wrong side of bed, that's all.'

And it was all right again. Being back in Melissa's good

71

graces left Ernestine weak with relief. These episodes terrified her, because they gave her a glimpse of the world without her cousin's love. Their alliance, so long taken for granted, was the shape of her life.

'Do you want some toast? There's damson jam.'

'You're a saint,' Melissa said, smiling like the sun coming out. 'What on earth would we do without you?'

'Starve,' Ernestine suggested, and they both laughed.

'I smelled the coffee – gimme it quick.' The room shrank as Frank came in, shaved and glossy, wrapped in a towelling robe. He dropped an affectionate kiss on the top of Ernestine's head. 'Jesus, that naughty apron again – '

He caressed her breasts with one hand, and grabbed a slice of bread with the other. Ernestine's glowing memories of the previous night burst into flames.

Then Frank saw Melissa, and froze with his mouth full.

Ernestine, suddenly aware of her cousin's semi-nudity, was surprised by a great pang of anguish. Even as she felt it, she recognized it as jealousy, and was shocked at herself. Was this what love did to a reasonable person?

Melissa, not in the least self-conscious, grinned. 'Don't beg my pardon, for God's sake. It's my fault for being such an indecent old tart.' Unhurried, without trying to pull down her T-shirt, she sauntered from the room.

Frank stared after her, his eyes trapped in the space where she had been. After God knew how long, he snapped out of his trance, turning back to Ernestine as if he only just finished speaking.

'By the way, you guys are out of hot water.'

Four

'Ern, did you remember the paper for the john?'

'Yes, and the peanut butter, before you ask.'

'All I can think of is that goddam cheese.'

'It's supposed to stink, Frank. That's the whole point.'

Frank and Ernestine were on their way back from Newmarket, in Will's muddy and dilapidated 2CV. During the
week they had been at the cottage, they had taken over the
task of shopping for the whole party. Frank had an acute
interest in food, and loved to watch Ernestine's expertise at
every stage, from buying the raw materials to laying the
finished product on the table. She was more than a cook.
She was an artist – Frank had never realized food could be
so blatantly sexy. Tomatoes suddenly became plump with
promise when she held them. Her garnishes fell into graceful patterns of their own accord, wherever she threw them.
Every morning, over her superlative fresh coffee, the two of
them discussed menus, with almost erotic intensity.

Now, driving down the winding lanes, loaded to the gun-
wales with provisions, Frank reflected on his new-found
talent for domesticity, and the incredible fact that he was
enjoying it. He was, he realized, in love – not with Ernestine
herself, perhaps, as much as the atmosphere of sensuality
and abundance she created around her. With no apparent
effort or drudgery, she laundered napkins, filled vases and
provided exquisite meals. And still she found the time to sit
for hours in the sunny garden, shelling peas into a bowl with
a novel propped on her knee. She shed nurture, Frank
thought, as magically as Hebe offering nectar. No other
woman looked as delicious as she did in the providing role.
Melissa was a clumsy amateur in a kitchen and poor Cecily

could manage nothing better than utilitarian vats of spaghetti. They all hated Ernestine's evenings off.

She was such a darling, too. Frank had never spent time with such a pleasurable and comfortable woman. Angrily, he contrasted her with his cold bitch of a mother and his arrogant sister. Ernestine exposed them, in all their meanness and petty vanity. Compared to them, she was the crown and epitome of femininity.

He had only intended to have a casual affair with her, and here he was, thinking how he would miss her when the houseparty broke up. He had found it amazingly easy to become addicted to her delicate curves, and the sight of her pretty face beside him when he woke. They made love at every opportunity, and with a restful lack of surrounding drama. With any luck, Frank mused, they would have time for a quick one when they got home, between unpacking the shopping and starting the lunch.

His grip tightened on the steering wheel. Whenever he thought of sex, he automatically thought of Melissa. Her skin was turning the colour of pale sand in the heat, and her eyes were slumberous with constant shagging – Will, lucky bastard, couldn't keep his hands off her. Of course, she belonged to Will. Frank accepted this. They were a pair, a major item, practically engaged.

But my God, the sight of her naked.

Melissa had a way of drifting round the cottage wearing almost nothing, as if she were alone. The previous morning, Frank had crashed in on her in the bath, and nearly swooned over the unexpected encounter with her breasts. She had only smiled, and asked him to pass her the loofah. At times like these – and there were plenty – Frank felt his blood slackening and his brain turning to soft cheese, and he had to rush off and fuck Ernestine with frantic urgency.

Ernie loved it, of course. If Frank had allowed himself to think more deeply, he might have felt guilty. But why should she care who he had on his mind, if she had his body? He glanced aside at her and felt fiercely protective. She was such a sweetheart, he wouldn't hurt her for the world.

74

They had reached the outskirts of Shenley, the sprawling village nearest Quenville. Frank turned the car into the short cut, which ran through the fields, skirting the village street. Whichever way you took, this was the least attractive part of the journey. Lopsided barns and derelict outhouses gave way to scrubby fragments of waste ground and bald coppices.

'Oh God,' Ernestine said suddenly, 'travellers. The farmer must be going crazy. I bet the whole village is up in arms.'

The roadside verge had changed overnight into a grotesque shanty town. Dented trailers and vans stood rotting in a sea of poisonous black mire, looking as if they had been taking root for years. There were heaps of rubbish everywhere – dismantled engines, rejected clothes, mouldering stumps of furniture. A chemical lavatory with the door hanging off leaned drunkenly against the fence.

Frank slowed to a crawl to avoid an evil-looking dog with a grey muzzle, which was carrying a dead rat across the road. Several dirty gypsy children were bouncing on an old car seat. Clouds of thick black smoke belched from a bonfire, upon which a group of ragged men were throwing tyres.

Disgusted, he put his foot down, and shot past the filthy settlement.

Ernestine drew in a sharp breath, and cried: 'Stop! Stop the car! Stop!'

Startled, he braked so suddenly that they both jerked forward, and a bag burst on the back seat in an explosion of escaped oranges.

'What the fu-'

'It's Giles.' She wrenched her door open. 'I just saw Giles.'

'Here? Don't be stupid – '

She was already running back down the road. Frank locked the car before following her – though these guys looked as if they would strip it down to the frame in five minutes anyway.

One man had detached himself from the group around

the fire. He put his arms around Ernestine and kissed her, while his companions looked on with black-browed indifference.

'Ernie! I knew you were around here – I hoped you'd run into us. And Frank, how are you?'

It took Frank a stunned moment to recognize Giles. Dirt lay on him in crusts. His light brown hair was matted and chalky with it, his fingernails were black. He was grimed in every seam. He wore unfamiliar jeans of plebian cut, and a discoloured gold earring which had turned one earlobe green.

Through the carapace of filth, he smiled a dazzling, ecstatic smile, then spoiled the effect by suddenly breaking into an agonizing fit of harsh, bass coughing.

'Oh Giles,' Ernestine thumped his back, 'you sound terrible. Where on earth have you been? We were so worried. Are you all right?'

Giles gasped himself to recovery, laughing away her concern. His eyes, Frank noticed, were as guileless as ever, but had a peculiar, other-wordly glaze.

'What're you on on, man? I wish you'd light it and pass it round.'

'Frank, right now I'm high on life. These have been the most brilliant, earth-shattering weeks of my life. I should have buggered off months ago.'

Ernestine lowered her voice. 'Are you actually – you know – living with these people?'

He took her hand. 'I'm one of them. And please don't stare like that, darling. They're the sanest people I ever met in my life. I've learned more wisdom in a few days than I did in years of expensive education.'

'Your dad had the river dragged. When the police wouldn't do it, he paid for it himself. Oh Giles, we saw him. He's out of his mind about you.'

Giles's smile faded. 'Wonderful what a guilty conscience will do, isn't it?'

'But he's so – '

'Ernie, that prick is not my father. I never want to see him again.'

'Tell him you're safe, at least!'

'You can, if you like. Say I've gone with the raggle-taggle gypsies, and he can stick his concern up his – '

'Oh for God's sake,' Frank burst out, 'this is ridiculous. Ernie, can we take him back with us?'

'Absolutely.'

Giles was laughing again, in a pitying way. 'No, no, no. Didn't you hear me? I've never been happier in my life.'

'What,' Frank demanded, 'with these cavemen? They're sub-human.'

'Poor,' Giles pointed out gently, 'that's all they are.'

'Bull. They don't even have normal-shaped heads. Jesus.'

'They've freed me. It's like being born again. I belong with the travellers now.'

Ernestine stroked his arm. 'Come and see us, anyway. We're right down the end of Dawn Lane, at the cottage with the green door. You could have a bath.'

Giles chuckled. 'I certainly need one. I must smell like a corpse.'

'That's putting it mildly.' Frank, now that the initial shock had worn off, was annoyed with Giles for causing so much trouble. 'How can you bear to live like these morons? You can't possibly have anything in common with them.'

'Frank, I wish I could make you understand. Give my love to Melissa, Ernie. Tell her I might drop by later.'

He turned back to his companions, and the foul curtain of black smoke closed around him.

The news that Giles had run off with the gypsies caused a sensation over lunch at the cottage.

'I guess I can see the lure of the open road in theory,' Frank said, 'but the reality is revolting. I think he's gone mad.'

'But is he okay?' Will asked, frowning anxiously. 'Did he seem depressed?'

'I've never seen him happier,' Ernestine told him.

'Well, it's the farmer I feel sorry for,' Cecily announced. 'The land's ruined, and there's not a thing he can do without hundreds of court orders.'

77

'You shouldn't have asked him here,' Melissa said. 'If those tinkers get to hear this place is empty half the year, they'll just wait to stroll in.'

Ernestine looked alarmed, but Craig cut in, with surprising firmness: 'Don't be so prejudiced. They can't help being homeless. Think of always being harassed and moved on. Think of being hated wherever you go.'

The others stared at him in amazement, as if a cat had spoken. Craig Lennox was usually so silent and so void of opinions that they forgot he was there for hours at a time. Why Cecily had taken up with him was a mystery – especially after his absurd misfortune at the ball, when he had been mugged for his clothes. But perhaps, Ernestine thought, they had been drawn together by their shared talent for calamity.

He subsided back into dimness as soon as the words were out of his mouth, and it was left to Cecily to interpret.

'Craig does a lot for the Labour Party. You must have seen him handing out his leaflets in St Aldates.'

'Must I?' Melissa wondered. 'No. But I don't think I'd remember Craig handing out leaflets if he dropped them naked from a balloon.'

'Mel – ' Ernestine murmured warningly, but she could not help laughing. Since Melissa had discovered that Craig was impervious to insults, her open rudeness to him had become breathtaking.

Frank found her barbs exquisitely funny, but Ernestine noticed they made Will uncomfortable. When Melissa was bitchy to Craig, the fog of infatuation around him lifted slightly. Now, a new and critical expression crept into his fair face as he watched her, and Ernestine found herself thinking: She'd better be careful.

The landscape wavered in the heat of the afternoon. Will had found the wormy croquet set, and was teaching Frank to play on the lawn. Melissa and Ernestine lay on their backs in the grass. They were supposed to be reading, but Melissa's mind was really on sunbathing, and Ernestine found that her awareness of Melissa's exposed body kept creeping between herself and the page. Did she really have to lounge around in that minuscule bikini? Frank kept looking at her, and you could hardly blame him. Still, it was pathetic to be jealous, and very insulting to Frank. No lover could be more affectionate. Whenever he came near her, he swooped down with kisses and embraces. He must not think she did not trust him.

Craig and Cecily leaned against the trunk of the apple tree, hand in hand. Ernestine distracted herself by musing on their sex life – a very audible sex life, which Melissa had said put her in mind of two dying mooses – and wondering why the idea of plain people making love automatically attracted hostility. Surely they had just as much right to romance. If you cut them, did they not bleed? Or, to put it another way, if you stroked them, did they not come? She was not sure she liked the picture of Craig coming.

Will was the first to see the two figures walking up the track to the gate.

'Giles!' He raised his hand in a Roman *Ave*, falsely hearty. 'Hi!'

Melissa shaded her eyes curiously. 'For God's sake, he's brought someone with him. Of all the nerve.'

'His tinker-bride,' Frank said. 'It figures. We should have guessed there'd be sex at the bottom of it.'

At the gate, Giles took his arm from around the waist of the tinker-bride, and kissed her cheek. As he walked up the long garden, she stayed leaning against the gate, watching them with disconcerting stillness. At that distance, all they could make out was that she was tall and skinny, with a shock of dark hair covering her face.

'Bloody hell,' Melissa said, standing up to survey Giles.

He grinned at her, delighted by her open distaste. 'Sorry about the pong, darling. Our Bedford van doesn't have an en suite bathroom.'

'Where do you wash, then?'

'We don't.'

'Oh bloody hell.' She took a step back.

Ernestine tugged at Giles's sleeve. 'I'm making tea. Would she like some? Do ask her in.'

Giles's jaunty self-possession suddenly collapsed. Never the type to blush, he crimsoned until his eyes watered. 'No. I mean, thanks. But – but she's not actually – I mean, she'd rather stay there.'

There was an awkward silence. They exchanged furtive, guilty glances, as if the woman's reluctance was some kind of judgement upon them.

Frank cleared his throat. 'Where did you meet her?'

'We weren't exactly introduced.' Giles managed a smile. 'She offered me a share of the van.'

'I spoke to Dan,' Will said, 'just to say you were all right.'

'Didn't tell him where to find me, I hope?' Recovering his briskness, Giles sat down on the grass. From his pocket he produced two skinny joints, and handed one to Melissa. 'Here. This should mask my body odour.'

'Oh Giles, you angel.' She was instantly all smiles, crouching on the lawn beside him.

'So tell me what's been going on. Are you and Will engaged yet?'

'I don't know. Are we, Will?'

Ernestine went back to the house to make the tea, leaving them all to gossip and laugh. Giles had stepped easily back into his old place in the circle, and the others were soon behaving as if he had never left, but she was uncomfortably aware of the silent, somehow accusing presence of the tinker-bride at the gate.

She was in exactly the same attitude when Ernestine returned to the garden with the tray of tea. Giles put a selection of her home-made rock cakes and biscuits on a plate and took them down to her.

It took a moment or two to dissipate the awkwardness of leaving Giles's woman to eat all alone, like a plague-carrier. Will, his pink eyelids fluttering, began to murmur something about bringing her in, but Giles cut him short.

'I'm sorry if it upsets your liberal conscience, Will, but this is what we'd both prefer.'

'Fine by me,' Melissa said. 'I can't make small talk with a social statistic. I haven't got a liberal conscience.'

There was general laughter, and Giles said: 'We all know that, dear girl.'

Ernestine joined in, but could not help wondering how their burst of laughter sounded to the exile.

'I meant to send you all postcards,' Giles was saying, 'but I've been in such turmoil, I've hardly had time to think about my old life.'

'Old life?' Will protested. 'C-come off it.'

'I'm serious. I've finished with Oxford, finished with my family, finished with the entire well-bred treadmill I've been trapped on since kindergarten. I'm free.'

Frank looked pained. 'What – you intend to spend your whole life living in a van? You could do anything, and you'll settle for that?'

Cecily said: 'All right, you might have had some unfair advantages. But giving them up won't help anyone.'

'And I assume you do want to help them,' Craig said, with more animation than any of them had ever seen in him. 'The question is, can you help the underclass by joining them?'

Giles slurped thirstily at his tea. 'I think I have to join them because I can't live in both worlds at the same time. You can't imagine how different they are. These are people who belong nowhere. They have nothing. They live from hand to mouth. They steal and fight and do drugs for survival, pure and simple – and survival means finding your next meal, and not being sure you own it until it's in your belly. The whole of so-called society turns its back on these people. They have no friends in the world except each other.'

Melissa looked vague and distant. Frank was irritated to be forced to face something he could not change. Will and Craig were nodding agreement. Cecily glanced into all their faces, trying to decide how to react.

Ernestine thought, with a sorrowful pang, how very difficult it was to remember that the 'underclass' were her fellow human beings, and not another species altogether. If you remembered it for too long, how could you bear it?

Craig asked: 'How did you find this lot?'

'Well, they found me really,' Giles said. 'I was very unhappy, and they were kind to me, so I went with them when they moved on.' He smiled, with the same slightly glassy-eyed expression Frank had noticed earlier. 'What cared I for my goose-feather bed?'

'All fine and dandy,' Craig said, 'but I think your approach is far too romantic – leaving Oxford and living rough, and all. Your friends need someone on the inside. Someone with the clout to influence society. Not another mouth to feed.'

'I can give them plenty in return.' Giles was stung. 'I can act as a kind of interpreter when they have dealings with what you call "the inside". Doctors, for instance, and Social Security officials. And scores of them are courting AIDS, because they've no idea they can get free needles and condoms. For God's sake – some of them can't even read and write – '

He erupted into a galvanic fit of coughing, which racked his body mercilessly and brought two hectic spots of colour up on his cheeks.

'You're sick,' Will said. 'You should see a doctor.'

'Rubbish.' Giles gasped and smacked his chest as the fit passed. 'Get this into your head, Will. I'm not lost – I'm found. Next time you see me, if you ever see me again, I shall be quite transformed.'

Round the bend in the lane, safely hidden from his friends at the cottage, Giles began to laugh so hard that he brought on another attack of coughing.

'Their faces!' He clutched at the hedge for support. 'And it's just as well you didn't come in, my duck. They thought you were a girl.'

'A girl? Get off,' said Johnny disbelievingly.

'Johnny, sweetheart, don't go all injured on me. They just assumed, you see, because I've always gone with girls before. And I was such a coward, I never got round to telling them. I reckoned I'd given them enough shocks for one day.'

Johnny shook back his mane of curling black hair in the petulant way he knew Giles found exciting. 'Did they try to make you stay with them?'

'Oh, of course. But I told you, I wouldn't let them get me. I'm with you now.'

'The girl in the bikini. That was Melissa, wasn't it?'

'That's right, the one who owns the ruined house.' Giles was deeply touched by Johnny's interest in his friends – he was avid for details of their lives, like a child begging for fairy stories. 'And Ernestine made the cakes and biscuits we had.'

'They were nice.'

Giles slung his arm round Johnny's shoulders. 'I do adore the way you say "noice".'

'Noice Goiles,' Johnny said, playing up his West Country accent.

They began to stroll back towards the travellers' site. 'The spotty one was the chap who had his suit nicked at the ball.'

Johnny's finely cut lips curved into a gleeful smile. 'Now, who'd do a thing like that?'

'Some joker. In the upper classes, deviant and anti-social acts are known as "japes", and that was a classic jape.'

'And what about the geezer with the yellow hair?' Johny's grey eyes were, briefly, sparks of concentrated malice.

Giles did not see it. 'That's Will, my dear old chum from Eton. He's as thick as thieves with Melissa, which rather surprises me. She usually has trouble sticking.'

'So they're a real couple, then?'

'Apparently. In love, and all that. I say, what a scream if they got married.' Giles halted, and pointed at a lopsided notice on a nearby fence. 'What does that say?'

Johnny stared at it, with an unfathomable smile. 'I dunno. "Keep Off", or "No Trespassing", or something.'

'Come on, Johnny, don't guess. What's the first letter?'

'F,' Johnny said, keeping his hilarity under control with some difficulty.

'Good boy. You could learn to read perfectly easily, you know, if you'd just put your mind to it. You're clever.'

'Thanks, teacher.' Johnny charged ahead, to hide his face.

'It says "Farm Shop, Next Right",' Giles caught him up, and grabbed his arm affectionately. 'I'll give you another lesson later.'

He had been almost pleased to discover that the beautiful gypsy was illiterate, because it seemed to offer a way of paying him back for his generosity. A simple, generous heart like Johnny's, Giles thought, is more precious than any amount of education. This tousled angel had appeared before him just when he had cried out for salvation.

The phone call with Dan, the day after the ball, had hurled him totally off balance. Afterwards, unable to return to his room at Christ Church, Giles had wandered in despair, trying to digest the new shape of his world. A fight with his father was one thing, but a fight with a vicious stranger who never wanted to see him again was a new and terrible experience. He was nobody, from nowhere. The sense of being an outcast weighed him down as if he had been carrying Tom Tower on his shoulders.

He had passed lighted windows and laughing groups of undergraduates, feeling like a spurned Ishmael, disowned by everyone. Eventually, as the night wore on, he had left the University district behind, and found himself in a run-down part of Cowley. In a patch of waste ground behind a disused factory building, he had seen the travellers, levering an old mattress onto a fire.

A little comforted by the leaping flames, Giles had sat himself down in the shadows to observe. In a strange way, he envied the travellers. They were dirty and savage, but they were a group. They belonged – if only to each other.

He whispered to himself: 'Who the hell am I?' and started to sob, with his shoulders bowed and his tears dripping on his knees.

Only gradually did he become conscious of the fact that someone was watching him. The figure seemed to have assembled itself beside him like a pillar of shadow, and in the first half-second after he saw him, Gile's stomach contracted with fear. The stranger's face flashed malevolence at him, and his senses screamed danger – but it had been nothing more than a trick of the light. As Giles drew the figure into focus, his automatic panic subsided.

The light from the flames shifted, and the face revealed itself as innocent and fragile, with slate-grey eyes of heart-breaking poignancy.

'What's the matter?' he had asked in his soft voice with its reassuring West Country burr. 'Why are you crying?' He sat down on the jagged wall beside Giles, and the warmth of his body was a soothing poultice to his misery.

The boy's name was Johnny Ferrars, and he was beautiful.

When he heard that Giles had nowhere to go, he invited him into the rusted Bedford Van he had just acquired as part of a cocaine deal. It contained a camping stove, a frayed sleeping bag and a couple of plastic carriers.

He was offering half of everything he possessed. Giles was overwhelmed by such bounty – he, who congratulated himself if he tossed a coin at a beggar in the street. And I thought I had troubles, he thought remorsefully. This boy would kill to have troubles like mine.

The shame, and his hunger for human kindness, stirred up desires he had never dreamed of. He kissed the spiked lashes and the delicate mouth, and floated into passion as the boy made love to him.

This was the moment of Giles's rebirth. Lying on the corrugated metal floor of the van, feeling Johnny's flesh beside him in the darkness, he had whispered: 'I feel as if my old self had been peeled away, like a snake shedding its skin.'

'Ever done it with a geezer before?'

'No.'

Johnny laughed. 'Took your cherry, did I?'

'It was wonderful. Not because it was a geezer, but because it was you.' And with greater tenderness than he had ever felt in his life, Giles questioned his new love – guessing the answers when Johnny's replies were too cautious.

'Did you go to school?'

'Here and there. When they made me. Didn't do me no good.'

'Johnny, can you read?'

There was such a long silence that Giles was afraid he had offended him.

Eventually, Johnny said, 'No. I never could.'

'I'd love to teach you – there's nothing to it.'

'This lot are moving tonight. I said I'd go with them.'

Giles rolled over, to take a mouthful of the gypsy angel's skinny chest. 'I'm coming too.'

Johnny crouched in a corner of the van, waiting for Giles's hoarse breathing to become regular. His cough kept him awake, but Johnny had laced his tea with some sleeping pills he had swapped with one of the women on the site for a blow job. He was getting mighty tired of the flower-child persona he had used to captivate Giles. The poor fool had lapped it up, but God, it was a drag. One of these days, he would give himself away – Giles had nearly caught him reading an old edition of the *Daily Telegraph*, wrapped round some chips. And one of these days, he would give in to the temptation of chewing the silly bastard's head off. Giles's sentimentality about the travellers, the open road, and the saintly life at the bottom of the heap got up his nose in a major way.

Thankfully, he would not need Giles much longer. He had learned, through him, that Melissa was back at Quenville, and persuaded the other travellers to pitch nearby. He had found the ideal position to spy on the girl who had eaten into his dreams. If he could, he would have climbed inside her head. He was desperate to know everything she thought, felt, did.

Giles's noisy breathing subsided into eerie silence.

Whoops, Johnny thought, hope I didn't give him too many.

As noiseless as a cat, he picked up the torch he kept hidden under the floor, and slid out of the van. He had spent the previous night exploring the ruins, and sniffing the air for a clue to that buried family fortune. He had been fascinated by the shattered tiles he crunched under his boots, and the elaborate patterns they made when he fitted the fragments together. Quenville was a brilliant place. He could have spent weeks examining every detail. No wonder Melissa was so crazy about it.

He had seen her last night, a white apparition, gliding hand in hand through the ruins with the stumbling Will. She had peeled off her long nightgown, and her naked body, in the unearthly, rose-scented glare of the moonlight, made Johnny catch his breath. Ceremonially, she spread a rug on the worn flagstones and lay down, fanning out her hair around her. She was like a clear pool in a desert. Johnny ached and burned to touch her.

She cried out for a right good seeing-to, he thought, chuckling to himself. She's certainly not getting it from him. The spectacle of Will splayed on top of her, grunting away, as pink as a prawn, was hilarious. Johnny was savagely delighted to witness the imbecilic face he made while thrusting, and to hear his pathetic cries of 'God, sorry, sorry – I'm c-c-coming!' when he clumsily toppled into orgasm.

Fine, if she needed his money. Johnny would have done exactly the same himself. If only they would do it again tonight. If only Will would run away, and leave him to fall between her legs, as he had done at the college ball. Did she remember? Did she ever think about him?

It was late. The cottage windows were dark. The tangle of verdure around Quenville shivered as a pair of stout badgers ran through it. Johnny risked switching on his torch to assess the condition of the upper floors. The bulging walls were lashed with thick stems of ivy and wild rose. Round the back, the masonry sagged ominously. There was a papery rustle of bats.

Melissa's family had been over every inch of the house, countless times, but the fact that they had found nothing only sharpened his belief that the treasure existed. He could smell opportunity, which had a teasing whiff to it, like sex. The others had not been ruthless enough, he decided. Like Melissa, they had cared too much about the house itself. He wanted to tear the stones apart, blasting every last moulding and shard of stained glass to dust. Quenville would not yield its secret, as long as they allowed it to stand. Johnny was feeling exceptionally lucky at the moment. Since the day he had come here to Quenville, all his plans had gone seamlessly. It was not luck he needed here, however. It was dynamite.

He switched off the torch, and picked his way across the weeds and rubble, making a circuit of the house. Melissa would have to understand, one of these days, that she must sacrifice her dreams of restoring Quenville if she wanted to get her hands on that treasure. Johnny could only do so much for her. The Lord helps those who help themselves, he thought, laughing as he recalled how often he had helped himself to things in the past.

He heard juicy stems snapping under someone's feet, and froze. She had come back. This time she approached in a storm of haste and whispers, tearing up roots and scattering leaves. Johnny slunk through the darkness towards the breathless gasps, and suddenly stopped short, nearly felled by a great pang of rage.

Here was Melissa, but the man with her was not Will. It was the American who went round with little Ernie. There was no ceremony this time. The two of them clawed desperately at each other, biting and wrestling like a pair of wild animals. Melissa's long elegant fingers tore at the buttons of Frank's bulging denim fly. Frank wrenched open her dress and sucked hungrily at her nipples.

He slammed her against one wall of the porch, hitched her legs around his waist and brutally entered her standing up, with the long grass licking at his exposed buttocks. His urgent, rhythmic pants, building to groans, made Johnny feel it was possible to die of jealousy. Frank and Melissa came together, in a plaintive duet of moans that seemed to go on for ever.

Silence fell. The sounds of the night reasserted themselves. Presently, Johnny heard the two of them whispering together.

'Jesus, what are we going to tell them?'

'Nothing – don't be crass. They won't even notice we've gone –'

'But we can't just – '

'Come on, Frank, come on – '

'No, we have to talk.'

'Talk?' hissed Melissa. 'What the hell about?'

'Us,' Frank said. 'Didn't that mean anything to you? Won't it change things?'

'Why should it?'

'Melissa, please – '

She raised her voice. 'Breathe one word of this to Will or Ernie, and I'll swear you're telling lies.'

'Hey, wait! I can't see a damn thing out here.' Frank ran after her.

Johnny listened to their retreat, only slightly mollified by the way Melissa had brushed him off. He saw, only too clearly, that this Frank was a far more potent threat to him than Will. He was handsome, he had a big dick and he belonged to Melissa's own world. When her obvious longing for him overwhelmed her, he would be able to do anything with her.

Johnny's head was so seething with fantasies about Frank's death, it felt about to explode.

'You bastard. You piece of shit. I'll pay you out for this.'

He muttered it through clenched teeth, but the force of his fury seemed to rise up in a swirling black cloud around him. A misshapen lump of red brick thumped down at his feet, like the first warning raindrop of a tempest. Another brick fell, then a section of the stone parapet. The ground lurched beneath his feet. Johnny looked up, in time to see the wall above him shiver and crack. It toppled, then crashed down on top of him. He felt one crushing spasm of pain, then nothing, nothing.

At first, he thought he had gone blind. He opened his eyes, and saw only a continuation of the blackness inside his smarting lids. Then he tried to move, and found his legs and chest pinned to the ground. He had a moment of sickening panic – I'm dead, I've been buried – and the freezing loneliness of all eternity lay before him.

He spat out a mouthful of brick dust, and his consciousness crept back. Cautiously, he moved his limbs, shedding a shower of rubble. Directly above him, he could see the moon, framed by a jagged ring of masonry. He moved the stone on his chest, wondering if he had broken a rib. Struggling, he sat up. There was something wet trickling down his face, and when it oozed into his mouth, he tasted blood.

Every muscle hurt, as if someone had pounded him all over with a hammer. His wet hands cautiously felt around the jagged walls of the crater he lay in. He was dizzy, furred with dust and keening with the shock and pain – but even as he did so, his mind was marshalling its forces to size up the situation.

A section of the flagstones had collapsed underneath him, brining down part of one wall on Johnny's head, and crashing through into a cellar, or a coal hole. God, he could have been killed.

He leaned over and vomited on the earthy floor beside him. The smell of his own warm bile rushing back to meet him was so disgusting that he threw up until he was drained and hollow. The last thing he remembered was his anger, and he could not help feeling he had conjured up the collapse himself. He was almost afraid of his own power, and in this rimy darkness, he shivered over the foolish joke he had made about selling his soul to the devil.

With shaking, bloody hands, he felt in his jeans pocket for a squashed packed of cigarettes, and lit one. His eyes were getting used to the gloom, and he recognized the outline of his torch, lying against one leg. He switched it on, and ran the feeble beam around his prison, looking for a way out. There was a single wooden door, bound fast by rusted iron bands. In any case, it probably led to even greater danger. He would need to hoist himself, somehow, back through the hole in the cellar's dank ceiling. And it was ten feet above him, at least.

'Shit,' Johnny said aloud. 'This is nice.'

He was stuck here until daylight. Someone at the cottage would hear him if he yelled – but what a way to be found.

Melissa would write him off as scum. A filthy vagrant. She would call the police without taking a second look at him. He had already heard what she thought of intruders.

'Oh, shit.'

He clicked off the torch, closed his eyes, and breathed slowly, to wrestle down his panic. This was an old trick of his which had got him out of a few tight corners in the past. He opened his eyes again, switched on his torch, and began examining his prison more calmly.

A fissure had opened out in the broken wall, dislodging brickwork and plaster. Johnny played the beam across it several times, before he realized there was something inside – a shape, an edge.

A box.

He remained motionless for several long minutes, hardly daring to believe it. Someone had hidden a box in a gap in the wall, and bricked it in to a depth of nearly a foot, so that you would assume it was solid from the outside.

Johnny was trembling, and his pulse thudded unbearably. He wanted to hold the moment, before the discovery swept into his life. He had found the treasure. He was going to be rich. He did not even dare to think of the possibilities. Jesus, his luck. The devil was a handsome employer, all right.

Feverishly, he scrabbled inside the fissure, seized the box, and managed to drag it out into the room. It was two or three feet square, made of heavy wood with brass trimmings, now almost black with age. There was a single lock at the front, and a thick rope lashing down the lid. The box looked like a pirate's treasure chest in a film.

Johnny did his breathing again, and his wild heart slowed enough to allow him to get to the treasure. He held his cigarette lighter to the rope, his teeth chattering with impatience. It might be gold bars, he thought, or diamonds. Maybe rings and necklaces, or heaps of Victorian sovereigns. The rope fell to the floor. He smashed the lock with one of the pieces of stone.

And his hands were gripping the lid. This is the bit where my life changes, he thought. Slowly, he opened the box. It groaned in protest, and one of the rotten hinges snapped.

There was nothing inside it but fucking paper.

The disappointment was so searing that he simply gaped, unable to take the pain all at once. Not even banknotes – just bundles of paper, covered in spidery writing and neatly bound with tape. Clutching at the final straw of hope, he plunged his hands into the bottom of the box, scattering the bundles around him, and found nothing more.

For almost the first time since infancy, Johnny shed tears. To come this close, only to see the dream melt away, was the sheerest torture. He lay on the cold floor, writhing and raging, until he was spent with fury, as dry and exhausted as a squeezed orange.

Eventually, he crouched amongst the debris, smoking another cigarette.

So it had been nothing but a stupid story, after all. Johnny drew the brittle packet of paper before him, and the tape crumbled away in his hands. He found himself holding an untidy pile of scraps, all in the same old-fashioned copperplate. Some appeared to be diaries, he noted, with quickening interest. And some were poems, written more neatly, as if the crazy old lady of Quenville had made fair copies of her ravings for posterity.

> I lay my jewels beneath this stone,
> To gaze on when I am alone.
> Hearts are fickle, loves untrue –
> These lie untouched by pain or rue.
>
> I'll never wear you now, I say;
> You'll know no more the gleam of day.
> I am too old, too coarse, too grey
> To shame your beauty with decay.

The pages from the diary were undated, and less easy to decipher. Johnny brought the torch closer. 'None shall know,' he read. 'My treasure shall be protected from venom and greed, and prying eyes. I went to look at it again today. I cannot go any more. I despise misers above all people. I do not have to see it, as long as I know it is there.'

Fastened to this sheet, with a pin that had bled rust into the yellowed paper, was another poem:

> The woman of impoverished heart
> Leaves all her chambers bare,
> To show her gaudy trinkets
> Upon her bosom fair.
>
> The woman of true riches
> Has caskets overflowing,
> But walks through mire in plain attire,
> To keep the world from knowing.

Well, well, Johnny was thinking, there might be something here after all. Had the old girl meant to leave clues? This was fascinating. And if he was fascinated, others would be too. He sifted the pages rapidly, catching more references to pearls and misers, and the delights of gloating in secret. It could all have been dismissed as madness, except for the final bundle of writings, bound more carefully than the rest.

The first was a letter, in a different script and meticulously folded.

Dr A. T. Aitcheson
Mulberry Grove
Shenley
Norfolk

My dear Rose,
   I do not think we shall have to worry for very much longer – without wishing to sound heartless, poor James is sinking fast. He is very agitated, and still frets that our sin cries out to heaven. That as a clergyman, he is the more blameworthy. I assure him the Great Judge cannot condemn a thing done for

compassion's sake, and am now easy that our affair
will die with him.

But he is asking for Joshua, and cannot be allowed
to see him. If James communicates our secret, it will
be most awkward.

Arthur

The second was another page of Rose Lamb's journal, dated
'St Mark's Day':

How old we are. I can scarcely believe that poor
James, who loved me so faithfully and thanklessly,
will soon be gone. I find myself wondering, if it had
all been different, might we have been happy? But I
regret nothing. I have looked into the future, and
know the time has come to bring my business to a
final settlement.

I feel that I shall soon follow James. He will get his
wish at last, if I am worthy to meet him in another
world. I am not afraid. Merely determined to be
ready. The place is sealed fast. I often sit there, for
where is the harm? Yesterday, I found primroses
growing there. All my papers shall be hidden. Joshua
shall not know, because he has already come into his
inheritance – I mean all the worst qualities in his
father. It was never my fate to love a man who did
not grieve me.

Johnny sat holding this document for a long time, feeling
that he was doing the most serious thinking of his life. It was
clear to him that the mystery of the treasure was not yet
solved, and that he held the key to it. But how could the
papers be of any use to him?

He could hand them over to Melissa. And that would be
the end of his involvement. He would get little or nothing
out of it as far as the real treasure was concerned, and he
would be no nearer winning power over Melissa. What I
really need, he thought, is these papers and Will Ivery's

money. I'd be made then. I'd own her, and whatever she found.

Dawn had begun to dilute the darkness. Johnny could see enough now to find an escape route. By straining his sore muscles to breaking point, he built the fallen stones high enough to scramble to the mouth of the crater. There was no way he could carry the box – and there was no way he was leaving it behind for someone else to find. He repacked the papers and, praying the rope would hold, knotted it around the chest. He clawed his way out into the fresh, dewy air with the rope in his hand, and nearly pulled his arms out of their sockets dragging the chest up after him.

Once free, he pushed the box well out of the range of further earthquakes, and threw himself down among the rough nettles and dandelions, to get back his strength.

Slowly, he was coming to the realization that, to get his hands on what he wanted, he would have to work hard and cultivate patience. It was time to get real.

He had no idea how he was to make the journey between the underclass and so-called normal society, but he knew he could do it. Being a total bastard was the only qualification anyone needed for success. 'Turn again, Whittington,' he murmured to himself, 'and kick their nuts off.'

Five

The following term, Giles returned to Oxford. Will, who ran
into him unexpectedly in St Aldates on the first day, was
smitten almost speechless with surprise.

'Giles – why didn't you tell me you were c-c-coming
back? What happened?'

Giles said, with hardly a trace of his old jauntiness: 'I've
been ill.'

'So I see. God, you look t-t-terrible!'

He forced a wintry smile. 'Thanks.'

'What was wrong?'

'Pneumonia.'

Will looked him up and down, shocked by the change in
him. Giles's rounded, ruddy cheeks had faded and dwin-
dled. His cherubic brown curls were cut short. He must
have lost a couple of stone, and his clothes hung on him. It
was on the tip of Will's tongue to ask why he was dressed
like that – he had never seen his disgraceful old friend looking so respectable. Giles wore corduroy trousers, a navy
jersey and – unbelievably – brogues. He might have been
any one of the tweedy Etonian giants swilling beer at The
Bear.

'You had that cough, when we saw you at Melissa's. That
was it, wasn't it?'

'Yes.'

'Christ, Giles – I mean, really,' Will groaned, 'you might
have known you couldn't take living with gypsies.'

Giles shrugged. 'There you are then. You were all right,
and I was wrong. See you sometime.'

'Wait a second!' Will grabbed his arm as Giles tried to
hurry away. 'When do you want to meet up? I'm taking Mel
out to dinner, but if you come to my room at about – '

'Sorry. I can't.'

'M-maybe lunchtime, then, in The Turf? Frank'll be there.'

Giles stopped trying to duck away, and faced him squarely. 'Look, I can't. I'm not ready to see anybody.'

'Aren't you well yet?'

'Perfectly well. I just can't face any of you.'

'For God's sake – '

'Will, please.' Giles eyes were red-rimmed and weary in his gaunt face. 'Can't you leave it there? I've been through too much.'

'What happened?'

His mouth hardened stubbornly. 'I'm not telling you. So please ask the others not to pester me.'

'Well, okay,' Will said, 'but the last time we saw you, you'd found the meaning of the universe, and you were going to spend the rest of your life on the open road. Did you get disillusioned? When did you decide to leave those people?'

'I didn't decide.' Giles was silent for a long time, then said: 'Do me a real favour – leave me alone for a while, eh? I'll tell you when I've got myself more together. Goodbye.'

'He made me feel like the G-g-gestapo,' Will complained later to Ernestine, 'and I was only trying to be supportive.'

'I saw him on Magdalen Bridge this morning,' she said, 'and I swear he deliberately avoided me. Perhaps he just feels a bit of a fool.'

'And so he should,' said Will.

Since taking up the post of Melissa's official lover, Will had acquired a more decisive edge. 'Less of a doormat' was how Melissa described it. Ernestine had noticed, however, that though he was no less soft-hearted, he showed it furtively, as if ashamed. She would never fathom that relationship.

Frank, for some reason, was annoyed by it. Ernestine was more deeply besotted with him than ever, and they were still – she assumed – a couple. This was a barbed pleasure, because Frank continued to behave as if they had fallen together in a friendly, temporary way, and the word love had never been mentioned between them. Frank's reluctance to take the depth of her feelings into account was the only flaw in her happiness.

But I can wait, she told herself; I must be grateful for what I have, and not expect too much. There had been a few days, during the holiday at the cottage, when his behaviour had been both puzzling and disturbing. He had been distant with her, and irritated by all the things about Will that he had once found endearing – the mildness, the stammer, the old-fashioned gentility. If Ernestine had been less in love with him, she might have said Frank was sulking.

It had passed, however. And if you overlooked the lack of formal romance, their relationship was wonderfully warm and easy. These were Frank's favourite words when he was with her. 'God, you're so easy!' he would sigh, usually with his mouth full, and Ernestine was determined to take this as a compliment. Just occasionally, she had a niggling sense that 'easy' was not a particularly flowery lover's tribute. But she was so unused to having a lover at all, she did not know what she ought to expect instead. Ears like shells and lips like cherries? If he ever came out with something like that, they would both die laughing. They loved to laugh, and the part of Frank that did not live on Tennyson and Arnold was enormous fun. 'Perhaps I'm not the romantic type,' she thought. It was really much more flattering when Frank gave her a smack and said 'Nice ass,' though it was not exactly material for a sonnet.

They saw each other every day, and Ernestine knew she was an object of surprised envy to scores of disappointed Oxford belles. This was good enough, until the relationship deepened into a commitment. She was sure it would one day. Could either of them imagine living without the other?

Frank had folded himself right into the centre of her concerns, making her life an extension of his own. It was Frank who persuaded her to go into business with her cooking skills. She had presented the Wild Young Bohemians with a stupendous feast for their first dinner of the term. They had all missed Giles, who refused to come, and felt that Craig Lennox was a poor substitute.

'I'll have to go easy in future,' she said regretfully. 'I mean, we may be a fashionable dining club, but these dinners are costing the Bohemians a fortune. We're not exactly the Bullingdon.'

Frank said: 'No, we eat far better than those guys. Why spend money, when you can make it?'

'Party Angels' began when Ernestine cooked a dinner for one of the don's wives. The saddle of lamb and timbale of potatoes and celeriac had been so successful that she soon found herself with more orders than she could handle. She bought Frank a bottle of vintage champagne with the profits, and the two of them spent a happy evening in her room, licking it out of each other's navels. Often, slicing and steaming in one of her customers' kitchens, she would send herself into an erotic trance, mulling over the unspeakably gorgeous sex she had had with Frank.

She found herself doing it one fine autumn afternoon, while icing a cake in the shape of Babar the Elephant for a child's birthday party. Smoothing green food colouring across Babar's marzipan suit, she sank deep into a memory of Frank's hands on her breasts, the night before. He couldn't have made love to her like that if it didn't mean something.

'I said, where are the sweets for the fairy-cakes?'

'Sorry, Cecily. In the Sainsbury's bag. Do half with Smarties and half with Jellytots, and don't let the icing get too dry.'

Cecily peered anxiously into the bowl of pink icing. 'Oh God, it's crusty – what shall I do?'

'Add a tiny bit of hot water. Here, let me.' She had employed Cecily as her assistant Party Angel, and was trying to teach her not to be a liability. Mostly, washing up was all she was good for. Even then, Ernestine had to be exceptionally calm, in case the poor soul got flustered and broke something.

'Thanks. Oh, I do wish I had half your talent, Ernie. Mummy and Daddy would be so pleased.' Cecily's parents lived in a large manor house in Brontë country, which they

99

ran as a country house hotel. Cecily, who had no gifts as a waitress or chambermaid, spent her vacations putting Silvo on the salt spoons, tying muslin mob-caps on the breakfast jams, and generally botching all the unskilled jobs nobody else wanted.

'Just ice the ones in the Thomas the Tank Engine cake cases,' Ernestine said, striving to keep her patience. 'No, no, not those – '

'Well, they've got engines on them,' Cecily protested.

'Fire engines. That's Fireman Sam. Look, I'll do them in a minute. You put the plastic dinosaurs in the going-home bags.'

In less than an hour, they would be invaded by a six-year-old birthday boy and twenty of his most intimate friends. Thankfully, Ernestine calculated, they were very nearly finished. The table was laid, ready for a storm of crisps and jellies. Val Archer, the vicar's wife, was still out swimming with the children. Father Mark Archer, the vicar, was shut in his study, counselling a student. Everything was under control.

Through the kitchen window of the large Headington vicarage, she could see scarlet leaves drifting past the climbing frame in the garden, and the unwieldy buttresses of the Victorian red brick church – too much like Quenville, she thought, with distaste. The vicarage was older, fully of tiny wellington boots, tricycles and cheerful family clutter. Ernestine considered it nearly perfect. This was the kind of house she would have herself, one day.

Across the tiled hall, the study door banged, and the vicar, a crumpled man with a rainbow sweater over his dog collar, came into the room. 'Hi. How are you getting on?'

'Fine.'

'Could you do me a huge favour? I've got to dash out, and my student needs more time.'

'You make him sound like an egg,' Cecily said.

Father Archer laughed, but looked slightly pained. 'If I send the poor chap in here for a minute, could you make him a cup of coffee?'

'Yes, of course.' Ernestine reached for the kettle. 'We'll all have one.'

'Fantastic.' He dived back into the hall.

'Hope it's not one of his loonies,' Ernestine said.

Mark Archer's hearty, jokey manner and degree in psychology had made him one of the principal refuges for undergraduates in crisis – everyone with a broken heart, an inability to cope with academic pressure or a hankering to throw themselves off the clock towers of their colleges ended up sobbing into Father Mark's Kleenex.

Cecily, said in a colourless voice barely tinged with reproof: 'He was ever so sweet to Craig when his mother died.'

Covered in shame, Ernestine began to search the cupboards for a decent bag of ground coffee.

In breezed the vicar again, pushing the student by the shoulder. 'Girls, this is my chum Giles.'

'Oh, my God,' said Cecily tactlessly.

Giles hung back in the doorway for a long moment, staring at them with a pinched, lost expression Ernestine had never seen on his face before. Then he grinned, with something approaching his usual cockiness.

'Well, well,' he said.

'Oh, you know each other? That's marvellous. Shan't be long, Giles, so make yourself at home.' Father Mark grabbed an anorak off a peg by the back door, and trotted away across the garden.

'Coffee's on,' Ernestine said.

Giles perched on one of the stools beside the kitchen counter. 'I'm glad you're making it, Ernie. Mark's is like cat-piss.'

They all laughed; Cecily too loudly.

'Can I help?' he asked.

Ernestine said, 'You can do the going-home bags. That'll liberate Cecily to put the crisps in bowls – oh Cec, not those. The red ones.'

Giles lit a cigarette. 'Pass me an ashtray.'

'Father Mark doesn't like smoking,' Cecily said.

'Yes, but I'm allowed to because my life is in turmoil. Not being able to smoke might push me over the edge. Relax – it's only tobacco.'

Ernestine giggled, delighted to hear the old Giles. 'They all get a dinosaur, a chocolate thing and a packet of balloons.'

'Balloons, eh? Thought they were condoms.' He began filling the bags, far more efficiently than Cecily had done.

Ernestine gave him a cup of coffee. 'We haven't seen you for ages. Why have you been hiding from us?'

'Oh God.' He was sheepish. 'I suppose Will's wounded?'

'He's worried about you. We all are.'

Giles sighed and rolled his eyes. 'My dear, I wish you'd all stop. It's incredibly fatiguing to know people are worried about one.'

'You needn't be so ungrateful,' Cecily said. 'Some of us think you owe us an explanation.'

Ernestine was irritated. 'No he doesn't. Why the hell should he? It's none of our business.'

He laughed rather sourly. 'It's okay, Ern – you don't have to be delicate with me. I had a bad experience, but I'm pretty well over it now.'

'We knew you were ill, when you came to see us. When did it get bad?'

Giles balanced his cigarette on the edge of his saucer, and went on mechanically filling the bags. Once again, Ernestine saw the bleak, strained look. 'Tell the truth, I don't really remember. They found me in a ditch, and I woke up in hospital, in an oxygen tent.'

'Oh, Giles!'

'What,' exclaimed Cecily, 'you mean, those people just dumped you? But you could've died – '

Over his head, shocked by his expression of pain, Ernestine telegraphed desperate shut-up signals. Giles looked up and saw them. He smiled, and Ernestine glimpsed a whole continent of misery and betrayal in his eyes. Whatever had happened to him, she realized, was too terrible to put into words.

'I nearly did die, apparently,' he said. 'The first thing I saw when I opened my eyes was Dad.'

Ernestine seized on this gratefully. 'So you've made it up? You're speaking again?'

'Yes. Poor old Dad, I've treated him like shit. I do see that now. I've changed, you see.'

'Reformed, you mean?' Cecily asked.

Ernestine groaned, but Giles was laughing again. 'You could say that. My little experience gave me a lot of time to think about the assumptions I make about other people. I realized I'd never even tried to understand Dad's point of view.'

'But I thought he wasn't your real Dad. Why are you pulling faces, Ernie? Everybody knows – '

'Don't worry, darling,' Giles said. 'The world needs people like Cecily to speak the unspeakable. And to sleep with them, if need be.'

Ernestine gave a great bellow of laughter. Cecily scowled, and muttered, 'There's no need to be mean about Craig, thank you – he was really nice to you.'

'Yes, he was. I apologize. And there has been another episode of the Ross family drama. Just when Dad and I decided it didn't matter who my real father was, his wife got pregnant. He insisted we have a blood test, and it turns out I am his real son after all. What a business, eh? We both feel extremely stupid.' Ignoring Cecily, he looked at Ernestine. He was very serious. 'Listen, I've had a terrible time. I've faced every kind of annihilation: physical, mental and spiritual. I can't talk about the details. But a lot of good things are coming out of it. When I saw you all in Norfolk, I told you I'd been reborn, and all that. Well, I had been – just not in the way I assumed. Tell Will.'

'So you split up with that woman,' Cecily said, 'the one who – '

Fortunately, this was the moment a convoy of space-wagons full of children was heard, crunching the gravel in the drive at the front of the vicarage.

'Here they come,' Giles said, crushing out his cigarette

and standing up, 'and here I go. Mark'll have me organizing games if I'm not careful. It's just the sort of thing he thinks will be good for me.'

'Will might want to know,' Ernestine said, 'why you had to confide in Father Mark, and not in him. I think it might hurt him a bit.'

'Oh, I needed more than tea and sympathy,' Giles said. 'I have to see Mark, because he's advising me about how to get accepted for ordination.'

'Sorry?' Ernestine gasped, sure she had misheard.

He smiled at them with bashful pride, like someone announcing an engagement or pregnancy. 'It's theological counselling I come for. I've decided I want to be a vicar.'

PART TWO

1991

A man had given all other bliss,
And all his worldly worth for this,
To waste his whole heart in one kiss
Upon her perfect lips

Tennyson, 'Sir Launcelot and Queen Guinevere'

One

Frank woke with a groan of self-pity, and freed his hot head from the folds of his duvet. His tongue felt like a carpet. His eyes were scorching in their parched sockets.

He lay beached on his mattress on the bare floorboards, drawing the view outside his huge, uncurtained window into focus. God, King's Cross was a depressing area – he always hated the loft in the mornings. In the best of circumstances, daylight did not improve the barren streets, the run-down council blocks or the disused gasometers. A hangover made them look like the last word in failure and degradation.

Far below, a steady stream of cars thundered towards the railway station. Inside the loft, Frank became aware of the agonizing sound that woke him every morning – Paul Dashwood, playing the violin to his marijuana plants. He tried to shout: 'Dash! Shut the hell up!' but his voice was reduced to a feeble croak.

When in London, he shared this prairie of a living space with Dash and Bella Fogarty, who were currently trying to take the London theatre scene by storm, with spectacular lack of success. Bella was unemployed, and Dash was appearing as Crispy the Carrot in an educational play about healthy eating. The thin partitions dividing this former factory floor meant you could hear a fly breaking wind from twenty feet away, and there was absolutely nothing Frank did not know about the private lives of the next Oliviers.

'Jesus, Dash,' Bella's voice complained distantly, 'give it a rest – you'll kill those frigging plants.'

From the far end of Frank's living space, gravelly snores were echoing in the girders of the ceiling. Will lay on his back in a sleeping bag, his mouth hanging open. Giles was slumped fully dressed on the battered sofa, with one hand dangling in the brimming ashtray.

The Wild Young Bohemians had been out on the town, recreating their old Oxford alliance to celebrate the forthcoming marriage of Will and Melissa. The girls had met at Will's flat, for dinner and a male stripper-gram. The men – dear, dear. Frank had dim memories of Giles and Dash 'mooning' out of the car window, and of hoisting Will up the stairs between them.

It had been their first meeting as a group since their grand dinner after the drama of finals. Frank ran it in his mind's eye like a film – their sense of release, following weeks of grinding, panic-stricken labour. How amazed they had been by Melissa's unremarkable second. Nobody had expected lazy Dash or uninspired Cecily to do anything better than scrape by, but Mel had been widely tipped for a first. If she had minded, however, she had not shown it. Or had he been so high on the triumph of his own brilliant first that he had not noticed?

Ernestine had done well, too, with an upper second that had missed being a first by a whisker. She had expressed her delight in a Roman feast of a dinner. After Dash's traditional toast, they had covered his house with so much broken glass that his Marxist landlords had threatened to call the police.

It had been the Bohemians' last wild cry, before the shades of the prison-house – adult life – closed around them. Frank, however, felt he had kept some of the vision splendid. When the others left Oxford, he had stayed. He was a Junior Research Fellow now, walloping English Literature into undergraduates, and using every spare minute to write. Exactly the life he had dreamed of, but the money was dreadful, and he had ended up dividing his time between this dump, and an equally dismal flat in Oxford. On a morning like this, viewed through the wrong end of a hangover, the trappings of his life seemed incredibly sordid.

His feet touched two plastic bags at the end of his mattress. Ernestine had been in, angel that she was. One bag contained Frank's clothes, washed and ironed. He sat up to examine the other one. Great – breakfast. Her mercy knew no bounds. But the resentful thought popped into his head before he could quash it: she's so busy being successful, she thinks she has to make it up to me.

She had filled the kettle, and spooned coffee into the enamel coffee pot on the big, old-fashioned electric stove in the corner. Frank tied a towel round his waist, and stumbled across the splintery floor to switch the kettle on. He was glad Ernestine had not stuck around to wake him up.

He wondered why the thought of her worried him, and recognized it as a leftover from the meeting with his parents the day before. The senior Darcys had descended on London to see their errant son. They were staying in a suite at the Savoy Hotel, and Frank had donned his Brooks Brothers suit to meet them for lunch in the River Room. He had not seen them for eighteen months, since his last visit home, and had never seen them outside their natural habitat. On the whole, he thought, they looked worse when transplanted. His father was stouter and redder, with a voice that made the cutlery rattle. Frank had not realized how used he had become to the English habit of mumbling in public, and had been annoyed by his father's bellowing.

'I mean, what the hell are your plans, Frank? Why should I go on paying you an allowance because being a teacher isn't lucrative enough?'

'I'm a Junior Fellow, Dad.'

'So what? We have universities too, you know. Come home. Get yourself tenure at Princeton or Yale – if they still take white males.'

'He needs to be in Oxford for his novel,' protested Mother, who had decided to treat Frank's English life as something artistic and genteel. 'And he'll be a professor one day.'

'I don't see any novel.'

'It's taking a while to mature,' Frank had said.

'You're getting too old to play the perpetual student. Look at Breda – she's a partner now, she has a beautiful apartment, a season ticket at the Met –' Breda was back in favour these days, if only for the purpose of telling off Frank.

'You can't expect him to hurry his book,' Mother had said. 'When it's finished, dear, send it over to me. I have a friend on one of my committees whose husband is practically head of the biggest publishers in New York.'

God, she's already planning the party for the damned thing, Frank thought now. While he waited for the kettle to boil, he went over to his desk beside the window, and looked over his notes. Here was his PhD: *Icily Regular, Splendidly Null; Unattainable Passivity and the Feminine Icon in Nineteenth-Century Verse*. And here was his novel – the same novel he had been slaving over since his Bohemian days. It would not come right. His heroine, a willowy beauty with long, nut-brown hair, obstinately refused to be captured in print. He could not get the essence of her.

Staring forlornly out at the gasworks, Frank allowed his thoughts to drift back to the night at Quenville, four years before, when he had made love to Melissa. The memory of this was the driving force behind his novel. He was still trying to find an explanation for her behaviour. Why had she come on to him one minute, and pushed him away the next?

She had not looked at him since, nor dropped a single hint that she even remembered. Sometimes, he wondered if he had dreamed the whole thing. Meanwhile, he had slid effortlessly into the relationship with Ernestine. It could not last for ever, of course. He had always assumed they would split up one day, when he met real passion. At the end of his novel, the American hero and the Melissa-esque heroine discovered their true, visceral bond and were united in eternal love. Nothing Melissa did could convince Frank that the bond did not exist deep down; a smouldering ember waiting to burst into flames.

The fact that Ernestine was proving a hard habit to break frightened him. Yes, he loved her, and this was just the trouble. If he was not careful, he would find himself listening to her timid hints about commitment – the word that, so far, he had avoided. Introducing her to his parents yesterday had brought his niggling discontent rushing to the surface.

Subconsciously, he had been counting on his parents disapproving of Ernestine. She was not rich, she was not a

Catholic, she was not American. She did not look like the New York belles of the Darcy circle: tall, perfectly made-up stick insects in black Karan or Klein.

She had rushed into the River Room yesterday, a Dresden figurine in a short Liberty silk dress. A forgotten pencil was skewered into the back of her curly brown hair, and there was a telephone number written in Biro on her wrist. Her handbag was too small, and she thumped her diary down in the middle of the table, spewing untidy scraps of paper. Ernie in a typical flurry, Frank had thought, doing eighteen things at once and revelling in it. He had waited for his parents to pucker their mouths in disappointment.

The moment had never arrived. They had been enchanted. Patricia had seen Ernestine's book on the *Sunday Times* bestseller list, and had already bought twenty copies in Hatchards, to send to all her friends.

'Ernestine, you are so clever. Francis will tell you, I was up half the night, poring over your menus.'

Francis senior chuckled richly. 'It should save me a small fortune.'

Ernestine's book, *Banquet on the Breadline*, was a collection of recipes, designed for working-class people on Income Support. Its emphasis on nutrition and extreme cheapness had been hailed with delight by middle-class, socially conscious gourmets.

'Will you be publishing in the States? Let me know. I can't wait to set the fashion for Breadline Banquets.'

'You'd better wait for the Spanish edition,' Frank had said grouchily, 'or the cook won't be able to read it.'

'Oh Frank,' Patricia had chided him gently, with a very palpable desire to impress Ernestine, 'how do you know I won't be trying the recipes myself?'

'It's not meant for people like you.'

'Well, I know, dear. Obviously, Ernestine is aiming to raise health awareness among the disadvantaged.'

'And how are they supposed to find out about it? Disadvantaged people can't buy books.'

'Yes, that has been a problem,' Ernestine had agreed

mildly. 'But I've got a meeting with an old friend from Oxford – Charlotte Spencer, Frank, you remember – who wants to make it into a television programme.'

'No!' exclaimed Patricia. 'How marvellous!'

'Then I'd reach a much wider audience.'

'And sell more books,' Francis senior had said, with satisfaction.

The television series was news to Frank, and not welcome news. Ernestine's good fortune had come without any particular effort or artistic talent, it seemed to him. What was cooking, after all? And he did not look forward to being known as the television cook's lucky resident stud. He could already hear the cracks about the way to a man's heart.

'Cute as a button,' his father had pronounced, after Ernestine had left them for her meeting.

'And so talented,' Patricia had said, smiling. 'We're staying at Aunt Geraldine's again this August. Do you think she would like to come?'

His parents' approval of Ernestine had made Frank feel trapped and panicky. He had not got around to explaining that this was not a relationship with an indefinite future, and now it looked as if he never would. The net was sneaking over his head. He would wake up one morning, and find himself shackled to a wife. And children. The horror of it. Ernestine's hints about babies were getting too heavy to ignore.

On the other hand, the thought of a life without her was even more depressing. No warm tendrils of curly hair on the pillow beside him, nobody to drop tissues in his hand or cups of tea on his desk while he worked. He would never have endured the loft without Ernestine's mercy-drops of food and washing. Face it, Frank, he lectured himself. This isn't freedom. It's assisted freedom. Fed and laundered freedom.

He was twenty-seven years old, and thirty was suddenly a serious possibility. Where was the passion he had promised himself? The picture of Melissa rose up before him, symbol of everything desirable and unattainable. Then he hated himself, for thinking slightingly of Ernie. A man who was not satisfied with such a woman did not deserve to be satisfied with anything.

On the other side of the room, Giles stretched and yawned, and sat up on the sofa rubbing his hair.

'Hi,' Frank called. 'How are you?'

'Dreadful. Simply dreadful. I never want to hear the word tequila again, as long as I live.'

'Me neither,' Frank said. 'Why did we start drinking it, anyway?'

Giles limped across the floor, scratching his unshaven chin. 'The worst benders are always caused by silly drinks, I find.' He picked up the bag of food. 'Good man, you've been out for supplies.'

'Not me. Ernie must've dropped by.'

'You are a lucky bastard.' He stepped into the tiny bathroom, opening off the kitchen area, to have a pee. 'You've certainly fallen on your feet with that girl,' he called over his shoulder.

'You're not kidding. She even remembered the milk.'

'Rather better than the dear old bridegroom, if you ask me.' Giles flushed the lavatory and came back into the kitchen, pulling off his jersey and donning a black clerical shirt with a roman collar. 'I've never understood what he sees in Melissa.'

'You mean, what Melissa sees in Will,' Frank said.

'No I don't. She's a nice enough girl, and gorgeous-looking and all that, but the idea of actually being married to her is enough to curdle the blood.'

'Why?'

'She's totally self-obsessed. Only room for one ego, in that relationship. Will lets her walk all over him.'

'He adores her,' Frank said wistfully. 'He's besotted with her.'

'God, yes. They both share the same hobby, anyway.' Giles ripped open a loaf of bread, and crammed the top slice into his mouth. 'Did we really end up at a dog-track in Walthamstow last night?'

Frank laughed. ''Fraid so, Vicar.'

'Ah, that would explain why I have fifty pounds in my pocket this morning. I must have been fortunate.'

'How's Will?'

'Dead to the world. What a good thing we had his stag night two weeks before the event. I wouldn't fancy having to get him to the church now.'

'I never heard anyone snore like that guy,' Frank said. 'I guess Mel's used to it.'

'It hasn't put her off yet.'

'Want some toast?'

'No thanks.' Giles snatched another slice of bread, and poured boiling water into the coffee pot. 'I've got to get back to Shadwell. I'm on duty at the drop-in centre for my methadone people.'

'I'll never get used to you doing good works down in the East End,' Frank said, 'like something out of Anthony Trollope.'

'There's nothing remotely Trollopian about chucking free condoms at drug addicts, I do assure you.'

'It's kind of weird, that's all. I mean, when you think of us all at Oxford, and what we've all become.' Frank sat down at his desk. 'We were all gilded youth back then. Now we're learning to live without the magic – all except Melissa and Will. Those two have managed to hold on to the charmed life. They're so perfect, it almost hurts me to look at them.'

*

'Bugger this,' Tess said, thrusting a gaudy flowered suit back on its rail. 'Let's go for a cig and a slice of gateau.'

'At least try on the blue,' Ernestine begged.

'It'll make me look like a circus elephant. And, ye gods, the price. What's wrong with my old purple?'

'Mum, for the last time, you cannot turn up at Mel's wedding in that ridiculous kaftan.'

They were in the department for the fuller figure at Dickins and Jones, where they had spent the past hour in a welter of printed silk tents. Tess's thick white hair had become wild and wispy. She was steaming inside her flowing poncho, and absently trying to untangle the two pairs of glasses she wore on chains around her neck.

'All right, but spare me a hat, for God's sake.'

Ernestine sighted. 'Everyone else will be wearing one.'

'Fat people shouldn't wear hats,' her mother said serenely. 'They always look like the lids of teapots.'

Tess was making her way towards the dainty white tables in the café. 'Hell's bells, my bloody feet.' Puffing, she lowered her bulk into a spindly velvet chair. 'I'm on strike.'

Ernestine sat down opposite her. 'You are not leaving this shop without an outfit for the wedding. I promised Mel.'

'Honestly, you two. You'll be telling Dad to wear morning dress next.'

'Damn right we will,' said Ernestine, borrowing a Frankism.

Tess laughed throatily, and fished one of her unfiltered cigarettes out of her handbag – a terrible handbag, Ernestine suddenly realized, shaped like a duck, with little flapping corduroy feet. That would have to be the next purchase.

She bought them each a large slice of chocolate cheesecake, hoping this would loosen Tess's iron grip on her chequebook. Mel and Will were getting married in Chelsea Old Church, near their exquisite flat off Cheyne Walk. She could not allow her poor old parents to turn up looking like a pair of refugees.

Tess dispatched her cake, lit another cigarette, and poured herself a second cup of tea. 'This wedding will give me a nervous breakdown,' she said. 'Thank God we're not paying for it.'

'It'll be gorgeous,' Ernestine said staunchly, though in her heart of hearts she was finding the whole thing rather dispiriting. 'Mel wants it to be the greatest day of her life.'

'Hmmm.' Tess pursed her lips. 'I didn't bring either of you up to believe a wedding was the be-all and end-all of a girl's life. I wish she'd put some of her energy into a career.'

'She doesn't have to,' Ernestine pointed out. 'Will's got more than enough money for both of them.'

'Come on, love. A career isn't only about money,'

'She's working on her thesis.'

'Oh yes.' Tess flicked her cigarette with a broad thumbnail grimed with clay from her pottery. 'Well, I'll tell you the truth, Ernie. All that stuff on Gothic Revival and how it led to Quenville gives me the willies.'

'It doesn't do any harm.'

'Doesn't it? Sometimes, she's her father all over again. Peter always used to speak about that dump as if he were going to inherit Blenheim Palace.'

Ernestine was curious. 'Is she a lot like him?'

'A little. But actually, she's more and more like Star.'

Star was Melissa's mother. Ernestine knew she had been a model, but Tess and George had always resisted going into details about her. Tess was full of stories about her brother, but these were mostly about their childhood. She tended to be guarded about his marriage. Now, however, possibly prompted by Melissa's wedding, she was in the mood to remininisce.

'Estelle,' she said. 'That was her real name, but she was always known as Star. She was quite incredibly pretty – I can see her now, shivering in the sitting room at the cottage when Peter brought her down for Christmas that first time. Poor thing. He was mad about her.'

'Mel's like her, isn't she?'

'Yes, though the eyes are Peter's, and the colouring. Star's hair was fairer – absolutely golden.' She sighed. 'Such a long time ago. I can't help wondering what they'd make of Melissa now, if they could see her. I hope they'd think I'd made a decent fist of bringing her up.'

'Course they would.'

'Peter would be pleased about the grand wedding. He believed in that sort of thing.'

'What about Star?'

The bulges of Tess's face rearranged themselves into a frown. 'I suppose so. I don't know.' She lapsed into silence.

Ernestine asked, as she had often longed to: 'Mum, did you like Star?'

The uncharacteristic silence continued. Tess eyed Ernestine speculatively, as if assessing her. At last, when Ernestine was half crazy with suspense, she said: 'Liking wasn't the sort of emotion you had about her. You sort of fell into her drama, and ended up adoring her, or – or not.'

'And you didn't.'

Tess sighed quietly. 'Look, you're not to repeat any of this to Melissa – I shouldn't even be telling you. But, no, I was never one of Star's adorers. I thought she was selfish. I thought she resented the fact that Peter was fond of me.' Her voice gathered force as the age-old antagonism welled up. 'George and I didn't fit into her picture of a glamorous lifestyle. We were too dowdy. And she made it pretty clear she resented the amount of time we spent down at the cottage. Grandpa let us all use it, but she wanted him to make it over to Peter.'

Ernestine found herself remembering, with a twitch of unease, Melissa's outburst about the cottage, all those years ago. 'Was that why he ended up leaving it to you, and not Melissa?'

Tess pounced on this. 'Yes – why, has she said something about it?'

'No,' lied Ernestine.

'Of course not. I'm being unfair. But there's no getting away from it – she is like her mother, in more than looks. She has the same talent for creating a dramatic atmosphere around her, without actually expending any vulgar effort.'

There was a critical, unforgiving edge to Tess's voice, which startled and disturbed her daughter. 'Mel's not mean, though. And she doesn't resent you having the cottage.'

Tess ignored this. 'Star wasn't a good mother. Which is an evil thing to say about anyone but, by God, it's true. She was furious when Melissa wasn't a boy. A boy was what she'd ordered, and she was used to getting what she wanted. She parked her baby on me whenever she could get away with it. Peter wasn't much better, but he would have matured, given time.'

'Which he didn't have,' Ernestine said, 'because he died. Perhaps Star would have improved too.'

'No she wouldn't,' Tess said, with surprising vehemence. 'She destroyed Peter, and she would probably have done exactly the same to Melissa.'

'How did she destroy him?'

Another silence. Tess said: 'Swear you won't say anything to Mel.'

And Ernestine realized there had been a secret lurking behind her parents' reluctance to discuss the past. 'I guessed there was something you didn't want us to know. I wish you'd tell me.'

'Dad will have my guts for garters, but I think you really ought to know. Just you – not Mel.'

'Me?'

'It was in the newspapers. I'm quite surprised we managed to hide the story for so long. We always told you girls that Peter and Star were killed in a car crash, on the way back from Glyndebourne.'

'Weren't they?'

'They'd certainly been to Glyndebourne.'

'And Peter had had too much to drink,' prompted Ernestine.

'Peter wasn't driving. It was Star.' Tess watched her reaction narrowly. 'She was drunk, and that was only the half of it.' She lit another cigarette from the stub of the last one. 'It's rather a relief to talk about it – we haven't even mentioned it since it happened. But Star killed Peter.'

'Because she crashed the car.'

'She went into the side of a lorry, and died instantly. But Peter wasn't in the car with her. They found him about a hundred yards down the road. I still can't think about it without feeling sick. Before he died, he'd tried to crawl to the wreck.' Tess's lips twitched angrily. 'There was a trail of blood.'

'But how on earth – '

'His blood was on the car, too. She'd run him over. Several times, the police reckoned. Ernie, just imagined how he died. Knowing the woman he loved wanted him dead. It haunted me for months.' She picked up a fork, and distractedly traced patterns on her empty plate. 'Mel used to wake up every night when she was teething – you never did – and I'd sit with her in my arms, beside the embers of the kitchen fire, playing it over and over. Wishing to God I'd been there. Or that I could have changed things. And I sat there clutching his child, refusing to admit that she was Star's child too.'

They were silent for a while, listening to the rattle of crockery and the murmur of conversations around them.

Ernestine asked: 'Why did she do it? Was she ill? Had she ever done anything like that before?'

'Not that I know, and we'll never find out now.'

'How horrible,' Ernestine said. 'Poor Melissa.'

Tess groaned softly. 'I flattered myself I'd never made any differences between you, but the differences were always there. You are not sisters; she is not my daughter. Lately, when I look at the pair of you, I see myself and Star.'

Ernestine was shocked. 'But Mel and I get on brilliantly. We're not enemies.'

Tess began picking up cake crumbs on the ends of her fingers, and licking them off distractedly. 'You're an adorer, Ernie. You and Will. She thrives in that climate. But I wouldn't like to see her if she ever stopped being adored.'

Ernestine gaped at her mother, bewildered and slightly scared. 'What do you mean?'

'Melissa is my baby and I love her,' Tess stated. 'I've protected her from the past and I trust you to do the same.'

'I won't say anything.'

'I know, darling. You're the sensible one, thank God. But I've been meaning to say this to you for ages – don't run round Mel too much. She uses you.'

'That's not true!' It was true, and Ernestine qualified it immediately. 'I mean, I'm happy to. I do it for love, not because she makes me. She gives back plenty in return. I mean, everything.'

'Bless you, I'm not running her down. She's a sweetheart, in her way. And I'll do anything to please her – I'll even waste a pile of money on a hideous frock for her wedding.' She swept her cigarettes and matches into her handbag. As she was lumbering to her feet, however, she murmured – almost as if she did not wish to be heard – 'Just don't get across her, that's all. She'll win, and you'll be hurt, as sure as eggs.'

Two

Melissa stood at the Georgian sash window, staring out at the Islington square where she and Ernestine had lived as children, and Ernestine lived still. Her silk veil lay in crests and drifts, cascading from her head to her feet like thick, low-lying mist. Through the delicate mesh, her brown hair gleamed, wound into a plain knot, and crowned with a wreath of real white rosebuds. Her dress was white silk, with a dull sheen that held a hundred shades of the clean spring light. Her figure was erect and graceful, seeming almost to float on the extravagant folds of her full skirt.

Ernestine, coming briskly into the bedroom, was suddenly thrown off balance by the spectacle of Melissa as a bride. Her cousin's beauty struck her with its full force. No, she thought, it was more than beauty. Melissa as a bride seemed to shed an aura of untouchable dignity; even purity.

To her surprise, she felt her throat tighten with the threat of tears. She did not consider herself sentimental about weddings, and had spent the past week in such a whirlwind of catering that she assumed she had baked out every last ounce of emotion. She was not prepared for this aching sense of loss, as if she were about to wave Melissa off on a long journey. Nonsense, of course. She was not losing her. But for a moment she found herself thinking of a virgin decked out for a ritual sacrifice.

'Mel,' she summoned a light, cheerful voice, 'Dad says the cars will be here in a minute.'

Melissa did not turn round. 'All right.'

'It must be quite weird to be back in your old room after all this time.'

Melissa murmured: 'I was – we have been – awfully happy here. Haven't we?'

She sounded like a bewildered child, trying its best to be brave in the face of the unknown. Touched, Ernestine shut the door and went over to her. Melissa turned her head, and her cousin saw the tracks of tears on her pale cheeks.

'Oh Mel, darling.' She took one of her hands, and cradled it tenderly in her own.

'I've been thinking about when we lived here. When we were little girls. It all suddenly seemed awfully far away.'

'Yes, I know what you mean,' Ernestine said, folding her fingers round the ridge of Melissa's diamond and sapphire engagement ring. 'It feels like the most incredible change. Rather silly, I suppose. I mean, you've been living with Will for ages. It'll go on just the same when all this is over.'

Melissa's face was expressionless, but two fresh tears dripped off her wet lashes. 'I'm scared, Ernie.'

Ernestine, remembering her thousands of prosaic responsibilities, realized she was on the point of allowing herself to fall into the mood Melissa had created. She was constantly on guard against this. And today, of all days, there would be more than enough sentimentality, without her wallowing in it too. 'Oh, now you're being dramatic. What on earth is there to be scared of – apart from falling on your fanny at the altar?'

The smallest hint of a smile tugged at Melissa's lips. 'Dearest Ernie. You're so good for me. You always have been.' She was solemn. 'Don't ever change.'

Ernestine laughed. 'What's brought this on?'

Melissa sighed, and turned her meditative gaze back to the square garden below. 'I suddenly wondered what I'd do without you. I realized how I've taken you for granted. Being married will somehow make it official. I'll be on my own, and I'm not actually complete without you.'

Ernestine, despite her resolve to be cheery, was deeply moved. 'I wonder if I'd be complete without you. It's funny how we've always slotted together.'

'We've had some bloody awful fights,' Melissa said. 'Sometimes, I hate your guts. Sometimes, I think you're a smug cow, and a po-faced old fusspot.'

'Well, I know.' Ernestine burst out laughing again. 'And I sometimes think you're a selfish, snobbish bitch. I've told you often enough.'

'But we blend. Don't we?'

'Yes.'

'I'm afraid of being without you,' Melissa said. 'I think I'm afraid of myself. I don't know who I'll turn out to be.' She looked searchingly into Ernestine's eyes. 'Am I talking rubbish?'

'Yes,' Ernestine said firmly. 'Total crap. Snap out of it, and come downstairs. Mum and Dad want to see you dressed up before we leave for church.'

'Wait,' Melissa scooped her tears away with the back of her hand, careful not to smudge her make-up. 'Let me have my moment of angst, there's a love. This is where I'm allowed to ponder my achievements, and peer into the future, and all that jazz. I'm allowed my traditional wedding nerves.'

'It's only Will. It's not as if you didn't know exactly who you're getting,' Ernestine pointed out.

'I've done well, haven't I? And it's the right thing to do – the right direction for my life to take – isn't it?'

'You tell me.'

'Yes. Yes.'

'There you are then,' Ernestine said robustly.

'I've been travelling towards it for such a long time,' Melissa said. 'I suppose it's natural to get cold feet when you're on the point of reaching a goal.'

'You couldn't have chosen a better one, Mel. Will's a darling.'

Melissa was scrutinizing Ernestine again. 'I think,' she pronounced, 'that he's rather like you. Isn't that funny? It's never occurred to me before. But you're out of the same factory.'

'What a compliment.'

'Both good people. Caring people.'

'Yeeuch,' said Ernestine. 'Boring people.'

After a rather disconcerting pause, Melissa said: 'No. Not

exactly. Though, of course, not as interesting as people who are selfish and naughty. It's just that you and Will share that certain quality – whatever it is – that I don't have. Maybe, deep down, that's the real reason I wanted to marry him – not what I assumed at all. Wouldn't that be nice?'

'You're off on one of your rambles again,' Ernestine said. 'I've no idea what you're talking about, and I haven't time to find out. I promised Will I wouldn't let you arrive late.'

'No, darling, wait.' Melissa seemed to shake herself out of a trance. She tugged up her skirt, and went to the pine dressing table. 'I got you a present.' From a drawer, she took a small jeweller's box and put it into Ernestine's hand. 'With my love. Because I do love you. And I never want to lose your love for me.'

It was a gold chain, with one irregular pearl hanging from it, like a tear.

Ernestine begged herself not to cry, but it was a battle. Melissa's rare avowal of love had absolutely pierced her with joy. 'Oh God, it's lovely – '

'Put in on – here, I'll fasten it.' Melissa's cool fingers fluttered in the back of her cousin's neck. 'Think of it as the bridesmaid's gift you would have had if you hadn't been too little to consider as a bridesmaid. I wasn't going to look like a beanpole on my wedding day.'

This was the old Melissa, at her most beguilingly heartless. Ernestine's exultation bubbled out in a shout of laughter. 'Bitch! Slag!'

They embraced; the tall white figure bending over the little one. Ernestine felt Melissa's heart fluttering beneath its carapace of silk, and rapturously inhaled her smell of Penhaligan's Night-Scented Stock and creamy roses. Suddenly, she knew why she was like Will. Tess had been right – both of them were adorers. But her mother did not need to worry about what would happen, if things changed. As far as Ernestine and Will were concerned, love never changed.

'"In gloss of satin and glimmer of pearls,"' Frank quoted to himself, gazing at Melissa, "Queen lily and rose in one".'

Across the room, Will and his bride stood hand in hand, smiling upon their guests through eyes unfocused with euphoria, as volleys of champagne corks popped around them. Such perfection, Frank thought, absently working his way through a nearby plate of smoked salmon canapes. Such youth, such hope, such bliss.

He poured himself a drink, from the bottle of Moet et Chandon he had appropriated for his own private use. He had not meant to get canned, but who could blame him? The large bathtub opening out of Will and Melissa's room was stuffed with seductive heaps of champagne bottles, embedded in an absolute glacier of melting ice. It was only two in the afternoon, and he was already doing backstroke in it. The perfect couple were launching themselves on a sea of bubbles.

Their Chelsea flat, where the reception was being held, was the ideal setting for this radiant nuptial tableau. The wide Edwardian bay windows commanded a view of the Thames, shining like a sheet of polished steel. The lofty rooms were symphonies of muted golds, blues and reds, designed to harmonize with John Pollard Seddon's original drawings of Quenville. Thirty-six of these, in identical gilt frames, hung in groups on the walls – details of carvings in sepia and terracotta, patterns for tiles in clear reds and blues, and designs for painted friezes, in yellows and aquamarines.

In pride of place, above the heavy marble chinmeyplace, was Seddon's watercolour vision of Quenville in its glory. Frank tried, and failed, to draw its gleaming turrets into focus. He was as drunk as a skunk, and headed for a wowser of a champagne hangover. But it was too late to worry about this now – after a while, you reached a point where you could drink more without making the hangover any worse. May as well be hanged for a sheep as for a lamb. And he had always found that champagne-thoughts had a peculiar clarity. Your better nature was the first thing to pass out, leaving your worse one free to point out all the things your better nature usually forbade you to notice.

He let the atmosphere of Will's flat drench his senses. Melissa had conceived the decoration as a homage to Quenville. She had spent a small fortune on Victorian Gothic furnishings and ornaments. The effect could easily have been like a mausoleum, with its dark, carved screens and embroidered ecclesiastical chairs, but Melissa had managed to create an atmosphere of easy, unshowy luxury. It was like herself, Frank thought – discreetly opulent, flagrantly beautiful, and imbued with mystery. Not one note jarred.

He could not help comparing her style with Ernestine's, whose taste in homemaking he had once considered perfect. It struck him now as stiflingly kitchen-centred and dull, lacking any hint of the exotic. His yearning for a poetic setting – for glamour, if he was honest – made him chafe against Ernestine's habit of wadding everything in comforts. She had used the money from her television deal to buy a flat in Belsize Park, and was designing herself a sort of Hampstead farmhouse, all warm tootsies and new-baked bread. She was so caught up in the pleasure of it, she had not yet noticed that the whole subject made Frank want to weep with boredom.

From comparing their homes it was only a short step to comparing the cousins themselves. Frank watched Ernestine darting about behind the buffet table she had slaved over, and did not feel the usual rush of warmth. That quivering energy, that constant atmosphere of bright daylight she lived in – he pictured her suddenly bustling through his mind, pulling open the curtains and determinedly flooding out every scrap of poetry.

For as long as he had known the pair of them, he realized, he had been drawing comparisons between Ernestine and Melissa. And if he was honest – really, brutally honest – Ernestine tended to come off worst.

Why? Taken in isolation, on her own merits, she was the prettiest of creatures, with the kindest of hearts and the sweetest of natures. The trouble was, he had always found it so damned difficult to take her in isolation. She came attached to Melissa, and this attachment threw a spotlight on the contrast between the prose of one and the poetry of the other.

She was laughing in a group of Oxford friends; a vivid figure, in a linen suit of the clear blue that suited her best. There was no mystery about Ernie; absolutely nothing to haunt or tantalize. It was incredibly mean to mind about this, but mind he did. Being bound to Ernestine seemed to doom him to a future without an atom of the unknown.

In the centre of the table was a magnificent wedding cake, smooth as fresh snow and patterned with a web of silver icing. Frank had sat in Tess and George's kitchen for several very tedious evenings, watching it take shape beneath her piping-bag and palette knife. Yes, Ernestine was brilliant, he thought. But brilliant at icing cakes – so what? In the end, despite the bestselling book and the projected TV series, wasn't there something slightly menial about cooking, after all? Melissa was simply above messing about with mixing bowls and wooden spoons.

'Well, Frankers, *quelle occasion splendide.*' Dash was at his elbow, dressed in a white three-piece suit and embroidered skullcap, and rather the worse for champagne.

'Buzz off, Dash,' Frank said. 'You bring down the whole tone of my suit, for God's sake.'

Dash chose not to hear. 'Doesn't all this rather fly to one's head, and fill it with hymeneal ideas?'

'No.'

'My dearest old dear, don't be such a poop. This is going to be the year of the wedding. Sing, Hymen, Hymen, *IO!*'

'What the hell are you talking about?'

Dash hiccoughed vinously, and swayed closer to Frank. 'Living with us as you do, I don't suppose you've missed a certain strain lately, between self and consort.'

This was putting it mildly. Dash and Bella had been having a week of such spectacular rows that Frank had taken to wearing wax earplugs at his desk. He grinned. 'Well, I tried. But with both of you screeching at the tops of your voices, I kind of surmised that I might be looking for new roommates. You won't be able to keep a baby in that dump.'

Dash giggled. 'Yes, I thought you'd guessed.'

'Guessed? Bella woke me at two in the morning, screaming the test was positive. And that she couldn't think how you'd done it, with a dick as small as yours.'

'That too, eh?' Dash snatched a fresh glass of champagne from a passing tray, and knocked it back. 'Let's say the news was a shock to both of us.'

'I haven't told anyone. Not even Ernie.'

'Frank, you're a perfect love. But we are now public. Bella and I have decided to get married.'

Frank laughed brutally. 'Jesus, you'll be sorry for this when you're sober.'

'What kind of reaction is that? I thought you'd be rushing off to propose to Ernestine, before the words were out of my mouth.'

'We're just dandy as we are, thanks.'

'But you've been together almost as long as we have! Face it – we're in the same boat. It's no good us bleating about losing our freedom, because we lost that ages ago. We might as well all accept reality together.' Bella was approaching, also full of champagne and arm in arm with Ernestine, and he added: 'Don't you think so, darling?'

Ernestine kissed his cheek. 'Congratulations. I'll do you a wedding cake, in the shape of a Greek tragedy mask. And you can save the top tier for the christening.'

Dash took Bella's hand. 'O future Mrs Dashwood, and mother of the infant Dashlet, should you be snorkelling down all that booze?'

'Fuck off,' said Bella.

'Pardon me, I was only trying to be a conscientious father.'

'Well, you'll be crap at it, so save your energy.'

He sighed. 'I must admit, the prospect doesn't exactly make me dance with joy. Craig and Cecily's brat seems a particularly disgusting specimen.'

They all looked over to the bay window across the room, where Craig and Cecily were taking a battery of plastic feeding bottles out of a pale blue changing-bag. They had been married straight after Oxford, and their three-month-old baby son was in a sling around Craig's neck, decorating his morning suit with a snail's trail of regurgitated milk. Bella, Dash and Frank shuddered. Frank could not see how anyone could like such a revolting little creature.

'Barely looks human, does it?' he murmured.

Ernestine laughed, as if he had meant to be funny. Her eyes, already dewy with the emotion generated by the wedding, became dewier when they rested on the child. 'Frank, honestly. He's a duck. How did Craig and Cec ever produce something that gorgeous?'

A film of sweat broke out under Frank's stiff collar. That look on her face made him feel he could hardly breathe. How the hell had he got himself into this position, when he had never once uttered the word 'Love', let alone 'commitment'? She thought she had him, and so did everyone else. Goodbye excitement, adventure, fulfilment. He wondered if Dash had been right, and his freedom was already long gone. If this was reality, there was no way he was going to accept it without a fight.

'Excuse me.' He fought his way across the thick carpet, through a forest of hats and morning suits.

Several friends smiled and waved, but Frank was too angry to stop. He lurched along to the end of the corridor, and into the spare bedroom, where the bed was piled with all the last-minute wedding presents Will and Melissa had not had time to open. The sight of the ribboned, pastel-coloured parcels deepened his frustration. He shut himself in the guest bathroom. An engraving of Landseer's *A Stag at Bay* hung above the lavatory cistern, and Frank stood staring at it for ages, his cock in his hand, long after he had finished peeing. The stricken stag, hounded and cornered, was himself – about to be torn by the slavering dogs of convention, unless he could find an escape.

He washed his face in cold water, and returned to the thronged drawing room, angrier and drunker than ever. Giles, without his dog collar in honour of the day, was pouring himself a drink from Frank's private bottle. His three-year-old half-sister clung to his pinstriped knees.

'Hi, Emily,' Frank said, with an attempt at geniality.

She gave him a censorious female glare.

Giles said: 'Em, go and find Mummy.'

'No.'

'Look, there's Daddy.' Giles grabbed at Dan Ross's arm as he passed. 'Give me a break, Dad. I can't shake her off.'

The unexpected birth of Emily had brought Dan out in an equally unexpected fever of doting fatherhood. 'She adores you. She wants to marry you.' He picked up the little girl, and bore her away towards the buffet. 'Come on, sweetie.'

'That's weddings for you,' Frank said. 'Every single guy in this room is suddenly beset with woman demanding marriage.'

Giles laughed. 'Emily's been wandering round in an old net curtain for weeks, marrying every male who comes to the house, from the postman upwards. It must be something in their hormones.'

'Tell me about it. Did you hear about Dash and Bella? Jesus.'

'They might as well make it official,' Giles said. 'Neither of them will ever get anyone else to put up with them.'

'How do you know?' Frank demanded. 'I mean, is that it? You fall into a relationship, and it's non-returnable if you don't send it back after thirty days?'

'The general idea,' Giles said, 'is that a relationship lasts because both parties wish it to.'

'That's garbage. And what the hell do you know, anyway? You haven't been near a woman since that scabrous gypsy tart. One dose, and you learned your lesson fast enough.'

Frank was too drunk to register the look of pain that flashed across Giles's face. He had broken the taboo, and mentioned the forbidden subject.

Giles asked. 'How much have you had?'

'Yes, Vicar,' Frank declared loudly, 'I am inebriated. I am having an attack of truth.'

Giles's voice was quiet. 'You're having an attack of being quite a considerable arsehole. Go and put your head under the cold tap.'

'Too late, I've tried that. Look, I know I'm being a shit. It won't wash off.'

'What won't?'

'The facts,' Frank declared. 'They've nearly got me.'

'This is pathetic, Frank,' Giles said. He did not raise his voice, and was even smiling slightly, but there was an angry tinge of red in his thin cheeks. 'Pull yourself together, for God's sake.'

'I'm pulling, I'm pulling.'

'Pull harder, then. I know what all this is in aid of. You're starting to realize that you'll lose Ernie unless you grow the hell up.'

'Now, wait a minute – '

'No, you wait. I've been meaning to say this for ages. Ernie's about the best thing that could happen to anybody. One of these days, if you're not careful, you'll make the biggest mistake of your life – and all because you're too bloody stupid to know when you're well off.'

The angry smile widened into one of greeting, and he went over to join Cecily and Craig. Frank was left alone, seething with fury. He longed to hit Giles, not least because he recognized some gleams of justice in what he had said. All right, he did treat Ernestine badly – when she deserved to be treasured and adored, and was as lovely as the day was long. She would make an absolutely perfect don's wife too, raising precocious tots in North Oxford. Why did he hate the idea so much? Maybe Giles was right, and his existential doom was nothing more than a pathetic failure to grow up.

Unable to bear the festive crowd any longer, he blundered out of the drawing room, looking for an escape. The kitchen was crowded by the three stout Spanish waitresses, who were washing plates and arranging coffee cups on trays. One of them gave Frank a gold-toothed smile, and gestured towards a door. Frank opened it.

He found himself in a windowless utility room. There, burnished and gleaming under a single bulb, the bride was rolling herself a joint on top of the tumble drier.

Melissa smiled up at him. 'Shhh – shut the door. My dear husband will go mad if he sees me.'

'Shall I leave?'

'No, no – just shut that bloody door.'

Frank did so, his tongue thickening with embarrassment. Enclosed in this space, so close to her folds of scented white silk and heaps of airy veiling, the memory of their one encounter at Quenville was uncomfortably immediate.

She lit her joint, and dragged on it in silence for some minutes, before handing it to Frank. His senses rushed to his mouth, as his lips touched the place where hers had been.

'What a day,' she said.

'Congratulations, by the way. This is all fabulous.' He cursed himself for missing the opportunity to kiss the bride.

'Isn't it? Ernie's worked so hard. You must be glad it's all over.'

'Yup, I've been on short commons for a month, while she spent night after night making things on sticks.'

'Well, now you get to eat them, at least.'

Frank laughed, unable to decide whether he liked or disliked this pally reference to his legendary appetite. Anything between them that assumed an intimacy without overtones of sex, he realized, made him wince. He would actually have preferred to be avoided.

He was suddenly angry, fired up by a longing to break down the barrier. 'You know, you look stunning. I've never seen you so beautiful. You're a goddess.'

'Oh Frank,' she said, indulgently but wearily, 'spare my blushes.'

'You're the platonic bride, Mel – dazzling in your vestal majesty. God, Will's a lucky man. If he wasn't my best friend, I'd punch his eye.' He had to force a smile as he said this, and was miserably aware that it came out as a snarl.

'You always could turn a compliment,' she said. 'Has all this given you ideas?'

His ideas were about kneeling at her feet, and kissing the warm folds between her ivory legs. Sweat broke out between his shoulder blades. 'Sorry?'

'I mean, ideas about Ernie.'

Suddenly, he no longer cared about the Chinese wall of silence they had maintained for the past four years. 'Not you, too. I can stand it from anyone but you.'

She raised her eyebrows enquiringly. 'Well, I'm sorry. I didn't think there was any problem between you – she hasn't said anything.'

'No. She wouldn't. As far as she's concerned, there isn't any problem.' He handed back the joint. 'Which is precisely the problem.'

'Oh, I see.' She looked vaguely, maddeningly amused. 'When did this all happen? When did the dream die?'

'There never was a dream,' he said. 'I was in love with Ernie, I still am – in a way – but I knew it couldn't be the real thing. Because I'd already had a taste of that.'

'Had you?'

'Don't mess me around, Mel. You know exactly what I'm talking about.'

'Deary dear.' She was smiling to herself. 'I was afraid you'd bring that up.'

'Well, excuse me,' he snapped. 'There was something incredible between us, and you killed it. We made love once, and then you acted like you had amnesia.'

At last, she raised her eyes to his. They were level and unabashed. 'I'm sorry. I'm afraid it was necessary.'

'Bullshit.'

'No, Frank, please listen. I should have explained at the time. I was taking an idiotic risk – I might have ruined my entire destiny.'

He asked: 'What bloody destiny?'

'Will, naturally. I already knew we'd get married.'

'So I was your passing fancy, was I? And all the time, you were head over heels in love with Will?'

'No, listen, listen –' She laid her hand on his sleeve. 'I wish I could make you understand. I was hugely attracted to you that time at the cottage. When we made love, I realized I had to stop it quickly, before I fell in any deeper.'

The romance of it all, suspended in his imagination and channelled into his novel for four years, assaulted him now with double force. He wanted to shout: I knew it! I knew it! She had never stopped wanting him.

'You mean,' he ventured, 'because I was with Ernie?'

Melissa shrugged. 'Partly. You two do go well together, you know.'

'Why? Because she's sweet and reliable and a good cook?'

'Do admit, Frank, these sort of things matter to you.'

He turned this over for a minute. 'I guess. But there's another side to me. It's the side you recognized, and Ernie – she can't help it – is strangling.'

She was silent for a moment, staring unblinkingly at him, the joint smoking like incense between her fingers. 'Perhaps there's another side to me too. I certainly felt I had to sacrifice something if I wanted my life to work out properly.'

Frank found himself sliding straight into the pages of his unfinished novel. He had written and rewritten this scene of mutual recognition, and knew exactly how it should end. The words came out in a rush. 'Don't you see, we have no right to deny the feeling between us? We only get one life – we shouldn't let anything stand in the way.'

'Oh Frank,' she said, sighing, 'you're awfully drunk.'

'Melissa –' he grabbed her hand, 'I love you. If you let yourself, I think you'd love me.'

'Love?' she echoed. 'For God's sake.' Her voice hardened. 'I was talking about lust. Why do people always try to dress it up as something else? I'll tell you something nobody else knows, not even Will. Love doesn't exist. It's an illusion. I've never been in love in my life, and I never will be.'

He heard her, but could not take it in. Such a beautiful creature could not mean it. 'But – but – you're in love with Will –'

'No I'm not,' she said serenely, 'though if you tell anyone, I'll deny it till I'm blue in the face. I don't love anyone in the world – unless you count Ernie and that's different. I like Will. I always have.'

'It's just what you call lust, then?'

She smiled, rather sourly. 'If you were a woman, would

you lust after Will? No, I simply weighed up what he could give me and what someone like you could give me. You're very sexy.' The statement was colourless and matter-of-fact. 'But I can't build a life on that. Will and I have a partnership. We have plans together. It's like you and Ernie – he anchors me. He supplies something I don't have. Lord knows what.'

Frank was at sea, mentally scrabbling to regain the image of Melissa he had nurtured and cherished for so long. 'And that's all it is to you?'

'My wedding day is a fine time to discuss it. But yes, actually. If you want all that love stuff, you'd better stick with poor old Ernie.'

'That's not love. That's domesticity and families, and June Allyson in a frilly apron – if I'd knowed you were a-coming I'd have baked a cake.' He knew he was babbling, but he had to lodge his final plea. 'One day, you'll know what I'm talking about. And then God help you.'

She crushed out the joint, and settled her billowing skirts. 'Goodness, I thought I was supposed to be the dramatic one.'

His grip on her hand tightened. He pressed the fine bones beneath the soft skin. 'You will, Melissa. You'll understand what you're throwing away.'

'You, you mean. Well, when that happens, you will of course be the first to know. Now, I've got guests, if you'll excuse me.'

'Mel –'

'Let me go. You're hurting.'

He dropped her hand. 'Sorry.'

'The kind of passion you're after only exists in fiction. Essentially, what you're looking at is a choice between a woman like Ernie or a woman like me – a boring warm heart, or a horrid cold one.'

Rustling her skirts against his legs in the confined space, Melissa opened the door and swept back to the kitchen. Frank hung back, hearing her laughing with the waitresses. She had dealt him a blow, but he was already recovering. He realized that she could have cured his passion if she had wanted, but that she had chosen to attack it with flames instead of the necessary cold water. The result was that he was more intrigued than ever – and wasn't that exactly what she had intended?

There was an insistent, throbbing pain behind his eyes, and a growing queasiness under his grey waistcoat. The champagne was starting to fight back. He needed some more.

In the drawing room, the wedding guests had moved on to coffee. Only half a dozen bottles of champagne remained, bobbing in the melted ice in the bath. Frank wrestled one open so clumsily that the cork escaped with a mighty bang, and flew against the medicine cabinet. The glasses had all been collected by the waitress. He grabbed one of the tumblers from the sink, shook out the toothbrush, and stumbled back into the drawing room.

He almost collided with Tess, who resembled a large Chesterfield sofa covered in flowered chiffon. She shot him an odd, uneasy look, and Frank realized it was because he was clutching the tooth-glass and swigging out of the neck of the bottle.

He made a strenuous effort to be collected and sober. 'No,' he informed Tess, 'this doesn't give me ideas. Not a single one.'

'Eh?'

She was baffled, but he was not going to explain. He was suddenly hungry, and fell on the buffet table – groaning with annoyance when he found it stripped of everything except the pristine wedding cake.

Plates of tiny petits fours, little miracles in chocolate and marzipan, were circulating with the trays of coffee. Frank wrenched one from the hands of a waitress, and cleared the dainties in seconds. God, he was famished. The cake, he knew, would be delicious. A large knife lay on the cloth beside it. Frank seized it, and held it over the smooth white and silver surface, deciding where to make the incision.

'Frank!' Ernestine snatched the knife away, amazed. 'What the hell are you doing?'

'Okay. You cut it, then.'

'No! Will and Melissa are supposed to cut it together – it's their wedding cake, for God's sake.'

'Fine. Get me something else to eat.'

'Something else to –' Her blue eyes widened. Frank saw himself reflected in them as a monster, and was intensely irritated.

'Well?' he demanded, in a low, clenched voice, 'Isn't that what you're so incredibly good at? Am I not talking to the great provider? Christ, if you don't come across with the food, what are you for?'

Her lips compressed, and her dimple indented her cheek angrily. She whispered: 'Oh, I get it. We're on about my television series again, aren't we? And how grievously it upsets the sacred lifestyle of Mr Frank Darcy. You scribble on a few essays, and the whole bloody world has to stop for your work. Meanwhile, I subsidize your intellectual pursuits, and my work is just a nuisance!'

Frank was aware that he was being hateful to her, and blamed her for making him do it. His frustration over Melissa had to find utterance or choke him. 'That's the deal, isn't it? I mean, how else do you show you care? Keep the domestic comforts coming, and you don't need to make any other effort to keep me. Jesus, Ern. You expect me just to fit in with you, whenever you have a window in your fucking diary –'

'Oh, it's miles beneath you, isn't it, living with a professional cook? You'll eat the grub, but I'm supposed to be grateful!'

The resentment, aggravated by the preparations for the wedding, had been building for weeks. Ernestine's book, Ernestine's projected television series, Ernestine's glossy appearances in various upmarket magazines – Ernestine's chronic lack of time, which she tried to cover with domestic attentions, as if he would not notice that she was managing extremely well without him.

'You think I'm a great big nothing,' he hissed. 'You think what I do is shit because I don't make any money and nobody writes me up in the *Independent*.'

137

'I think you are a selfish fart, Frank, having a tantrum because the little woman can't wait on you twenty-four hours a day. And you're drunk. How dare you spoil Mel's wedding like this?'

He turned away from her, and she stared after his broad back, making a supreme effort not to burst into tears. They had come right to the brink of facing the submerged tensions between them. Why couldn't he be pleased for her?

Perhaps he had stopped loving her. Perhaps he had never started. Suddenly, the prospect of life without him made her giddy with emotional vertigo. Somehow keeping a social smile soldered to her face, she wove through the guests.

Across the hall from the drawing room was Will's study, which he used when he brought work home from the bank. She darted inside, and leaned against the door. The room looked out on to the narrow courtyard at the back of he building, and was gloomy. Melissa had had no hand in the decoration. It had a masculine striped wallpaper and heavy leather chairs, now heaped with coats and handbags.

Ernestine allowed her shoulders to relax, and released her tears with a loud, convulsive sob.

'Ernie?' She had not seen Will, sitting in the large swivel chair at the window.

She jumped, and gasped: 'God – I'm so sorry. I didn't know – you startled me – '

For a moment, he looked as strained and guilty as she did, and she fleetingly wondered what on earth he was doing here, all alone. As he approached her, however, his freckled face softened into kindness and concern. 'What's the m-matter?'

Ernestine hastily wiped her eyes. 'Oh, nothing, really – '

'Come here.' Gently, he folded his arms around her.

She pressed her face against his shoulder and wept. His body felt solid and inexpressibly safe. Will was a confidant and a comforter, and knew the business of all his friends. There was no point in trying to hide anything from him.

'It's Frank, isn't it?'

'He's had too much to drink, that's all.'

Will stroked her back. 'Don't make excuses for him.'

'Really, I'm being silly. We're all a bit over-emotional today.'

'Frank doesn't like weddings. They scare him. That's probably why he's behaving like a prick.'

'I try so hard to please him. Too hard. Because I hate it when he goes into one of his moods.'

'Ignore them,' Will said. 'They always blow over.'

'Maybe. But while they're happening – oh Will, it feels so horrible.' She pulled away from him, and rooted in her tight sleeve for a tissue. 'And then I forget everything I ever knew about fairness and what's due to me. I'll just do anything to get his love back.'

'What did he say exactly?'

She tried to laugh. 'You shouldn't have to worry about this, on your wedding day. It's just what I get, for being a B who falls in love with an A.'

'What?'

She laughed shakily. 'A-people are the beautiful ones, the desirable ones. B-people are more or less everyone else, in a lower league altogether. I'm a B, and if I had any sense, I'd fall for someone in my own group. When Bs love As, they have to pay for it – A-people are allowed to be difficult and to demand more. Well, Frank's obviously an A.'

He was smiling, but the smile did not reach up to his eyes. 'What do the A-people get out of it?'

'In Frank's case, dinner, washing, all-round valeting. Adoration.'

Will said: 'I'm a B. And Mel's definitely an A. What a shame we couldn't have fallen in love with each other, eh? Leave those two to find another couple of poor bloody second-rate Bs.' Realizing what he was saying, the tidal blush overwhelmed his freckles. 'Oh God, I don't mean you're not g-gorgeous – '

Their eyes met. Ernestine was aware, for the first time, of his maleness. They were assessing each other, she realized; wondering why God had given them libidos which apparently required so much complicated maintenance, when they might have loved one another instead and been content. As Melissa had said, they were alike – so alike that they had both invested everything in people who could never entirely repay the outlay.

'I know what you mean,' she assured him. 'Our trouble is, we actually enjoy servicing our A-people.'

'Ready to catch them, should they fall,' he said.

'Yes.' Ernestine blew her nose. 'You could argue we have a tad more control of things that way.'

'C-could you?' Will asked. He looked as if he were trying to work out a piece of complicated mental arithmetic. 'Wish to God I could control Mel.'

'You call the shots more than you realize. She needs you, Will. I'm so glad you're married.'

'I hope –' he began. He stopped, glanced at his watch, and cleared his throat. 'Lord, I think we ought to be cutting the cake. I'd better find my wife.' He leaned forward, and awkwardly brushed her cheek with his lips. 'I haven't had a chance to thank you properly. You've worked so hard.'

'I enjoyed it.'

'Frank doesn't deserve you. You're an A, if ever I met one.'

Ernestine forced a laugh, desperate to lighten the mood. 'A B-plus, then.'

'No – one day, you'll meet someone who worships the ground you tread on, Ernie. And then Frank had b-better watch out.'

'Oh, Will. Look, I'm sorry I spoiled your wedding by blubbing all over your suit. I'll put a piece of the cake under my pillow tonight and see if I dream about a true love who isn't Frank. I hope I don't – any true love of mine is just bound to be a troublesome A, and better the devil you know.'

In the drawing room, the waitresses were already circulating with the champagne which had been held back for the final toast. An air of weariness hung over the guests. Hats and buttonholes were wilting, and there were open yawns. Cecily's baby could be heard from the bedroom, wailing like a sawmill.

Melissa grabbed Will's arm. 'There you are – where did you slope off to? Let's get this over with.'

They took up their positions behind the wedding cake, and both their hands closed round the hilt of the knife. Their friends huddled round, ready to applaud the moment.

Ernestine searched for Frank, and saw him on the extreme edge of the crowd, sprawled on a large sofa with his collar and cravat on the cushion beside him. Giles perched on the arm. They were both toasting the bride and groom in large glasses of water.

She wanted to avoid him – not because she was angry, but because she was meditating the right approach. Frank beckoned her over, however, and squeezed her hand.

'I just threw up,' he said.

It was all right. Smiling with relief, Ernestine said: 'Poor you.'

'No, don't waste your sympathy. Chide me, spurn me. I acknowledge my transgressions, my sin is ever before me.'

Giles was laughing. 'Your lunch is ever before you. You utterly pebble-dashed that bathroom.'

'I can't believe I did it,' Frank moaned. 'How old am I, for God's sake? I thought I grew out of drunken barfing before I went to college.'

'You're a horrible man, and a total waste of my time.' Ernestine caressed his damp hair. 'Are you all right, love? Can I get you anything?'

He sagged against her. 'Can I come home with you tonight? I can't handle the loft.'

'Of course. You know Mum and Dad won't mind.'

Frank waited until Giles had moved away, then put his arm around Ernestine. 'I got rid of a load of nasty stuff just now,' he murmured. 'I'm so sorry, sweetheart.'

She cradled his head against her breasts, and caught Will watching her from the other side of the room. She grinned at him. Without smiling back, he silently raised his glass in a salute.

Three

The note lay open on Will's blotter, where anyone might have seen it. In letters large enough to post in a newsagent's window, it said: 'I GIVE YOU EVERYTHING. YOU HAVE GOT GONORRHOEA.'

Very, very fortunately, Will was first out of the morning meeting. He snatched up the paper, clapped it into his desk diary and whisked into his chair with a hammering heart. When Alex and Hamish strolled in a few moments later, they found him bent studiously over a German bank report, a heavy lock of bright yellow hair obscuring his terrified face.

Panic. Total and utter panic. Inside his head, he was screeching, 'Ruined! Ruined!' like a wronged maiden in a Victorian melodrama. Disaster yawned before him. He saw himself telling his shocked GP, or sitting in a sordid clinic full of foreign sailors. If he had a dose of the clap and it ever got out, he would have to emigrate. He could never live with embarrassment on such a scale.

Almost immediately, however, he recognized this as another of the evil creature's jokes – like the non-existent disgusting photographs, or the director who had allegedly seen Will and his paramour in an obscure restaurant, or the fictitious policeman whom the little wretch reckoned knew Will's name.

He broke out in a sweat of relief and breathed easier, but it was no good. He could not go on like this, at the mercy of a lover who seemed determined to destroy him. He suppressed a longing to lay his weary head down on the desk and moan aloud. Three months. That was all it had taken. In the three short months since his wedding, Will had watched in amazement as his own life careered wildly out of control. He had behaved like a complete fool, and the bugger of it was, he was still doing it – his blood heated with desire for his tormentor, even as he cast around for an escape.

There was one small nugget of satisfaction. His tormentor had obviously thought this latest tease would upset Will's marriage, but what a miscalculation. If he had somehow managed to give Melissa the clap, it would be the immaculate clap, conceived by the Holy Ghost. Bitterly, he thought back to his wedding day, and the admiring friends who had toasted the perfect couple. What would they say, if they knew the bride and groom had not slept together for more than a year?

The trouble was, Will's friends needed to admire him, because they had got so addicted to burdening him with their troubles. Since Oxford, he had been the father-confessor of the Bohemians, counselling them on their broken hearts while his own lay in bits and pieces. There was nobody he could confess to. Frank, Giles, Ernie, guess what – I'm embroiled in a totally destructive affair with a psychopath, and I can't get out because I love it.

Come on, he urged himself, get a grip. He tilted back his head, and refocused on the scene around him. The partitioned space he shared with Alex and Hamish was part of a vast, rolling plain of open-plan office, on the eighteenth floor of the bank's crystal tower. Will's desk was beside the glass wall, which smeared a muted, brownish light over the untidy vista of the City, and gave him a vertigo-inducing view down into the gleaming canyons of the Square Mile. Under his feet – literally under his feet, which had taken months of getting used to – London lay in an untidy jumble, as if a child had shaken a bag of buildings out on the floor. Will fixed his gaze on the dome of St Pauls's, in the foreground of the familiar diorama.

This was the last straw, he decided, and the proverbial camel's back had finally broken. It had come to a choice between the addictive danger and the chance he still had to build a life with Melissa. He flinched away from the pain of the decision, but knew he had to make it. This time he honestly, honestly meant it.

He could not think clearly in the false, dustless climate of the tower. He put on his jacket, tucked his Filofax under his elbow, and shut himself inside the mirrored lift. It halted on the tenth floor, the last place on earth Will wanted to be just now. How extraordinary, he thought, that two entirely different sets of emotions could exist together in the same person. In the moments it took for the lift doors to open and close, he was hopeful/fearful; aroused/sickened; desiring/disgusted – a ragbag of contradictions.

This glimpse of the tenth floor made Will think of the earth's crust parting, to reveal the damned toiling in the craters of the underworld. Here was the dealing room, in which bullet-headed barrow boys dealt with the coarsest aspects of the bank's trading.

Before the birth of his obsession, Will had regarded the dealing room with a kind of fascinated repulsion. It was a bear pit, vibrating with the din of aggressive jungle cries. Banks of screens flashed around the walls, and in long rows on the unpartitioned desks. Hundreds of young men, in shirt sleeves and garish braces, bawled into telephones. Cleaners, bent like reapers, worked their way across the floor with black binbags, gathering squashed cans and dismembered sandwiches from the ashy carpet. Will felt naked and exposed, and shivered with relief when the lift whisked him down to the ground floor. Being seen now would knock all his resolution sideways. He knew that even his lover's smell could melt him to wax.

Beyond the monstrous revolving doors of the bank, the air was damp and laden with diesel fumes. The tide of scurrying ants with briefcases had thinned. Will found a table in a deserted coffee shop opposite the Old Bailey, and ordered a cappuccino. When it arrived, he stirred it carefully, and opened his diary. On its public pages, his descent was charted in code – asterisks, cryptic clues and columns of figures. Now, he would go back to the beginning, for the long reckoning-up.

'Return' meant their return from Venice, where Melissa and Will had spent their honeymoon. Will had clung to a desperate and – as it turned out – forlorn hope that the most romantic place on earth could work a miracle.

'It can't be helped,' Melissa had said. 'I didn't expect anything.' The words were comforting, but her tone was icy. She had gone to the window of their hotel room to watch the moonlight rippling across the Grand Canal. A hot breeze had stirred the filmy net curtains around her.

'I was so sure,' he had pleaded. 'I thought it had to make a difference. I wanted to consummate our marriage more than anything in the world. Oh God, I'm sorry, I'm so sorry. You deserve so much more – '

From the balcony, the freezing voice floated back to him: 'Don't whine at me. It makes me feel guilty – and I certainly don't deserve that, after sucking my jaw numb.'

She could be very cruel. Like Ernie, Will had learned to withdraw until the mood passed. He made himself a cup of tea, lay down on the bed, and eventually fell asleep, with his nose squashed in the Ruth Rendell he had bought at the airport. When he awoke, he saw Melissa sitting in an armchair beside the open window, still gazing out at the gondolas on the water.

He stumbled out of bed, and went to her. Mutely, she turned her face towards him, and showed him that she was crying. Not a muscle in her face moved, but her tears drenched her blue, blue eyes and made two moonlit tracks across her face.

The rush of tenderness was like a bursting dam. On the rare occasions Melissa showed him her vulnerable side, he was utterly unmanned. He would have killed to protect her. This was, he always felt, the real Melissa who had bewitched him that night at Quenville – behind the cool detachment, an anxious child, clinging neurotically to her dreams.

'My sweetheart.' He had folded her in his naked arms.

She whispered: 'Is there something I'm not doing? Is there a particular way I should be turning you on?'

She had asked this once or twice before. Will laughed

ruefully. 'Oh, darling. You mean dressing up as a traffic warden, or thrashing me with a rubber hose? I almost wish it were that simple.'

She smiled, and he was encouraged to add: 'I'm afraid I don't know what's wrong with me. The last thing I want is for you to imagine it's your fault. You are quite staggeringly beautiful, Mel, and in normal circumstances you could give a corpse a hard on, I should think. So don't cry, angel. Please d-don't.'

'I'm always afraid it's something to do with me. Because your body knows I'm not really good enough.'

'Angel, you're far too good. I'm still amazed that you're truly my wife – Across the seven stars, O grace to farty old me.'

The Tennysonian reference made her laugh. She said, with her soul in her voice, 'God, I wish we were at Quenville now. We never had any trouble there. We went at it like stoats.'

'We'll go there. I'll take you, the minute we get back.'

'More and more, I see that it's our spiritual home. And then I'm terrified that something will stop us living there.'

He had a standard reply, which he crooned out automatically as he caressed her hair: 'Nothing will stop us. Everything will be fine.'

They sat together in the big hotel armchair for ages, lulled by the whisper and slap of water; the eternal sound of Venice. Melissa did not cling to him, but curled herself into his embrace, an animal creeping into its refuge. Usually, he enjoyed the feeling of protectiveness and peace this gave him. Tonight, however, he was conscious of a niggling irritation.

He was sick of the Quenville game. He loathed the place. He was never going to sink his inheritance into that heap of rubble. Melissa had to understand this, and get rid of her morbid obsession once and for all – or neither of them had a snowball's chance of happiness. Unfortunately, falling into the fantasy in the first rush of passion, it had taken him some time to realize she was serious. She truly believed she had got him to agree to restoring Quenville, and the more she believed, the more he rebelled.

In the months leading up to the wedding, Will had discovered dreams of his own. He imagined Melissa as a boxed jewel, in a golden country manor with worn flagstones and Labradors. Wellingtons beside the back door. Runner beans flourishing in a sheltered old kitchen garden. He had not yet dared to mention it to Melissa, but this dream fleshed out a little every day, until he saw it as their salvation – the antidote to Quenville. In a setting he controlled, with an atmosphere created by his own nature, he was sure he would be able to make love again.

That was for the future, when they returned to their life in London. Will and Melissa got through the rest of the honeymoon with little friction and less warmth. It had been a dull affair from Will's point of view, with Melissa glued to Ruskin's *Stones of Venice*, insisting they spent their time tramping round churches and doges' palaces. He had put up with it because it took her mind off what she was not getting at night. He began to see that this was the reason he always gave into her – because he had failed her and had to compensate somehow.

Now Will flicked through the pages of his diary, sipping his coffee. He thought he could pinpoint the exact moment the trouble had started. The page contained only the name and number of an antique dealer, but it deserved to be marked with a white stone. It was the evening Will had fallen into captivity.

The day had begun with a row, which blew up while Will was ironing himself a shirt in the kitchen. They only ever actively quarrelled over two things, which were really one thing – money and Quenville. Other women spent their husband's money on jewels or clothes. Melissa had running accounts with several incredibly expensive antiquarian booksellers, who supplied her with precious volumes by and about Pugin, Ruskin and Barry. Her chums at Sotheby's and Christie's telephoned her whenever they had a Victorian Gothic rood-screen, or a fine sideboard with marquetry panels designed by Holman Hunt. This morning, she had casually informed him that he was about to get a bill for seven brass altar lamps, ripped from some dump of a redundant church.

They had one blistering row about the price – nearly three thousand pounds – and another when Melissa had proposed hanging the ghastly things above their bed. She had lolled against the kitchen counter in one of her skimpy T-shirts, peeling an orange, while Will slammed the ironing-board like a nagging housewife.

She had won, of course. One of these days, he would be killed in his sleep by a brass lamp falling on his head, but anything was better than Melissa's cold displeasure. He could not cope with it, and she knew it. As the day wore on, Will had accepted that he would end up paying for the lamps. There would be a scene, where he had to beg her forgiveness for his anger, then everything would slip back into its ordinary, bearable state of misery.

He could not quite face this immediately after a harassing day at the bank, so he had gone to a wine bar in Moorgate, where he often took refuge. Jammed into a wall of pinstriped backs, he had sat on a tall stool, gazing at his melancholy reflection in the mirror behind the bar. I can't even be a convincing barfly, he thought. Whoever heard of a man drowning his sorrows in orange juice? Set 'em up, Joe. Drinking, like sex, was evidently not his thing.

Looking back on this averagely miserable, unremarkable evening, Will tried to work out at what point his subconscious had become conscious. It was as if someone had suddenly opened a door and let in a chilling draught. He had found himself looking at another face in the smoked mirror, and realizing that he was being watched.

He had seen the young man before. Sometimes, he was in the lift in the mornings. He appeared to work in the dealing room on the tenth floor, and Will's conscious mind thought him common and disagreeable. Standing too close to the young man made him nervous. This evening, standing close to him again, Will suddenly knew why. The man was beautiful. Good God, he was as beautiful as an orchid or a tiger lily, this cocky oik knocking back house champagne like lager – it was absolutely outrageous. He was tall and slight, with sharp shoulders and elbows, and curly black hair shorn to a point in the nape of his neck. His lips and nostrils had a delicacy which struck Will as cruel. His eyes were remarkable; clear grey, marbled with streaks of a darker grey that was almost black.

And they made Will nervous, because they were always watching him. They seemed to burn into his soul like lasers, full of malice and secret knowledge. It dawned on Will that they had been watching him for ages. The moment he met them, he was lost.

Will had left the bar without finishing his drink, but it was too late. They had not exchanged a word, yet the face was branded on his mind. In a single second, the poison had entered his bloodstream.

After that, he had searched for the face every day. Seeing it was horrible, but missing it was worse. Will would upbraid himself for being over-dramatic, then catch a look or a smell that sent him into a ferment of delicious fear. He was meshed in a weird, telepathic game; a secret conversation that tormented him in the bank's echoing stairwells and noisy staff restaurants. Part of Will longed to escape, and was afraid of the young man. Another part of him threw out fantasies about meeting him, which staggered Will with their perversion and caused faint, Lazarus-like twitchings in his loins.

There was nothing marked in the diary, but the date of the catastrophe was engraved in Will's memory. As the weeks passed, the baleful influence of the stranger from the dealing room had blurred the edges between fantasy and reality, and prompted him to do all kinds of reckless things. Sooner or later, Melissa was bound to notice.

And one evening, she confronted him with the photographs he had shut in his desk, half-hoping she would find them. Quite casually, she had thrown them down on the kitchen counter.

'What are these?'

He had felt his pink skin sizzling guiltily. 'Oh, an estate agent sent them.'

'Why?'

'I – I must have sounded interested, I suppose.'

'In this shit?' She held up a picture of a farmhouse, glowing in the folds of a Cotswold landscape.

'I think it's lovely, actually.'

'Green welly and Aga land,' Melissa had said, laughing. 'Five beds, near Tetbury. God, I'm glad we're not stuck for a house. Tetbury is the anal sphincter of the arsehole of beyond.'

Will said: 'I quite like it, actually. It's an awful lot prettier than all those turnip fields and sugar refineries in Norfolk.'

She did not seem to have heard. 'Anyway, we can't afford it. We need every penny we can lay our hands on for Quenville.'

'I've been thinking –' Will began feebly.

'So have I.' She distracted him with a delightful smile, showing the dimple in her cheek. 'Now we've got this place set up, we really should talk about starting work on our real home. I've found a good firm of surveyors in King's Lynn. They'll come tomorrow afternoon, if you don't mind me spending the night at the cottage.'

'I do,' Will blurted out. 'I do m-mind.'

Melissa was making one of her rare attempts at supper. She flicked him playfully with a wet head of lettuce. 'Oh darling, will you miss me so dreadfully? I'm moved beyond measure.'

It was a pity to spoil her mood, but it had to be said. 'Mel, listen. I think we should hold b-back on Quenville for a while.'

Her smile did not waver, but there was a hair's-breadth pause. 'Oh, it's only an assessment. It won't cost much.'

'Yes, but what about the future?' He cleared his throat. 'We need to talk about how much I – we – are proposed to shell out, once we start talking to b-b-builders and things.'

'The money's still there, isn't it?' There was the faintest underlay of anxiety. 'Will, if I really did spend too much on those lamps, you should have made me send them back.'

'No, no.' The childishness of this nearly disarmed him. 'Darling, you can have all the lamps you want. But we need to think about this properly.'

'We thought about it ages ago. We've always known what needed to be done.'

'Precisely. I mean, we could be looking at m-millions, for Christ's sake.'

Her face took on the awful, blank stillness he had learned to dread. 'Yes, I dare say it will. But you've got millions, haven't you? And you promised.'

'I don't remember promising anything. I might have said some day.'

She threw the lettuce into the sink. 'Perhaps you'd like to explain the difference between "some day" and "never".'

'Look, I only meant I'm not ready to go bankrupt now.'

'When, then.'

'M-Mel – '

'You either mean some particular day, or you mean you want to back out of restoring Quenville, full stop.'

'Well, you know,' Will murmured feebly, 'it was never terribly practical. I always took it as a sort of joke – '

'Am I laughing?' Her eyes were slivers of glass, cold as charity.

Will seemed to feel the frost right in the marrow of his bones, but he persisted. 'Don't you think we should start being practical? We both love the idea of living in the country. I just feel we'd be a hell of a lot more comfortable in a place we could move into straight away. Not some building site which just eats money. A better investment.'

'And what do you propose I should do with my building site?'

'I'm not saying we should do anything hasty. Let's just add up what the land is worth and see how that would affect our capital.'

With slow, fluid movements, she reached out for her packet of cigarettes and lit one. She was calm, arching her eyebrows at him enquiringly.

'You want me to sell Quenville?'

'No-not exactly. Oh, what the hell. Yes I do.' He was losing patience. 'Sell the bloody place, and let's buy a house that doesn't look as if it was designed by Prince Albert on an acid trip.'

'Ha ha.'

'If you must live in a Gothic mausoleum, I'll buy you St Pancras Station. At least it'll be handy for the train.'

She breathed out a plume of smoke. 'Have you finished? Are there any more little digs at my taste – which you've never bothered to complain about before?'

He was getting frightened. 'Sorry. I wasn't trying to insult you.'

Too late. Melissa never lost her temper, but he had pushed her to the point where her tongue could carve his self-esteem to ribbons. 'You want to discuss it, Will. So let's discuss it. At the top of the agenda is the fact that you are a lying shitbag.'

'B-but I never made any commitment – '

'So you were just letting me make a fool of myself, telling you all my dreams. You thought you'd found a great way to make me do what you want. I even married you, for God's sake.'

'That wasn't the only reason, presumably. The fact that you thought I'd committed myself to restoring your house.' The moment he said it, the whole world darkened. Well, I've been a fool, he thought. Obviously it had been the only reason. He had assumed there was something else for Melissa to love, besides the contents of his Coutts and Co bank account – there had to be, he had reasoned to himself, because nobody would go to such lengths for a miserable ruin. He had reckoned without Melissa's incredible tenacity. He held his breath, ready for the tidal wave of pain to crash over him. He had never faced pain like this.

Astonished by the sheer unreality of the situation, he stared at her, waiting to be contradicted.

'You think a lot of yourself,' Melissa remarked.

'I don't,' he murmured. 'I'm n-nothing. Aren't I?'

She shrugged impatiently. 'Now you're being ridiculous.

Of course your money wasn't the only reason I married you – I could have married someone a hell of a lot richer. But you allowed me to believe our minds were working together. That we wanted the same kind of future. If that future is different all of a sudden, I've got some serious thinking to do.'

'I fell in love with you. I love you.'

'Will, I come in a package. You can't just take the bits you want. If you can't see the importance of Quenville, you don't know me at all.'

There was a silence. Melissa crushed out her cigarette. 'Why do you think I've been so patient about the fact that you can't fuck me? I make concessions too.'

Not real, Will's mind was saying, not happening. They had stepped into the landscape of a nightmare. 'I've seen a doctor,' he said breathlessly. 'He told me we should get some therapy. Both of us.'

Melissa gave a loud groan of boredom. 'Do me a favour. There's nothing the matter with me.'

'But if we d-did, and it worked – that would make a d-difference, wouldn't it?'

'What,' she said, 'you imagine a good seeing-to would shag Quenville right out of me?'

'No!' Will hated her coarseness. It was like a cheesegrater scraping across his nerves.

'I don't require compensation for not getting laid,' Melissa said. Her eyes had become vague and slightly out of focus. Will recognized this as a sign of deep, corrosive anger. 'I didn't marry you for sex.'

'All the same,' he muttered, 'it must be frustrating for you.'

'Not really. Sex is only like food. If there's nothing in the fridge, you pop out to McDonald's. Don't you?'

There was a paper bag of cherries on the kitchen counter. Melissa began to eat them, spitting the red stones into the palm of her hand. Will watched her helplessly, winded as if something had slammed into his solar plexus. She was challenging him to ask her what she meant. The revelation loomed between them, and Will was suddenly desperate not to find out. He knew the limits of what he could bear, and instinctively steered away from the worst humiliation of all.

'I'm sorry,' he said, as he always did in the end. 'Get your surveyor. It can't do any harm.'

'No,' Melissa said.

His lips had begun to work with the threat of tears. He was on eggshells. 'Please don't let's get to the point where we threaten each other. Our relationship doesn't depend on what we do with your house. You know you don't m-mean it.'

Delicately, Melissa laid the cherry stones on the chopping board and counted them out, murmuring to herself; 'One, I love. Two, I love. Three, I love, I say. Four, I love with all my heart. Five, I cast away.'

A night of anguish was followed by a day of resentment. Will hung about at the office as long as he could, then ended up in the wine bar. Melissa had gone to the cottage to meet her surveyor. He had no reason to go home.

Melissa had seriously alarmed him. Now he was left to deal with the knowledge that he was too much of a coward to call her bluff and put his foot down. This is a mess, he thought. I am twenty-six years old, and I have made a dog's breakfast of my life. I'll do anything to keep her, but what's in it for me?

He took out his credit card and propped it on the bar in front of him, as he had seen other men do. The barman hurried over, and he ordered a bottle of vintage Bollinger, at a ridiculous price. Let's try the getting drunk option, he thought.

It was hard work, when you were not having fun. Doggedly attacking his third glass, he stared at his reflection in the long, smoked mirror, and knew exactly what he would see.

He was there at the other end of the bar, coolly pouring his own champagne, and incongruously reading *The Economist*. For once, he was not looking at Will, and Will now had enough alcohol inside him to decide he found this annoying.

His colleague, Alex, dived through the throng, puffing a cigar and full of loud bonhomie. He played squash with the dealers and arbitrageurs, and knew everyone at the bank.

'Alex —' Will grabbed his cuff.

'Bolly, Willikins? Can I believe my eyes?' Alex turned his attention away from signalling the barman. 'Are they out of orange juice?'

'Do you know that guy?'

'Which one? Oh you mean the cider drinker.'

'Eh?'

'The lads named him after that unspeakable old Wurzels' hit —' Alex brayed it out tunelessly: ' "Oi am a coider-drinker, ooh-arr ooh-arr" — because of his shit-kicker West Country accent. He's Johnny something. Ferrars, I think.'

The barman was in front of them. 'Yes, sir.'

'Another go at the '78, please.' Before Will could learn any more, Alex was fighting his way back to his table.

Will refilled his glass, gazing at the cider drinker's sharp profile, which was apparently absorbing a long article about the South Korean economy. He was beginning to be maddened by this Ferrars's lack of attention. It was an incredible cheek on the one hand, and shamefully wounding on the other. His sense of humbled invisibility increased. By the time the bottle was down to its last two inches of suds, Will regarded himself with a mixture of deep dislike and profound pity.

It was half-past ten. The group of drinkers at the tables had thinned. The two of them were alone at the bar. Johnny slapped *The Economist* shut, and said, without turning round: 'Ready, then?'

'S-sorry?'

'Your place or mine?' Johnny's marbled eyes were laughing at him, reading Will's secrets.

Will was, for the first time, really, seriously frightened. 'I don't quite understand —' He tried to climb down from his bar stool, and slithered clumsily. Johnny shot forward, and his hand clasped Will's elbow to steady him. His grip was very strong, and hurt a little.

'Give us your car keys, then.' Johnny reached into Will's jacket and neatly lifted out the keys to his BMW. Almost in the same movement, he picked Will's gold credit card off the bar, and it vanished into his pocket.

'I d-d-don't think I'm really fit to drive,' Will mumbled. 'I think I m-might throw up.'

'Not on me, you won't. Or I'll make you eat it.' His voice, with its cider drinker's accent, was guttural, teasing, threatening. He kept hold of Will's arm, yanking him roughly out of the wine bar as if he had arrested him.

Will did not tell him which was his car, or where he had parked it, but Johnny knew anyway. He manhandled Will roughly down the ill-lit steps to the bank's underground car park, and smoked a cigarette with an air of disgusted boredom while Will vomited all over the Chairman's parking space.

Eventually, he stubbed out the cigarette on a No Smoking sign on the wall, and climbed into Will's car. Will clung to a concrete pillar, waiting for the nauseous mantle of sweat inside his clothes to cool.

He knew he should run away, and that he would not. The fascination was like a drug. This was the first time they had exchanged a word, but Will felt they had already gone too far. Too far into what? He was stumbling blindly towards some preordained horror or bliss, and if someone had appeared to save him, he would have resisted. He got into the car beside Johnny. It was full of the smell of his aftershave, which Will found spicy and common, and hypnotically delicious.

Johnny drove with more than confidence. Will was thrown forward at red lights, and flinched as his tyres screamed round corners. When they reached the Embankment, Johnny's foot hit the floor. They tore off so fast, and committed such atrocities of overtaking and driving down the wrong side of the road that Will's damp fingers were knotted together in a nervous palsy.

By the time they were in the subdued, carpeted hall of his block of flats, Will felt a little calmer. They were on his territory now, and that was bound to tilt the balance of power.

The moment the front door closed behind him, however, Johnny surveyed the flat with offhand mastery. He began to move round, cat-footed, switching on Melissa's handsome Victorian lamps. They created pools of concentrated yellow light, which picked out gleams of red and gold in the shadowed upper half of the cavernous drawing room.

Will, realizing he seemed far less at home than his guest, stumbled over to the bay window, to draw the curtains against the watchful lights of the river.

'Too late,' Johnny said. 'I think that police launch saw us.' He chortled unkindly. The sound of his voice instantly made the whole room as strange as a dream.

'Look,' Will forced out, 'what do you want, exactly?'

'This'll do.' There were bottles and glasses inside the marquetry sideboard. Johnny helped himself to Cognac. Arrogantly raking his fingers through his curly hair – knowing, of course, that Will's eyes were glued to him – he sauntered along the shelves flanking the fireplace, reading the spines of the books.

'L-look, it's awfully nice of you to take me home. But I don't want you to think – I'm afraid we might have got our lines crossed somewhere.'

Johnny was not listening. Will had to scuttle after him as he strode into the bedroom, and flicked on the two lamps on either side of Will and Melissa's bed. It was huge, with an elaborately carved headboard. Behind it, Melissa had hung a reproduction, prodigiously expensive, of a William Morris tapestry. Her seven lamps hung above the damask counterpane on dull chains of laquered brass.

'Brilliant place,' Johnny said. 'Like a film.'

The wardrobe door hung open, spewing clothes. Melissa had obviously packed for the cottage in a hurry, leaving turmoil in her wake. Johnny leaned over to a fat velvet armchair in front of the chimneypiece, and hooked up one of the T-shirts Melissa wore in bed. It was faded pink, limp and creased. Johnny held it to his nose and sniffed.

'No!' Will shouted, in agony. 'Put it down!' He swallowed several times in an attempt to sound reasonable. 'Please. It's my wife's.'

'Didn't think it was yours,' Johnny said, sniffing again. He tossed the shirt on the chair contemptuously. 'Oh, calm down, for Christ's sake. What are you so scared of?'

Will squeaked: 'I'm not scared – '

'Yes, you are. You want me to leave.'

'I wish you would. I mean, if you d-don't mind, only it's getting late – '

Johnny grinned, showing front teeth with prominent, vampiric canines. 'Come on. What d'you think I'll do to you?'

His extraordinary beauty – the crisp definition of his hair-line, his eyebrows black as jet in his white face – tore from Will his last pretence of defiance. He whispered: 'I'm afraid you'll hurt me.'

'Oh, I'll hurt you, all right,' Johnny said. 'Never you fear.'

With deliberate, businesslike movements, he drained his glass, placed it on the mantelpiece, and took off his jacket. Keeping his insolent gaze fixed on Will, he ripped off his tie and shrugged his braces off his shoulders. Will registered that they were ghastly braces; bright yellow with a pattern of fat red hearts. Johnny opened his flies, plunged his hand inside and took his cock into his hand.

'Suck it,' he said.

Will thought he might faint. The embarrassment made his ears sing. 'I think you've made a mistake,' he began. 'I'm terribly sorry, but this isn't what I – '

The blow landed on his cheekbone. The flowers on the carpet rushed up at him, and his chin caught the brass fender as he fell. He found himself floundering on the floor, moaning with pain, and making an enormous perspective of Johnny looming above him.

'Suck it.'

'No, no – '

Johnny's steel fist slammed into his mouth. Will felt the inside of his lip bursting against his teeth like a grape, and tasted blood on his tongue.

'Don't mess me about,' Johnny said. 'This is what you want, isn't it?'

Will whinnied: 'Yes!' Submission brought vast relief and exhilaration. He gathered his aching limbs into a kneeling position, and closed his eyes as Johnny's semi-hard penis thrust into his bleeding mouth. It swelled against his tongue, and made him gag as it pushed against the back of his throat. But the smell of Johnny's groin charged through him like electricity. He sucked hungrily, utterly at the mercy of his desire. Johnny was hard now, and all Will's senses were in his own rocklike erection. With muffled yelps of urgency, his hands scrabbled blindly for his flies.

'No you don't,' Johnny said. His hand slammed into the back of Will's head, tearing his hair by the roots. Johnny ground into him, nearly choking him. At the point of suffocation, Will bucked and howled beneath the force of a shattering orgasm.

He lay at Johnny's feet, abject and twitching. His spasms died away, and the part of his consciousness that was not enslaved wanted to die of shame. But his subconscious was in charge now. At his wedding, Will had vowed to worship Melissa with his body. Dimly, he realized now what that promise had truly meant. For all the loneliness and despair in his mind, his body commanded him to worship Johnny.

'Take your clothes off,' Johnny said. He left the room, and came back a moment later with the brandy bottle. He refilled his glass, while Will obediently removed his crumpled, stained pinstriped suit, shirt and tie. He waited, feeling as naked as if he had taken off his flesh and stood with all his beating internal organs exposed.

'Right,' said Johnny, 'on the bed.'

The next hour was a fiery baptism of humiliation. Will did not see how he was to go on living, after suffering such outrages. Later, when he was left alone, he had done his level best to forget the absurdity of being lashed face down to his bed, his wrists and ankles bound with a selection of his silk ties. Mindful of his neighbours, he had buried his screams in the pillows. Yet he had come twice more, in a raging fever of pure, animal pleasure.

Eventually, Johnny untied him and ordered him through

an encore that filled him with disgust, even as he sobbed out a final orgasm that made him think he was having a cardiac arrest.

Johnny was still hard. He looked at his watch, calmly began to masturbate, and ejaculated with barely a tremor over the armchair. Will saw his juices foaming over Melissa's pink T-shirt, and burst into pathetic, babyish tears.

It was over. Will dared to struggle off his devastated bed and put on his dressing gown.

'Johnny –' he uttered his name for the first time. 'You're going now, aren't you?'

'If you want me to. I only do what you want.'

'We – we – can't do this again.'

'That's what you think now.'

'How will you get home?'

Johnny grinned wolfishly. 'Can't wait, can you?' He stooped, to pick Will's wallet out of his jacket. 'I'll get a taxi.' Will had about seventy pounds in cash. Johnny took it all. 'See you.'

Not if I can help it, Will thought. What had got into him? Left alone, he fled into the safety of his kitchen, and made himself a cup of tea, splashing its surface with tears. Then he stripped the bed, bundled the sheets into the washing machine, and ran himself a searing hot bath. Wiping the fog from the bathroom mirror, he faced his reflection. His lower lip was crusted with dried blood. One of his eyes was white and puffy, and there was a purple swelling on his cheekbone.

The next morning, he had phoned in sick, unable to rick displaying his wounds at the bank, or meeting Johnny. In sackcloth and ashes, he told Melissa he had got drunk and fallen down the steps of the underground car park.

She had believed him. 'Oh God, Will, you know you can't drink. I made you do it, didn't I? I'm sorry, darling.'

The meeting with the surveyor at Quenville had, apparently, gone well. In her sweetest mood, she sat him down in a comfortable chair, and made him an omelette. Will realized Melissa was being so nice firstly because she was genuinely sorry for being beastly to him before she left, and secondly because she wanted to show him how pleasant life could be when she got her own way about Quenville.

If only he had had the sense to let her win from the start. Gratefully cutting the burned bits off the omelette, he told himself this harmony was worth any amount of money, and shuddered over the dreadful sin he had committed against her.

'Blimey, what you have done to yourself?' Alex asked, when he sloped back into the bank the following day.

'Fell down the car park steps.'

'Yes, well. You were exceedingly pissed.'

'Never again,' Will said.

Alex and Hamish had both laughed at this. Everything was back to normal. He could breathe again, and pretend it had not happened. There had been a dangerous moment that lunchtime, when he had run into Johnny in the lift, but Johnny had looked straight through him – as if the whole thing had been a dream.

Will had begun to feel safe, and that was when the memories welled up to torment him. Without warning, he would recall some piece of filth from their encounter, and find himself drifting into a trance of erotic longing.

Reviewing his downfall in the café, he turned over the pages of his diary, to remind himself of the days he had spent pining at his desk and rediscovering the adolescent affliction of getting sudden erections in unsuitable situations. With hindsight, he supposed the crumbling of his resolve had been inevitable; he was, after all, possessed.

One scant week after swearing never to speak to Johnny again, he had sidled up to him at the wine bar, and whispered: 'I must see you.' They had gone to Johnny's place, a bare and functional flat in Crouch End, with featureless white walls and beige carpets. Will surrendered himself to the humiliation like a starving man falling on a piece of raw meat.

There were no more bruises, but Johnny knew how to cause pain without leaving a mark. By great exercise of self-control, Will managed to keep their trysts down to one a week. Occasionally, despite his fear of the man, he was surprised by surges of sentimental tenderness; like a whining dog slobbering over the hand that beat it. Who was Johnny, and what drove him? Was he capable of love?

This was Will's honeymoon, during which he managed to think of Johnny as a romantic, even sympathetic figure. He was soon disillusioned. Someone from his personal bank rang him at work to check the amounts that had been spent on his credit card.

Will had three credit cards, and realized that he had not seen this particular one for ages. He was scandalized when the woman on the phone told him that his next monthly bill would be for nearly thirty thousand pounds. He was on the point of telling her his card had been stolen – and suddenly remembered, with a sickening lurch of the stomach, where he had last seen it.

'Fine – everything's fine,' he had gabbled. 'No problem.'

And his battered heart had cracked at last.

'Of course I've got your credit card,' Johnny said, genuinely surprised when Will confronted him. 'You don't think I do all this for love, do you?'

He was sitting cross-legged beside the horrible coffee table in his flat, slicing lines of cocaine on its glass top. It was a Saturday, and in spite of himself, Will was riveted by Johnny's dishevelled weekend costume of faded jeans and Doc Marten boots. Paradoxically, casual clothes made him look better bred, Will decided. Not the least embarrassing thing about public meetings with Johnny was the fact that he always looked common in a suit and tie.

He leaned forward, and vacuumed up a line through a new fifty-pound note. 'I just took what's owing. I reckoned you'd work it out for yourself.'

'But so much! In less than a month!' Will pleaded. 'What have you done with it?'

'None of your fucking business what I do with my own money. But if you must know, I paid off a chunk of my mortgage and bought a second-hand Mercedes, and the rest of it went on snout-candy.' He gestured at the table. 'Go on, have a line on me. Just to show you I'm a businessman who knows the value of greasing up to the customers.'

'You're a shit,' Will said. He hated Johnny. He wished he would die. 'I'm cancelling that card.'

Johnny smiled vivaciously. 'Fine. I take cash.'

'I'm not giving you any more m-money.'

'All right. I'll tell everyone at the bank what you get up to after hours.'

Will was shaking. 'You'll lose your job.'

'So what? I'm brilliant on the House Book. I'll get another job, no question. But you?' He scratched his gums and poised the banknote above the next white line. 'Everyone who knows you in the whole world will also know that you like being roughed up and –'

'Stop it!' Will roared. 'Let me go!'

'Your wife might be interested too.'

'No! You wouldn't! Johnny, please – '

'You'd better leave me the credit card, Will. It's simpler all round – I do your signature so beautifully. And you know you'll be back whining for the treatment sooner or later.'

'Oh God, you bastard. You evil bastard. You want to destroy me.'

'Stop moaning. It's extra if I get bored.'

Loathing him from his soul, Will flopped down on Johnny's ugly leather sofa and buried his head in his hands. 'How much? I have to know that, at least. So I can plan.'

'I'll send you an itemized bill, if you like,' Johnny snorted his next line and caressed his bulging flies. 'Right, I'm ready. This stuff makes me as hard as the Russian alphabet.'

'I can't,' Will had said. 'The p-party's over. I don't want to do any more.'

Johnny dealt Will a mighty wallop across the face. 'I'm afraid you'll be walking into a door on your way home, you poor darling.'

Visible injuries that required explanations were Will's punishment for disobedience. Even Melissa, whose interest in his body was minimal, could not fail to notice bloody noses and black eyes. Will hated lying. He hated living in a constant climate of fear. He hated stumbling on the artistic lies his torturer found so hilarious. He hated Johnny.

In the café, he closed his diary and began to calculate the cost of escape.

Four

' – over on BBC1, the *Nine O'Clock News*. Here on BBC2, Ernestine Bennet invites you to a *Banquet on the Breadline*.'

'Frank!' Dash yelled across the loft, 'It's starting!'

Dash, Bella and Giles were squeezed on to the sagging sofa in front of Dash's small, fuzzy television. Cartons of takeaway Indian food lay on the bare floorboards at their feet. As the jaunty theme tune piped out over a credit-sequence of dancing tomatoes, they roared in unison: 'Frank!'

'Okay, okay.' Frank hurried across to the fridge, carrying a four-pack of Budweiser. 'Move over, Giles.' He pushed in next to him, passing out the beers.

'I can't watch,' Bella said. 'I mean, suppose it's dreadful? What on earth do we say?'

'Shhh,' Giles hissed, with his mouth full of ochre-coloured curry.

A studio kitchen appeared, artfully cluttered and homely. And there, among the ropes of onions and mismatched but photogenic saucepans, was Ernestine.

The four of them burst into frantic cheers. Dash took his can of beer, and opened it in a celebratory fountain of yeasty foam. Then they settled down to stare at the screen, and Ernestine's sweet voice echoed through the room, telling them that they did not need to be rich to dine upon nectar and ambrosia.

'You know,' Dash said, in a surprised whisper, 'she looks beautiful. Seriously beautiful.'

'Course she does,' Frank said loyally. But he was surprised too. Secretly, he had been rehearsing sympathetic speeches about the unkind camera, and not to worry. But for a moment, he hardly recognized the glossy creature on the screen, smiling so winningly in her crisp scarlet apron.

The camera flattered her delicate curves into a compact, toothsome sensuality. It emphasized the stained-glass blue of her eyes and the childlike perfection of her mouth. It coaxed out broad cheekbones, which gave her an air of melting serenity, like a Leonardo madonna. Altogether, Frank realized, she looked delightful. He found himself remembering the night of the ball, when she had appeared transformed in delphinium blue, and felt a throb of attraction which was immediately cancelled out by an unpleasant sense of alienation and exclusion.

Frank had privately expected the programme to be an embarrassment. He had seen himself kindly hiding bad reviews, and imploring friends not to mention it. But it turned out to be rather good. Ernestine showed the camera a cornucopia of leafy vegetables, juicy chickens and bottle of olive oil, explaining that this would make a week's delicious meals for a family of four, and actually cost less than fat-laden convenience foods. Junk, she claimed, was only cheaper in the short term. People on limited budgets did not realize that they could afford to be experimental.

Spellbound, forking up their takeaway curries and bhajis, her friends watched her giving her list of essential ingredients.

'The secret lies in the old-fashioned concept of the stock-pot; something that was once found in virtually every kitchen. The carcase of this chicken will form the basis of soups and even casseroles. And the beauty of stock is that it can be made with virtually anything. If a chicken seems too pricey, ask your butcher for a ham bone. Or simply make a vegetable stock with any raw scraps and a few herbs.'

Neatly, she scraped and chopped, and stirred seething saucepans.

' – mix a spoonful of flour into the warmed olive oil; pour in the pint of your stock, a little at a time to mix it well, then add a good squirt of tomato puree and – if you fancy it – a drop of red wine. Now, it's ready to pour over your raw, seasoned pot vegetables. It should take around an hour and a

half at gas mark five, and if you want to see the finished product – '

' – here's one I prepared earlier,' chanted Giles, Dash and
Bella, rocking with laughter.

'Quiet!' ordered Frank.

'People are always telling me,' Ernestine was saying, in
close-up, 'that they know fish is a healthy option, but they
simply can't afford it.'

'I think that was me, actually,' Bella said. 'Ernie wanted
me to eat fish for the baby, and I said it cost too much. I also
said I couldn't stand the meaningful way they glare at you on
the chopping board.'

Cut to Ernestine on location, in front of the wet fish
counter at Sainsbury's, where a man in a white hat allowed
her to prod slabs of herring and mackerel. Back in the
studio, a cheerful pan of bouillabaisse bubbled on the stove.
Ernestine showed them how to boil fish heads for stock, and
flung in various cheap, unlovely parts of the piscine popu-
lation.

'Really delicious,' she assured them. 'I wish you could
smell it.'

Cut to a block of council flats, somewhere in Tottenham.
Standing on a bleak, concrete walkway, she promised the
camera a weekly visit to a family who achieved healthful
meals on Income Support.

'Great,' said Dash, 'the prole-spot. I've been looking forward to this. She said it was agony finding oiks who could
cook.'

On the other side of the chosen prole's snowy net curtains, Ernestine discussed yams and breadfruits with a
handsome West Indian woman. The woman had four pretty
children, a bright taste in aprons and a joyous, whooping
laugh. She addressed Ernestine throughout as 'Darlin''.

'God, they must have rung a casting agency,' Dash said.

Frank nodded. 'Bloody condescending – they didn't want
to frighten the punters with a lot of unattractive poor guys.
Next week's is even worse, apparently. An Indian family
from Southall, who make like the Punjabi Waltons.'

'Couldn't they find any nice, smiley white families?' asked Bella.

'Nope. They all eat shit and look like mutants.'

'Quite true,' Giles said sadly. 'I was all set to offer her some of my customers, until I heard what they wanted.'

A rapid assurance that all recipes could be obtained on a fact sheet for the price of a stamp, and it was over. Dash, Bella and Giles burst into cheers and whistles.

'Right.' Frank levered himself up from the sofa. 'I'll go call her. Make some coffee, someone.'

'Send oodles of love,' Dash called after him. 'Tell her she's fab and her programme is divine.'

The phone was on Frank's desk, beside the draughty window. He sat down, in front of the manuscript of his novel. It was furred with dust – the wellspring of inspiration had been depressingly dry lately. He had stopped taking it with him to Oxford.

George answered the phone. 'Ah, Frank. Wasn't she magnificent? Just a minute, I'll fetch her.'

Frank could picture George and Tess squinting earnestly at their daughter's performance. They watched television with a ceremonial air, as if such an unfamiliar activity required extra concentration. It was preceded by a great palaver of finding spectacles, gravely checking the channel in the *Guardian*, and providing themselves with microscopic helpings of alcohol. If they saw a commercial, they laughed like children, and said: 'Oh, isn't that clever?'

Frank wondered at what point this – like their innocent stinginess – had ceased to be endearing. He listened to the sounds of footsteps and shouts in the Islington house, and suddenly felt weary. Congratulations and assurances were called for, and he had no relish for the role of faithful supporter. Absurdly, he was almost offended, because she did not need his protection.

'Darling,' Ernie picked up the phone, breathless and excited. 'Was it all right?'

'It was great.'

'Honestly?'

She was waiting for him to elaborate. 'You looked gorgeous. So did the food. And the West Indian family were terrific.'

'Weren't they? She was such a nice woman. God, I was so nervous – I just couldn't face watching myself with you, and the whole crowd. I hope you understand.'

'Sure. They send love, by the way.'

She gabbled on happily. 'I was behind the sofa for most of it. God, I thought, who the hell is that sawn-off little squirrel?'

'Really, you looked gorgeous.'

Frank could see this exchange of self-deprecations and compliments stretching into infinity. 'Listen, I'd better go. Will I see you tomorrow?'

'Well, I've got a meeting at lunchtime.'

'What meeting?'

'A woman from the *Sunday Times* is coming to interview me – isn't that a scream?'

'Hilarious.' Frank did not think it was a scream. Where was all this going to end? Paradoxically, Ernestine's success made him feel both too close to her, and too distant. He had no part in it, except cheering from the sidelines. His own concerns and ambitions were shrivelling away into nothing. He had made penitent efforts to be nice to Ernie after his shocking behaviour at the wedding, but it was getting harder not to blame her success for his own lack of it. 'If you're too busy – '

'Oh darling, of course I'm not too busy,' Ernestine said, in the indulgent tone he disliked intensely. 'Tell you what, I'll be round to cook your breakfast. The full works. Then you can come to the flat with me – they're delivering the Aga at long last. I'm so excited. You are free, aren't you?'

'Sure. You know my schedule better than my students.'

'I love you,' she said, as she had started doing lately.

He ignored this. 'So long, hon.'

After he had put the phone down, he sat for a few minutes, tracing patterns in the dust on his novel. Reflected in the window, he could see Giles and Bella making coffee at the stove behind him, chatting happily as they scavenged in the cupboard for biscuits, just as they had done as students. On the surface, these three were still wild young bohemians. But Dash and Bella were about to become parents, and move into a house reluctantly provided by Bella's father. Giles was about to be a fully-fledged vicar, with his own parish in the East End.

Frank was the only one who had not changed. He had a surge of fondness for his ramshackle academic lifestyle, and realized he did not want to lose it.

I'm not ready to grow up, he thought. I've got stuff to do first.

And his imagination sailed off on its inevitable course of literary fame and fortune, which always ended at the feet of Melissa.

'Right. That's the last, and I've probably got a hernia.'

'Thanks, darling. Sit down, and have a glass of wine.'

Frank tipped a pile of books off a stripped-pine kitchen chair, and sat down, wiping his wet forehead. There were dark patches of sweat on his grey T-shirt. He had spent the entire day toiling up and down the tall house in Belsize Park, between a hired van and Ernestine's new attic flat. Her belongings spilled out of grimy tea-chests, across the blond wood floor of the spacious open-plan kitchen and sitting room.

Beaming, she surveyed her new home. 'I had no idea I owned so much. Isn't it funny, when you move? However nice you think your possessions are, the boxes seem to contain nothing but odd wellies and dented colanders.'

'Just don't expect me to start sorting through them. I'm bushed.'

'Well, I've managed to get the dinner on. Why don't you have a shower? The water's hot.'

'Okay.' Frank dug into his jeans pockets for a squashed pack of Marlboro. 'Is there an ashtray?'

'Use this.' Ernestine put an old saucer in front of him, and continued her dazed, happy wandering. Her keen blue eyes were radiant. 'Don't you love it? I wanted it to look a bit like your loft.'

He lit a cigarette 'You're crazy. It doesn't look anything like that hovel.'

'The atmosphere – you know. So free and bohemian.'

Frank looked around at the immaculate surfaces, gleaming under the recessed spotlamps that studded the sloping white ceiling. His nostrils stung with the smells of raw paint and plaster. Anything less like the loft could not be imagined. He poured himself a glass of white wine from a bottle on the huge, waxed kitchen table.

'Is it nearly ready? I'm starving.'

In the midst of the chaos, Ernestine had prepared a large green salad. Two fillets of salmon lay in a glass dish on the counter, and a knob of butter was skating across the surface of a cast-iron frying pan on the hob.

'Give me ten minutes,' she said, tying on the inevitable apron. 'I'll just seal these over the heat, Elizabeth David-style, then poach them in a spot of the white wine.'

Frank did not give a shit what she was going to do with the salmon. Spare me, he longed to say – you're not on TV now, for God's sake. He crushed out his cigarette pettishly, and was further annoyed by the apprehensive glance she shot him out of the corner of her eye. The glance said, plainer than the plainest words, that he was being a difficult bastard and spoiling her innocent pleasure. He did not care.

He went into the large, carpeted bathroom where – at his suggestion – Ernestine had installed a powerful shower, with a proper glass door. English people knew very little about personal hygiene, he thought, and absolutely nothing about showers. For years, he had suffered under lukewarm dribbles, behind clammy plastic curtains that stuck to his haunches.

Even the luxury of a real shower, however, was not enough to improve his mood. He flung his sweaty clothes into a heap on the floor, for Ernestine to put in her new washing machine, and moodily stepped under the fierce jet of hot water.

Afterwards, he flung on the white towelling bathrobe Ernestine had kept for him at her parents' house, which was already hanging on the back of the door, next to her yellow one. If he was really honest with himself, he resented Ernie's success like hell. *Banquet on the Breadline* had now been running for five weeks. Viewing figures were enormous, and her face regularly beamed from the pages of Sunday supplements. It was not jealousy, exactly. He merely felt obliterated – tagging along uselessly behind someone who did not need him.

'Nearly ready,' Ernestine said, without turning round, when he went back to the kitchen. He poured himself more wine.

'When did you get the lights wired, by the way?'

'Will fixed them. Didn't I tell you?'

'No.'

Ernestine flipped the salmon fillets on to plates. 'You don't mind, do you? Only you never seemed to get round to it, and Will actually enjoys things like that.'

'Bully for him,' Frank said sourly.

'He came round the day before yesterday, when you were in Oxford.'

'How's Mel?'

'Oh, he was on his own. He was rather odd, actually – very nervous. He cheered up a bit after a glass or two of wine.'

'Will doesn't drink,' Frank protested.

'He does now, apparently.' She set down their plates of salmon, and sat opposite him, still in her apron. 'You look glorious in that robe – by far the most desirable feature of this desirable residence.'

Shovelling food with his fork, Frank said: 'Just don't think of me as a fixture.'

Ernestine was startled. She tried to laugh. 'Of course you are.'

Their eyes met. Hers were anxious, his defiant.

'This is your flat,' he said.

'Well, but you'll be here too. It's the perfect London base

for you. If you're not paying rent on the loft, you'll be able to get somewhere nicer in Oxford.'

'Don't count on it.'

'What?'

He realized he had been too harsh, and his tone softened. 'We have to talk.'

'Oh God,' Ernestine murmured, 'I hate it when you go all American. You mean, you want to talk about something horrid.'

'Grow up, Ern. I could say I hate it when you go all British, and panic about discussing emotions. We really have to talk.'

'About what?'

Frank laid down his fork. 'Okay. It's about this flat. I'm not ready to move in with you.'

'But living together was the whole idea –'

He raised his hand. 'Your idea. Not mine. I need my own space.'

'Darling, I'll make sure you have loads of space!'

'Oh, sure. Physical space. Come on – don't make this tougher than it needs to be. I'm talking about the emotional space I need to finish my novel.'

Two fat tears brimmed out of her eyes. 'And I don't give it to you.'

'Oh, honey.' Those swimming blue eyes made him wretched. He was battling for survival, but there was no need to be cruel. 'You're fabulous, and I'm a lucky man, and all that. But I won't be able to breathe up here. I've got to live to my own timetable. To free my creativity.'

'But you hate the loft!'

'You're missing the point. I'm not ready to surrender my freedom. That's what it comes down to.'

'Oh, I see.'

She carried on eating her salmon mechanically, as if chewing barbed wire. She had the air of brittle optimism with which she covered fear, and a palpable determination to make the best of whatever he threw at her. Misfortune had to be very bad before Ernestine would accept it as such. She could outstare the blackest cloud, insisting against all the evidence that she could see a silver lining.

After a pause, she said: 'So you want to carry on as we are?'

The chance to seize his freedom was there, and Frank backed away from it. 'Yes. Of course.'

'You're not saying you – you want to stop seeing me?'

He took refuge in anger. 'Jesus, I only said I wasn't ready to move in. Why does that have to mean I want to split up? Aren't I worth seeing, unless I'm in residence. Or do you mean you want to stop seeing me?'

This was mean, because it forced Ernestine to placate him. Sure enough, her eyes widened in dismay, and she stammered out: 'God, no – Frank, please – you know I'll be happy to go on just as before. You can stay here whenever you want – but I won't force you – '

Frank decided they had gone far enough for one night. He sensed that Ernestine was on the brink of saying she loved him, and headed her off with brutal cheeriness. 'Hey, you'll see enough of me.'

They finished their meal, with Frank studiously ignoring her lingering, pleading looks. He had stopped himself at the edge, and did not want to go any further – for the moment.

Reviewing all his ancient fondness for Ernestine, and the discomfort of letting her go, he calculated that he had better make love to her tonight.

He was dog-tired after carrying all those boxes, but his reliable old Quenville memory fired his blood. When Ernestine went down on him later, he closed his eyes and sketched her cousin's face around her lips and tongue. The white bedroom walls and flower-patterned duvet faded, and a moonlit ruin rose up in their place.

Five

Will stood on the brow of the hill, staring down at the chimneys of the house in the green hollow below. The warm breeze carried a balsamic scent of leaves and grass, overlaid with a faint whiff of the nearby cow-byre, pleasantly rural in the lazy, wavering late summer heat.

In the glare of noon, the house was as still as the Sleeping Beauty's castle. Captivated, Will watched the only moving thing in the smiling landscape; a drowsy bee, its striped fur packed with pollen.

The atmosphere fell upon him like a blessing. For the first time in months, he was flooded with peace and hope. Through a leafy screen, he saw a porch of soft, golden Cotswold stone, and imagined Melissa gliding out under the roses. No, it was more than imagination. He could absolutely see her, shading her heavy-lidded blue eyes against the light. The hallucinatory clarity of the vision was a sign that this was going to happen.

Never once had he been able to visualize her at a restored Quenville. Up at the other end of the lane, the estate agent's car was pulling into the dried ruts beside Will's Range Rover – but the man would have the easiest job of his life. Seeing the house would be the merest formality. Will knew he had found his home; the harbour where his battered ship could rest. Absurdly, the insides of his eyelids stung with thankful tears. He and Melissa had been given another chance.

'Mel?' He dropped his car keys on the hall table, sternly telling himself to be firm. The visionary optimism of the afternoon had not faded, but he could not pretend that communicating it to Melissa would be easy.

'Hi,' a voice called from the kitchen.

It was Ernestine. He found her at the hob, stirring a fragrant pan of chicken and herbs, and it was the most natural thing in the world to drop a kiss on the nape of her neck.

'Ernie – what are you doing here?'

'You invited me to dinner.'

'I didn't expect you to cook it. Where's Mel?'

Ernestine grinned. 'At Waitrose in the King's Road, I sincerely hope. She forgot to get virtually everything on my list.'

Several familiar, buried thoughts flitted across Will's subconscious mind. First, that it was nicer to come home to Ernestine than Melissa. Second, that it was a pity they had never managed to fancy one another. Third, that Frank was a lucky bastard. He suddenly felt extraordinarily happy, and the permanent burden of Johnny seemed to ease a little.

He sat down on a high stool, and snatched up a slice of red pepper from a plate. 'God, she's hopeless. Can I help?'

'You can stop picking, for a start.'

He laughed. 'Sorry. Like a glass of wine?'

'I'd love one. Then you can keep me company.'

'What a chore.' Will opened the fridge and selected a bottle of Ernestine's favourite Sancerre. He poured them both large glasses. 'Cheers.'

'You're very sprightly, Will.'

'Well, yes. I've had a m-m-arvellous day, actually.'

'Oh?'

Will fixed his eyes on her small, neat hands, as they sprinkled chopped tarragon into the pan. He had meant to keep quiet until he had discussed his plan with Melissa, but could not resist the luxury of telling Ernestine. 'I've been out to the Cotswolds, to the most gorgeous little village about ten miles outside Cirencester. Do you know Cirencester?'

'No.'

'It's lovely. And you could eat the surrounding countryside on toast.'

'What were you doing there?'

'Falling in love. With a house, before you jump to conclusions.'

'A house?'

'A seventeenth-century manor. It's called Monksby, and the owners have restored it stunningly. You'd salivate over the kitchen.'

'Hang on.' Ernestine did not stop working, but she was puzzled, almost anxious. 'What on earth are you doing, looking at manor houses? Mel hasn't mentioned this.'

'She doesn't know.'

There was a disconcerting silence.

Ernestine said: 'You'd better not tell her. Or I predict Big Trouble. You know there's only one house in the world she cares about.'

'Ah, but she hasn't seen Monksby. The minute she does – '

'Will, dearest Will. Ground Control to Major Will. Aren't you forgetting a tiny little thing called Quenville?'

He sighed fretfully. 'I wish I c-could.'

'But restoring Quenville is the dearest wish of your heart.'

'When have you ever heard me say that?'

Ernestine frowned. 'I just assumed, you know.'

'A lot of people have assumed things about me,' Will said.

She covered her bubbling pan, picked up her wine glass and leaned against the kitchen counter. 'All right. Start at the beginning.'

It was amazing, Will thought, what being listened to – properly listened to – could do for his confidence.

'I might as well start at the end,' he said. 'I made an offer on that house this afternoon.'

'Oh my God. You didn't.'

'Three-quarters of a million pounds – not much, for a slice of paradise. And nothing at all, compared to the cost of rebuilding Quenville.'

'Oh my God.'

'Just a sec – I'll show you.' He darted out to the hall, and returned with a glossy brochure which he thrust at her. 'That's the view from the front. You can just see the roof of the dovecote, on the right.'

'A dovecote – oh, it's perfect!'

He chuckled happily. 'Knew you'd adore it.'

'Well, of course. Anyone would.' She handed back the brochure. 'Anyone who doesn't have a bee in her bonnet about Victorian Gothic and John Pollard Seddon.'

'I never want,' Will said, with unaccustomed violence, 'to hear that fucker's name again in all my life.'

Her eyes were round with astonishment. 'If you know how to make her stop saying it, I wish you'd tell me.'

'I'm not joking, Ernie. The fantasy has got to stop, before we both go barmy. We need to draw a line underneath it and start again. I've been doing a hell of a lot of thinking lately.'

There was another silence, during which Ernestine gazed at him, full of compassion. Eventually, she softly said: 'I should have talked to you properly the other night, instead of drivelling on about my own concerns. I could see perfectly well that you were bothered about something. Is it Mel?'

'It's always Mel,' Will said. 'N-no, that's not fair. I've had a few problems at the b-b-bank.' He raised his voice, as if that would quench the fiery blush that surged up his neck. 'But they've made me realize, we need to sort out the terms of our whole relationship. I love her. And we're not happy.'

'Sweet William,' Ernestine murmured, 'I'm so sorry.'

He braced his sagging shoulders. 'I'm not asking for sympathy. Moving off to Monksby will give us that chance to love each other. Or n-not.'

'She loves you, I promise. I know her. She's told me how much she needs you.'

Will smiled suddenly. 'God, yes. A-people like her couldn't make a move without us poor Bs.'

Glad to be offered a chance to change the subject, Ernestine laughed, and said: 'You were so nice to me that day.'

'I still refuse to accept that you're a B. Frank's behaving, I hope?'

Her smile wavered a fraction. 'Oh, we muddle on. But I'm afraid it'll take more than a manor in the Cotswolds to solve our difficulties.'

'Such as?'

'It's the age-old problem. As ancient as Petrarch and

Laura, or Dante and Beatrice. One loves a lot, and the other doesn't. Or not quite so much.'

'Aren't we a pair?' Will mused.

She swept the sliced peppers into the pan, momentarily bathing them both in delicious vapours. 'Perfectly matched, like bookends. Pity we can't elope, or something.'

'Frank doesn't realize how much he loves you, that's his problem. If we did elope, he'd coming running after you like a shot.'

'That's an experiment I don't care to try. I'm just doing my best to tailor my expectations to what he's prepared to give me.'

'Well, you shouldn't,' he declared, with surprising firmness. 'Stick out for what you really want, and tell him to bugger off if he doesn't like it.'

'Is that what you're going to do with Mel?'

His jaw hardened stubbornly. 'I have to.'

'Rather drastic.'

'I wish I could make her understand. D'you know, I think I had a sort of spiritual experience at that house this afternoon. Don't laugh.'

'I won't.'

'It was almost like a premonition. I mean, I don't really believe in that sort of thing. But I had this certainty –' he emphasized the word – 'when I first saw the place. I just knew we were going to live there. And – this sounds completely mad – that I was going to find an incredible peace there. Only peace is too quiet to describe it. A kind of revelation, a fulfilment.' Will slopped more wine into his glass, encouraged by Ernestine's rapt face. 'There was one particular moment. The agent showed me into the main bedroom. Mullioned windows and roses round them – roses, roses, everywhere. The sweet kind that smell of guest soap – nothing like those vicious bastards at Quenville. And my heart just – you know. Lifted up.' He grinned sheepishly. 'God, I'm talking rubbish.'

'And Mel was part of all this.'

'Oh, definitely. I could practically see her. So though I

haven't a clue what any of it means, I have to follow my instincts.'

Ernestine sighed, and shook her head. 'She'll murder you.'

'No, I really don't think she will. She believes in destiny. And I just felt that not buying this house would be denying fate. Of course she'll cut up rough at first, poor thing. You know what that Quenville crap means to her. But she'll come round, and we'll live at Monksby.' He took her hand. 'Ernie, I swear, I've never been so sure of anything in my life.'

'If you can't give me my house, just what the fuck are you for?'

Melissa's rage erupted like a volcano. The bathroom mirror cracked from side to side, like the Lady of Shallot's, as she sent an alabaster vase crashing into her own demented reflection. She had swept the remains of the dinner party off the table, and the drawing room carpet was littered with fragments of grapes and cheese.

It had been a stupid time to tell her. All evening, she had been holding forth to Frank about the surveyor's report at Quenville. Frank had ignored Ernestine's tactful attempts to change the subject. Whenever Melissa was around, he was deaf and blind. Now, Will knew why.

'If I'd been interested in shagging, I would have married Frank Darcy. His cock's ten times the size of yours – even supposing you could get yours up. Do you know what I think? You're a poof. You'd shag him yourself, given half a chance.'

'Mel – '

'Find another poof to share your wet dream. You'll never get me to live there – I won't look at it. Fine, buy your house – you'll be moving there on your own – '

'Oh, that's meant to be a punishment, is it? Living without an evil-tempered b-bitch who only cares about my wallet?' He stumbled round the flat after her, while she methodically smashed glasses and plates, as if deliberately working off her fury. 'D'you think I gave a shit about what you've done with Frank Darcy? I'll tell you what – I'm s-sorry for the man. He's bloody lucky he's got a bollock left to his name. Your fanny's got fangs – do you know that? No wonder I can't get it up – '

Will was frightened by her anger, and absolutely terrified by his own. When he caught his own scarlet, bawling reflection in the Pugin mirror, he saw a stranger. As if from a great distance, he heard the obscene torrent pouring out of his mouth, and was disgusted to realize that he sounded just like Johnny Ferrars. Some outside force had seized control of his tongue, and he could not stop.

'Two million quid! To rebuild a house I don't even fucking like! Well, you're m-mad – What are you doing?'

She had begun to tear her precious Seddon sketches off the walls. 'I'm going to Quenville,' she yelled at him. 'I'm going home!'

'Do what you like!' he yelled back at her. 'I'm f-f-finished with you, you evil bitch. Find some other silly tit to pay your bills!'

He picked up her lead paperweight in the shape of the Albert Memorial, and smashed it against the glass of the Seddon pictures, one by one, in a storm of splinters, with such savage, exquisite satisfaction that he felt a charge of sexual excitement. The hated images of architraves and bas-reliefs fragmented and distorted in shards of cobalt terra-cotta.

Melissa shrieked, like a vampire being shown a crucifix, and leaped on Will with her claws extended. He pushed her roughly away, and – as the crowning revenge – hurled the paperweight into the watercolour of Quenville, above the fireplace. She cried out then as if he had hurled it at her. She screamed and screamed, with a terrible edge of despair, and collapsed on the hearthrug, holding her head in her hands.

With the appalling energy of his anger pulsing through him, Will tugged open his flies and fell on top of her, prising open her limbs so that she lay trapped underneath him. She was wearing a summer dress of flimsy silk, and silk knickers which he tore off, basely thrilled by the sound of the ripping fabric.

In a fever of the misery and anger that had been building up since he first met her, he smacked her hard across her lovely face, and pushed his erection into her. After a few ferocious thrusts, he climaxed with a head full of confused images – blue eyes, grey eyes, softness, hardness. Johnny and Melissa, fusing into one irresistible erotic enemy.

She left him stretched out on the Persian runner in the hall, too stunned to move. She dived into the bedroom, and re-emerged hastily dressed in jeans and one of Will's shirts. He clutched at her foot when she made for the front door, and she kicked his hand away. The slam of the door reverberated into a deafening, empty silence.

And he was alone, hatred utterly spent. Why, why, why was love so impossible? How had he – a nice enough man, with a genuine wish to be kind – ended up beating and rap-ing the woman he would die for? The dream of escape to Monksby, far away from the baleful influence of Johnny Ferrars, crumbled to ashes. He did not deserve to be happy with Melissa now. If he was really as wicked as this, he had better die and have done with it.

He wept, half wishing he could lie there until he ceased to exist. Eventually, the pressure in his bladder forced him to move. He limped to the bathroom, still shaking with sobs. Afterwards, he lay down on the sofa, with a whisky in the only tumbler Melissa had not smashed, and mopped the slick of mucus off his face with one of her fleur-de-lis Pugin cushions. In this position, he waited for sorrowful sleep to overtake his exhausted body, wishing it would last for ever.

He woke suddenly, with a wildly beating heart. Addled with sleep and grieving, his brain took a moment to register that the telephone was shrilling at him under an overturned lamp in the corner. Shivering, he struggled towards it, nearly skidding on a lump of Camembert – Melissa had, at some point, flung the cheeseboard from one end of the room to the other.

'Yes?'

Her voice in his ear was cool and clipped. 'It's me.'

'Mel? Where are you?'

She asked; 'Are you still angry?'

'Darling, I'm so sorry – '

'Look, save it.'

'But I've got to t-t-tell you – '

'Before you do that that, you've got to come and get me, I'm afraid.'

Will found it an extraordinary relief to return to his role of protector. 'Where on earth are you?'

'I've written off the BMW.'

'Jesus – are you hurt?'

She sighed, as if bored. 'Oh, no. I went into a bollard.'

'Mel, don't meander off on one of your digressions. Just tell me where you are.'

'I'm at Heston service station. On the M4.'

'Where? What the hell are you doing there?'

'It's a long story,' she said, 'and I'm running out of money.'

Will rubbed his eyes and looked at his watch. It was half-past three. 'I'm on my way. Stay there.'

'I'm not likely to go anywhere.'

'Just don't talk to anyone. I'm leaving now –' The pips were going, and he recklessly gabbled: 'I love you,' before slamming down the phone and scrabbling in the wreckage for his car keys.

He was high on sheer thankfulness as he drove through ghostly, empty streets towards West London. He had not lost her. But God – was she all right? His guilty imagination threw out nightmarish scenarios in which Melissa was snatched from him just before the moment of reconciliation.

Marvellous, he told himself resignedly; you don't appear to be able to live without her. You're as much of an obsessive as she is.

Not for the first time, he wondered what, exactly, drove

him. Surely not sex, since he had not been able to get it up for months. The woman did not love him, and did he even love her in the accepted sense of the word? He hated himself for what he had done to her, and his heart grew heavier as he weighed up the probable cost of absolution.

Lorries and vans thundered along the motorway in the hideous orange glare of the overhead lights. Will dodged the cars bound for the airport, every sense peeled for the Heston turn-off. The airport, he thought – was that where she had been headed?

He followed the luminous sign to the service station, and immediately saw his BMW, stranded on the verge of the sliproad. One of the back wings had been so severely crushed that it was almost inside out, and he felt an after-shock of nausea as he pictured the impact. He had nearly lost her – nearly been the cause of her death.

The car park was deserted, with only a few cars basking in the thin chiaroscuro cast by the cheerless windows of the restaurant. Suddenly so desperate for a sight of Melissa that he was nearly sick, Will pelted across the damp concrete.

She was at a Formica table right against the window, smoking and reading a garish paperback. Will fell against the glass. For one second, she stared at him, with a curious mixture of sadness and calculation, then jumped up to meet him at the door.

They clasped each other wordlessly beside the checkout, in the most fervent embrace of their lives. Will smelled chips, baking under hot lamps, and his stomach rumbled loudly.

'I don't believe it,' he said. 'I can't possibly be hungry again.'

Melissa smiled, showing her disarming dimple. 'Go on, have something. I won't tell Ernie.'

'What'll you have?'

'Tea. I'm over in the smoking section.'

'Righto.' There was white noise between Will's ears. He had to keep reminding himself that this was real. Amidst the plastic foliage, poison-green under the fluorescent lights, he loaded a tray with delectable rubbish, and went to join Melissa.

'Well.' He had no idea how to begin, but the tearing open of Cellophane packets created a diversion.

Melissa poured a packet of sugar into her tea, and lit another cigarette. 'You saw the car, I suppose?'

'Yes. Don't worry about it. I'll ring the recovery service later.'

'Oh, Will. You're a saint.'

'It doesn't matter. The ashtrays were full, anyway.'

This bashful offering of a joke was received with another smile, balm to Will's soul.

He asked: 'How long have you been here?'

She shrugged. 'No idea.'

They sipped tea in silence, both aware that they were approaching the barrier.

'I thought you'd gone to Norfolk,' Will said.

'I changed my mind.'

'Were you m-making for the airport?'

She chuckled suddenly. 'It would've been typical of me, wouldn't it? So dramatic. And of course, I was so fucking angry.'

Will put down his jam doughnut, and mumbled, through lips gritted with granulated sugar: 'I'm sure they're not badly damaged, darling. Your Seddons. I'm sure they can be restored.'

'Oh, yes.'

'It was an evil thing to do. I can't b-begin to make it up to you. I just want you to let me try.'

Melissa leaned across the narrow table towards him, her blue eyes calm. 'Don't apologize. I'm the one who should be grovelling.'

'You? I can't bear it. I'm a shit, a bastard – '

'Oh, Will. How good you are. You don't have to be so good. Why do you let me get away with being so bloody awful to you?'

'Because I love you.'

'I've taken huge advantage of that, haven't I?'

'That's what love is.'

'I was going to Cirencester. I had some loopy idea about seeing your house.'

He groaned. 'Look, I don't know what got into me. I should have told you – '

'Do you realize what you did tonight?' she asked. 'You smashed Quenville. And once that was out of the way, you fucked me.'

'God, I'm sorry. I'm so sorry – '

'Stop apologizing. You did something incredibly significant.'

'Did I?'

'You broke the spell. You smashed the Golden Bowl.'

Sensing it was vital to understand, Will said, as neutrally as possible: 'You've l-lost me, I'm afraid.'

She pushed back her heavy hair. 'You never needed to go to a therapist. You needed to break Quenville. I see that now.'

'Oh.' This was a dream. Will tried to organize his thoughts, to take in exactly what she was saying. Had she, all this time, been waiting for him to rape her?

'Oh, Will,' she said, smiling over his bewilderment, 'I'm not saying we have to trash the flat every time we make love. Basically, I came up against your limit. You forced me to choose between you and Quenville – and I've ended up choosing you.'

He could not reply, not daring to believe it could be this simple.

'Maybe I was testing you,' she went on, lowering her eyes. 'And it took a godalmighty fight to make me see how much I really need you. I think I came back to my senses when I nearly killed myself in the car. I couldn't help thinking of my parents. It was like a sign.'

He reached over and covered her hands with his own. 'You and your signs.'

'But you believe in destiny too, or you wouldn't have found that house.'

'I was totally out of order. I had absolutely no right to

make an offer on the place, and you mustn't think of it as a condition.'

'No, I'm not – but I do want to see it. Really and truly.'

'And what about Quenville?'

Melissa sighed, as if the weight of the world rested on her shoulders. 'I don't know. Sell it.'

'Wait a minute. Let's not rush into anything.' Euphoria swelled inside him, as he tasted the chance to create his paradise around her. 'We need to think –'

'I've thought,' she stated. 'And I've decided that we've got to do something radical. What we need is an escape.'

Sometimes, she had an uncanny way of instinctively reaching for the truth. Escape – for reasons she could not possibly know – was the overwhelming reason that had driven Will towards his dream.

They would escape together, like the Start-Rite kids, down the straight, sunlit road.

Six

The poor swan sang, as down her head she lay –
   Where my heart fails at last,
And my blood mingles with the sun's death-ray,
   There place my tomb and seal it fast.

Johnny took a deep drag of his joint, and tried to recall if
there was a place, at or near Quenville, where the rays of
sunset pooled precisely enough to mark where Rose had
buried her treasure. He had the mad old cow's dreadful
poems off by heart now, and the more he pored over them,
the more convinced he was that they were full of clues.

The papers he had stolen from Quenville were strewn
across his ugly leather sofa, giving off a faint, earthy scent of
the tomb. Mentally dissecting each word for every possible
shade of meaning had become one of his favourite relaxa-
tions. He would probe at the enigma until the day he found
the secret code which would make the whole mystery spring
open.

On this evening, he had left his answering-machine on
and poured himself a handsome shot of brandy. A Bach
Sonata for solo violin soared from his CD player, like the
valedictory partita of Rose's dying swan. It had been a present from one or other of his lovers – they were always trying
to clean him up with cultural soap and water. During his
ascent to respectability, Johnny had digested large quantities
of classical music, worthy books and grainy French films.
Next to his beauty, his most effective weapon had been his
improvability. Male or female, they had all got off on taming
the savage ignorance of the poor gypsy boy. One old geezer
had even taken him to Bayreuth for *The Ring* cycle.

Johnny had greatly appreciated *The Ring*, though he had been careful to conceal his pleasure from his patron. Instinct had told him that it would lessen his power. As a general rule, it never did to reveal the full extent of his intelligence.

And in the end, every single thing he had learned had come back to Quenville and Melissa. Every sensation or piece of knowledge fed that central purpose. The house, the treasure and the woman had become indistinguishable, and Johnny could not shake off the superstitious believe that if he possessed one, he would possess them all.

Quite a career I've had, he thought, since the day I found this lot. He weighed a bundle of the papers in his hand, as if to convince himself that it had all been worthwhile. Forging a life on the right side of the law had brought him the kind of safety net other people took for granted. He had a job, a house, a car, a driving licence. Even a passport, for God's sake. He existed.

These days, he bought books instead of nicking them, though he sometimes lifted a volume or two for old times' sake – to keep his hand in. His own money, honestly earned if you counted his job an honest one, had provided all the volumes he had hankered after when he was poor. He had been like a colt turned loose in a spring meadow. Novels, poems, plays and histories lay in heaps around his unremarkable, semi-furnished flat. How stupid they were; all those well-meaning types who had assumed that culture automatically brought moral improvement. I am as much of a shit as ever, he thought. Now I'm a literate shit – that's all.

The husband of a connection, incredibly eager to forget a busy weekend as a threesome, had furnished him with his first contact in the city. Johnny had presented a CV as richly embroidered as the Bayeux Tapestry. Half-truths being more effective than outright lies, he had been perfectly open about his youthful criminal record. It amounted, on paper, to a couple of minor teenage misdemeanours, and one short stretch for the time he had walloped a Sikh newsagent with a baseball bat.

What God knew about his real, hidden record would have

made their hair curl – but who was asking God? Copiously oiled with charm, Johnny had won a chance and proved himself too valuable to overlook. Ironically, he had turned out to be far more effective at making money on behalf of other people than he had been for himself. He worked on the House Book, maintaining the yield of stocks and shares traded by the dealing room of the bank, and watched with amusement the theoretical sums that daily slipped past him on his screen.

And all this time he had been stalking his quarry. Moving to the bank where Will worked had been beautifully easy. The salary and commissions were better too. He did not much like all the cider-drinker jokes about his accent, but his reputation as a hard man kept the yobs more or less in line. Sometimes, he found himself rather enjoying his job, and wondering if he should not be satisfied with getting this far. The doubts seldom lasted long, however. Short of his main objective, there was no such thing as Enough.

He looked at his watch, and began to stack the Quenville papers back in their box.

Punctual almost to the second, he heard Will's key in the front door – he must have been waiting outside, in the car. Poor halfwit. He made a dramatic sort of entrance, tense and breathless, as if he thought he was winning at last.

'Evening,' Johnny said. 'Good day at the office, dear?'

Will took up a formal pose in the middle of the room.

'Johnny. There's something I want to t-talk about.'

'Aren't you even going to kiss me?'

'I'm being serious.'

'Suit yourself. Want a drink?'

'No.'

'Oh, go on. You paid for it.'

'It's this whole – arrangement,' Will said. "I've had enough. I want to get out.'

'I wonder,' Johnny mused, 'how you propose to do that?' He ripped apart a cigarette, and tossed its entrails on the glass table, to roll himself another joint.

'There must be some room for negotiation.'

'Well, I don't know. There might be.'

'I'd appeal to your better nature,' Will said, with a surge of bitterness, 'if I thought you had one. You're the most evil person I've ever m-met, do you know that? I want to stop seeing you, and get myself out of this whole mess, because I've been given a chance to find a bit of happiness. But you don't want anyone to be happy. You get a kick out of causing pain – oh yes, I've got the measure of you, all right.'

Johnny only said: 'Sticks and stones,' but he flicked one watchful glance of purest acid out of the corner of his eye, as he asked himself if Will could possibly know anything really damaging.

'I know,' Will announced, 'that you're sick. You're incapable of love to such a degree that it amounts to a mental illness. You're not normal. I used to be curious about you. I thought there must be some way of touching you. Do you have a heart?'

Johnny held the flame of his lighter against his lump of Moroccan. 'I have an organ that beats. There's a muscle in my chest that you could shoot or stab – if you had the bottle. But you're asking, do I have a thing that's capable of going soft and lowering the price? Well, sorry. I sure as fuck don't have that sort of heart.'

'You're very cruel,' Will said. He seemed to think he was revealing something of devastating importance.

'Yes.' To Johnny, it was merely a fact beyond dispute. Will might as well have told him he had curly hair or grey eyes.

'Do you c-care about anyone? Have you ever?'

Johnny licked the cigarette paper, and lit his finished joint. 'I used to have a social worker once who sounded like you.'

This rare, personal detail immediately diluted Will's anger with doubt. He sat down on the leather chair opposite Johnny, leaning forward with his elbows on his knees.

'Was this social worker someone you liked?'

'He liked me,' Johnny said.

'Something must have come out of it, then.'

191

'We got quite close.'

'Oh, Johnny. I wish you'd let me get close.'

Johnny stifled a snort of laughter. This game was too easy. Go on, you kindly, posh, Etonian heart – bleed. 'Well, I'll tell you what came out of it. I learned a lesson I've never forgotten.'

Will let out a tremulous breath, as if approaching the last resting place of the Holy Grail, 'Yes?'

'Never fuck anyone in social services – they can't pay chickenshit.'

'For Christ's sake!' Will's anger came flooding back, with interest. 'Why can't you ever be serious?'

'Getting nothing but a tenner and a bag of chips is serious, if it's all that stands between you and the gutter. But I'll do you a big favour, and spare you all the sob-stuff. Let's talk business, if you insist. You want to stop seeing me.'

'I really mean it this time.'

'So I gather,' Johnny said.

Will's eyes widened. Relief made him look pathetic. 'You d-do?'

'One of the geezers from your department told me about the new house.'

Will was startled, and flinched. 'Yes.'

'Very nice. Off to make a fresh start. No more bending over and biting the carpet.'

'It's our last hope, Johnny. Please, please don't spoil everything.' Will leaned further forward, his palms spread in supplication. 'I realize there will be a price. You know how much I've got, and I'm willing to p-pay virtually anything.'

Johnny's eyes were glittering with excitement. He was so near now, he was getting a hard on.

'Funnily enough,' he said, 'I've got a nice figure in mind.'

'How m-much?'

Johnny lounged back on the sofa, thrusting out his groin so that Will could see the outline of his erection.

'I want to fuck your wife.'

Seven

The fruit cup was the colour of a garnet with the sun behind it. Gems of orange, lemon and strawberry starred its glassy surface. Sprigs of fresh mint floated like water lilies.

Melissa was pouring two bottles of vodka into the immense glass punchbowl, watched by Ernestine. They were both laughing.

'Don't you dare tell Will,' Melissa warned. 'I want people to remember this party, thank you.'

'Remember it? You might as well give them a general anaesthetic at the door. Look, I was only following orders. Will was worried about people driving home.'

'I don't mean to insult your talent. It's lovely fruit cup, dear, and alcohol will only improve it.'

'I haven't seen you. I disclaim all responsibility.'

'Here.' Melissa ladled out two glasses of her witch's brew. 'This'll loosen your drawers.'

Ernestine raised her class ceremoniously. 'To your new home.' She took a sip, and spluttered: 'God's truth!'

They both went into such paroxysms of laughter that they had to lean against the rail of the Aga. A familiar happiness bubbled up in Ernestine as she realized how long it was since she and Melissa had giggled together like this. Despite the nagging unhappiness of the past few weeks, and all the unspoken fears about her future with Frank, she felt a twitch of optimism. It had a great deal to do, she thought, with the loveliness of Monksby – the warm, beating heart of the old house, which made the spiked, sinister towers of Quenville seem like a bad dream.

The kitchen at Monksby, meticulously restored by its previous owners, was a thing of beauty. The peculiarly rich light of the late season daubed the whitewashed walls with gold, and turned the rows of copper pans into discs of fire.

Ernestine had been besotted with Will's dream since she had helped the pair of them to move in, three weeks before. She had been startled by the effortless way their lives had shifted into the new pattern. The Chelsea flat was to be put on the market. In the meantime, Will camped there for several nights a week, among the remaining sticks of furniture. Everything else had come to Monksby, and the summery atmosphere of the house had subtly changed the character of Melissa's fetishes. Her collection of Victorian Gothic (including the reframed Seddon pictures) looked merely handsome and charming here; their exoticism all but cancelled out by the sheltered wholesomeness of the setting.

As Will had predicted, the kitchen was Ernestine's idea of paradise. Working on the lunch for the housewarming party, she had found herself designing the meal for the sheer, sensuous pleasure of texture and colour, as if arranging a still life.

The long work surfaces were a riot of every shade in creation, from tender green salads and scarlet tomatoes to deep brown pies – all laid out on huge cobalt and white willow-pattern plates.

The glass door stood open, and the laughter of the assembling guests drifted in from the stone terrace and shady garden outside. The summer green of the trees was enriched with the beginnings of autumnal ochres and reds, but the day was as warm as July. Cars filed down the rutted lane in a steady stream, disgorging festive passengers in light, fluttering silks and linens. Will's sunburned face and neck were salmon pink against the flaring yellow of his hair. They could hear him shouting out in the paddock, organizing the parking.

This, thought Ernestine, is perfect. She stuffed a chilled smoked mackerel roulade into her mouth, to blunt a stab of envy. Melissa, in a silk shift of bright coral, which heightened the eerie blue of her eyes, exuded calm contentment. Will's dream appeared to have come true. Ernestine had no idea how the miracle had come about, but she had given up trying to understand this relationship.

'So nice of you to do all this,' Melissa said, gazing round at the feast as if seeing it for the first time. 'We're vastly honoured.'

'Think of it as my housewarming present. Besides which, I never can resist interfering. If you'd hired caterers, I would have been in agonies.'

'Is the punch ready?' Will bounced in energetically, fanning himself with his panama hat. 'I think we should start nudging people away from the champagne.'

'Here you are, darling,' Melissa said. She plunged a glass jug into the ruby liquid. 'Fill them up with this.' One eye briefly narrowed in the ghost of a wink, and Ernestine had to stifle her yelps of guilty mirth in a tea towel.

Will took a sip from the jug, and innocently pronounced: 'Delicious. What's the matter?' He laughed provisionally, waiting to share the joke.

'Nothing,' Melissa said tenderly. 'Pure silliness.' Her body moulded itself to his for a moment, as he put his arm round her and kissed her cheek. Ernestine noticed the new expression on her face – not a mirroring of his obvious happiness, exactly, but a kind of intense, gloating pleasure in it.

After he had dashed back into the sunshine with the jug, she said: 'I've never seen old Will so radiant.'

'He adores it here,' Melissa said.

'You made a sacrifice for him. A huge sacrifice.'

'Have I?'

'I mean, giving up restoring Quenville. I know what it must have cost you.'

Melissa smiled thoughtfully. 'It wasn't really a sacrifice. Life's been so much easier since I decided to take my stab at making Will happy. You know how discord exhausts me.'

'Very true,' Ernestine said, 'but this is the first time I've ever seen you caving in. Normally, everyone else is exhausted by discord long before you are.'

'It was worth it,' Melissa said. 'You only have to look at poor Will to know. Oh, Ernie – don't say it.'

'Don't say what?'

'That you'll never understand me as long as you live. You always say that.'

'I shan't say a thing, old dear. But if you want to hit me with a feather, I'll fall down. That's all.'

There was a lull in the stream of cars. Will found Frank in the far corner of the paddock, resting against the mossy trunk of a big oak tree. In repose, staring moodily at the steep swell of the meadow on the other side of the hedge, he looked so much older that Will suddenly felt shy. This air-brushed American beauty, every expensive inch of him buffed and polished, was chewing a blade of dried grass between his dazzling teeth, with a distant frown that made him seem infinitely more mature than his callow Oxford contemporaries. Or were they all more mature nowadays?

The uneasy feeling was dispelled when Frank saw him approaching, and grinned. 'What the hell is that? I told you to get me another drink.'

Will kneeled down beside him, and poured the punch into Frank's empty champagne glass. 'Mel was all for rivers of booze, but I don't want to get everyone pissed.'

Frank tipped it back, coughed, and said: 'Phew. Hate to break it to you, pal, but this is definitely laced.'

'Laced?'

'As in laced with some form of intoxicating liquor.'

'Oh,' Will said, 'that's why they were laughing.' He smiled to himself affectionately. 'She really is the l-limit.'

'Give me some more. I'm parched.'

'Well – '

'Oh Will, for fuck's sake,' Frank snapped, 'Ernie's driving us back, okay?'

Will was startled. 'All right. Only asked.'

'Sorry.' Frank let out a gusty, fretful sigh. 'I just had one of those moments when I know exactly what everyone is going to say – as if I'd dreamed it all the night before.'

Will settled himself more comfortably against the tree, beside the hard bulk of Frank's shoulder, and said amiably: 'Yes, we're hardly packed with surprises, after all this time.'

'Mel can always surprise me,' Frank said.

'Oh, but you even get used to that. And honestly, do you want to live in a turmoil of surprises all the time? I think there's a lot to be said for predictability.'

Frank's crisp black brows knitted ominously. 'It's my idea of hell.'

'Are you – you know – all right?' In an attempt to lighten the tone, Will added: 'Why so pale and wan, fond l-l-lover?'

'You won't care. You've already been bagged by Ernie.'

'What? What do you mean?'

Frank knocked back another glass of the spiked punch. 'No offence, old sport. But this is exactly my point about predictability. You ask if I'm okay. I say, no. You ask why. I say, because I'm suffocating in a relationship that's going nowhere – and you give me a lecture about being such a shit to Ernie.'

'Oh.'

'You're married to her cousin. You're inevitably going to end up taking sides.'

'But Frank, I – '

'No, I'm not blaming you. It's just kind of awkward, when my best friends have an interest in keeping us together.'

They sat in silence, listening to the murmur of open-air conversation rising from the shaded arbours of the garden.

Will said: 'I'm terrifically fond of Ernie. I hate it when you're mean about her.'

'Are you fond of me?'

To his intense embarrassment and dismay, Will suddenly remembered Melissa's barb about him wanting to shag Frank himself. With Frank's face so close that he could see the black dots on his chin where he shaved, he had to struggle to beat off the physical awareness before it turned into something dangerous. 'Of course.'

'Then you ought to try to see it from my point of view. Sure, Ernie's marvellous and wonderful and a saint, and all that shit. But I can't love her to order.'

'And you d-don't?'

'Want me to be honest?'

'Yes.'

'I'm bored. I'm trapped.'

Will was blinking rapidly, a sign of deep thought. 'I think you do love Ernie,' he said, 'more than you realize.'

'Of course I do. How could anyone not love her?'

There was another silence, during which they avoided one another's eyes.

'I'll say it for you.' Frank was aggressive. 'Poor little Ernie. What a misfortune, to be stuck on someone who can't appreciate her.'

'Look, Frank – I swear I won't lecture – but let Ernie down l-lightly. If you have to let her down at all.'

'I wasn't planning to throw her out of the window.'

'Seriously.'

'There's no kind way of kissing someone off,' Frank said. 'Just rest assured, if we ever get to that point, I'll look for the way that's least unkind.'

'I can't bear the thought of her being hurt.'

'You think I like it?' Frank's indignation had subsided, and he looked rueful. 'She trusts me, she even admires me, and I'm trying to betray her.' He slapped the trunk of the oak. 'I leaned my back unto an oak, I thought it was a trusty tree.' He leaped to his feet in one strong, confident movement. 'Let's go find something to eat. You won't catch me biting that hand, until it's fed me.'

Far less gracefully, Will struggled up after him, and the two of them began to stroll across the paddock towards the house.

A lithe, youthful figure detached itself from the crowd on the terrace, and ran down the steps to meet them.

'Will, this is unbelievable. You could sell tickets.' Giles, incongruous in his black clerical shirt and roman collar, gave Will a smacking kiss on the cheek.

Frank said: 'I didn't see Fancy Dress on the invitation.'

'Fuck off. I came straight from a meeting with my bishop.'

'Was it all right?' Will knew the business of all his friends. 'Did you get it?'

Giles favoured them with a cherubic, beaming smile of

triumph. 'He loves my Shadwell project. He adores my methadone Masses and my syringe-and-condom coffee mornings. It'll take me several years to scrape the pooh off my tongue, but the grovelling paid off.'

'Congratulations?'

Frank asked: 'Why are we congratulating you? Did you get promoted?'

'You are addressing the Vicar of St Benet's, Poplar. Saved from the wreckers' ball at the eleventh hour, specially for my latest project.'

'Oh. I thought they'd made you Chaplain of All Souls, at the very least.'

'Frank, you have a worldly mind, and I pity you. St Benet's is going to be a centre for the dislocated and dis-possessed – positively the sludge and silt at the very bottom of society.' He took a thirsty swig of Melissa's mixture. 'The homeless, the alkies, the crackheads, the shitheads. Basic-ally, if no one else will give you the time of day, you're welcome *chez moi*.'

'Thanks, Father. I'll bear that in mind.'

'I tell you, my sons, I'd rather be the Vicar of St Benet's than the Dean of St Paul's.'

'That's wonderful,' Will said, 'and I suppose you'll want some money.'

'Naturally.'

'Remind me later, will you?'

Frank, who could never talk about Giles's good works for long without discomfort, was gazing round at the revellers. 'God, Will, your parties are like drowning. My whole life is flashing past my eyes.'

'Why do you always invite poor old Cecily and her boring tit of a husband?' Giles had switched back into Oxford mode. 'There's kindness, Will – and there's sheer maso-chism.'

This was much better, and Frank snorted with laughter. 'Who let those guys breed?'

'I have thought of holding special Masses for nerds,' Giles said, 'but I couldn't get my bishop to buy it.'

Will was smiling, in spite of himself. 'You mean sods. They're Wild Young Bohemians, and we swore we wouldn't lose touch.'

'I'm trying to decide,' Giles announced, 'whether we've all totally changed since the Bohemians, or whether everyone is depressingly the same.'

'I've changed,' Will said.

'No, you've only reverted to what you were always going to be. The part-time country squire.'

'Actually, I might be going full time. I haven't told Mel, but I'm toying with the idea of leaving the bank. I'm getting bloody tired of dashing up and down the motorway.'

Giles and Frank exchanged looks of surprise, and Frank said: 'I thought you liked it.'

Will chose his words carefully. 'It's been going badly l-lately. Getting on top of me, rather.'

'Well, you certainly look happier,' Giles said. 'Doesn't he, Frankers?'

'Huh. Happy vicars and country gents rusticating on their acres – I'd better pull my finger out or I'll be on a walking-frame before I finish that novel.' He chuckled. 'The minute I get somewhere, real life makes a mockery of my fiction.'

As Frank was to remember for ages afterwards, real life proved his point. He saw a young man coming towards them across the lawn, neatly dodging the crowds. He had a fleeting impression of wonderfully defined colouring, a handsome head of curly hair, and a mean-looking mouth.

The newcomer stepped into their group, and softly said: 'Hello, Giles.'

Giles turned to meet the marbled grey eyes, and fainted.

'Get out,' Will hissed. 'Now, Johnny.'

'Nice place,' Johnny said, with an appreciative glance round the kitchen. He was wearing white jeans and a white linen shirt, and looked like the hero of an Edwardian school story. Every trace of vulgarity had been erased. Will's fingers trembled as they tore the foil off a bottle of wine.

'What in the n-n-name of God are you doing here? I mean, how dare you?'

'I didn't get my invitation. Anyone would think you'd been avoiding me, Will.'

'Look,' Will blurted out desperately, 'I said I'd be in touch. I've been too busy lately, all right? But that doesn't give you the right to barge in here while I'm holding a party.'

'We've got some unfinished business,' Johnny said. 'You owe me. I've come to collect.'

Will's soft lips trembled. 'No.'

Johnny bared his vampire's teeth in a gleeful smile. 'Oh, you've changed your mind, have you?'

'I never agreed to anything. I said I needed time to think. For God's sake, be reasonable. At least consider the other offers.'

'I told you, this is what I want. Then I'll leave you alone.'

Two tears rolled down Will's ruddy cheeks. He wiped them away angrily with the back of his hand. 'It's impossible. She doesn't know anything about it. How am I supposed to tell her? And she does have feelings, you know. How the hell am I supposed to make her do it?'

'Oh, you don't need to worry,' Johnny said. He pinched Will's bottom playfully, hard enough to bruise. 'You can leave that side of it to me.'

Ernestine hurried into the room, bearing a tray of empty glasses.

'Well,' Johnny said, letting his hand linger on Will's buttock, 'if it isn't Ernie.'

She stared at him, taken aback by the confident way he addressed her, as if he knew all her secrets. 'Sorry, have we met?'

'I've seen you on the television. Your show is terrific.'

Will was so amazed to hear gracious words from those lips that it took him a moment to remember his manners. 'Er – this is Johnny, Ernie. From the b-b-bank. He sort of works with me.'

'Johnny Ferrars.' He took Ernestine's hand, and looked boldly down into her eyes. 'Is Giles all right?'

'Oh, do you know Giles?' she relaxed. 'Yes, we made him lie down in the spare room. Poor thing, he's mortified. Says he can't imagine what got into him.'

'He doesn't strike me as the delicate type,' Johnny said. 'Eh, Will?'

'I d-don't understand.' Will no longer cared that Ernestine was in the room with them. 'When did you meet him?'

'Long before he got that collar. Actually, I think I was his first mission.'

'He does such marvellous work,' Ernestine said. 'And I still can't get used to it. Somehow, it seems out of character.'

'I hope he perks up later. I'd like to see him again. It's been a while.'

'Have you eaten?'

'No.'

Ernestine handed him a plate. 'The large pie is veal and ham. There's vegetable terrine and leek pie. Plus cheese, of course.'

'Is that the pie you did on the telly?'

'Yes, actually.'

'I'll try that, then.' He cut himself a large slice of the raised veal and ham pie, and attacked it without the formalities of plate, napkin or fork. 'Don't worry about me, Will,' he said sweetly, with his mouth full. 'I'll find my own way around.'

He stepped out of the glass doors. For a moment, his white figure was a burning brand as he stood in a pool of bright sunlight, looking round. Then he folded himself into the crowd on the terrace.

Ernestine absently hacked off a chunk of stilton. 'He seems nice.'

'He's not,' Will said.

'Sorry?'

He forced a smile. 'Nothing. Have you seen Mel recently?'

'She was in the herb garden just now.'

'Excuse me. I need to speak to her.'

Johnny never could get over the novelty of blending into scenes like this. A few years ago, they would have called the police or set the dogs on him as soon as look at him. Now, he was winding through the knots of people without causing a ripple of unease. He brushed shoulders and bumped backs – what a tidy sum he might have made, if he had still been in the business of picking pockets. It was all he could do not to lift a couple of wallets just to see if he still had the touch.

But who steals a purse steals trash, he thought, whisking a quotation from his supple and capacious memory. And he had reached a far higher level of larceny. The poet in him appreciated the beauty of the setting; an ideal backdrop for this ultimate scrumping of someone else's apples. His blood was racing with excitement, sparkling in his veins like champagne.

At the end of the lawn, he paused before a blistered wooden door set in the mellow stone wall, and glanced over his shoulder. Will was out on the terrace, staring after him with his hand shading his anxious eyes.

Here I am, Johnny thought, I'll wait till you catch me up. The idea of Will following him made his cock twitch with delicious anticipation. It would be too perfect – to replay the scene at the Oxford ball with the roles of performer and audience reversed. All the pent-up energy he had been storing since that mystical encounter was poised to explode.

He took another glass of punch from a passing tray, and a glass for Melissa, then paused to calm the fierce hammering of his heart.

Was he nervous? No – he had seen too many seriously frightening and disgusting things in his time to be afraid of something like this. Unless he was afraid of rejection, but nobody ever did reject him. Was he very vain? Johnny found this notion interesting, and turned it over for a second or two. Vanity had nothing to do with it. The superstitious side of his nature was aware of being pushed inexorably towards something that had lain dormant for years. He could not have turned back now to save his life.

The warped, creaking door in the wall opened into an overgrown kitchen garden, gorging itself on the afternoon sunlight. There, waist-high among the tall ranks of plants, was Melissa; her coral dress a shocking splash of colour against the hundred shades of green.

There were no paths. Johnny walked towards her down an earthy thread of track. Juicy tendrils plucked his sleeves as he passed them. Snail shells crunched under his shoes. His head, already light with desire, swam in scents of thyme and rosemary.

She raised her head as he approached, and held him in her serene blue stare. Her eyes were languid and wanton.

'Brought you a drink,' he said.

'Thanks.' Her heavy hair had a treacly sheen. When he bent forward to give her the glass, he caught its musky, flowery scent. Their hands touched briefly, and the feel of her flesh sent a shudder of pleasure through him, as if she had wrapped her fingers round his erection.

'Do I know you?' she asked.

'I work at the bank, with Will.'

'No, that's not it.' She took a sip of punch, and he watched her soft lips kissing the glass. 'It'll come back to me in a minute.'

'Nice house,' he said.

She bent down for a moment, plucked a leaf and held it to her nose. 'I like it.'

'No you don't.'

Melissa's expression of guarded interest sparked into active curiosity. 'I do. I think it's lovely.'

'You hate it.'

'This could get silly,' she said. 'Oh yes I do – oh no you don't. Like a pantomime. Why shouldn't I like my own house?'

'You don't have to stay. All sorts of things you can do.'

She stared at him, crushing the leaf between her finger-tips. They were locked in each other's gazes. The current running between them made Johnny catch his breath. The sap-scented silence stretched between them.

After a pause that seemed to last for hours, she murmured: 'Oh my God. It's you.'

And Johnny kissed her, sighing with exultation as the missing piece slotted into his soul.

Once again, her acceptance was unquestioning and absolute. He pulled her roughly against him. She arched her back, pressing herself into his groin.

Time stopped while he sucked at her mouth. Melissa started it again, by jerking her head away, and saying: 'In the house.'

Beyond the walled garden, the crowded lawn passed Johnny like the landscape of some bizarre dream. Melissa kept hold of his hands. Johnny had a massive and highly noticeable erection. Neither cared a damn if anyone saw them.

The Jacobean staircase at Monksby was of dark, uncarpeted oak. In the deserted upstairs passage, doubly quiet because of the distant voices outside, daubs of sunlight made a mosaic of the worn Persian rungs. Johnny recognized them from the Chelsea flat. The seven altar lamps, under which he had violated Will, hung above the same ponderous, carved bed – but the character of the room was different. Creamy roses climbed through the open lattice, and over the stone sills. A pall of sensuality hung over the place, as if those seven lamps had dispersed a magical incense.

They were urgent, but undressed with sober, unhurried intent. The recent heat had warmed Melissa's skin to a deep peachy gold. She was without flaw or blemish. She stretched her naked body on the bed. Johnny pulled her knees apart. The pale lips of her vagina opened; a rose with a jewel at its centre.

Drugged with delight, he flicked his tongue around her clitoris. He was aware of her sobs and moans, and the tensing of her buttocks as she pushed herself into his hot mouth. He was drowning in sweetness, and he entered her with a loud, desperate groan of pleasure.

This was more than sex. This was a giving and receiving of power, which would make them both immortal. Scowling with concentration, he built his thrusts into a violent rhythm. The bed bucked and bounced beneath them.

Melissa's sleepy gasps deepened. Her eyes widened with

a kind of astonished recognition, and she came with a great cry of despair. Tears of repletion dripped from her long lashes. Johnny surrendered to the tidal wave of his orgasm, which crashed through his body until he thought the ecstasy would burst his heart.

The roaring tempest in his head subsided. He lay on top of her, twitching with every beat of his pulse. Gradually, he became aware of the calling, laughing voices outside. She had set him on fire, and he would never stop burning.

He rolled over on to his back, and gazed round at the sun-lit bedroom with stupid contentment. Melissa raised herself on one elbow, her face inches above his. Johnny had read of people 'glowing', but this feebly expressed her phosphorescent radiance. He had fucked out all her languor. She was the sleeping beauty, brought to life by the Prince's kiss.

She whispered: 'I don't know your name.'

'Johnny.'

'Johnny what?'

'Ferrars.'

'Do you smoke, Johnny darling?'

'Not half.'

She reached out for the carved satinwood night-table beside the bed, and pulled open a drawer. 'This is the very best, even good enough for you. King's Cross Gold, grown under lamps by a friend.'

She took out a fat joint and lit it, settling herself comfortably on the pillows beside him. 'Will hates me doing this. He's so square, he's positively a cube.'

'You only married him for his dosh.'

'Good heavens, yes. Why else?'

Johnny let out a lazy laugh. 'Does he fuck you?'

'Just about. You can't imagine the work I have to do.'

He took the joint from her. 'Oh, I can. We must compare notes some day.'

She was laughing too. 'This is a dream. A very dirty dream. I can't believe this conversation. Do you know everything about me?'

'Everything.'

'You're heavenly. I've never come like that in my life.'

'That's how the fates meant you to come.'

'Yes,' she breathed. 'Oh, yes.'

They passed the joint between them, until they had smoked it down to the roach. Melissa stubbed it out in a china ashtray. Then she knelt above him, and the warm masses of her hair fell across his face. He closed his eyes, and shut out every sensation except the heat of her mouth as it closed on his penis.

If an angel could make love, he thought, it would give head like Melissa. In his mind, he saw the stone angel at Quenville, and imagined it softened into melting feathered whiteness, caressing him until he was shouting for mercy. She lowered herself on his erection, and galloped them both to a roaring orgasm which ploughed the bedclothes into chaos.

Afterwards, she examined the blobs of his sperm on the counterpane, laughing to herself as she rubbed them with the tip of her finger.

'Deary me,' she said, 'I've got some explaining to do.'

'You'll think of something.'

'I usually do. The wonderful thing about old Will is his credulity. Oh –' She spread her legs. 'Look what you've done to me.' The folds of her vagina were tinged with a hectic flush. 'You're so right. I was designed for sex like that.'

She stood up, and looked at him intently. 'That was you, wasn't it? That night at the ball, when I was so stoned.'

'Yes,' he said. 'I've been chasing that fuck for years.'

'And I've been waiting for you. Don't disappear again.'

'I won't.'

Melissa pulled on her knickers, and sheathed herself in her silk dress. 'I'd better get back to my guests. What a bore.'

Johnny said, 'The boredom's over now.'

'Oh, Johnny. Handsome, winsome Johnny.' Lightly, she kissed his damp, limp penis.

One more lingering look, and she was gone.

Johnny lay on his back, letting the late afternoon breeze

fan his naked body through the open casement. He had reached the pinnacle of physical fulfilment, he thought; what other kind of fulfilment was there?

There was a sudden sound – something between a honk and a snuffle, hastily suppressed with a choke.

'Jesus,' Johnny said. 'I forgot about you.'

He got off the bed, stretched luxuriously until his bones cracked, and followed the sound to a louvre door of golden pine. It opened on a bathroom, dominated by an antique cast-iron tub on clawed feet.

Will was curled on the bathmat against the lavatory bowl, stifling his convulsive sobs in his corduroy knees. Slowly, he raised his head. His scarlet face shone with tears and mucus.

Johnny burst into peal after peal of hysterical laughter. He had never seen anything so exquisitely funny. The thought of Will eavesdropping on that magnificent performance made him weep and howl and clutch his sides.

'Remember, viewers,' he gasped, 'don't try that at home without a grown-up!'

Giles had escaped to the furthest corner of the paddock, as much for other people's sake as for his own. Everyone was monumentally embarrassed by the fact that he had fainted, and his being dressed as a vicar made it worse. He embodied that most outmoded cliché, the swooning Victorian curate. If he had not been embroiled in such a nightmare of horror, he would have been amused. As it was, he wondered if he would ever smile again.

You fool, he murmured to himself; how could you have kidded yourself it was all behind you? The blinding sight of Johnny Ferrars, creeping up on him like a demon from his unconscious suddenly made flesh, had warned him that no atonement could wipe away the stain across his life.

He replayed the moments before his fate had caught up with him, marvelling that he could have been so filled with happy optimism. How, in the name of heaven, could he carry on, with this lesion disabling his soul? A decent man would have gone straight back to the bishop, said a fond farewell to his cherished project for the homeless and turned in his collar. In the past, he had managed to convince himself that his guilt did not give him the right to deprive those who needed his help. But had this been a sort of excuse? The reappearance of Johnny had pitched him straight back into the part of his past that he had dedicated the rest of his life to erasing.

He was not at all surprised to see the white-clad figure making its way across the paddock towards him. There was a terrible, pagan feeling of fate about the whole meeting, and he had known he would be found. Passively, he watched Johnny vaulting over the fence into the meadow, and sauntering up to the grassy hollow where he stood.

'Hello,' he said. He knew then that there was more to this than his guilt. He could not help the hurt and betrayal bleeding into his voice.

Johnny smiled at him, in the old, heartbreaking way. 'Hello, Giles. That was quite a welcome.'

'You gave me the shock of my life. What on earth are you doing here?'

'I've got a proper job these days. I work in Will's bank.'

'They let you near other people's money? God Almighty.'

'It's dirty work, but someone's got to do it. I didn't have enough O levels to clean toilets.'

'Ha-ha,' Giles said. 'Well, you've caught up with me. What do you want?'

Johnny manufactured a look of injured innocence, shot with the purest malevolence. 'Nothing! Just wanted to say hi. Talk about old times.'

Giles lowered his eyes. 'Spare me the games, eh?'

'On my life, Giles – on yours, if you prefer – I haven't come here to make trouble for you.' He lit a cigarette. 'It's well weird, seeing you in that get-up. I'd never have had you down for a priest in a million years. Didn't even know you were a Catholic.'

'I'm not,' Giles said. 'Not a Roman, I mean. I'm High Anglican.'

Johnny chuckled. 'How typical. You do everything at half-cock, you do. Can't even get religion properly. Still, that's a few years less in purgatory for me. We're not supposed to shag priests, no matter how hard they beg.'

Giles's mouth twisted in disgust. 'I don't believe this. Are you telling me you're a Roman Catholic?'

'Yep. Spent a year having the shit beaten out of me by the Christian Brothers. I was even a boat-boy.'

'I'm amazed the plaster saints didn't scream at the sight of you.'

'No, no, Giles. Us proper Catholics have a different deal – we get to commit more and bigger sins before they catch up with us.'

'Are you actually saying you're still a believer?'

Johnny smiled wickedly. 'Haven't you ever read "The Hound of Heaven"? Fabulous stuff. "I fled Him, down the nights and down the days;/ I fled Him, down the arches of the years;/ I fled Him, down the labyrinthine ways".'

'Shut up.' Giles was white and shaking with anger. 'If the Hound of Heaven ever catches you, I hope he bites your arse off.'

'Father! Really!'

'That's one thing you did for me, Johnny, and I ought to thank you for it. You showed me the reality of human evil. Without you, I might have been tempted to take the trendy view that it doesn't exist. I'd never have known God, if I hadn't seen the opposition.'

Johnny lounged against the fence. 'Pity you're not a real priest. You'd have loved to hear my confession. But you don't believe in that.'

'No.'

His voice dripped honey, sweet and caressing. 'So you've never told anyone.'

'I've got a confessor. But no, I've never told a living soul what really happened, and I don't think I ever will. I'm a fraud and a hypocrite. It makes nonsense of everything that matters to me. I only hope the afterlife is ecumenical, Johnny – it'd be some comfort to burn in hell next to you.'

Johnny chuckled appreciatively, as if Giles had said it to please him. 'You'll be there long before I am.'

'I can wait.'

'Long, long before. You might die quite soon.'

'I'm not ill,' Giles said. 'I only passed out.'

The honeyed voice dropped intimately. 'That vicar's conscience of yours has a terrible terminal smell to it. I shouldn't like it to get you into trouble.'

The threat hung in the air between them. For a long moment, Giles looked into the depths of the dark grey eyes, and saw the stark simplicity of Johnny's meaning.

'Don't worry,' he muttered. 'I'm not holy enough to chuck everything away now. I'm a dedicated coward, as well as a hypocrite.'

'That's all right, then.' Johnny leaned forward to plant an insolent kiss on his lips. 'Look after yourself.'

Left alone again, Giles surveyed the rottenness of his soul. The past could never be erased. He heard the pounding feet of Heaven's Hound catching up with him, and felt its hot breath on his back.

'"They beat –'" he recited to himself, gazing across the green sward where the sheep grazed in tranquil safety. '"And a Voice beat/ More instant than the Feet –"'

He made himself acknowledge the bitterest punishment; the eternal, perishing loneliness of the sin that is never confessed or repented.

'All things betray thee, who betrayest Me.'

Eight

Frank met his shaved, laundered reflection in the dark hall mirror, and smiled at himself. New loafers, Argyll socks (matching), grey flannel trousers, light blue shirt with button-down collar and navy blazer. God, but you're lovely. Anyone could see why the woman at the publisher's had taken such a shine to his proposal.

'I love your style,' she had said, leaving a significant pause before adding: 'Your writing style, that is. So sexy. So entertaining. And you're working on a novel, too? Gosh. How on earth do you find the time for your academic work?'

After meeting her, Frank had scooted back to his academic work, to hear an essay by a student who very clearly fancied him. The teaching side was sometimes a bit of a grind, but – if he were honest – marvellous for his ego. When he felt slighted or diminished by Ernestine's public persona, it was extremely comforting to assume his role of college sex symbol. It wasn't only the students, either. The previous night, at top table, he had had his thigh caressed by a very passable female don. He was whistling to himself as he checked through the piles of letters on the radiator.

The dilapidated stairwell of the converted terraced house off the Cowley Road, where he lived in term time, brought him down somewhat. This part of Oxford, too near car factories and thundering ring roads, was worlds removed from the City of bells and dreaming spires. Well, perhaps his father would loosen up a little Darcy money for a decent house, now that the family name was appearing on a book. He was getting tired of camping out in the same, dismal hinterlands as his students.

Bounding up the stairs to his top-floor flat, he smelled

meat and herbs, and his senses automatically lifted with pleasure. Ernestine. She had a beautiful new flat and a hit TV series, but the stars in their courses could not stop her making her pilgrimages up the motorway to Oxford.

The pleasure was followed by a nagging sense of guilt, which stopped him short at his own door. Matters between them were no longer restful or simple. She had changed, or he had. The relationship had, somehow, been thrown out of balance. They had been growing in different directions for some time, but Frank dated his most profound discontent from his encounter with Melissa at the wedding. She had awakened the longing that had slept in his blood for four years, until he was in a hopeless state of confusion about his feelings for the two cousins. Which one did he truly love – what the hell was 'true love' anyway? Mystery, beguilement, erotic torture? Or sweetness, light and sanity?

Ernie, sweetheart, darling, he found himself thinking – set me free. This may not be noble or good, or even sensible, but if I don't get out, I'll go crazy.

In his moments of greatest isolation, he could almost feel that Melissa had poisoned him, infecting him with a fearful restlessness and discontent.

Squaring his shoulders, he opened the door. The flat was a depressing two-rooms-and-bathroom job, with the kitchen part strung out along one wall of the sitting room. This meant working and reading in a permanent welter of dirty cups and pans. Only Ernestine had the patience and skill to make it halfway civilized.

'Hi, love,' she said.

She was at his desk, making notes on the script of the Christmas edition of *Banquet on the Breadline*. The smell came from a pan of stew on the hob, surrounded by Post-its and clearly one of her professional experiments.

'Hi.' He dropped a kiss on her springy hair, inwardly chafing at the middle-aged domesticity of it all.

It was like kissing a hummingbird, quivering with energy. Ernestine, busy and capable, glowed with the joy of doing a thousand things at once.

'I did your shirts,' she said, glancing up with a brief, pre-occupied smile. 'They're on the bedroom doorknob. And I stopped by at Sainsbury's for you – everything in your fridge was mouldy.'

All this is my fault, he thought ruefully. I showed her I liked all this domestic stuff. She wanted to please me, and I turned her into this parody of herself. He could not picture Melissa peeking in fridges, or trawling round supermarkets.

'Hey, guess what,' he said. 'I just got myself a publisher.'

'What?' She looked up properly this time, dropping her pen. And the moment she did this, Frank realized that what he really disliked was the spectacle of her immersed in her work. He felt a greater heel than ever – positively the stiletto of heels.

'It's not the novel. It's a book based on the thesis. You know. *Icily Regular, Splendidly Null*, blah blah. I'm jazzing it up into popular lit crit, all pretty Victorian paintings and sultry poems.'

'Frank, that's wonderful! You should have told me – '

'Should I? Would you have had the time to listen?'

Her smile froze. 'Well, of course – '

He winced away from those round blue eyes, so innocent in their stubbornness. 'Honey, can we talk? I mean, without you writing a Hollywood film script.'

This time, something in the quality of his voice told her the blade was about to fall. And give her her due, she pushed her work aside at once, with an obvious determination to be brave.

'Okay.' He took the chair opposite her, and rubbed his face wearily. 'How do I do this?'

There was a short, charged silence, after which Ernestine said: 'Don't ask me. I'm not going to do it for you.'

Frank fixed his gaze on the cheap pine surface of the table. 'It's not about me loving you any less, because I'll always love you. But it's stopped working.'

'No, it hasn't – '

'Ernie, please. Admit you know something's wrong.'

'All right,' she said cautiously. 'I know something's wrong with you. You're not happy with me.'

He sighed. 'Listen, I'm not suggesting we should go for a big, dramatic split. You're too big a part of my life for that. But we've got to change the terms round here, and give each other more – freedom. That's all.'

She asked: 'To do what?'

'Well, to work, for instance. I come home, and you've moved all my papers. I open a book, and a frigging recipe falls out of it. And I'm not allowed to gripe about it, because your work makes money and mine doesn't. I need more space.'

'Oh, space,' she said dully. 'American-speak for "any space that doesn't have you in it".'

'Hey!' This was so true that looking wounded and indignant was the only possible response.

'You're not in love with me any more. If you ever were.'

'Don't over-simplify. Maybe I don't love you in the way you wanted. You're the best friend I ever had, and I can't imagine my life without you. You're a part of me. But – '

And that 'but' lay between them, silently reeling into all kinds of unspeakable admissions.

Ernestine laid her hands on the table, and cleared her throat in a businesslike manner. 'What are you suggesting, exactly? Are we breaking up?'

'No! No – we're lowering the heat, that's all. We're still together, but we're not making assumptions about the future.'

'I can't give you what you want,' she said, her face flooding with pain. 'I've never managed to find out what that is, and I don't think you know either. But in the long term, it obviously isn't me.'

Frank groaned. 'Does this have to be such a crisis? All I'm saying is, I love you – but I'm not ready to buy the whole package. Houses, weddings, kids.'

She stood up. 'I'm going to make a cup of tea,' she announced. 'And you're not going to stop me. We're going to do this in a civilized manner. A model of its kind.' She put the kettle on.

'I'm not good enough for you,' Frank said. 'You deserve

someone better. And if you ever find him, well – I'll try not to stand in your way.'

Now that self-revelation was no longer a risk, Ernestine let him have the truth with both barrels. 'Let me translate. I'm not good enough for you. You think you deserve someone better, and you don't want me in the way.'

'No!' Frank shouted desperately.

'I'm never going to find anyone else, Frank, I'm afraid. You're the man I love. I've loved you since the day Mel stood you up at the ball, and you picked me a rose – do you remember?'

'Naturally I do. C'mon, Ern.'

She spooned tea into the teapot, dangerously still. 'I'm not the sort of person who's in love one minute and out of love the next. I'm afraid nobody else will do.'

'Is that supposed to make me feel bad?' he blazed. 'Well, it does. Okay? Ouch. How can you know who you'll love in the future?' For the first time, he tried to visualize Ernestine loving someone else, and the idea terrified him. Besides which, he hated shouting, because he reminded himself of his father. He breathed deeply, and said, in what he hoped was a more reasonable voice: 'Just a little more freedom, to find out who we really are. Is that so terrible?'

She put a mug of tea in front of him. 'Let's be practical. We won't be drastic, but we'll give each other's keys back. I'll call you before I come round, and you can tell me if it's not convenient.'

'You're amazing,' he said humbly.

'Aren't I?' Her face was pink and strained. Suddenly, she smacked the table, and blurted out: 'I'm doing it again. Holding back, pushing down. Bending over backwards to meet your terms. I always do that with you, because I'm so scared of losing you. I've probably repressed so much anger in the past year, I'll get cancer.'

They gaped at each other – he was as astonished as she was.

'Actually,' she said, 'I don't feel remotely civilized.'

'This is healthy, Ern. Let it out.'

She snatched up the cup of tea and hurled it on the floor, peppering them both with splashes of boiling water. 'Fuck off, Frank. It's not healthy at all. Ever since I've known you, it's been Mel, Mel, Mel. I'm sick of being used as your season ticket to Mel. I'm sick of the way you sniff round her, and drop to your knees whenever she gives you the time of day. You go on and on about how sensitive she is, as if I had no feelings at all. You'd have stopped sleeping with me ages ago if you thought there was a cat's chance she'd have you instead.'

'What the hell are you – '

'Just fuck off!' Ernestine had started to weep furiously. She bundled together the pages of her script, and grabbed her handbag. 'More freedom? I'll give you more freedom. It's over.'

'No! No!'

'And don't you dare go near her. You might not give a fart about losing me – well, let's see how you like it if it means losing Mel too.'

'Wait – '

She slammed the door behind her, and he heard her noisy sobs exploding as she stumbled down the stairs.

When her anger had subsided, it left her with an almost postcoital feeling of physical catharsis. She stopped her car at a café on the Cirencester road, patched up her swollen face in the Ladies, and bought herself a disgusting pork pie to stop up her wretched hollowness.

Back in the car, with a box of tissues on the seat beside her, a feeling of horrified embarrassment began to dawn on her, as she replayed what she had said to Frank. She could hardly believe she had displayed such childishness, such pettiness. She had not thrown a scene like that since she and Mel were tiny, and she had kicked up a fuss because her new wellies were blue and she wanted Mel's red ones.

Underneath this humiliation lay a continent of fear. How was she to bear her life without the man she loved? To make it worse, Frank had never looked so beautiful – his shining hair, those hot blue Irish eyes, that body to die for. They had

217

been right, all those people who had thought him far too good for her. He was the A-person par excellence, way out of her league. And, she had thrown him away, the man she had loved to desperation.

There was a dangerous moment when she found a half-eaten packet of chocolate he had left in the glove compartment, and another when she switched on Radio Four and got *Poetry Please*. A lugubrious male voice intoned: 'The day breaks not, it is my heart,/ Because that thou and I must part,' and she needed windscreen wipers for her streaming eyes.

She wanted Melissa. Actually, she wanted Will. He was so comforting, so strong. His shoulder was built for sobbing into. Rehearsing the story she would tell him took the edge off the pain. Unconsciously, she was postponing her next burst of grief until she had an audience.

The weather was still unseasonably hot, with barely a hint of autumn. Ernestine steered her Metro through sleeping, heat-soaked lanes. Reaching Monksby, she parked at the top of the track that wound down to the house. The engine whispered away into the humming silence. Every hedge-leaf and blade of grass was still.

Ernestine gathered her tissues and her bag, locked her car and stood for moment, gazing down into the valley. The peace fell upon her, scented and timeless. Like a hurt child limping home to its mother, she started down the track, praying Will and Melissa would be there to meet her. She needed tea and sympathy in that sunny kitchen.

Thank heaven, both cars were in the paddock. She knocked on the front door to announce herself, and it swung open. Perhaps they were outside. Decorative pictures slotted into her mind, of Melissa at the dovecote, and Will tidying his herb garden. He was, supposedly, 'on leave' from the bank, but Ernestine knew he would never go back. He was talking about turning Monksby herbs into a business – a charming hobby, since he did not need the money. Ernestine found herself deeply comforted by the idea of his always being there when she needed him.

She clattered into the silent house. 'Hello?'

Columns of dust whirled in the tall shafts of sunlight. The place seemed to contain acres of shining, polished emptiness. Her footsteps, as she moved across the worn flagstones to the kitchen, had a lonely echo.

The kitchen was also deserted, and painfully tidy. Every surface was stripped and immaculate, as if someone – surely not Melissa? – had put their whole soul into cleaning it. The Aga rail was festooned with damp cloths, and there was a faint smell of bleach. The door to the terrace was locked. Ernestine looked through the glass, and saw a forgotten coffee mug on the wrought-iron table, pinning down an old newspaper warped with dew.

'Come on, you two,' she murmured to herself, 'where are you?'

Unable to help colonizing, she automatically filled and switched on the electric kettle and went to the cupboard for the cafetiere. There were three neat stacks of ten-pence coins on the kitchen table. Ernestine saw that there was a note underneath them: 'THE MONEY YOU WANTED.'

'Mel?' she called. 'Will?'

This, barely recognizable as such at the time, was the first chilly draught of unease. For the rest of her life, Ernestine would play and replay the dreamlike unfolding of the next few minutes.

'Mel?' She began to climb the stairs, her senses peeled for any sound.

The door to the bedroom stood open. Ernestine nearly gasped aloud with relief when she saw Will stretched on the bed. For several minutes, she stood watching him in the doorway, wondering if it would be mean to wake him.

The room was drowsy with the powdery smell of late roses. Will lay with his face turned to the open casement. Ernestine crept towards him. Beside him, on the night-table, stood an empty glass and an empty half-bottle of whisky.

Will was drinking too much these days. Unless he had a cold, or something.

It took her God knew how long to fit the fragments together. One of Will's hands was curled round a little plastic drum of paracetamol, also empty. Yes, he was ill.

But how still he was.

How pale he was.

One frozen moment of disbelief, then Ernestine let out her breath in a great, stricken howl; as if this could recall Will's vanished spirit from its long flight across the summer meadows.

Nine

Strangers had taken possession of the house, filling it with alien voices, but these could not disturb the vast silence radiating from the awful thing that lay under those seven lamps upstairs.

Why, why, why? The question tolled in Ernestine's mind like a great funeral bell. It made her almost frantic to think of the misery Will must have suffered, and the fact that he was now beyond human comfort. What agony, what bloody sweat had he endured in the lonely hour before he ended his life?

She kept glancing down at the palm of her hand, half expecting it to look different. It was smarting from the memory of touching Will's frozen cheek, and she would never get it warm again.

Death had begun to smooth his freckled face into smiling serenity. Will had been so much like himself that it was impossible to believe she could not wake him. Then she had felt the incredible coldness of his flesh, and confronted the fact that the smile had not been generated by any emotion of Will's.

In a few days, he would be bright green and grinning like a lunatic, and that would not have anything to do with Will's emotions either. The thing upstairs had once been Will, and was Will no longer.

The chocolate biscuit in her mouth turned to ashes. Why the hell was she eating anyway? Revolted, she spat it out into a piece of kitchen towel.

Above her head, the voices murmured and the footsteps creaked. They had all been as kind as possible – one of them had even made her a cup of tea. But Ernestine wished they would stop assuming she was about to go to pieces. Somehow, she had to get herself braced and under control before Melissa came home.

This was the worst day of her life; so bad that she could not actually bring herself to think about the future. Yet she could still find a grain of consolation in the providence that had brought her here to cushion the blow. Every scrap of animosity or jealousy she had every felt about Melissa was submerged in a great, throbbing wave of tenderness. All her love for her cousin had been reborn and reinvented, because if ever Melissa needed her, she needed her now.

Unconsciously, she was concentrating upon Melissa as a way of holding herself together. If she was self-forgetful, this was a blessing – Ernestine did not want to remember herself. She was frightened of Mel's reaction. Under that coolness, nearer the surface than anyone suspected, lay a kind of wild fragility; something that could shatter like spun glass.

As far as possible, for all their sakes, she must be spared. The police had wanted to know if Will had left a note. There had been nothing in the bedroom, but Ernestine felt sure he had – Will couldn't nip out for a pint of milk without leaving a full account of his movements. It was essential to find it first so that she could take the full impact of whatever it contained.

She went into the drawing room, wincing over its normality and the books Will had left, half-read, on his favourite side of the sofa. It was an effort to remember that he could not walk in and find her snooping. He had a large rolltop desk; a clumsy thing disliked by Melissa. The key was kept in a japanned box on the mantelpiece. Ernestine unlocked it, and was almost disabled by the living sense of Will that rushed out to meet her. Each pigeonhole was, typically, in apple-pie order.

The single sheet of paper, bearing a few neat lines crowded at the top, lay on the leather blotter. Ernestine had to read the familiar writing several times, before she could make sense of something this senseless.

I have to do this for both our sakes. It hasn't worked. It will be tough for you at first, but in the long run you'll have a better life without me. Love, Will.

And that was all. For Ernestine, it carried eerie echoes of the last conversation she had had with Frank. It expressed, in a nutshell, everything he had tried to make her understand for ages. How bizarre, that it was addressed to Melissa.

But this could not be right. Gentle Will, who had loved the very air Melissa breathed, seemed to be saying this was all her fault. He must have known what it would do to her.

It'll kill her, Ernestine thought, that's all. Oh Will, how could you?

A car crunched the gravel outside. Ernestine saw the next few minutes in a sort of strobe-effect of panic. The slender, reed-like figure took in the ambulance and police car parked outside and dashed into the house, head bowed. There must have been a moment when she was told, but Ernestine could never recall it afterwards.

Everything was obliterated by the film of horror that settled across Melissa's eyes as she broke against the breaking news. Then the cousins were sobbing in each other's arms.

'Wait, darling –' Ernestine begged, 'my poor love – '

She would see it until she died, printed on her memory whenever she closed her eyes. They were bringing Will downstairs in a kind of bag you hung winter coats in to keep off the moths.

Nothing would stop Melissa rushing up to the landing, and tugging down the zip to expose his face.

'Oh, poor – poor – poor –' she crooned, stroking his icy cheek.

Ernestine saw how awful it was on the faces of the policemen. They plucked her off him, fighting and begging. One of them restrained her, while they carried the body into the ambulance.

Melissa broke into frenzied, thrashing sobs, and struggled

against Ernestine as if possessed. The doctor sunk a syringe into her arm. Gradually, while the other policeman guided the ambulance up the narrow track, she subsided like a deflating balloon, to the point of letting Ernestine guide her to the sofa and cover her convulsing body with a blanket.

Ernestine sat stroking her hair, watching her lashes meet over her terrified eyes. Only then was she aware of the shaking in her own limbs, plus a guilty relief that the first storm had passed.

The doctor asked: 'Are you two going to be all right?'

She found a voice, surprisingly forceful. 'Did you really have to creep up on her like that? She's not a rogue elephant.'

'Will you be able to cope on your own?'

'Yes, it'll be much better if we're alone when she wakes.' Ernestine craved a huge shot of alcohol, but had no intention of giving into it with all these people watching. 'I'll be taking her back to London as soon as I can. I'll leave the number, of course.'

Get out, she wanted to implore, just get out.

With maddening slowness, the strangers got themselves into their cars and drove off up the drive. Ernestine stood at the drawing-room window, listening to the sound of wheels dying away in the distance. The immense silence of the darkening countryside reasserted itself, emphasized by the sobs that tore mechanically into Melissa's sleep.

Craving light as much as alcohol, Ernestine took the brandy bottle into the kitchen, and slowly sipped her drink on a high stool, watching the reassuring blink of the digital clock on the oven.

She could have telephoned Frank. She should ring her parents. But the thought of dispensing more comfort and reassurance filled her with weariness. Where was the person who would look after her? She allowed herself a pang of acute self-pity for bearing the weight alone. Will's parents were both dead – his mother had died two years before – and she was selfishly glad to be spared the task of telling them. What would they say to their son, if there was a next world where they would meet again?

The cafetiere she had pulled out, a lifetime ago, still stood on the work surface. Ernestine found comfort in making herself an incredibly strong cup of coffee. It made her cement-lined stomach lurch uneasily, but the caffeine poured energy into her veins.

After a long, long time spent clutching the empty cup, she saw light stream across the hall. Ernestine hurried back to the drawing room, still holding the cup, and met Melissa rolling, drunken and wild-haired, towards the door. She had switched on the big lamp beside the sofa, and thrown off the blanket. Her eyes were puffy and owlish, but she was no longer hysterical.

Ernestine put an arm round her shoulders, and led her out to the kitchen.

'Let me get you something, darling. You should have some tea.'

'Coffee,' Melissa croaked; 'the smell woke me. Is there any left?'

Relieved to have something to do, Ernestine guided her into a big, cushioned carver's chair at the large table. 'I'll make some fresh.'

Melissa's head drooped forward into her hands. Her wrists seemed too thin to support it. She murmured: 'It's real, isn't it?'

'Mel – '

'God. What have I done?'

'Look, you're not to blame yourself.' Ernestine felt this sounded feeble, but could not help thinking of Will's note. Evidently, something had happened between them.

How the hell am I supposed to do this bit?

She sat down beside Melissa, carefully placing the cups of coffee. 'You have to know, darling. I hate to have to tell you, but someone's bound to if I don't. He left a note.'

Melissa raised her head. 'He says it's all because of me. Doesn't he?'

'They took it away, but I made a copy. Do you – do you think you want to see it?'

'No. I can guess.' The full, perfect lips buckled distressfully. The tears cascading from the blue eyes tore at

225

Ernestine's nerves. Words like 'distress' and 'grief' were too weak – she felt she was seeing her cousin's heart breaking. 'I never meant to hurt him, Ernie. I'd kill myself, if that would save him. I must be very evil.'

'Don't. Stop it. You're not evil.'

'You don't understand. I loved him because of his goodness, and something in me hurt that goodness. I destroy the things I love most.'

'No, no. Stop it – '

'Did you ever see anything so good as his face? Or so sad?'

Ernestine said: 'But he was smiling – peaceful.'

'All corpses smile,' Melissa said, shaming this platitudinous attempt at comfort. 'I could see the sadness.' Her head rested on her folded arms, and her thin shoulders shook.

Ernestine stroked her back. 'He told me, the day he first saw this place, that he'd had a sort of vision of finding peace here – ultimate peace, I mean.'

'D-did he? Truly?'

'Try to think of that, love. Forget the note – he can't have been in his right mind. He'd never want you to feel like this. You know how he adored you.'

It was the wrong thing to say. The sobs intensified, until Ernestine could almost see the raw, bleeding edges of the shattered heart.

'Darling, get some things together – or I'll do it – and we'll go to Mum's. You shouldn't be here.'

'Please – I don't want to leave. Please – '

'Mel, for God's sake!'

'He's still here. I can't leave while he's still here.' Her head jerked up. 'Was the window open?'

'What window?'

'The bedroom – did I leave it open?'

'Yes, it was open.'

'Are you sure?'

'Positive.'

Melissa breathed out a tremulous sigh of relief. 'He won't be trapped, then.'

'You're scaring me,' Ernestine said.

She rubbed her wet eyes. 'Don't worry. I won't go barmy. I can cope, as long as you're here.'

This statement, uttered with such confident simplicity, made Ernestine feel she could walk through fire for her cousin. 'I'm here, Mel. I'll be here.'

Suddenly, Melissa grabbed at her hand with fingers that felt like claws. She had tensed to iron. 'What's that?'

Ernestine followed her gaze to the three piles of coins, lying forgotten where she had found them.

'Nothing –' she began. Then, remembering the scrap underneath bearing poor Will's writing, she added more firmly, 'Nothing,' and stood up to remove it.

Melissa was too quick for her. She leaped out of her chair, and pounced on the note hungrily, scattering the coins.

'For a parking meter or something,' Ernestine offered, trying to sound casual. 'Some change. That's all.'

There was a silence, during which Melissa was frozen to stone. Eventually, she said, in a different voice: 'Did the police see this?'

'I don't think so.'

'Don't you understand?' Melissa looked terrified, appalled. 'Three pounds, in ten-pence coins.'

'So?'

They both jumped as the phone shrilled into the quietness. 'It's probably Mum,' Ernestine said. 'I gave the police her number.'

'No!' Melissa tightened her grip. 'Don't answer it.'

'But what if it's – '

'No! Let it ring!' Her nails dug into the soft flesh on Ernestine's arm. The phone rang and rang, a vicious intrusion that made them both weep with pain.

'Thirty pieces of silver,' Melissa whispered.

Ernestine felt herself being cast out of the land of common sense. The still small voice which told her this was ridiculous was drowned in the crashing tempest of a typical – and, in the circumstances, forgivable – Melissa drama. She watched, hypnotized, as Melissa's mouth distorted into a howl of despair.

PART THREE

But what a weight, O God!
Was that one coffin to bear!
Like a coffin of lead!
And I carry it everywhere.

I have made a vow in my heart,
Whatever the friends may say,
Never to carry a corpse
Again, to my dying day.

Thomas Ashe, 'Corpse-Bearing'

PART THREE

One

Will's funeral was a grisly parody of his wedding; a photograph seen in negative. The same friends who had showered him with rice and confetti in the sunshine, five months before, now shivered in the dank October drizzle outside the same church, watching his shining coffin being loaded into the hearse.

Frank had been one of the bearers. Almost hyperventilating with nerves, he had crept along the aisle, one hand clasping a brass coffin handle and the other gripping the shoulder of Giles. He had been afraid to stand up straight because he was taller than the other five. Behind him, in similar agonies, the sawn-off Paul Dashwood had strained on the balls of his feet. Both were so terrified of dropping the body that they had exchanged glances of naked, unashamed relief when the undertaker's man helped them to place the coffin on the trestles.

Then, when the burden had been lifted from his body, Frank carried the full weight on his soul. In his worst moments, he had imagined Will's dead limbs lolling and thudding against the wooden shell. This had not happened, but he was suddenly haunted by the knowledge that the only remnant of his beloved friend lay a few feet away from him, cold hands folded on his still breast.

He stared round the congregation for comfort, and saw them all making special, solemn faces above black ties and sober suits. It all struck him as ridiculous; a charade. The absence of Will was a gigantic embarrassment – like having a loud, rude conversation about someone in the next room. The strangest thing was that, despite the coffin, he had a strong sense of Will being present and alive somewhere else.

He wished he could cry. Giles sniffed audibly in the pew beside him, and Frank felt rather jealous of him. Anyway, were vicars supposed to cry at funerals? Reprovingly, he whipped out his handkerchief, and pressed it into Giles's wet fist. All he could make himself feel was a savage longing to shout and laugh and get drunk – anything, to remove the crushing weight of Will's coffin.

The service seemed to have been designed to make everyone as confused and wretched as possible. On the one hand, the priest talked of reconciliation and 'celebration', and implied that exhibitions of mourning were in bad taste. On the other hand, the hymns and readings were as heart-rending as possible, calculated to set the entire church gulping and blowing their noses.

Frank's weeping started during the slow movement of Elgar's Violin Concerto, but even as he snatched his hand-kerchief back from Giles, he resented this blatant manipulation of his emotions. Of course he was crying. Anyone would cry over the Elgar, whether or not they had loved Will.

A countertenor they had known slightly at Oxford, whose astonished squeak of a voice suggested a permanent search for his testicles, sang Psalm 121: 'I will lift up mine eyes unto the hills, from whence cometh my help.' Frank was assaulted by a memory of how he, Giles and Will had laughed madly at this man during a madrigal concert, and wept in good earnest.

Then Dash, in his beautiful, soulful baritone, read the piece of Tennyson chosen by Melissa:

> Thy voice is on the rolling air;
> I hear thee where the waters run;
> Thou standest in the rising sun,
> And in the setting thou are fair.

Melissa stood across the aisle, in the opposite pew, next to Ernestine. Frank had not seen her since Will's death. He had been deeply shocked by Ernestine's outburst on the day of their split – and who was he, anyway, to disturb the poor widow? Now, he risked a look at her sharp, pale profile; and his head filled with stars.

All the rags of longing and imagination which had tormented him for years suddenly swept together, into one holy revelation of worship. She was haggard, and plainly dressed in a black suit which did not fit her well. But Frank was blinded by her spiritual clothing of shimmering samite, white as the fleshy bells of the Madonna lilies she had placed on her husband's coffin.

She could not have epitomized grief so perfectly if she had not loved Will. He knew he had been right not to believe her when she fed him that nonsense about love and lust at her wedding. How could such a creature not know love?

The sheer poetry of the tragedy took his breath away. Will had died, he realized, for nothing less than the love of this woman. Loving Melissa had been the death of his friend. He found that he was no longer angry with Will for hurting her so cruelly. He had too much respect for an Icarus who had flown too near the sun, and wore the winding sheet of burned plumage. In death, he had a certain sacrificial grandeur.

These thoughts were not consciously processed. They simply slotted, fully formed, into Frank's mind; the final pieces in a complicated mosaic of jewelled fragments which now made a dazzling whole. In the time it took to turn his head, he had crossed the barrier.

The immediate effect was like a cloak of lightning, which made him intensely aware of all the best elements in the love he felt for his friends. Iron bands loosed, chips of ice melted, scabs of shabbiness and selfishness peeled away, leaving exquisite tenderness. He put his arm around Giles's shoulders, moved by the purest desire to comfort.

Good God, he thought, with a shock of awe – I wonder if this is how it felt to be Will?

When it was over, the undertakers' men shouldered the coffin, and the mourners followed it out of the church. Melissa, Ernestine, Tess and George climbed into a waiting

233

limousine to accompany Will to the cemetery. Others prepared to follow in their own cars. The rest had to get through an awkward hiatus, before they assembled at the Chelsea flat for the funeral baked meats.

Frank felt utterly scraped and drained, and perversely cheerful. He blew his nose, and whispered to Giles: 'I can't face to earth-to-earth graveside bit. Let's go to the pub.'

Giles was staring at the hearse. 'What the bloody hell is that?'

Insulting the austere beauty of Melissa's Madonna lilies was a floral tribute of astonishing hideousness and vulgarity – 'Will' spelled out in pink and purple letters a foot high.

'I thought all the other flowers were sent to the cemetery,' Giles said. 'I wonder how that thing got past. The undertakers must have cocked up.'

'It's gross,' Frank said. 'Poor Melissa.'

Funeral rituals were one part of the British class system he had never quite grasped. Only by reading the shocked faces of the other mourners did he realize that a terrible violation had occurred. The ghastly flowers blew a loud raspberry into the sweet symphony of good taste.

'Ye gods,' said Giles, 'it makes him look like some East End gangland boss.'

'Hey, where's the champion of the working class? I guess St Peter will know he went to Eton.'

'You're absolutely right, Frank. I'm a snob. I deserve to be tarred and feathered, and forced to wear Terylene.'

The two black cars swept round the corner, and the crowd on the pavement relaxed. Cigarettes were lit, and small groups formed. The schoolfriends, the Oxford friends, the friends from the bank scattered like so many blobs of spilled mercury, because they no longer had Will to bind them together. Bella, who was seven months pregnant, stood on guard beside Dash while he held forth about his latest job in an advertisement: 'I jump out of a photocopier dressed as a goblin and perform a little dance. Utterly asinine, but it's more fulfilling than playing a carrot, and the money – '

Cecily addressed a knot of Will's dowdier Oxford acquaintances, whom Melissa always called the 'charity cases': 'He had the classic suicide profile, of course. It's the self-effacing types who are most prone to depression – '

Stout Alex was puffing a cigar, and trumpeting, ' – and there was that bloke from Warburg's who chucked himself under a train. They simply can't take the pace – '

'Hail and farewell, old Will,' Frank said. 'I hope he thinks we gave him a good send-off. Wherever he is.'

He expected Giles to say something priestly. Instead, he muttered: 'This whole thing stinks. Men like Will don't kill themselves.'

'Well, a man like Will just did,' Frank said.

'Doesn't it strike you as remotely fishy? Oh, come on.' Giles sighed. 'I need to find that drink – assuming you're buying.'

'Oh, nice! I'm a penniless academic.'

'And I, may I remind you, am a starving slum parson.' He turned up the collar of his coat, and joined the file of people sloping off towards the pub.

Frank, momentarily distracted, jostled against someone coming out of the church porch, and said: 'Sorry – '

He met a pair of grey eyes, two discs of startling hostility. Not until he was pushing into the crowded bar behind Giles did he remember where he had seen them before.

Giles shrank defensively into the chimney breast. Johnny Ferrars, head to foot in black to the extent of a crepe armband, was handing round cheese sandwiches as if he owned the place. Nobody knew him, but assumed someone else must. The terrible flowers had certainly come from him, and the armband – the likes of which had not been seen since George V lay in state – was a calculated piece of impertinence.

The sheer sauce of the man would have been comical if the intrusion had not been so sinister. Giles, who had made great efforts not to connect Johnny's appearance at Monksby with Will's death, felt himself transformed into one icy shudder of fear, and virtually had to nail his feet to the floor to stop himself running away.

Will's more distant friends and colleagues were fleeing with very little ceremony – a gulp of wine, a word to Melissa, and they could not wait to get back to the land of the living. The Chelsea flat, stripped of furniture and ornaments after the move to Monksby, was too sad a reminder of the loss of its master. The reaper had begun his winnowing among them, and they did not want to know they were not immortal.

The presence of Johnny, so aggressively and obviously alive, added to the deadness of Will. That man, Giles thought, is a fiend. He owed it to the innocents who did not know the beast's true nature to watch him – though how he was supposed to fight him, God knew. Hold up a crucifix?

This is silly, Giles lectured himself. Maybe he has changed. Maybe I imagined the whole thing. Maybe he was only teasing me that time at Monksby, with his dark hints and threats. What possible reason could he have for hurting any of us?

He studied Melissa, who stood against one arid wall, listlessly holding her untouched glass of red wine. Giles was shocked to see how the dewy edges of her beauty had crumbled. Her dry hair was ineptly twisted into a long braid. Her skin was the colour of parchment, and her blue gaze – unbelievably dimmed – seemed to be turned inwards in a trance of self-hatred.

Before Giles could make up his mind to approach her, she placed her glass on one of the inadequate tables, and slipped out of the room.

Johnny, bored with the game of handing round the sandwiches, had started to eat them. Still chewing and holding the plate, he sauntered up to Giles.

'All right, Father?' He smiled in a friendly way, but Giles could not miss the long-remembered metallic gleam of malice.

'Not really,' Giles said. 'This is a nightmare.'

'Do you know,' Johnny said conversationally, 'this is the

first funeral I've ever been to? Can't see the point, myself. I mean, it's a bit late for all the eulogies, when he's already a pre-packed dinner for maggots.'

'We didn't do it for Will, exactly. Funerals are for the people left behind.' Giles discovered, not so deep inside him, a cowardly desire not to annoy Johnny. Slightly deeper down, he was dismayed that part of him still remembered Johnny as the first – the only – person he had ever been in love with. His heart seemed to yearn towards the angelic gypsy youth hidden under the sharp black suit. He had to remind himself that the Johnny he had loved had never really existed. Was it, he wondered, particularly difficult to accept and believe in the wickedness of people who were beautiful?

'I can't see,' Johnny said, 'how that arse-aching service could be much of a comfort to Melissa. She doesn't look any happier.'

'You obviously know them both quite well.'

Johnny smiled to himself – again with the gleam of secret malice. 'Oh, yes.'

'I think this whole business has torn her apart.'

'She'll get over it,' Johnny said.

'Sorry?' Giles decided he had misheard.

'Her little struggle with virtue. She wasn't built for decency.'

'That's a horrible thing to say,' Giles said in a voice that came out as a whinge.

'I can say it to you, Giles. I know it won't go any further. Don't I?'

Johnny's smile was as lovely as ever, but Giles was sure now that he had not imagined the implied menace of their last meeting. He left a couple of beats, before steering himself out of danger.

'We've all been torn apart, actually. The worst of it is having to revise everything we thought we knew about Will.'

'Nobody knows much about anyone,' Johnny said.

'Look, you say you knew him well. Do you honestly believe he killed himself?'

Johnny was gazing across the room, but the question snapped his full attention back to Giles. For a fraction of a second he was as watchful and calculating as a cornered rat. Then he smiled again. 'No,' he said. 'I don't.'

All kinds of nasty thoughts trooped through Giles's mind, exactly as Johnny had intended they should. These were immediately chased by an angry conviction that he was being wound up, but that left an evil taste, nonetheless.

He added: 'In fact, I'd swear in court he didn't. What a good thing it didn't come to that. Hey, wait –' He held Giles's cuff, to prevent him walking away. 'I wanted to ask you about that American bloke.'

'Frank Darcy,' Giles said. He restrained a longing to jerk his arm away rudely.

'Has he left Ernie, or what?'

'They've split up, yes.'

'Is he shagging someone else?'

'I don't think so.' Giles hated himself beyond measure for letting Johnny use his power to extract information about his friends. 'I gather it was all pretty civilized.'

'Bollocks,' said Johnny.

'Look, it's none of your business. Or mine.'

'Has that bugger started sniffing round Melissa yet? Because that's what he's after.' His voice became confidential, caressing. 'If you're such a pal of his, Giles, you'd better warn him not to waste his time.'

Ernestine was across the room in the curtainless bay window, talking to Craig and Cecily. Noticing that Giles and Johnny were looking at her, she came over to join them.

'Hello, Giles. And – it's Johnny, isn't it? Terribly nice of you to come.'

'It was,' Johnny announced gravely, 'the least I could do.'

Giles, though reeling from the latest threat, had enough spare compassion to notice Ernestine's reddened eyes. He would have liked to take her in his arms. Since Johnny was watching, he squeezed her hand instead. 'You poor darling – they've left it all to you to deal with, as usual. Why didn't you phone me?'

'There wasn't much to do, actually. Dad dealt with the undertakers, and Mum found a firm for the sandwiches. I resisted the temptation to do the catering myself.'

'Good for you,' Giles said. 'You had enough to worry about without staying up all night buttering bridge rolls. Dad and Nina send love, by the way. They've gone away filming, or they'd be here. Dad was really fond of Will.'

'How's Melissa?' Johnny asked, suavely ignoring Giles's scowl of annoyance. 'I suppose you've been spending most of your time looking after her?'

Ernestine's eyes widened slightly, in obvious surprise that Johnny was on such familiar terms with her circle. 'Well, it sounds stupid to say she's taking it badly, when there's no other way to take it. But she has been odd. I wish you'd talk to her, Giles. We can't seem to shake her back into herself. She's locked into one of her dramas, only this time it's about a million times worse. She's sitting in the bedroom now, just gawping at the wallpaper. If this was a film, she'd be on a cliff, staring out at a storm-tossed sea.'

Johnny handed Ernestine the empty plate. 'Excuse me.'

Giles snapped: 'Where do you think you're going?'

The brindled grey eyes were reproachful. 'For a leak.'

'It's the first on your right,' Ernestine said.

'Thanks.'

Careful to close the door of the drawing room behind him, Johnny crossed the passage, and went into the bedroom without knocking.

Melissa sat on the extreme edge of the striped double bed, diminished by the bareness of the walls and her black clothes. When she saw Johnny, she whispered: 'No – I can't see you. Go away!'

'There's gratitude for you,' Johnny said.

'Leave me alone.'

'How long are you going to keep this up? I told you I'd be ringing you that night, and you couldn't even answer the fucking phone.'

'Ernie was there,' Melissa said dully.

'Nice way to treat me, after all I went through.'

Her mouth quivered. 'When I look at you, or even think about you, I don't know how to live with myself.'

'I thought it was you you couldn't live with.'

'There's something inside me I don't know,' she murmured. 'I'm so scared, Johnny. If I'd known before –'

'Known what?'

She raised her fearful eyes to his face. 'I found something. I was looking through the mess on George's desk, and I found a piece of newspaper about my parents.' Her voice dipped to a whisper. 'They never told me. I wish they had. Oh, I wish they had.'

'Talk sense.'

'I made Tess admit it. My mother – before she died – my mother killed my father. Don't you see? That bit of me. I never understood it, and it was her.'

'Crap.'

'I thought I knew what I was doing. Now I don't know anything about me at all.'

Johnny stood beside her, looming over her. 'Lost all interest in it, have you?'

She tilted up her head and, as she met his gaze, could not prevent desire sparking her own eyes. 'I've never had sex like that in my life,' she said, 'as you know very well. But don't you see, that's what killed him?'

'Whisky and paracetamol killed him,' Johnny said. 'And going guilty on me certainly won't bring him back.'

'I know.' Melissa lowered her eyes tragically. 'But everything's ruined now. If I could only have made him understand.'

'I've brought you something.' Johnny sat down on the bed, and drew an envelope out of his breast pocket. 'Here.'

Melissa opened it, and found a yellowed sheet of paper covered in a spidery scrawl of sepia copperplate. After staring at it for a few moments, she read aloud:

> 'Truly, can these dry bones live?
> And can this clay,
> On that last day,

As flesh again, forgive?

Yes, for rebirth cleans the heart.
So I can show,
And he may know,
Why God said we must part.

Dearest, though I hurt you sore
And wronged your love,
To meet above
We leave grief on the shore.'

Slowly, as she let the message soak into her, Melissa's eyes filled with tears. In a hushed, awed voice, she asked: 'Who wrote this?'

'Rose Lamb.'

'I knew it, I knew it! Oh Johnny, where did you get it?'

'At Quenville, of course. There are loads more too.'

'It's a sign,' Melissa said. She had shaken off her despair, like a snake shedding its skin. 'I believe in signs, and this is telling me, as clear as anything, not to give up. Not for Will's sake – not for anyone's.'

'Same terms then?'

She actually smiled at this. 'You don't need to use those letters to bribe me. I've tried to change, but it's no use. I can't go anywhere without you, ever again.'

Through the open door, Frank saw her lips opening for Johnny's tongue, and her legs opening for his hand. He was winded by the second revelation of the day – that alongside his chivalric worship, he was possessed of something far more lethal. Frank Darcy was turning out to be not such a nice guy after all.

Two

' – actually told us that Mel didn't want to see us. Said our whining liberalism was only a cover for our chronic meanness. Whining liberalism! He actually used those very words!'

George's litany of complaints accompanied Ernestine down the garden path to the lane where she had parked her car. It rumbled on while she unloaded the last box, and followed her back into the cottage kitchen.

'I said, why can't she tell us all this herself? And he said because she had too much else on her mind. So then Mum tackled Mel.'

'And got bitched at for my pains.' Tess, veiled in cigarette smoke beside the sink, took up the litany. 'She went on and on about how we'd always hated her, because we wouldn't let them stay here while they're at Quenville. Oh, you can stay, I said – but I'm not having that ghastly man in my house. And then she accused me of trying to spoil everything now she'd found happiness for the first time in her life.'

'So I said, Excuse me,' George chimed in, 'we thought you'd found happiness when you married Will – or did I tog up in a bloody penguin suit for nothing? I mean, carrying on like that, with the poor chap not cold in his grave – '

'We needn't have wasted all that worry,' Tess said grimly. 'She wasn't stricken with grief, it turns out. She was pining for that horrible young man.'

Ernestine was tired. She had not had a good night's sleep since Will's death and Frank's defection. She had spent the day packing three months' supplies into her car and ferrying them down to Norfolk. And she had been pounced on the minute she arrived by her hurt, maddened parents.

'Look,' she said wearily, 'this is all part and parcel of the grieving process, Mum. You know how she flips her lid sometimes. You know she can't cope without a man. Johnny obviously fulfils a need.' She began unpacking her favourite pans and knives, and stowing them in the cupboard with her mother's bent, crusted second-home utensils.

Tess snorted angrily. 'Come on, love. This isn't just any man she's put in poor Will's place. It's the rudest, nastiest, shiftiest – and where the hell does he come from, anyway? She was seeing him, you know. Before Will died. Well, now that suicide note's explained, isn't it?'

'Mum! You don't know – '

'Oh, yes I do. He told me! She didn't deny it, either. Frankly, I think it's indecent.'

'You mean, people in the village think it's indecent,' Ernestine said, with her head deep in the cupboard.

George groaned. 'What does she see in him?'

'I've only met him a couple of times, but he seemed all right to me.'

'You wait,' George said.

'You like him because he's good-looking,' Tess said. 'You've always been daft about good looks. That's why you got into such a lather about Frank.'

'Are you saying I only love Frank because of his looks?' Ernestine pulled her head out of the cupboard so fast, she banged it on the shelf. 'Is that all you think of me?'

'The red wine – gone,' mourned George. 'The lawn-mower – gone. The whisky – gone.'

Ernestine massaged her temples, wondering why they were all quarrelling. 'Dad, that whisky was ancient. He's probably used it to clean windows.'

'You agree with Mel, then,' Tess said hotly. 'You think we're mean.'

'Well, you always were a little near, Mum. I'm sure they'll pay you back.'

'It's Star all over again,' Tess said, finally blurting out the real source of hurt. 'When we came down on Friday, it was like turning the clock back, wasn't it, George? Finding the cottage turned upside down, half the crockery missing, wet towels everywhere – this is exactly why we tried to keep it from her. I might have known she'd take it out on us.'

Ernestine longed to scream. She had moved down to the cottage to write her new book in peace, and already she was in the middle of a battle zone.

'I'm here now. I'll look after everything. Now, why don't you let me make you some supper?'

'Oh, darling,' Tess was contrite. 'After that journey – '

'You two go off to the pub. Give me a minute to turn round.'

'We're in the way,' George quavered.

'George, shut up. Let's leave Ernie in peace.' Thankfully Tess dropped the knife with which she was inexpertly carving some muddy parsnips. 'I'm not going to turn down a decent supper.'

The two of them, armed with torches, trotted down the dark lane towards the Quenville Arms in Shenley, to drown their grievances in Tolly Cobbold ale.

The descent of silence was so blissful that Ernestine sighed aloud. Perhaps now she could begin to work out how she was supposed to write a cookery book, when she had fallen so utterly out of love with food.

All the foundation stones of her life had crashed. Nothing was in its right place any more. She scarcely knew herself; wherever she turned, it had all shrivelled to ashes. Frank had accused her of running off to Norfolk for an orgy of feeling sorry for herself. Well, why not? Who was going to do it for her?

Ernestine was deathly tired of being marvellous. This was, she realized, why she could not share the general indignation about Johnny Ferrars. Was he really such a shit? She did not want to know. He had taken on the burden of Melissa's emotions, and that was all she cared about.

I'm only thinking about myself for a change, she thought defiantly. That's what Frank means by self-pitying. But if he thinks I'm going to get into a panic about Mel, just because he doesn't like Johnny –

She missed Frank. He had gone to New York a few days before, to attend his sister's gay wedding to her analyst. Since their split, Ernestine and Frank had got into the habit of long nightly telephone calls – friendship without the sex. Perhaps it was good for her to have this crutch removed. If only, she thought, I didn't like Frank so much. Unlike a lot of English men, he had a feminine gift for friendship. He saw nothing odd in walking about for hours with the receiver clamped under his chin, content to run up the phone bill with long, cosy silences. It had turned out to be a split by gentle, almost imperceptible degrees. After her outburst over Melissa, they had been miraculously civilized. The trouble was, Ernestine had not yet dared to think how she would feel when Frank took up with someone else.

To bury this nagging fear, she switched on the radio and charged through the kitchen, restoring order. By the end of *The Archers*, she had hidden her boxes in the sitting room, hacked the baked blobs off the cooker and put on a pan of vegetable stew. If this was going to be her house for the next three months, it was bloody well going to be comfortable. Those filthy gingham curtains were going into the bin, for a start. She no longer saw the cottage through a haze of its sacred childhood associations. She did not wish to be reminded of the summer she had fallen in love with Frank.

There was a light tap at the back door.

'Ernie! You are alone, aren't you?' Melissa came in, bringing a gust of cold autumn air. 'I saw the torch wobbling off down the road.' She waved a bottle of champagne. 'This is for you, darling. Housewarming present.'

She was like a stained-glass window with the sun behind it; giving light and radiance. Ernestine had never seen her cousin's beauty in such shining splendour. Her long hair gleamed in the dim overhead light, and her eyes looked almost turquoise against the rosy tan of her skin.

'Oh, it's going to be so much fun, having you down the road.' She opened the champagne, and poured two generous tumblers full. 'So much nicer than those two old wart hogs. I can't tell you how awful they've been.'

Ernestine heard several alarm bells shrilling in this speech. She decided to tackle them one at a time. 'Has it really got that bad with Mum and Dad?'

'We're not on speakers. They've been such total shits to Johnny.'

'Did he really call them whining liberals?'

'Not till George called him a parasite.'

'And just what is all this about my being down the road?'

'Sit down, sit down.' Melissa urged her towards a chair as if she were the hostess and Ernestine the guest. 'Didn't you hear? We're living at Quenville. What does this portend? Yes, we're starting work. As soon as Will's money goes through probate, or something.'

Ernestine scowled softly. 'Oh God, builders everywhere. I might as well have stayed in bloody London.'

'They'll be miles away – they won't bother you. Oh Ernie, I'm so happy!' Melissa laughed. '"O coz, coz, coz, my pretty little coz, that thou didst know how many fathom deep I am in love!" I haven't seen you for so long. It seems like ages, anyway.'

The sour taste in Ernestine's mouth intensified. 'You were never cut out for perpetual mourning, I suppose.'

'Deary me,' Melissa said softly. 'I seem to detect a whiff of disapproval. You want to tell me I'm a fickle little tramp because my husband's not – to borrow George's revolting phrase – cold in his grave.'

'Oh, no – '

'Come on, Ernie. Get it out.'

Ernestine sighed. 'All right. It seems bloody unfair that you're the one with a dead husband and you're happy, when I'm miserable.'

'About Frank?' Melissa was in her 'awake' mode, and her wondrous eyes were keen.

'And Will. I miss him so dreadfully.'

'You think I don't?'

'Well, what am I meant to think? With you being fathom deep in love, and all.' Ernestine could not suppress a knife edge of bitterness in her voice.

Her cousin went on regarding her with unwavering, pitying serenity. 'It's very important to me that you understand what's happened,' she pronounced.

'I'm not sure I want to. You always end up convincing me that black's white.'

'It was meant. I knew it as soon as Johnny showed me the letters.'

'Oh, fuck – not signs and wonders again,' Ernestine said rudely. 'I though you'd grown out of all that when you and Will moved to Monksby.'

Melissa shook her head sadly. 'I tried very hard, but that's when it all came unstuck. When Johnny gave me Rose's poems, it was like a missing piece of myself, slotting back into place.'

'How did he get hold of them, anyway?'

'He found them, and saved them for me. We are two halves of the same whole, darling. I'm more alive now than I've ever been in my life.'

Ernestine sipped her champagne, unconsciously slipping nearer the comfortable state of being won over. 'Of course I'm glad you're happy. But don't you feel dreadful about Will?'

'I feel –' Melissa began carefully, 'I feel he knows properly at last, wherever he is. And forgives me.'

'For seeing Johnny, before he died?'

'Yes. But, darling, he was seeing someone else too, you know.'

Ernestine slammed down her glass. 'Will? What nonsense.'

'Perfectly true, I'm afraid.'

'Okay, who was it then?'

'I'm not going to tell you. I didn't want to disillusion you about poor Sir Bors, but you really must see I'm not such an evil slut after all.'

Tears prickled behind Ernestine's eyelids. They sat in silence, while she digested this new revelation. The old refrain rang in her head – that she had never fathomed that relationship, and never would.

'Well,' she said eventually, 'if it is true, it'll teach me not to sit in judgement, I suppose.'

'I can't cope without you, Ernie. Especially now he's gone. Johnny can't fill that place for me.'

It was a huge relief to Ernestine to hear this. When she was at odds with Melissa, nothing went right.

'I'm still here for you,' she said.

'Thanks, darling. There is one small thing you can do for me.'

In spite of herself, Ernestine could not help laughing. There was something so transparent about Melissa on the make. 'Let's have it, then.'

'The thing is, we're staying in a trailer with the sketchiest supplies of water and light. And heat. Would it disturb you terribly if we nipped in sometimes for a bath?'

'Sometimes, as in how many times?'

'Every day, actually. This was why we had such a row with Tess and George. They wouldn't let us live here – and they hadn't promised it to you then. And they couldn't see why we were living in such squalor when I've so much money.'

'They've got a point,' Ernestine said.

Melissa sighed impatiently. 'There isn't a hotel for miles, and we can't rent a cottage. Nobody will let us have one. The whole village has got me down as a scarlet woman because I took up with my fancy man so soon after Will's death. Such old hags.' Her look of lofty injury invited Ernestine to agree with her – no, assumed she would.

'I came down here for peace,' Ernestine said. This seemed the height of assertiveness, and she brought it out with a tremendous effort.

Melissa, however, only nodded sympathetically. 'You need it, darling. Now that you've split up with Frank, you really should try to discover your own desires.'

'Yes, that's what I'm trying – oh, of course I don't mind, Mel. If you'll just give me some idea when to expect you.'

Melissa beamed at her, one blaze of beauty. 'I think it'll be easier if we sort of leave it open.'

Ernestine, despite her irritation, was laughing again.

248

'Easier for whom?' But as usual, she was letting Melissa win her own way, on her terms. In the teeth of all her grim determination to be self-sufficient, she felt the familiar rising of her spirits as she basked in Melissa's good graces. Perhaps it might be fun to have her so nearby.

'Well, all right. As long as I don't end up cooking for you.'

'Johnny will be disappointed – he's such a fan of yours.'

'No, Mel. No, no, no. That's as far as I go.'

'You're an angel. We're going to have such a good time.' She leaped up. 'We're so happy, we've gallons to spare.'

She slipped through the kitchen door, and was swallowed by the darkness. Ernestine went to the window, and saw the firefly light of her torch bobbing across the fields towards Quenville. Now that night had fallen, she could see where, for the first time in generations, Melissa had set the lamps burning in her ruined house.

She thought of Will, and was sorrier for his sorrow now that she knew about his disloyalty. But Melissa had been so precious to him – maybe he really was happier now.

'I didn't tell her it was you,' Melissa said. 'No point in shocking her – I want access to that bath.'

Johnny, stark naked, was sitting on the narrow bed in the trailer rolling a joint. 'All right then, was it?'

'I can always get round her. She says she won't cook for us, but of course she will.'

He glanced up at her out of the tops of his eyes, amused. 'Sure of her, aren't you?'

'It's good to have something in this life you can be sure of.' Melissa lay down beside him, smiling. 'I can't be sure of you.'

'You're not doing badly. I'm living in a trailer with you, and I thought I'd left all that behind years ago.'

'Would you rather be in a hotel?'

'No. There's too much to do here.'

Melissa caressed his crisp hair. 'Not for a while. I haven't even spoken to the architect yet. And there's the survey, and finding the builders.'

Johnny lit the joint, and got off the bed. 'You're not thinking.' Rose's papers were spread across a small, Formica-covered folding table. He paddled his hands through them, squinting through smoke. 'There's stuff to do first, before anyone else moves in. It seems to me, you've never had a proper look round these grounds.'

Melissa laughed. 'We've only been looking for about a hundred years.'

'You were all crap at it, though, weren't you? Didn't find this box, for a start.'

'No, but it was bricked up, behind a wall.'

He turned flinty eyes to her. 'This is not some game of fucking hunt the slipper. We're not peeking under rugs any more. We need some pickaxes and a jackhammer.'

Melissa stopped lounging, and sat up. 'I'm not doing anything that might damage the house.'

'I've been looking at the plan,' Johnny went on, as if he had not heard her. He shook out Seddon's original floor plan, shedding Rose's letters like leaves. 'We should go through the place, wall by wall. And if anything doesn't measure up, we make a bloody great hole.'

'No! I said no! I won't tear Quenville apart, to find something that may not even exist.'

'That treasure exists,' Johnny said. 'I've studied these papers long enough to know Rose was writing about something real. And I'm going to get it, if I have to blow the place to atoms.'

She had become very still. She whispered: 'I won't let you.'

Johnny arched his perfect eyebrows at her meaningfully. 'You'll do as you're told.'

She reached across the cramped trailer and grabbed his hand. 'Please, Johnny – I've worked so hard to get to this point of restoring Quenville. It's more important to me than anything.'

Johnny detached his hand neatly from hers. 'Let's get something settled now. If I decide to knock down your house, I will.'

250

'No – '

He grabbed her chin, forcing her to look up at him. 'Listen. Suppose it was a question of Quenville or me. Which would you choose?'

Melissa's gaze did not waver. 'You. Of course.'

This made him laugh, and he dropped her chin. 'Lying mare. You'd dump me in a second. But you never will. Because it's one luxury you can't afford. Understand?'

'I love you, Johnny,' she said humbly. 'I don't want Quenville at all if I can't have you. But I'd rather have both.'

'Well, and so you will. Leave it to me. I won't say trust me, since you're not an absolute fool. Just realize we both want the same thing, more or less.'

'It's a big thing for me to know I love someone.' Melissa was solemn. 'To find the person I'd do anything for – I mean anything.'

'Don't kid yourself you've done it all for me,' Johnny said, as if giving a piece of friendly advice.

'Oh, but I – '

'Do me a fucking favour. Living with you is like living with myself. You're all angles, you. Now, get us a drink.'

'All right.' She did not move. Curled on the tumbled bed, with her knees tucked under her chin, she stared at Johnny while he pulled a heavy cannabis-smelling jersey over his curly head. Presently, she said, conversationally: 'I am in love with you, you know. You've taught me what the word means.'

He planted his bare buttocks on the vinyl bench nailed to the wall beside the table. 'Let's open that champagne.'

'I gave it to Ernie.'

'Fuck.'

She relaxed into a delighted laugh. 'You do have the most conventional picture of the good life, darling. Will brandy do?'

'Yes, if you put it in a glass. I hate drinking the stuff out of mugs.'

'Very good, my lord.'

The tiny steel sink, into which water trickled in a rusty

251

thread, was heaped with dirty crockery, takeaway cartons and discarded underwear. Melissa disinterred a half-full bottle of Martell, and two smeared tumblers.

'God, you're a slut,' Johnny said.

'You clean it, if it bothers you.'

'I bet old Will was a dab hand with a duster.'

'Mmm. He was my first line of defence when the cleaning lady couldn't come.' She made room for the glasses on the table, and squeezed on to the bench beside him. 'You've been reading them. You're as bad an obsessive as I am.'

'Up to a point,' Johnny said. 'I don't waste so much time with romance.'

'Well, you're not like Rose.' She picked a sheet from the pile in front of them. 'All that dreary stuff about Endymion and the moon-goddess. Sexual fantasies Victorian-style.'

'You're wrong. This is exactly where we should be starting. Don't you see?' Johnny seldom allowed himself the weakness of sounding excited, but his voice gained a little in intensity. 'That story is her code for the hiding of the treasure. Time and again she takes the trouble to mention real places round here – hedges, fences, fields. They're signposts. Look –' He held up one of the papers, and read: '"Most beautiful of men, I saw thee sleeping/ Where the whortleberries red/ O'er thy Morpheus-drowsed head/ A frosty winter's watch are keeping."'

Melissa was staring into his face. '"Most beautiful of men",' she said, smiling. 'You surely don't think we should be searching for a clump of hundred-year-old whortleberries?'

He laughed. 'Until we get a map where X marks the spot, it'll have to do.'

She sighed. 'You're so determined. Can't you ever just sit and be, and not think about buried treasure for five minutes?'

'That's rich, from a woman who shouts "Seddon! Seddon!" when she comes.'

'I do not.'

His eyes raked watchfully over her face, so close to his.

'You've gone through all this to get back to Quenville. And now you're here, you just want to sit and be.'

'Oh God. You're going to say you don't understand me, just like all the others.'

'Am I?' His face inches away from hers, he smiled his most ferocious smile and pulled her hand on to his hardening penis. 'No, no. I understand you only too well.'

'Oh Ernie, do be careful!' Will held the bottom of the ladder. Ernestine was climbing, but the ceiling of her flat had melted, and the top of the ladder was miles above her, wreathed in clouds. 'Ernie, do be careful. Do be careful.'

She snapped awake, her heart lurching. The cramped childhood bedroom she had shared with Melissa gradually reassembled around her, the edges of the furniture blurred in the darkness, but Will's face was still printed on her mind.

He had begged her not to put the lights up herself. She had glanced down and seen his forehead furrowed by an anxious frown. 'Let me do it. Oh, do be careful.'

As the vividness of the memory faded, the sense of loss bit into her. She switched on the dim lamp with the toadstool shade beside the bed, and stared groggily at her watch.

Four in the morning.

She rolled off the narrow mattress and crept down the creaking staircase, careful not to disturb her parents across the landing. The kitchen had the cold, reluctant atmosphere of a room disturbed at the wrong time. It smelled of her parents' cigarettes. They had left a pan of cocoa on the hotplate. It had a skin on it like cellulite, and Ernestine's newly rebellious stomach shuddered in protest.

This was the worst time; the part of the night when loneliness and grief held their demon's revel like ghosts on Walpurgis Night. If she had been alone in her own home, she would have dispelled them both with the World Service. She had spent untold hours of insomnia recently, weeping through jolly quiz shows which somehow seemed, at that godless hour, heart-rendingly brave and poignant, a tiny spark of cheeriness keeping the darkness at bay.

But she was not alone, and did not want to wake her parents. She was left with the aftertaste of Will, and a puzzling sense that he was nearby. While she waited for the kettle to boil (and kettles took hours to boil during these vigils), she thought about Melissa's revelation.

So poor Will had been unfaithful. Of course, it explained a lot. So why did she feel somehow agitated, as if Will was asking for her help?

His voice, activated by her dream, would not be quiet. 'Do be careful, Ernie. Do be careful.'

Three

The church hall was a scarred, breeze-block building covered with graffiti, next to the shabby red-brick church. Dirty iron grilles, fastened with immense padlocks, covered the windows. Frank, standing in the middle of the lino floor, experienced a giddy moment of dislocation.

Suddenly, he could only see the pair of them from the outside, their figures ghastly under the flickering fluorescent strips. Frank and Giles, those former wild young bohemians. When had they turned into two serious men? And if he had trouble recognizing himself, what the hell did he have to do with this priest?

Giles, in the black clerical shirt and dog collar Frank disliked so intensely, was stacking disabled plastic chairs against the wall. His fresh face, still so absurdly guileless with its turned-up nose and gummy smile, looked exhausted. But Frank could not bring himself to help.

'Sorry to keep you hanging about,' Giles said. 'It takes ages to get the buggers out, and even longer to clear up after them.'

'So, let me guess,' Frank said. 'The Boy Scouts, right?'

Giles smiled distractedly. 'Homeless night. Alcoholics, mostly.'

'Oh.'

'Thanks for coming over.'

'No problem. But I can't stay long – I've got to make the last train back to Oxford.'

'I do appreciate it.' Giles hefted another pile of chairs. 'How was the the States?'

'Foreign. I don't belong there any more. I felt like I'd just alighted from a spaceship.'

255

'Wedding all right?'

'Two lesbians, taking vows in front of a gay nun. When I got back to Heathrow, I almost kissed the tarmac.'

'You're too conventional, Frank. I think it sounds great.'

'Well, the drugs were okay. Best grass I ever had in my life. Breda grows it at her place in Connecticut. You'd have loved it.'

Giles laughed. 'Not these days. A man in my position, and all that.'

'I guess.' Frank could have wept.

'I pretend not to notice when the customers bring in hash, but I can hardly ask for a toke. It's heartbreaking, actually – they're always offering.'

'Oh, bless them.'

There was a sudden crash from one of the iron grilles. A thick, toothless voice roared: 'Father! Oy! Fa-ther!'

Frank flinched, but Giles only groaned to himself. 'Great.'

'I know you're there. Come out! Bas-TARD!'

Crash, crash, crash.

Giles shouted: 'Ed, we're closed. Fuck off.'

'I'll tell your fuckin' bishop you said fuck off.'

'Who's he going to listen to, me or you?' Giles dropped the last pile of chairs against the wall. 'Go on, fuck off.'

The grille crashed like a cage of a wild beast. 'Bas-TARD! I'm comin to get you, Bas-TARD!'

Frank whispered, 'Want me to call the police?'

'God, no.' Giles was surprised. 'It's only Edbanger. He's been off guzzling aftershave or brakefluid or something, and he hates to miss the meeting, that's all. No real harm in him.'

'I'm going'-cutoff-your-BOLLOCKS!'

Giles sighed and rolled his eyes. 'Yes, it's been another quiet evening at St Benet's. I thought my luck was in when nobody threw up. I should have known.'

'Holy shit.' Frank was disgusted, and mortified to find himself scared – particularly when Giles was so cool.

One final crash, then silence.

'He's gone,' Giles said. 'Help me take out the rubbish, then we'll get a curry, if you're hungry.'

'I already ate, thanks.'

'Very wise.'

There was an almighty thud from the double doors at the front of the hall, dying away in a silvery shower of broken glass. A man swaggered into the hall, and stood swaying, trying to focus his bleared eyes. His face, puffy and striped with filth, peered out of a greasy balaclava. He wore three overcoats, each visible through the holes of the one above, and his stink rushed ahead of him like a breaker smacking across the shingle.

'I want my meetin'. I want my cuppa tea.'

Giles put his hands on his hips. 'I told you, we're closed.'

Ed let out a long growl. 'Wanta prayer.'

'Prayers are finished,' Giles said calmly. 'You know when we start, Ed. Come back tomorrow.'

'No! No-o-o-o!'

'Off you go.' Giles moved towards him, calm and unhurried.

'Father, I got nowhere to sleep – '

'What nonsense. You've got that lovely box under the viaduct.'

Frank let out a snort of shocked, nervous laughter.

'I got fuckin' NOWHERE!'

'Forget it. I am not going back to plead your case at the Refuge. If you can't keep a couple of rules, they've got a perfect right to –'

Ed staggered forward and punched Giles in the face, hard enough to lay him out on his back and send his body skating across the floor.

Galvanized into action, Frank dropped his briefcase and seized Ed's arm. 'Okay, pal. Out, before I call the police.'

Giles sat up. A ribbon of blood tricked out of his nose and splashed on the floor. 'Don't, Frank –'

Ed's face laboriously underwent a gear-change into grief. 'I hurt him!' he moaned. 'I hurt my vicar! I hurt him – '

He allowed himself to be hustled out into the street, sobbing wretchedly. 'I hurt him – I love him – '

The stink was making Frank's eyes water. It was beyond belief that one human body could smell so dreadful. 'Piss off.'

Ed clumsily tried to get past Frank, back into the church hall. 'I want Father – '

Frank, screwing up his face with distaste, pressed a five-pound note into the black hand. Ed, distracted, stopped his yelling and keening to study it. After a few moments of cheese-breathed silence, he slowly shuffled away along the rows of empty market stalls. Frank watched until his tattered figure had merged into the dark chaos of flapping tarpaulins and flying rags of newspaper.

He found Giles still sitting on the floor, pressing a wad of bloody tissue to his nose. Half a dozen scarlet spots were daubed on the lino around him.

'You okay?'

'Fine.' Giles struggled to his feet. 'Where's Ed?'

'Gone.'

'Did you give him money?'

'Yes. Am I not allowed to feed the animals?'

'I wish you'd given it to me, that's all.' Giles removed the tissues and sniffed experimentally. 'I wouldn't have squandered it all on Woodpecker Cider. Was he fighting?'

'No, full of sorrow that he'd whacked Father.' Frank glanced down at the spots of blood. 'D'you swear you're okay?'

'I swear.'

Between them they ferried out the binbags full of paper cups and cigarette ends, and the heavy basket where Giles kept his supplies of milk, tea, coffee and sugar.

Frank waited, looking anxiously up and down the street, while Giles kicked the broken glass into the gutter and banged the grille across the door. The poverty and desolation of this slice of East London made him feel he was standing at the world's end. Once more, he was unsettled by the sense that he was searching for Giles and failing to find him.

Giles padlocked the doors with a huge bunch of keys, and

led Frank along an alley down the side of the hall. They toiled with the rickety metal staircase to another door, treble-locked. There was more waiting as Giles searched through his keys, then the door opened on to a hallway the size of a coffin, aggressively and hideously wallpapered.

Frank did not even try to hide his disapproval. 'They expect you to live here?'

'I keep meaning to do something about it, but I've been too busy.' Giles took him into the mean kitchen, just big enough for a sink, a stove and a Formica table.

'Poverty, chastity, obedience,' Frank said.

'Coffee?'

'Sure. Thanks.'

'You'll have to sit down, or I'll have to climb over you to fill the kettle.'

Frank sat on a plastic chair, which groaned alarmingly under his weight. He lit a cigarette. 'Is it – you know – safe?'

'You mean, from the the likes of Ed and his friends?' The stove was the old-fashioned kind, with gas rings that lit with a bang. Giles tossed the spent match into a saucer and slammed the kettle on. 'Probably not. The last bloke here had a breakdown after he was knifed.'

'Oh, nice. God Almighty, Giles.'

'Look, most of them are just like anyone else. You get to know the difference between the Eds and the one or two who are really dangerous.'

'He seemed dangerous enough to me.'

Giles spooned instant coffee into two mugs. He grinned at Frank over his shoulder. 'Honestly. You quickly learn to get past your generalized prejudices, and recognize the smell of genuine evil.'

'Is there such a thing?'

Giles's smile switched off, leaving his tired face bleak. 'Actually, that's sort of why I wanted to see you.'

'I'm intrigued.' He made a face as the thin brew was plonked down in front of him, and ungratefully said: 'Wow, I miss Ernie.'

'Didn't I always say?' A ghost of a smile returned. 'I was in half a mind to have a try myself, you know, when we were all at Oxford. Bit of a disappointment when you got in first.'

'Get out of here. You and Ernie? You weren't fit to lace her shoes.'

'No.' He gazed sadly down at the surface of his coffee.

'Anyway, let's have it. Why was it so important to see me?'

'It sounds mad. But it's about Melissa.'

Frank, without moving, instantly bristled. 'Yes?'

Giles groaned to himself, and wearily massaged his temples. 'Listen, Frank. Please don't be offended – but you and Melissa.'

'What?' he barked, and Giles winced.

'I'm telling you all this because you're the only person I can trust. But it'll be no use at all unless you can somehow overcome the fact that you're still crazy about her.'

'You don't know what you're talking about.'

'We've all known for years,' Giles said. 'It was the main problem between you and Ernie.'

Frank's heart lurched. 'Of all the evil things to say – '

'Listen to me, please listen! If you want to help Melissa now, there mustn't be any hidden agendas. It's too serious.'

'Okay, okay.' Frank had been stung on a very sore place, but made an effort to wrestle down his anger. He had never seen Giles in such deadly earnest. 'You can trust me. I promise not to ride into town for a shoot-out. I assume this is about the obnoxious little creep who muscled in on Will's funeral.'

'Johnny Ferrars.'

'Yes, I caught him groping her.'

Giles said: 'Sensitivity never was her strong point.'

'She's vulnerable right now.' Frank was stern. 'You never really liked her. Did she turn you down too?'

'I may not idolize her, as you do, but I'm terrifically fond of her.' Giles lit one of Frank's cigarettes. 'That's why I can't stand by and watch this business with Ferrars.'

Frank sighed irritably. 'If she likes him, there's fuck all we can do about it.'

'She says he's the great love of her life.'

'My God. Severe infarction of the taste muscle,' Frank said. 'I thought he had asshole written all over him.'

Giles could not look at him. He was frowning down at the surface of the table. 'You know I said I've learned how to recognize real evil? Well, Johnny Ferrars is really evil.'

'Hey, come on!'

'I know him, all right?' Giles was suddenly fierce. 'I wish I could forget it – I've tried hard enough. I'm not going to tell you how I got the measure of him, because I can't. But Frank,' his eyes filled with tears, 'I had an affair with him.'

Frank's stunned system worked to take in this latest shock. The world he carried in his head, which was as regular and orderly as the Ptolemaic universe, was rocking on its foundations. He hated and feared the spoiling of that comfortable picture of his Oxford idyll and his English friends – Good Sir Bors dead, saintly Sir Percival having a homosexual affair.

He had to swallow several times, before he could bring himself to speak. 'I think,' he said, 'I must be very old-fashioned. Very innocent. Incredibly blind. Oh, hey – '

Giles's head had sunk into his folded arms. He was sobbing. Frank hated himself for his reflexive reluctance to touch him. Unable to help overdoing a certain husky, changing-room masculinity, he slung his arm around him. 'It's okay, it's okay. Jesus, you must have hated me for sneering at Breda's gay wedding like I did.'

'That's the thing, you see. I'm not really gay.' Giles gently shook himself free, and mopped his eyes with the bloody tissue he had used for his nose.

'You're like him, then. You swing both ways.'

'Since Johnny, I haven't swung any way at all. I can't tell you why. It was too – well, I just can't.'

Picking his words with tweezers, Frank said: 'Are we talking about AIDS here? Is that why you're so worried about Melissa?'

Giles said: 'No. I had the test afterwards. He was clean when I had him.'

'Well, thank God.' Frank shuddered with relief.

'Basically, I'm worried about Mel because I know exactly what he's like. What he can do. He's a creature without love – without the least idea what it means. I think it amounts to a kind of mental sickness in him. There's an old definition of hell as a place without God. Well, Johnny is a person without God. There isn't anything he won't do.'

'But what can he do to Mel?'

Giles dropped his voice. 'You remember he turned up that day at Monksby? Every time I think of it, I simply can't believe in Will's suicide.'

'What are you saying? What?'

'You know as well as I do, Will wasn't the type to kill himself. We've got to get at the truth.' Giles's eyes filled again. He forced a miserable laugh. 'Sir Bors is dead, Sir Percival is too much of a coward. This is a job for Sir Galahad.'

Four

The rat squinted at Ernestine with an air of sordid slyness and shifty gutter wisdom. It was long and grey, with matted, greasy fur, and was nosing along the runnels in the draining board.

For an endless, frozen moment, Ernestine stared at it. Her heart hammered in her throat and she felt sick. There was no point in telling herself that her horror of rats was unreasonable. Some substratum of her consciousness, independent of all reason, recognized them as creatures of nightmare, inhabitants of the underworld.

She picked up the rolling pin from the table, brandishing it ineffectually in the hope that the rat might feel threatened, and backed out of the kitchen on legs of jelly.

'Johnny!' Her voice came out in a feeble pipe.

No reply. She blundered up the narrow staircase and banged on the bathroom door. 'Johnny!'

Still no reply. She was wary of Johnny and never spoke to him during his visits to the cottage if she could help it, but this was an emergency. She pushed open the door.

Johnny lay in the bath with a joint hanging from his lips, in a cloud of marijuana smoke. His eyes were closed and his ears were sealed with a Walkman. Ernestine heard the tinny clash of music through the phones. On the extreme edge of her consciousness, she registered his nakedness, but this could not shock her when there was a rat downstairs.

'Johnny!'

Slowly, his lush lashes parted enough to reveal the glint of his eyes. He did not seem at all surprised to find Ernestine standing over him, near tears, clutching a rolling pin.

He unhooked his earphones. 'Hello.' His expression reminded her disagreeably of the rat's.

She was too glad he was here to care. 'Oh God, oh God, there's a rat – a rat in the kitchen – oh please get it out, oh please –'

Johnny laughed. 'Have you asked it politely?'

'It's walking about on the draining board – please, Johnny, I hate the things – '

'And I'm supposed to deal with it? Nah. You just wanted a sight of my cock.'

'It's huge!' Ernestine babbled.

Johnny roared unkindly. 'Thanks.'

'The rat! I meant the rat! You bloody bastard, stop laughing at me!' Ernestine turned scarlet and burst into furious tears. 'Just get out of that bath and do something!'

'Okay, okay. If you really mind that fucking much –' Ungraciously, Johnny climbed out of the bath and reached for a towel. Hot water poured off his taut body on to the inadequate candlewick mat. Keeping his bold, unwavering gaze fixed upon Ernestine, he rubbed himself with a towel, paying special attention to his genitals.

She had subsided into frightened sobs, which struck even her as foolish. 'Hurry – oh, hurry – I'm so scared it will run and hide and I won't know where it's gone – '

'Look, belt up, will you?' He pulled on a skimpy pair of underpants and his frayed jeans. 'And gimme that rolling pin. I keep thinking you're going to deck me with it.' He snatched it away from her, roughly but not too unkindly.

Ernestine followed him downstairs and cravenly hovered in the hall behind the door while he went into the kitchen. She heard his bare feet padding across the flags.

'Cor. Big bugger, isn't he?'

'Wh-what are you going to do?'

'Squash 'im.' Perhaps unconsciously, he had slipped into a West Country accent as thick as silage.

'No,' Ernestine moaned, 'don't hurt it!'

He startled her by suddenly yanking the door open in her face. 'Get rid of it, but don't hurt it. Fine. I'll give it a cup of tea while you call the RSPCA.'

She was very close to him, her nose a few inches from his

collarbone. She raised her eyes to his face. 'Can't you get rid of it without hurting it?'

Their gazes locked. Johnny's annoyance slowly melted into a look of deep curiosity, then surprised, reluctant amusement, quite unmixed with scorn. 'Why not hurt it, if you hate it so much?'

'That's not the rat's fault.'

'You're mad, you.'

There was a skittering sort of thud, as the rat jumped into the sink. Ernestine let out a great sob of anguish, and grabbed Johnny's arm. 'Oh God, oh God – '

He prised off her hand. Her fingernails had left red marks.

'You silly cow,' he said, laughing. He had started to enjoy himself. While Ernestine clung, weeping, to the doorframe, he advanced towards the sink. 'The little sods'll bite you, given half a chance.'

Clamping the shrivelled roach of his joint between his lips, he picked up a large saucepan from the table and tipped out the peeled carrots it contained. With the end of the rolling pin, he deftly scooped the rat into the pan.

'There you are.' Laughing more than ever, he suddenly made a dive towards Ernestine and thrust the saucepan under her nose.

She saw the rat clawing the sides of its prison in despair, and her head filled with nauseous mist.

'Shit,' Johnny said. He looked fascinated. 'You really do hate them, don't you?'

Dimly, through the mist, she saw him take the saucepan through the back door, into the garden. She sat down on the stairs to recover. Normality returned and she regained enough of a grip to look at herself. I am, she thought, a hysterical idiot.

'All right. He's gone.' Johnny came back into the kitchen, slammed the door and turned the saucepan upside down to prove it was empty. 'I put him down the drain. You left the cover off.'

Weak with mingled shame and sheepishness, Ernestine

crept into the kitchen. 'So I did. I was pouring down some disinfectant yesterday, and I forgot to put it back. Oh Johnny, thank you so much! I'm so glad you were here.'

He frowned at her, baffled, as if she had spoken a foreign language. She could sense him sifting her words for hidden meanings. 'It was nothing.'

She managed a shaky laugh. 'Not to me, it wasn't. I've got an absolute phobia about rats.'

He spat out his roach, and dug a squashed packet of cigarettes from his jeans pocket. 'You wouldn't last five seconds out in the real world.'

'You – you used to live rough, didn't you?'

'Still do, thanks to your dear little cousin.'

The awareness of his body rushed back to Ernestine, and she covered her sudden shyness with bustling. 'Would you like some coffee?'

For a moment he was suspicious. 'Well, okay.' He sat down at the table.

Ernestine put the kettle on, trying not to look into the sink where the horror had been, and spooned fresh coffee into the cafetiere. Without looking at him she was piercingly conscious of Johnny. She remembered Tess saying she liked him because he was good-looking, and a warm blush bathed her cheeks. The protective shields were down, and she was forced to admit that she found her cousin's half-naked lover quite amazingly handsome. If she were not careful she would start imagining the two of them in bed.

'Coffee is the least I can do,' she said, with forced cheeriness. 'Actually, you deserve a twenty-one-gun salute and the freedom of the City.'

'Get off. No big deal.'

'I suppose you learned not to mind them.'

He considered this, eyeing her cautiously. 'Well, I never exactly liked them. Used to wake up sometimes, when they jumped on my sleeping bag. A couple of them ate my stash, once. Got totally stoned and started coughing.'

'Ugh.'

'Does that make you feel faint again?'

266

'Don't remind me. Sorry I was such a wimp. Sugar?'

'Three.'

She set down their cups and joined him at the table. 'I don't know how you endured it.'

Johnny said: 'It's the humans you have to watch.'

'I always think I can handle people. Rats make me totally helpless.'

Johnny said: 'Times like this, you must miss that American bloke. You need a man around the place.'

She sighed. 'I ought to say something feminist about coping on my own, but I'm afraid you're probably right. On the surface I'm fine. And then something like this reminds me I'm not coping at all.'

He was listening, and she could not help expanding. 'Perhaps it wasn't such a wonderful idea, hiding away down here. I can't work. I can't eat. Half the time, I don't know myself.'

'You're waiting for Frank to change his mind.'

'No,' Ernestine said, all the more firmly because it was not true. 'It's all over. We're still friends – '

'Bollocks,' said Johnny.

'Sorry?'

'You can't be friends with a man who dumped you. You either hate the bastard or you've still got the hots for him.'

Ernestine said: 'I don't hate him.'

'Just like rats.' Johnny laughed savagely. 'Get rid of him, but don't hurt him. Didn't you want to pay him back?'

'Why should I?'

'Because he fancies your cousin, for a start.'

She was shocked; less by Johnny's rudeness than his exposure of the part of herself she most disliked and feared. All her life, she had struggled against those niggling stabs of jealousy. Will's death, on the day she and Frank had split up, had come like a punishment for her outburst about Melissa.

'There's nothing I can do about that,' she said.

'You could make him suffer.'

'What would be the point?'

He watched her thoughtfully, sipping his coffee. 'I don't

understand you. What d'you expect for being so saintly – a fucking medal?'

Ernestine snapped: 'I'm not trying to be saintly.' This was exactly the way Melissa liked to needle her. 'I just don't see what good revenge would do me. All right?'

'You might enjoy it.'

She smiled, taking this as a joke. 'No, I've just enough sense left to see that it's not really about Frank. I miss Will.'

Johnny was silent for a long time, scrutinizing her as if she were a specimen under a microscope. 'You really liked him.'

'I loved him. Not in the – the sexual sense.'

'What other sense is there?'

'He was so good.' She brought out the word with tremendous emphasis, not noticing the sceptical twist of Johnny's mouth. 'So – constant. A force of goodness, like an anchor. We all took it for granted. And then, when it was taken away, we were all at sea. If I'm honest, I think I'm angry with him. I found his body, you know.'

'Yes.'

'It was a kind of betrayal. I can't let him go without an explanation. Why did he do it? Mel says he was having an affair – you knew about that, I suppose.'

Johnny smiled – a beautiful, melancholy smile, tinged with regret for the whole human condition. 'Well, yes.'

'Why didn't he tell us? We wouldn't have been angry. We might have been able to help.'

'Oh, no,' Johnny said. 'Don't think that.'

'You're right. I should let him go.' She realized Johnny was looking at her oddly, with an unfathomable expression – puzzlement, disquiet, curiosity. She smiled. 'God, listen to me. Pouring out my sorrows like the Ancient Mariner. I'm terribly sorry.'

'I don't mind.'

'It's tremendously nice of you.'

'Is it?'

'You've been wonderful. Tell you what, why don't you and Mel come over for supper tonight? I've been meaning to ask you for ages.'

Johnny's eyes narrowed, suspicious but amused. 'All right,' he said. 'Don't see why not.'

Melissa ran in through the back door without knocking. The first Ernestine knew of her arrival was her cousin's arms flung round her waist.

'Ernie. Oh my Lord, look at you!' Laughing, Melissa grabbed the top of Ernestine's skirt. 'I haven't seen you for yonks – you're always hiding when I come in for my bath. You could get two of you in this thing. Have you been dieting?'

'No –'

'You're wasting away.'

Ernestine took a step back, and looked down at her body as if seeing it for the first time. 'I thought my clothes were going baggy in the wash, or something.'

'When did you ever hear of clothes doing that?'

Ernestine giggled. 'Not mine, at any rate. Hello, Johnny.'

He was hanging back in the doorway, watching the cousins together. 'Hello.'

'Darling, do shut that door. It's freezing. We haven't been warm for weeks.'

'You don't have to stay in that trailer,' Ernestine said.

'What, are you asking us to move in here?'

'No.'

Melissa drew a chair up to the Rayburn, and huddled against it. Her wondrous eyes were dilated and glittering. 'Mean old fanny-breath.'

'Sticks and stones,' Ernestine said.

'Seriously, though –'

'Seriously, Mel. I absolutely promised Mum I wouldn't give into you. So forget it.'

'Worth a try,' Melissa said. Luxuriously, she pulled the sleeves of her jersey over her hands, and held them out to the warmth. It was November, and the winds that swept across the flat fields had fangs. 'I wasn't built for the gypsy life. It's all right for Johnny – he's used to it.'

'Doesn't mean I like it,' Johnny said. He was holding a

269

bottle of wine, and he banged about the kitchen drawers until he found a corkscrew. With the eternal joint hanging from his lips, he opened the wine.

Ernestine set three glasses in front of him, wondering how to get over the awkwardness of seeing him again after the incident of the rat.

'How's it going?' She addressed the question to the space between them.

Melissa replied: 'Brilliantly. The builders should be coming in the day after tomorrow to shore up the foundations. We can't do a thing until the place is vaguely safe. One wall will have to be taken down – but Nigel thinks we can reassemble it with the same bricks.' Nigel was Melissa's oracle, the London architect and surveyor she retained at vast expense.

Johnny slopped out the wine, and gave a glass to Melissa.

'Thanks,' she said. 'Did I tell you, Ernie, we've got a buyer for the lease of the Chelsea flat?'

'Oh good. What about Monksby?'

'It's the wrong time of year to sell country houses, apparently.'

'I wish I could afford it,' Ernestine said. 'Do move out of my way, Mel – I want to baste the pheasants.'

Melissa groaned childishly, but Johnny said: 'Let her baste the fuckers. I'm starving.'

She obeyed him at once.

Ernestine, secretly surprised to see her cousin so biddable, opened the oven. Two fat hen pheasants, their breasts covered in strips of bacon, sizzled on a bed of roasted potatoes. She prodded them with a skewer to assess the colour of the juices. Her expert eye did not fail her, but she missed the old sensual delight; the physical tingling of her salivary glands as she smelled her creations. The pheasant was good, but good was all it was. Since Will's death, she had lost her mystical pleasure in blends of juices and herbs.

'Smells great,' Johnny said. Their eyes met, and he grinned at her. 'First real food we've been near in ages.'

Ernestine laughed. 'Don't expect any sympathy from me. You two could eat at Claridge's, if you fancied.'

'You've been listening to Tess,' Melissa said. 'She's dead against me restoring Quenville – that's what it's all about.'

'Splash out on a camping stove, then.'

'Darling, can you honestly see me cooking on a camping stove?'

'They stink the place out,' Johnny said. He threw himself down on a chair, and flung up his muddy feet on the seat of another. 'If you'd ever lived with the travellers, you'd know never to cook inside a trailer.'

'Really? Why not?' Ernestine, busy setting the table, was interested.

Johnny laughed, with sudden animation. 'Hell of a lot you know about living on the breadline.'

'I wish you'd tell me about it.'

Melissa pushed Johnny's legs off the second chair and sat down at the table beside him. 'Oh Ernie, don't start one of your tedious conversations about food.'

'I don't mind,' Johnny drawled, still smiling.

'Well, I do.' Melissa glanced peevishly from Ernestine to Johnny. 'Let's just eat it.'

Ernestine turned her back on them, to carve the birds on the counter. 'Sorry, but this is just the kind of thing I need for my next book. It's got to be different – to go in deeper. I don't want to degenerate into a recipe-machine. You know – *Picnic on the Breadline, Christmas on the Breadline, Henley Regatta on the Breadline*. That's what my publishers expect, but I want to find out more about how people on the poverty-line really eat. And help them to do it better.' She put steaming plates in front of Melissa and Johnny. 'I'm a woman with a mission.'

'God, how dull,' Melissa said.

Johnny immediately began to eat. 'You're setting up as the saviour of the scum, are you?'

'Not exactly. There must be something they can teach me.'

'Shoplifting. Drug use.'

'No, I'm serious.' Ernestine sat down opposite him. 'It's another country, another world. I'd like to take down that barrier.'

'Have you asked anybody from the wrong side of the good old welfare net what kind of help they actually want?'

She was crestfallen. 'No. I've never met any of them.'

'Except me, and I've reformed.' He smiled at her with friendly slyness. 'You just thank your lucky stars.'

Melissa raised her drooping head. 'Suppose you'd met us both before you got reformed. What would you have done to us?'

'What makes you think – ' Ernestine began indignantly.

'Well, let me see.' He looked at Melissa, and the spark of understanding that crackled between them was almost visible.

'Raped us?'

'Of course.'

'Both of us?'

'Why not?'

Melissa gazed at him in rapture. 'Which first?'

'You. You're the prettiest.'

She rocked backwards, laughing and clapping her hands. 'Sorry, Ernie.'

Ernestine smiled, rather uneasily. 'I'll live.'

'I wouldn't have minded being raped by you,' Melissa said.

'Oh yes you would, the way I did it.'

This was, Ernestine decided, their peculiar way of expressing affection. She dredged up a laugh. 'If Mel had liked it, would that have spoiled it for you?'

Johnny gave her one brief glance which seemed to cut right to the marrow of her bones. 'Nah, when I rape something, I don't care what noises it makes.'

'Isn't he a shit?' Melissa asked proudly. 'I honestly believe he misses raping and stealing.'

'I don't miss having it done to me,' Johnny said. 'But I've put all that behind me now.'

'In front of you, you mean,' Melissa said. They both laughed.

Ernestine was out of her depth – shocked, if she was honest. She could understand why her parents had been so upset by this relationship. Johnny brought out a shadow side of Melissa which was doubly disturbing because it was so recognisably, quintessentially Melissa-ish.

Like a bad taste on her tongue came the familiar fear of discovering that her cousin was, after all, as horrible as she sometimes appeared. The loneliness of this idea was unbearable. To conquer it, she would have to make an effort to like and understand Johnny.

'Did you become respectable before or after working at the bank?'

'I've left,' Johnny said. He picked up the remains of his pheasant, and tore at the flesh with his strong teeth. 'I'm a gentleman of leisure now. Your dad thinks I'm living off Mel.'

'Nothing will convince him,' Melissa said, lighting a ciga- rette over her untouched plate. 'I tried to tell him the truth – that I've actually been living off Johnny, until Will's money goes through probate. There's been some ridiculous delay. There are loads of bequests to sort out – I dare say you can imagine. Everyone from Will's old nanny to our cleaning lady. He left thirty thousand pound to Giles, for his mis- sion.'

Ernestine's eyes smarted. 'How like him.'

'Yes,' Melissa said dismissively, 'bless him. It all takes ages to sort out, though. Thank God, Johnny's loaded.'

'Oh?'

'Something I picked up in the City,' Johnny said. 'Let's say I made a killing.'

Melissa, in the middle of taking a sip of wine, choked on a great yodel of laughter.

He watched, chewing, while Ernestine thumped her cousin's back and poured her a glass of water.

'Oh, Johnny. You're sublime,' Melissa rasped, wiping her streaming eyes with her napkin.

'Have you two lovebirds had enough?' Ernestine heard herself with dislike – disapproving and repressive.

'Darling.' Melissa took her hand, to stop her getting up and clearing the table. 'How sweet you've been to us. This is delicious. Frank really was a fool to let you go.'

This blatant attempt to mollify her by including her emphasized the fact that she was excluded – a gooseberry – and Ernestine was insulted. 'I wish everyone would stop talking about Frank as a kind of ambulant stomach,' she complained. 'He does have other emotional requirements, besides food.'

'Have you heard from him recently?'

This was a tender point. Frank had not phoned since his return from America. After leaving a message each on his London and Oxford answering-machines, Ernestine was determined not to pursue him any more.

'He's fine.'

'Give him my love, when you next speak to him. I do think you're wonderful, being so civilized.'

Ernestine said: 'Don't. I hate being wonderful.'

'Go on, then,' Johnny said, reaching over for Melissa's pheasant. 'Give yourself a treat. Take some revenge, like I said this morning.'

'What?' Melissa's eyes lost their dreamy, being-nice glaze. 'What were you talking about this morning?'

Johnny searched in his pockets, and produced a small plastic bag full of grass. 'We got quite philosophical, as a matter of fact. Ernie was trying to explain why she wouldn't let me kill that rat.' He chuckled, and favoured Ernestine with a genuinely friendly smile. 'Still beyond me, I'm afraid.'

Unexpectedly warmed by his casual use of her name, Ernestine relaxed. 'I always think it must be awful to be a rat,' she said. 'Imagine being born automatically loathsome. I didn't see why the frightful thing should suffer, just because I was scared of him.'

'Soppy date,' Melissa said.

'Ever so sweet, if you can afford it.' Johnny began to assemble a fat joint, which Melissa watched keenly. 'If you lived with a whole swarm of them, you'd soon start squashing them like flies. The little buggers take chunks out of the kids.'

'That's disgusting! Can't people ring the council, or something?'

'Hello, I'm one of the travellers from the illegal site on the rubbish dump, and I'd like to complain about the shocking conditions.' Johnny chuckled, enjoying Ernestine's shocked face. 'Do yourself a favour, and stick to Henley Regatta. You don't want to write about all that shit.'

'Aren't there any sorts of traditional recipes?'

Melissa sighed fretfully. 'Johnny, hurry up.'

He ignored her. 'Well, when my nan got pissed, she used to talk about living with the gypsies in Ireland. They stopped at a farm to help with the harvest, and the women would ask the farmer to let them stay long enough to make some food for the children. Nan reckoned it was a lump of suet pastry, wrapped round meat or apples, and cooked in the embers of the fire. She said it was delicious. Big enough to feed twenty of you.'

'That's it!' Ernestine was intrigued. 'Exactly what I need! Did you ever taste it?'

He lit his joint. Melissa instantly snatched it away and took a long, sulky drag. He scarcely noticed.

'Not me,' he said. 'The old bag was well past it by the time I knew her.'

'Do you think I could find someone who'd tell me more about those times?'

'Probably. As long as you cross their palms with silver, and don't believe half of what they tell you. They'll be whining beggars, who'll call you "lidy" and say you've the lucky face. You'll want to hit them.'

'Of course I won't.'

'All right, but you'd better not look to me for help. I've left all that behind. They come up to me in the street these days, and try to give me sprigs of fucking white heather. God, it makes me laugh.' He took the joint back from Melissa, and held it out to Ernestine. 'Want some?'

She was so surprised, she almost said yes. 'No thanks. It must be odd for you to be on the receiving end for a change.'

'Not half. I let them drone on about my lucky face, and how I'm a sweet young gent, then I tell them to sod off.' He chortled to himself appreciatively. 'God, I love it.'

'I've often wondered about those old ladies,' Ernestine said, absently picking at her plate. 'Is it all nonsense? There's one in Belsize Park who always shouts things at me when I pass, and she hits rather a lot of bull's-eyes.'

'Oh, for God's sake,' Melissa said scornfully. 'I suppose you gave her money once. They never forget that.'

'Well, I did. But just after Will died and – you know – splitting up with Frank, she called out: He'll come back, darling. And there was no way she could have known.'

Melissa said: 'She only had to see your face, you wally. You're so gullible.'

'There was one,' Johnny said, 'who made me think. This stinking old cow who hangs about outside Moorgate tube station, thrusting heather at anything in a suit. I was on my way to the bank, packed into a whole crowd, and she starts yelling at me, "I know who you are, don't you come near me, don't you look at me with your evil eye." Made my day, that did.'

Ernestine, mesmerized, searched Johnny's face. 'What did she see?'

'Fuck knows,' Johnny said. 'I just wish I could bottle it and sell it.'

Melissa stood up abruptly, and moved off towards the back door. 'Time we were going,' she said, without looking round. 'Thanks for dinner.' The door slammed behind her. She had not waited for Johnny.

'I couldn't stand it any longer. Poor old thing, she can be so boring. And I swear, she's getting worse.' The beam of Melissa's torch snagged at the Catseyes on the narrow road back to Quenville.

Johnny strode beside her, his hands buried in his pockets. The keen wind blew showers of sparks from the end of the joint in his mouth. 'Great food,' he said.

In the darkness, Melissa's voice floated at him. 'Glad you enjoyed it.'

'Hope she asks us again. I'm sick of curry.'

'God, Johnny. I didn't expect to find you like all the rest – tiresomely hung up on eating.'

'What's up with you, eh?'

Melissa snapped: 'Nothing.'

'Why've you got the hump all of a sudden?'

'I detest that expression.'

'And I detest people with the hump, Lady Muck. Lighten up, or you'll be sleeping outside tonight.'

Her voice took on a plaintive tinge. 'Don't you care that I was miserable?'

'Nope.'

'Aren't you even interested to know why?'

'Nope.'

'The worst thing about Ernie is the effect she has on other people. If you could have seen yourself – telling stories about the gypsies and their horrid domestic habits. You suddenly struck me as appallingly commonplace and ordinary. I had to get out of that house, before you began to bore me too.'

'Oh, I get it,' Johnny said. He chuckled. 'You're jealous.'

'Of Ernie?' Melissa's voice lashed at him, outraged. 'Jealous? That shows how stupid you are.'

'I talked to her. You couldn't take it.' He stated this calmly, without animosity, but managed to make it sound both sinister and cruel. 'But I talk to whoever I like, and you'd better get used to it.'

'I simply fail to see why you want to talk to poor Ernie.' She was trying to sound lofty, in a voice trembling with pathos. 'Obviously, one's sorry for her – but you're never sorry for anyone.'

'Shut it,' Johnny said. 'You're being boring now, and if you carry on, you'll feel the back of my hand.'

'You wouldn't dare!'

He sighed heavily. 'Don't make me, Mel, there's a good girl.'

They turned off the road, and the tarmac changed to rutted mire as they hit the track to the ruined house. The one light burning in the trailer made the black towers blacker. In silence, they trudged on.

When they reached the door of their Portakabin, Melissa

suddenly turned on Johnny as if about to attack him. He braced himself defensively, but she flung herself into his arms. She was crying.

'I'm sorry, I'm sorry. Don't leave me.'

Her hair, musky and silken, fell across his face.

Their lovemaking began, as it often did, like a fight – biting, wrestling, clawing. Johnny gave himself up to the overriding, unquenchable lust that utterly possessed him whenever he held Melissa – delicious, alarming torture-by-orgasm. They fucked, half-clad, in the doorway, sprawling out into the cold night air. Then, when the first agonizing urgency had subsided, they stripped and did it again on the hard shelf of a bed. Johnny ploughed into her from behind, his hot hands clasping her breasts. She adored this position, and her sobs of pleasure sharpened his own climax. As they came together, they seemed to merge into one pulsing animal, and to crash back to earth in unison like a pair of spent rockets.

Afterwards, Melissa lay in a drowsy stupor, sighing as she stroked her vagina with a tissue.

Johnny hauled on his jeans, and one of the interchangeable jerseys they shared. 'I'm going out for a slash.'

'Mmmm.' She was dropping blissfully into sleep.

He went to the edge of the jungle of weeds, where he would be sheltered from the wind, and sighed with satisfaction as control returned to his body.

Alone in the cold November darkness, with the wind whistling and sawing through the leaves around him, Johnny suddenly realized why he felt so good. Making love to Melissa had exorcized something that had been bothering him all day; a restless, niggling feeling of discomfort.

For some reason, he had caught himself wanting to do something kind for Ernestine.

Why?

She was very pretty, but could not hold a candle to Melissa. The nearest he could get to defining this feeling was that it was like being pinched or tickled in some incredibly intimate place, and that it was impossible to decide

278

whether the sensation was delightful or repulsive. That morning, when Ernestine had insisted upon being grateful to him, Johnny had been reminded – very distantly – of various encounters he had sponged out of his memory because they carried the threat of lost power.

If he was afraid of anything, he was afraid of this. He remembered his very first time at Quenville, when the peachy little parcel in the flowery frock had left food for an unknown man because he was hungry.

The sentimentallity of it made Johnny feel slightly sick. Amazingly, this woman had lulled him into liking her harmless company. Fucking Melissa had returned him to himself, and brought him vast relief.

In future, he told himself, he would concentrate on the business in hand, and leave pretty Ernie to be eaten by the rats. Why should he care?

He had struck Melissa as 'appallingly commonplace and boring'. How right she had been – that woman was his true self, and he was a fool if he forgot it. Grinning, he ran back to the trailer and shut the door, leaving only the smallest, vaguest regret to die out in the night air.

Five

Scarlet-cheeked, her head haloed in clouds of her own breath, Ernestine was digging round the roots of a small, lopsided fir tree. She wore new jeans, bought to fit her diminished frame, and a huge grey jersey which hung on her thin shoulders and arms like a burst balloon.

Johnny leaned against the fence of the cottage garden to watch her. He had known that sooner or later, he would end up drifting down to the cottage. Over the past few weeks, while Melissa blissed out on restoration, he had fallen into a peculiar friendship with Ernestine which was like nothing he had ever known.

The point was, neither seemed to want anything in particular from the other – or, if they were playing angles, they were not sharp ones. Johnny had got over the shock of realizing that he was capable of taking pleasure in her company. It had turned out to be laughably harmless, posing no threat whatsoever to his autonomy.

The fact that he simply liked her carried no dangers, and brought all kinds of practical advantages. Melissa, once she had got over her ludicrous fit of jealousy, approved. 'How clever of you to get round her,' she often said. 'See if you can coax out another supper tonight.'

Both needed the warm cottage more than ever. A hard frost had slammed down on the countryside like a mailed fist, furring every blade of grass with white and making glaciers of the earthworks around Quenville. Johnny and Melissa woke in their icy trailer every morning to a view of raped soil, uprooted plants and two petrified bulldozers. Johnny had welcomed the chance to comb through freshly exposed foundations and wall cavities, but Melissa was furious that the frost had halted the work.

Johnny had been relieved that morning when she buggered off to London. Her blind obsession with the house was grating on him, and he was without the usual compensation of sex because he had caught a stinking cold. His chest was tight and painful, his head ached, his ears sang giddily, and he had sneezed his nostrils raw. All he wanted in the world was warm feet and whisky.

Melissa did not take kindly to having her lily-white hand brushed off his balls. 'Stop coughing,' she kept saying. 'Stop sniffing.' The previous night, they had irritated each other to the pitch of a vicious row, which had turned exciting and built to a finale of seismic sex. Melissa had driven away with a smile a mile wide. Johnny had woken up hoarse as a raven, and exhausted.

Eventually he had dragged himself out of bed, and gone in search of Ernestine. Just the sight of her was enough to simmer down his temper a degree or two. He sneezed violently, and she saw him.

'Hi, Johnny.'

'What are you up to, then?'

'This pathetic twig is our Christmas tree. I'm about to put it in a tub, and I wish I'd just gone and bought one. It's tougher than I thought.'

'Want a hand?'

She grinned. 'Yes, that was a hint. The ground's frozen solid.'

He climbed over the fence, and took the spade. While he hacked at the tangle of roots, she held the stem of the tree in her gloved hands, ouching absently when the needles worked into her fingers. A large terracotta tub stood outside the back door, with a bag of potting compost beside it. They lowered in the tree, and Johnny helped her to shake the compost and pat it down.

'Well,' she said critically, 'it'll have to do. I wish it hadn't grown on only one side.'

Johnny was amused by her gravity, as if she were deciding the fate of the nations, and diverted by this window on a 'typical' family Christmas.

Ernie said: 'Let's just hope the lights work. Mum's constitutionally incapable of putting them away properly.'

'Shall I help you lug it inside?'

'That's kind of you.'

'No it isn't. I want a cup of tea.'

She was smiling, teasing him. 'Can I ask you another favour first?'

'Oh, here we go. Okay.'

'I've got to get some holly from the coppice, and if you come with me, I'll only have to make one trip.'

'So what'll you give me?'

She giggled. 'What do you want?'

'Blow job.'

'Too many calories. Glass of mulled wine and a mince pie?'

'Done.'

They had fallen into the habit of this sexless sexual banter as a way of getting over Ernestine's awkwardness at having seen him naked. It served to underline the physical distance between them, and their lack of mutual combustion. Sex with Ernestine was, interestingly, beyond Johnny's imagination. Of course, he had tried. But what a joke. It was restful, he had found, to be with someone who did not expect The Treatment.

Huddling deeper into his three jerseys and donkey jacket, he followed her across the hard brown field towards a clump of trees. It was a white, clear afternoon. A red disc of winter sun hung in the immense Norfolk sky.

'Where's Melissa?'

Johnny watched the wreaths of their breath mingling and curling upwards. 'London. She's meeting that poofy architect, and taking him to a plaster-moulders.'

'She must be annoyed by all the delay.'

'That's putting it mildly. She's a right boil on my bum at the moment.' He felt for a cigarette, hoping it would warm him. 'How long will your parents be staying?'

'A week. We've always spent Christmas down here. Melissa and I hated it when we were teenagers.'

'I'll bet.'

Ernestine shot him an uneasy glance. 'I don't suppose you're looking forward to it. I mean, it'll put the house rather out of bounds.'

He shrugged. 'Mel can come, if she wants.'

'Johnny, you can't spend Christmas all by yourself in that trailer!'

'Why not?'

'You'll be so lonely – '

'Na-a-ah!' He reacted with scorn. 'Me? What's going to be so great about it anyway?'

'The food, for one thing,' Ernestine said.

'You'll send me some.'

'Will I, indeed? And there's the television. Though watching with Mum and Dad can be rather a trial – Dad asks such daft questions. Still, you know. Bog-standard English country Christmas. All of us wearing funny hats and drinking port, and trying not to miss Will.' She sighed heavily, and trailed off with: 'Oh, you know.'

'I don't,' Johnny said. 'I've never done a bog-standard Christmas.'

She looked surprised, and a little guilty. 'Of course, you don't have a family.'

'I've spent years trying to avoid organized yuletides,' Johnny said. 'Christmas day in the workhouse, or related institutions, has pretty well bashed the festive spirit out of me.'

'Weren't they kind to you?'

He chuckled. 'Too kind, that was the problem. One day a year, when everybody suddenly remembers you and gets off on being nice to you. I could have taken the turkey and stuff, but not the screws walking round wearing bits of tinsel.' He caught the compassion in her blue eyes, and added: 'Heart bleeding yet?'

'Oh no, I – '

'I don't get it, I really don't. All you types hate your family Christmases like poison, then you feel sorry for me, because I've never had one.'

He was laughing, and Ernestine joined in. 'You're right,'

283

she said, 'they can be the sheerest torture. And it'll be horrid this year, without Will. He always came down with Mel for part of the holiday.'

'And what about Frank?'

'He always goes back to the States. His dad's dropping hints about buying him a house if he toes the line this time.'

'Huh,' Johnny said dismissively, 'all right for some.'

They had reached the coppice, its black branches pierced by red lances of sunlight. With the bitter air withering their skin, and the birds cawing and wheeling above them, they began to clip long stems of holly.

Ernestine handed Johnny the secateurs, and pointed out the stems where the blood-red berries clustered most thickly under the glossy green leaves. The sun was dipping and the sky turning to pewter as the short winter afternoon declined. Each gingerly clutching a thorny sheaf, Ernestine and Johnny made their way back across the frozen furrows to the cottage.

The warmth of the kitchen rushed to meet them like an embrace. Johnny dumped his holly on the floor, and thankfully made for the Rayburn. Ernestine, who had not inherited her mother's parsimony, had every appliance in the house belting out heat. The sitting room, across the narrow hall, was fragrant with woodsmoke from the snapping log fire. Ernestine peeled off her gloves with a sigh, and walked round switching on lamps.

Johnny gave himself up to a galvanic fit of sneezing.

Ernestine, in the middle of assembling ingredients for the mulled wine, handed him a piece of kitchen towel. 'Awful cold you've got there.'

'Not half.'

'That trailer can't be doing it any good.'

'You're not kidding. I'm so iced up, it takes me half an hour to piss.'

'Go and have a bath,' Ernestine said. 'The wine will take a minute or so, and the water should be scorching.'

'Brilliant.' Johnny sneezed again. 'Bring the wine up, if you like, and have another gander at my pecker.'

She smiled. 'No thanks. I've seen that particular tourist attraction – and like the Leaning Tower of Pisa, once is enough.'

This wrested a laugh out of him. She could be a lot of fun when she chose. Obviously, Ernestine was a bit straight, but why did Melissa think she was so boring? His spirits rising as his body thawed, he ran himself a blistering bath, from which he emerged like a lobster.

Wearing only one of his jerseys, he went downstairs, following the smells of wine and cinnamon.

'In here!'

She was sitting on the hearthrug, nursing a plate of mince pies and a jug of mulled wine beside the leaping flames. In a tight circle of lamplight, her cheeks were touched with pink. She smiled, and held out a glass. Johnny saw the reflection of the fire dancing in her eyes. He pulled a cushion out of an armchair, and sat down on the rug beside her.

'Feeling better?'

'God, yes. Haven't had a cold like this in years. Banking must've turned me soft.'

'Can I get you an aspirin, or something? You look as if you might have a temperature.'

'I'm fine,' Johnny said. 'Thanks.' He took one of the mince pies, trying to analyse what he found odd and novel about this situation. People had fussed over him before. But their consideration had always formed part of a sexual transaction. Some of them had got off on warming towels for him and scrubbing his back. Look at Will, he thought. Always panting to take care of poor little Johnny – with an erection you could have hung your hat on.

The memories tasted sour, and were more than usually difficult to banish. For some reason, having these thoughts in the presence of Ernestine hurt him. The soft golden light around them was connected with her, and he could not bear to spoil it. What with the cold, and Melissa's exhausting similarity to himself, he was worn out. Being here with Ernestine suddenly made him feel like a boat that has crossed the bar into harbour.

He yawned noisily. 'This is lovely.'

She was watching him over the rim of her glass, with a mixture of caution and something approaching tenderness. 'I do find it odd, the way you talk about your past.'

'Odd?'

'I mean, as if you were talking about someone else.'

'Well,' he said. 'I like moving on. Being able to cast off the past gives you power. I think about it, but you're right – it all happened to someone else.'

'Have you changed so much?'

'If you'd met me ten years ago, you wouldn't recognize me.'

Her voice was gentle, but reproving. 'Don't start on about how you would have raped me and nicked my handbag. I'm not Melissa. Your wickedness doesn't thrill me. If you were really as wicked as all that, you wouldn't have helped me this afternoon. You wouldn't be sitting here now.'

'I had a motive, though. Drink and a warm. You could have done anything with me.'

Ernestine said: 'Look, if my asking about your history offends you, I won't do it. I'm not after titillation or lies, or a guilt-trip. I'm not a board of middle-class social workers, and I'm not interested in improving you. Though there's certainly room for it. I want the truth, or nothing.'

'Oh, I'm beyond redemption,' he said lightly.

'Seriously.'

He met her level blue gaze. 'This is as serious as I get.' He sneezed again.

Ernestine said: 'For God's sake, Johnny. You shouldn't be out on a day like this.'

'I'm never ill. Don't know how to handle it.'

She refilled his glass. 'Stay here, beside the fire. I'll leave a note in the trailer for Mel, telling her to come to supper.'

'She won't come,' Johnny said.

'Why not?'

'She doesn't want you to see her black eye.'

He said it matter-of-factly, but watched her reaction with intense interest.

286

Plainly, Ernestine was horrified. It occurred to him that this was the first time she had ever met a man who admitted to hitting a woman. He wanted to say, 'Fascinating, Captain,' like Mr Spock commenting on an alien species.

'What happened?' She was waiting to hear that she had jumped to the wrong conclusion.

He smiled angelically, and said: 'I walloped her.'

It was most intriguing to see the expressions of alarm, anxiety and censure flitting across that sweet, peach-bloom face.

'Is she all right? Oh God, poor Mel – '

'She asked for it.'

Ernestine sat up sharply on her haunches. 'Don't give me that.'

'Would you prefer me to say she walked into a door?'

'I mean, how could you?'

'You wanted the truth, Ernie. We went at it hammer and tongs, until I gave her the back of my hand. She richly deserved it, I promise you.'

'No woman deserves it. Or asks for it. She must be devastated, and you just sit there – '

'No, love. She's not devastated. As a matter of fact, she was having a good laugh about it this morning, when she saw what a shiner she'd got. She said, you'd better tell Ern I walked into a door or she'll never let you near the cottage again.'

Ernestine was scowling at him miserably. 'I wish I did have the bottle to throw you out. They were all right about you: you obviously are a shit, after all. And I tried to defend you.'

Johnny's fingers tightened round the hot glass. He was sick. That was why he felt so strange – why he had this lump suddenly lying on his heart, like a marble stone.

She had tried to defend him. She had unmanned him, mocked him – as if he needed defending from Melissa's stupid family. He ought to have been furious with her. And instead, he wanted to pick up her hands, and use them to cool his burning temples.

Something must have shown on his face, since Ernestine's scowl melted a fraction. In a gentler voice, she asked: 'When you'd hurt her, didn't you feel ashamed? You know how much she loves you – weren't you at all sorry afterwards?'

He felt it like a knife tearing a jagged gash in the sky of his world; an invasion by some outside force. The incredible thought had come to him that he would never give Ernestine a black eye. More, that he would pulverize anyone who did.

The feeling was upsetting – not unpleasant, but frightening in its peculiarity. It passed when he rooted out his dope tin, and tore his eyes away from Ernestine's face to roll himself a joint.

She sighed. 'I like you too much, that's the trouble. I'm so suggestible – always being led up the garden path. Do you know who you remind me of? Mel. You have the same way of admitting to dreadful things, without showing the least remorse. Making it nearly impossible to criticize.'

'Go ahead and condemn me if you like,' he said. 'I'm used to it. I know I'm still alive if I'm annoying someone.'

Ernestine collapsed back into a sitting position, and took a sip of her wine. She had forgiven him. They were silent, listening to the whispering of the logs on the fire, until Johnny had lit his joint. He drew on it hungrily, and she waited for his fierce fit of coughing to die down.

Then she said: 'Were you always like this?'

'I reckon so. I was a bloody nuisance before I could walk. The other women on the site were forever complaining to my nan.'

'Your grandmother?'

'No. She was a drunken old Irish biddy, who agreed to take care of me for a few days, and got stuck with me when my mother buggered off for good.'

'How old were you?'

'Dunno. Six months. A year.'

'You poor little thing!'

Her indignation made him laugh. 'I don't remember. I just grew up with Nan. In travellers' sites round Plymouth way – which is why I sound like I've got a mouth full of cow-shit.'

'Actually, I like your accent.'

'Yes, it's come in handy.'

There was another pause, then she began again. 'She must have loved you, your nan.'

'Get off. She was always cussing me for being landed on her. Only reason she never dumped me was because I made her a fortune out begging – "Give us a few pence for the baby," type of thing.'

'Didn't the social services do anything?'

Johnny laughed long and hard at this one. It had a bitter ring, which made Ernestine wince.

'Oh, what a lovely middle-class question! Call the social, and everything will be all right. We spent most of our time and energy avoiding the sods.'

'But you went to school?'

'Not if I could help it. I bunked off until they sent someone after me. Then I got a handsome clout from the old woman for making her the focus of unwelcome attention.'

'So how long did you stay with her?'

Johnny leaned against the sofa. Lapped in warmth, with the sky darkening outside, he found he could edit the details as he went along. Let her have a taste, if that was what she wanted. 'When I was twelve, I came back one day to find an ambulance outside, and someone told me they'd found her dead. Not terribly surprising, when you consider she had a liver the size of a fucking bungalow – could that old bag drink, or what? Anyway, I legged it, before anyone snooped round asking questions about my welfare.'

'What did you do?'

He shrugged, bored. 'Lived rough. Slept in alleys, or on other people's floors. I was on the game for a while. Mostly hand-and-blows for small change. I'm not that way inclined, given a choice, and I didn't fancy having a tradesman's entrance like the Blackwall Tunnel.'

'And then?'

He could not see her face in the shadows, but she sounded mesmerized.

'Then,' he said, 'I naturally got caught with my dirty little fingers in a newsagent's till. They washed me, tried me, slammed me into borstal for a stretch. Then I was put in care. Then a Catholic institution for delinquent youths, where I scrubbed bogs, peeled potatoes, and had a nice sideline doing rude things to the Fathers. Some of them were right perverts.'

A log cracked loudly, shooting out a tongue of flame. In the flash of light, Johnny saw the silver tracks of tears on Ernestine's face.

'What? What is it?' Before he knew what he was doing, he leaned forward and took both her hands in his. He had never given a toss about other people's tears, but each one of hers seemed to fall directly on his parched soul.

'It's so sad, Johnny. It just breaks my heart to think of a little child being cast into such a life.'

Other people had said it was sad, but not like this. Other people were sorry for him because they felt it turned messing around with him into a good deed. In Ernestine, he sensed someone reaching out to touch him, as an equal, with real compassion for the sorrows of that lost child – reminding him, totally against his will, that the lost child was still living inside him.

He held her hands tightly. 'I hated every second of it. The captivity, the stench of authority, the knowledge that I was cleverer than everyone who thought they had the right to boss me around. Not one of them was smart enough to twig when they were being used. Except – '

One memory assaulted him.

When he was fifteen, there had been an upheaval at the Catholic institution. Several of the Fathers, known very intimately to Johnny, had left suddenly, in a sulphurous gust of scandal.

Under the new regime, there were no gifts for obliging boat-boys; no cosy assignations in studies, no pinches on the bottom for rapacious people who looked like Renaissance St Sebastians. The new Headmaster, a chilly thread of a man in rimless glasses, had called Johnny into his study, to tell him he had his eye upon him.

'Sit down, John.'

Johnny sat, thrown by the new angle on the room, which he had mostly seen from a bending-over perspective. He had glanced round for the man's weapons and seen not so much as a ruler. Instantly, he had been uneasy.

'John, I've been going through your file. It makes for dismal reading.' He had leaned forward. 'You're not happy here, are you?'

For once in his life, Johnny had been lost for words. Who had said anything about happiness? Was that compulsory here too?

The Headmaster had leaned further. 'Shall I tell you what I see between these damning lines? I see a boy of above average intelligence, who might be anything he chose if he could lose his bad attitude. Because, you know, it's yourself you injure in the end.'

Johnny had relaxed a fraction, having heard this lecture many times before.

'Have you had any kind of contact with your mother since she left you?'

'No.'

'Your grandmother died a few years ago. How did you feel about that?'

'She weren't my grandmother.'

'Was not,' the Headmaster had corrected sharply. 'I know all about your reading habit. And if you really can understand Tennyson and Keats, you must have a perfectly adequate grasp of English grammar. There's no need to play the guttersnipe with me. Did you love your – the woman who brought you up?'

'No.'

'Was she unkind to you?'

'Not specially.' Johnny had felt his shoulders knotting with tension. The man was pushing him towards something he did not want to consider.

'There must have been someone you cared for – or who cared for you. Doesn't the word Love mean anything to you?'

'Sex.' This was an attempt to push the man away, but he brushed it aside.

'Sex has nothing to do with the kind of love I mean.'

'You mean God.' Johnny was openly scornful now.

'Partly, yes. I'm talking about the love of God as it is manifested in human beings. When I look at your record, John, what strikes me most forcefully is the lack of love in your life. A world without love is a kind of hell. Love is God, and hell is often defined as a place without God. That is where I think you have been living.'

Johnny had been aware of the ferocious, incomprehensible pain he felt when he read this sort of thing in books. It was a hundred times worse when applied to himself.

'Do you remember anything at all about your mother?'

'No.'

'No kisses, or caresses?'

Johnny had felt himself turning scarlet with anger. 'Get off.'

'Well,' the Headmaster said, 'well, of course. How could you be tender, when you know nothing of tenderness? How could you have anything but contempt for the feelings of others, when you have known only contempt and rejection? How could you be decent, when nobody has been decent to you? Or anything but cruel, when others have corrupted you with their cruelty all your days?'

His expression had changed. The cold, white face now wore a look of compassion, which made Johnny physically queasy.

'Society has failed you, John. This school has failed you. I hope we can change all that. I want you to know that I refuse to see you as a bad person. Nobody is beyond redemption.'

And it was at this point that Johnny had exploded, and done the terrible, appalling thing that had made him run from that school as if the Hound of Heaven itself was snapping at his heels. For the rest of his life, he had tried to forget it.

He had remembered Nan telling him about his mother: 'She give you a kiss, and off she fucked.' He had felt his mother's kiss as a burning brand on his forehead, the first and last kiss of love he had ever received, and he had burst into tears.

The Headmaster had counted this a great success, and been kind to Johnny afterwards, in a detached way – sending him into his own bathroom to wash his face, and letting him smoke a cigarette in his immaculate study.

And he had not been able to see what he had done. Johnny had been possessed with a desperate, inarticulate rage, because this clever bastard had tricked him into weakness. He had been forced to weep out all his power.

So, while the Headmaster had congratulated himself on his talent for reaching even the hardest heart, Johnny had set fire to the gym. It had made a terrific blaze, which could be seen for miles. From a distant hillside, Johnny had watched it, rejoicing as his strength poured back.

Ernestine's tears had the same, panic-inducing effect. Worse, because he could not bring himself to hurt her. At last, he had run up against something he could neither understand nor deal with.

'Johnny?'

Her hands were resting in his. He dropped them as if they burned, and stood up.

'I've got to go.'

'Are you all right?'

He called over his shoulder: 'Thanks,' and leaped back into the frost, more cruel now that night had fallen.

And something more painful than frost gnawed at his bones now. A part of himself he had never met before exulted that he had made Ernestine cry. He wanted to hold the tears in the palm of his hand, those precious jewels that had been shed for him, as if he deserved them.

Another part was fighting and clawing like a beast in chains. He could feel the breath of the terrible, slavering hound, raising the short hairs on his neck.

His eyes were adjusting to the blackness. He stumbled along the track towards the desolation of Quenville, suddenly choking on a sense of himself as a tragic figure. No –

293

nothing as dignified as tragic. He was actually pathetic; a mewling halfwit, who had been cut down to the level of all those he despised. The truth had been walking beside him for ages, and now he made himself look at it.

He had fallen in love with Ernestine.

The feverish gnats' whine in his head surged into an angels' chorus; the ground was falling away beneath his feet. God, he was sick; he had gone mad. He had to save himself, before everything he believed in blew to atoms.

A light glowed in the trailer, and Melissa's muddy car was parked, lopsided, in the broken earth. Johnny halted, knowing he had to get a grip on himself before he went inside. A wretched sob jolted out of him, and he angrily dashed away the sudden tears that warmed his frozen cheeks.

It had happened at last. He had come against a thing he wanted, with no idea how to get it. His normal methods would not work here. With Melissa, it had been a clear case of hunger for sexual possession – he would have raped her, if necessary. But that kind of sexual possession was not what he wanted from Ernestine. With no real idea what he did want, exactly, he knew that his normal methods did not apply – because they would only have destroyed whatever it was he desired.

Teeth chattering in the cold, Johnny called up all his powers of resistance. He must forget this, as he had made himself forget so much else. He thought about the fortune that lay beneath these shattered stones. He thought of the perpetual invitation in Melissa's long eyes; the way she arched and purred at the lightest touch of his fingers; the way the caress of her tongue could turn him into a demon.

Part of the problem, he saw, was that his ridiculous cold had dulled his sexual responses, and let in all this garbage about Ernestine. Drawing Melissa in focus sent the old charge through his blood.

His tears, and the memory of Ernestine's, were seared away as his energy returned. He bounded up the steps of the trailer. Melissa was bending over the table. Her air of housewifely concentration mocked the great purple welt over her left eye, and the fact that she was slicing lines of cocaine with one of Johnny's razor-blades.

She raised her head, and smiled an invitation through her cascade of shining hair. Johnny tugged off her jeans, oblivious to her complaints about the draught from the open door, and fastened his mouth on her, shaking with greed.

Six

In acres of cold whiteness, Melissa stood, her arms raised in exultation. She was sparkling, glowing, pulsing with energy. This was her creation, though the miracle still existed mainly in her eyes.

'Wonderful,' Ernestine said. Her voice swooped and echoed through the space, bounding off the drying cornices and the rough, grey concrete floor.

She supposed it was wonderful, and struggled against a puzzling sense of anticlimax. Somehow, Quenville had lost its brooding mystery in a welter of cement and plaster. Something vital was missing.

Ernestine had not realized how much progress had been made at Quenville since Christmas. It was now early March, and for weeks she had heard across the fields the crashing, grinding and drilling of Melissa's dream coming true. The dream was intensely private. This was one of the very rare occasions she had been invited to share it. And the transformation stunned her.

The jungle of weeds had been swept away, ripping the veil from Quenville's crippled façade. The bulging west wall had been rebuilt stone by stone, and there were piebald patches where the old bricks had been beyond saving. The great, forbidding staircase rested on monstrous wooden props. The mullioned windows had been unblocked to let the cold grey light pour in. Ernestine's head swam with the scents of paint, new wood and mortar.

'My drawing room,' Melissa said. 'The wood blocks are coming for the floor as soon as they've finished shoring up the other storeys.' She gestured impatiently. 'Of course, you can't judge it now. Wait till the murals are done, as the

296

crowning glory. Darling, you'll swoon. Just imagine Seddon's drawings, towering over one whole wall.'

'Goodness,' Ernestine said faintly. She was glad she would not have to live with all those sinewy thighs and fleshy flowers looming over her sitting room. So depressing, if you fancied watching television with your supper on a tray. Not that Melissa ever would, however. She had never done anything normal in her life, and obviously did not intend to start now.

'"Paradise and the Peri",' Melissa continued, her eyes unfocused with passion. '"One Morn, a Peri at the gate of Eden stood, disconsolate." Now, don't you think it's interesting that he should have chosen such a theme? The spirit trapped in her low state, yearning to be immortal? I think he was making a sly reference to the old brewer's social pretensions. You know – doomed to salivate, just at the gates of paradise.'

'How much is this lot costing?'

'A fucking fortune,' Johnny said, from the wastes of the window recess, far away on the other side of the room.

Ernestine turned to look at him, a smile hovering on her lips, ready to be deployed. It died, when she saw he was still wrapped in The Mood. These days, Johnny seemed unable to decide whether he was her best friend or worst enemy. They would have weeks of companionship, and then, without warning, The Mood would descend. Ernestine would be lulled into laying out his coffee-cup and looking forward to his dropping into the cottage, only to be baffled by avoidance and snarling surliness. This particular Mood had been festering away for a record-breaking ten days. What was the matter with him?

'Two fortunes,' Melissa said airily. 'His and mine. Thousands upon thousands, until my cheque-writing hand is practically crippled.' Her avid eyes made a circuit of the room, then landed on her cousin. 'It's worth it, though. Isn't it?'

'Yes. Always assuming you don't end up going bankrupt, and turning it into a bed-and-breakfast. When do you think you'll be able to move out of the trailer?'

'Summer, we hope. I'd still love to get into that cottage of yours, but what with Tess guarding the door, the chain-smoking old angel with the flaming sword – '

Christmas had been marked with a row between Melissa, Tess and George, which Ernestine had worsened by sticking up for Johnny. Relations with the elders were now extremely rocky.

'Still, you're there,' Melissa said, giving Ernestine's hand an affectionate squeeze, 'and that's lovely. Isn't it, Johnny?'

'Hmmmm,' Johnny grunted.

'But Ern, how I neglect you these days. I never see you, and here you are, wasting away! Are you quite well?'

Ernestine's mirror told her she was looking better than well. Positively pretty, in fact, in the new clothes she always ended up buying, whenever she drove into town. Johnny had told her, too, when his good side was uppermost.

'You're pretty today,' he would say, stating it as a bald fact. And Ernestine would laugh – not least because he made her feel like the Queen of Sheba.

How very typical of Melissa, she thought, to be blind to the improvement in her cousin; to interpret it as something insulting. Increasingly, Ernestine was conscious of hanging back on the periphery of Melissa's drama, instead of hankering for a part of it as she had done all her life – cameo, extra, walk-on, anything. Nowadays, she did not care for the pedestrian character roles on offer.

Drily, she said: 'I'm fine, actually. Living out here must suit me.'

'Does it?' Melissa's interest was already veering away. 'Do be careful, darling. Your sort look better with bosoms.'

Reluctantly, Ernestine laughed – but her Melissa-laugh was less admiring than usual. 'My God, I must be boring.'

'Oh, don't be silly. Come and see the mouldings for the library dildo – which is what dear Johnny calls the dado.'

'Of course,' Ernestine exclaimed suddenly. She tried addressing it to Johnny, but he turned his back on her. 'I've been trying to work out what's missing. What's happened to the Quenville angel?'

'It had to come down, while they were doing the porch. So we took the opportunity to scrub its face.' Melissa's voice was sailing away towards the library, on the other side of the hall. 'Johnny, take Ernie out to see the angel.'

'No,' Johnny said.

She had not heard. Her footsteps hammered across the hard new floor.

Slowly, slowly, Johnny turned away from the rubble-strewn view outside the window, and faced Ernestine.

She whispered: 'Please – ' not talking about the angel.

Johnny knew she was not. He shrugged rudely, however, and muttered: 'Come on, then.'

He led her out of the house, over sagging bags of sand and cement, to a bald and blackened patch of earth that had been snatched back from the weeds.

Here – shockingly – the Quenville angel kneeled with arms outstretched; six feet high, its massive wings and huge sandalled feet all out of proportion. It seemed about to topple forward, and Ernestine touched it gingerly. The weatherworn face had been scrubbed to the texture of dirty granulated sugar.

'I used to dream about this when I was little,' she said. 'I absolutely hate it.'

Johnny was watching her, and she risked meeting his eyes. They were hot and angry. His hair had grown down to his shoulders, and despite the coating of black stubble on his chin, given a pair of wings, he and the angel could have changed places.

'It looks like you,' Ernestine said. 'Not that I hate you.'

'Well then.'

'Johnny, what have I done?'

'Eh? What've you done about what?'

'Come on. You've been horrid to me these last few days.' She surprised herself by ending on a breathless half-sob. 'You know you have. And if I've done something wrong – '

'Look, don't cry!' he hissed. 'Don't fucking cry!'

'I'm not. I swear. If you'd only say – '

'Because,' he spat, 'I'm scared of what you're doing to me. All right?'

'Me?'

He let out a long sigh of infinite weariness. 'When I'm with you, I see the point of being normal.'

'Why is that so terrible?'

'It's too late, Ernie. I should have met you years ago. Meeting you now is a joke. You turn me upside down until I start to think you might be right – which means I'm wrong. And if I'm wrong, I'm lost, and I'll never be able to get near you. And then you gaze at me – why am I scared of you?' he demanded with sudden vehemence. 'Why aren't you scared of me? Don't you realize I could hurt you?'

Ernestine said: 'But you won't.'

'Won't? Don't you understand? I – I just bloody can't?'

As they stared at one another, Ernestine felt her soul rushing out towards him. He was a vortex, drawing her in. She could see far, far beyond his angel's face to the Johnny imprisoned inside.

This was nothing like the scented romance of falling in love with Frank, all those years ago. It was sorrow and danger; it was being pushed to the brink of the pit. What she saw in Johnny's eyes broke her soft heart – she could almost feel its jagged edge scraping against her ribs when she tried to draw a proper breath.

Johnny whispered: 'I love you.'

She knew this was the first time in his life he had ever uttered the words. They fell on her like a witch's spell, melting away all her solid layers of conventional morality.

'I love you, I love you,' he said. 'I love you.'

He clutched her against his chest, and she listened to his heart beating. Lightly, their lips touched.

From the house, Melissa's voice sang: 'Johnny! Ernie! Where are you?'

Too late. She had lost them both for ever.

For the second time in her life, Ernestine stood in the cottage garden, digesting the realization that she was in love. For want of a better word.

When she fell in love with Frank, there had been no

better word required. That had been all flowers and fragrance, a sunlit idyll in a bubble of stationary time. She had felt young, and loving Johnny made her feel old.

The two weeks that had passed since their first embrace at Quenville had not been golden. She had walked home alone, soaring like an angel, utterly transformed. But far from resolving the tension between them, Johnny's declaration had only added to the complications.

For a start, there was Melissa. Johnny had never said – had never needed to say – that he could not give Melissa up. They held one another in a desperate physical passion, which he could not give up any more than he could give up eating or drinking. Melissa and Johnny touched each other, and it was like a potent drug. They were addicted.

Ernestine understood this, without being told. She also understood that Melissa represented more than sex. She represented Quenville, riches, victory – the obsessive longing for the buried treasure that was the fault-line running through Johnny's entire personality, right to the marrow of his bones.

Johnny's love for Ernestine had been wrenched from him, utterly against his will. It filled a part of himself he had not known he had, and did not like having. When he held her against his beating heart, it had been a release. Gently, fearfully, he had explored rays of sweetness and sadness in himself. He spent hours at the cottage with her, or pacing the sodden lanes around Quenville, charming her with his harsh humour, his halting memories. He was marvellous company, balm to Ernestine's loneliness. And he made her feel treasured and admired – balm to the wound Frank had made by his rejection. Johnny had also healed the awful wound made by Will's death.

Though she no longer shovelled in food as if it could kill all her pain, Johnny had helped her to recapture her pleasure in the tools of her trade. Once more, she could cradle an onion in the palm of her hand, and delight in the way it filled its tight brown skin. She could bake a tray of hard russet apples into a toothsome symphony of fragrant cinnamon and plump raisins, and elevate soups to masterpieces with hedge-herbs. Thanks to Johnny, she had regained her missing power, her sixth sense.

But he had never kissed her properly, let alone had sex with her. Ernestine, enslaved by his beauty, would pour her whole soul into her hand if he pressed it. Yet she accepted the peculiar chastity of their relationship without question.

For one thing, it meant something to Johnny that they did not have sex. More importantly, it helped Ernestine to convince herself that she was not betraying Melissa. It was certainly not a betrayal, in any way that Melissa would understand.

Happiness? No, this was not what Ernestine meant by happiness. Gazing round the garden, its bare twigs mellowing under a particularly mild March sun, she admitted that waiting for Johnny to walk through the gate made her pulse beat in a way that brought only care and anxiety.

Nothing was solved. Under these terms, no future was possible. They were living on stolen time – and with an uneasy sense of a looming crisis waiting to happen.

Oh, don't be silly, Ernestine lectured herself, you're getting as bad as Mel.

She was constantly trying to decide exactly what she felt for Johnny. If this was real love, it hurt like hell. She held something in her hands that was infinitely sad, infinitely fragile. And how could she lose the awareness of that other part of Johnny, fenced off from his relationship with her?

Frowning to herself, she ducked back into the kitchen, slamming the door, and returned to the pan of onions she was caramelizing on the Rayburn. The coffee was in the pot, the cups laid out on the table, beside a dish of chocolate brownies à la Ernie – star turn of the television series, fast attaining classic status, and Johnny's favourite. Hardly the set-dressing for an illicit romantic meeting.

As she dreamily stirred the onions with the spatula, a scrap of her classical education returned, to throw a garish, Melissa-ish light on the problem; Philoctetes, hero of the Trojan war, whose arrows could never miss, whose wounded foot could never heal. Despite his power, the wound smelt so ghastly, they had parked him on some remote island or other.

Johnny's wound was his past, and while she did not know the details, she could not ignore the stink. It pervaded all her tenderness for him. Should she know the truth? Would it make any difference? Should it?

'Morning.' Johnny sidled in through the back door. 'Found you these.' He thrust out a bunch of early daffodils, bright green, just faintly streaked with yellow at the buds.

'They're gorgeous.' He made her feel like some venerated Victorian heroine; the kind Frank was always writing about. 'It must be spring. Thanks.'

He dropped them into a glass jar, drying on the draining board, and switched on the kettle. 'Brownies. Brill.'

'I made them for you.'

He grinned at her. 'Of course you did.'

She could not help laughing at his casual arrogance – God, he sounded like Melissa sometimes. 'Trust dear old Ern to express herself in comestibles. Will once said I was one half of a perfect woman – the bit you want to come home to.'

'Who was the other half? Melissa, I suppose.'

'Yes. It was a joke we had – what a shame we couldn't fancy each other, and leave the pyrotechnics to Mel and Frank.'

'It bothers me,' Johnny said, 'the way I see you two cousins. Two sides of love, if you like. And I can't control either of them.'

'You wouldn't be the first to see us like that.' They had had this sort of conversation before. 'It's been our curse, I sometimes think. Mel generally comes out best. In the battle between the luxurious and the necessary, the luxurious usually wins, I find.'

'But you don't seem jealous of her,' Johnny observed, his mouth full of brownie.

'It's the wrong word. With you – with us, I mean – I have wondered if I should start being jealous of her.' Ernestine felt her cheeks burning, as she trod gingerly round the unbroached topic of sex. 'And I have to be honest, I do rather relish the fact that for once, I'm the one who's been preferred.'

He stated: 'You must stop thinking of you and her as two halves of the same woman. You're worth ten of her.'

'You don't have to say that. It's not true.'

'It is. You're good, and she's bad.'

'Bad! Oh, Johnny, really – '

She glanced laughingly at him over her shoulder, and was rattled to see that he was serious. His brindled eyes had never been pinned on her with such intent.

'She's a bad woman, Ernie. I meant it. Trust me to know what I'm talking about.'

'Well, she can be selfish sometimes, and manipulative – '

'No, no, no!' He waved this aside impatiently. 'Listen to me. Watch your back.'

All Ernestine's instincts went against this sort of melodrama, yet there was a force in Johnny's warning which made her blood curdle.

'She'd never do anything to me.'

He said: 'She'd do anything to anyone.'

'You're being silly.' Ernestine turned, rather crossly, back to her saucepan, to catch the onions before they burned. Didn't he see, there was no way on earth she could hear a word against Melissa now, when she had betrayed her?

With his eyes still pinned on her, Johnny felt in his pockets for his cigarettes. He lit one, and gazed at her in tense silence, for some minutes.

Eventually, he said: 'One of the first things that struck me about the difference between you two was the way you both talked about Will. You were really shredded when he died, weren't you?'

'Yes. It felt like the end of the world. But he wasn't my husband, and I know you can never judge a relationship like that from the outside.'

'Come on, Ern. You're not writing an article for the *Guardian*. Say what you really feel.'

This sort of demand made her extremely uncomfortable. Frank had said, and Johnny was constantly saying, that she was incapable of separating what she really felt from what she 'ought' to feel. She frowned unhappily. 'I was very angry with her, for not – I don't know – mourning longer. He was such a darling.'

Johnny smiled the secret, feral smile that she had come to dread. It gusted over a great whiff of his stinking wound.

She clanked the pan off the hotplate, in a sudden fit of irritation. 'You know something else, I can tell. Well, I'm not interested in any more sordid revelations. Will's dead, and I'll remember him how I like, thanks.'

His face had tensed to watchful apprehension. There was another spell of silence, while Ernestine scraped her treacle-coloured onions into a pastry case.

In a small, unfamiliar voice, he said: 'You wouldn't love me, if you knew.'

'Then bloody well don't tell me! What's the point?'

'I dunno. You might need the truth, some day.'

She wiped her hands and turned to face him squarely. 'You've made me fall in love with you, totally against my better judgement, and that's all the truth I can handle. Okay?' She seized a jug of eggs, and beat them as if they had done her an injury. 'Yes, I really think I do love you, but look what I've done. Mel is one of the people I love most in the world, practically a part of me, and I've stolen her man. Try to imagine how that makes me feel.'

'I don't belong to her.'

Ernestine snapped: 'You do. She's crazy about you. I've never seen her go overboard like this before. Do you know, I honestly believe she'd die for you?'

He frowned, and sank into another long spell of silence, during which Ernestine added cream and black pepper to the eggs, poured them into the pastry case, coarsely grated Parmesan over the top and slammed it into the Aga.

Why was she angry? If she was honest, not just because of what he was making her do to Melissa. A shudder of sexual longing streaked through her, swelling her clitoris and pinching her nipples. She was one great, palpitating ache, desperate for his touch.

If I'm so bloody wonderful and marvellous and beautiful, and worth ten of Melissa, why does he fuck her and not me?

She hated herself for having this thought, but it did not lessen her annoyance when Johnny suddenly said: 'I'd die for you.'

'Thank you. That won't be necessary.' She was bustling with a cloth now, as she had used to do when Frank nettled her. Frank – oh God. At times like this, she bitterly missed having a normal relationship, with a normal man. You were always meant to be the sensible one, she thought to herself, so how on earth did you get yourself into this mess?

'Ernie.' His level voice commanded her to look at him, and she could not help obeying. 'I mean it,' he said. 'Don't forget it. If ever I had to protect you with my life, I'd chuck it down without a word.'

She would have liked to brush it off with a laugh. But he held her in that transforming gaze of his, guaranteed to rip her sore heart to shreds. These were the moments when he netted and enslaved her with a glimpse of the fallen angel; the forlorn Peri barred from Paradise.

His avowal filled the space between their bodies, until Melissa shattered the spell.

Like a demented Botticelli Primavera, she leaped into the kitchen, cheeks pink and eyes blazing. 'Johnny – '

Ernestine thought she would die of guilt, but there was nothing for Melissa to see. And even if they had been banging naked on the table, she would not have noticed. Ignoring her cousin, she swooped down on Johnny, her hand outstretched.

'Look! Look!'

'Shit,' Johnny said. He snatched the prize from her palm. 'You've found it.'

'Nearly – as good as. We haven't a second to spare – '

It was a ring; blackened and misshapen, but with a deathless sparkle that caught the light through layers of dirt.

Instantly, as if charged with electricity, Johnny was

quivering with nervous energy. 'A diamond. Shit, shit. And there's some engraving. Is that Rose's name? Was there anything else? Where did you find it? Shit, I thought I'd combed every inch – '

'Near the coppice.' Melissa was speaking very fast, but with superb control. 'I took a flier over some stupid branch and there it was, right by my nose. The plough must have turned it up. Thank God the farmer didn't pinch it first.'

'The coppice? That's miles away – '

'Johnny, Johnny, use your head. A hundred years ago, that field used to belong to Quenville. We always thought she buried it, but we were assuming it'd be in the house – '

Ernestine said: 'You can't go digging up Ray Smith's field. He'll go mad.'

Neither had heard her. She might as well have been a ghost.

'We have to buy it,' Johnny said. 'And everything else that used to belong to Quenville.'

'But how? If we go to him directly, he'll smell a rat, he'll take us to the cleaner's. Should we do it through an agent, or a solicitor?' Distractedly, she threw her hands up over her eyes. 'You realize, if we get this ring valued anywhere nearer than London, it'll be all over the village? Oh God, oh God. I don't know what to do.'

'Hey – ' Johnny took her in his arms, with something approaching real tenderness. 'Calm down. We're nearly there.'

Over Melissa's head, nestled against his collarbone, he caught Ernestine's eye and smiled.

He was a wolf with fiendish eyes, distorted and possessed by greed. Ernestine searched for the man who had vowed to lay down his life for her, and he was not there. This was, she realized, not another Johnny. It was the real Johnny. She had not noticed how near she had stepped to the edge, and now it was too late. She was already in the pit and falling, falling, falling.

Seven

Out across the flat fields, the single light at Quenville burned on.

Giles braced his jaw, to stop his teeth chattering. He had crawled to the nearest church for comfort, but the sinister shapes of the graves by night made him mortally afraid. The rustlings in the yew hedge only intensified the thick rural silence, reminding him there was not another human soul between himself and that solitary warning light.

The sense of evil he had carried from London hovered round him, a poisonous fog. High in Shenley church tower, the clock tolled the lonely half-hour between eleven and midnight. He longed for the return of the day, and wrestled with the waves upon waves of superstitious horror that made every hair on his body bristle in a silent scream of alarm.

He had nothing to fear from the sleeping dead, who neither knew nor cared about the agonies of doubt and worry that had tortured Giles over the past months. It was the living he must fear.

Had Johnny guessed why he was there? Had he heard anything? The man could vaporize and seep through key-holes. Giles gave full, supernatural credit to those striped grey eyes in their barbed-wire lashes. Mixed with the guilt, the self-loathing and remorse, he felt the old pain of betrayal. Part of him still yearned – would always yearn – to recapture the mythical Johnny he had loved. He looked forward to the capture and kill with dread that contained a certain sexual thrill of anticipation.

He pushed open the lych gate. The ragged purple clouds across the moon parted, and he could make out the edges of the buttresses. The cold spring rain had stopped, and a

308

boisterous night wind carried smells of raw earth and unmatured pastures. Wishing he had worn something warmer before he belted away up the M11, Giles inched along the cinder path between the lopsided tombstones.

Seven hours from now, noisome Edbanger would be fuming outside the locked door of St Benet's, wondering why his beloved Father had failed to show up for early Mass. It would be 25 April, the Feast of St Mark, and Giles liked to keep saints' days.

He felt a sudden nostalgia for Ed's tiresome devotion, and wished he could have said goodbye. Without a clue what his next move ought to be, Giles knew he could not return to his church. They would all know, soon enough, that types like sottish old Ed, for all their surface grime, were cleaner than their parish priest.

He had reached the church porch, and his fingers fumbled on the scaly iron latch. He sat down on the stone bench, knocking his shoulder against an ancient marble stoup, which contained a green stain of holy water.

Enclosed by the mildewed air, colder than charity, Giles faced the vast question of his future. He had lived with the guilt for so long that he had almost become used to the great holes it had burned in his psyche. Yet – incredibly – he had managed to convince himself that he could square his faith and his conscience with a refusal to confess or atone.

What a bloody fool I've been, he thought.

By trying, at long last, to do the right thing, he had risked blundering into a far greater sacrifice than he had intended. If he had stayed a coward and done the wrong thing, he would not now be breaking into a clammy panic every time a twig snapped.

Above him, the church clock chimed the quarter. The past was all around him, and he was assailed by an Oxford memory of Frank reading poetry to his friends, lying on a tartan rug in the meadow, absently swatting midges with his brawny, unpoetic hand. It had been Keats, which sounded peculiar and oddly arresting when read in a patrician American accent.

'The Eve of St Mark'. Country people, a footnote had explained, once believed that if you sat in the church porch at midnight, on St Mark's Eve, you would see the spirits of all who were going to die in the next twelve months.

They had had quite a discussion about what they would do if any of them saw a vision of a person they knew. A very lively discussion, since death had been a glorious joke in those days. Ernie had said you could not possibly go and tell the person what you had seen. If it were true, she argued, what would be the point of upsetting the poor soul, and ruining the last few months of a life that was going to end anyway? And if it were not true, why depress them? Frank had agreed with her, but Giles, Will and Melissa had been all for rushing straight to the unfortunate person, to urge them to make one final bid for life. At the very least, Melissa had pointed out, they would take more care when crossing the road, and that might be all it took to save them.

A deep shudder shook through Giles, from the soles of his feet to the ends of his hair. He saw the spirits in his mind's eye; a ghostly procession of souls taking temporary leave of sleeping bodies as a rehearsal for the final severance. Old people and young, all bearing the mark of the Reaper's blade.

If he had come here at this time last year, he might have seen poor Will. He could imagine him trotting up the path, checking his watch and settling the knot in his tie – typically, absurdly anxious not to be late, even for this Mass of the Doomed.

Giles's scalp crawled. Who might he see tonight?

Not Melissa, please. Not this final punishment. He had tried so hard to warn her.

Of all Melissa's immediate circle, Giles had been the least enslaved. The others tended to treat her as a creature apart and unattainable, and Giles had usually found her highly attainable. Their relationship, before Will had staked his claim, had been friendly and fun. Giles, because he asked for nothing, had brought out her best side. His refusal to take any of her bullshit meant that she could give free rein to her enchanting, insouciant selfishness. God, how she had made him laugh sometimes, curled on the single bed in his college room, describing the antics of her various adorers. Terrific in the sack, too.

In those days, given the choice, he would have preferred Ernestine – if only she had not been quite so firmly and conspicuously on the side of the angels. Dallying with Melissa had carried no responsibilities. No stash-hiding, no pretending not to know the Oxford low-lifers who greeted him by name in the Corn. With Melissa, he could be his disgraceful self.

He remembered the evening, a few days before the Commem Ball, when he had told her exactly how much money Will had. And how, with a charming smile, she had said: 'In that case, he'll do very nicely.' Life for Melissa had been a refreshingly simple business. When you wanted money, you made yourself fall in love with a man who had some. She could not imagine the state of wanting anything, and not being in a position to get it.

But she had bitten off more than she could chew with Johnny Ferrars, and it was all Giles's fault. Since the terrible day at Monksby, when Johnny had crashed back into his life, Giles had lived with the knowledge that he had brought evil into the golden circle.

It had been eating into his brain like a maggot. Frank had not understood because Giles had not been brave enough to tell him everything. Finally, the previous day, he had been unable to bear the torture of guilt and fear any longer.

In a way, facing the very worst was a kind of relief. Calmer than he had been for months, he had locked up the church and his flat, and climbed into his moribund old Beetle. Paul Dashwood had bequeathed it to him, after Bella's parents had presented them with a new Volvo containing a childseat – Mr and Mrs Dashwood, as they now were, lived in meek respectability in Finchley with a baby daughter.

Clattering up the motorway, Giles had reflected that he was now the last Bohemian to own a dreadful car. Even

Frank, so determined to cling to his student days, had succumbed to a gleaming new Saab.

He had tried to ring Frank, to tell him what he was about to do, but term had not yet started, and Frank's answering-machine had informed him that he was 'incommunicado', finishing his book. Probably just as well. Giles had only wanted the sound of his voice for moral support.

Minutes before leaving, he had impulsively called his father, with some vague idea of enjoying the last moments of a relationship that was about to change catastrophically. In fact, he had got Nina, and then ended up having an involved, incoherent conversation with his little half-sister.

'Are you wearing your steeple, Giles?'

'You mean my collar, darling. Yes, I am.'

'Do you take it off in the bath? I'm going to have a bath, Giles, and I expect I'll wear my new Barbie pyjamas afterwards. Come and see me, if you like.'

'Sorry, duck. I've got to go somewhere else.'

'All right. Good night, Giles.'

'Good night, Emily.'

Good night, good night, little Emily. The brazen innocence of this unfinished, unspoiled being had made him feel awful.

After that, he had taken the precaution of ringing Melissa on her portable.

'Yes, I'd love to see you.' It had not occurred to her to ask why Giles would be 'just passing' the middle of nowhere. 'Johnny's going out, and Ernie's in London, so I'm desperate for company. Be an angel, and stop off at the curry house in Shenley on your way. I'd like a tarka dal, a mushroom bhaji, a mixed raita with cucumber.'

What a sublime cheek she had. Even at this extremity, Giles had been unable to help chuckling. Of course, he had stopped at the Indian takeaway, where he had often bought greasy bags of curry for Johnny during their summer idyll. The fact that the place had not changed made him see, with full force, the changes in himself.

He groaned aloud as the unmade track leading to Quenville scraped his exhaust-pipe. Damaging his car was absolutely the last thing he needed. The sight of the house, however, knocked every other consideration out of his mind.

He had remembered Quenville as a sinister hulk; a spiked jumble of black towers. As the car lurched to a halt in front of the trailer, he gaped at Melissa's miracle. A glaring white light burned in one of the huge, naked windows on the ground floor; making the room a dazzling box.

He was standing, half out of his car, transfixed, when Melissa flung open the trailer.

'Giles. How fab.' She was as shockingly stunning as her house, in a soft shift of golden suede, with two slim gold bangles on one arm. They clinked together as she flung up her hand to sweep back her hair. 'What do you think?'

'Magnificent. God, it's amazing. I had no idea – '

'Didn't I always say?' She ran towards him, planting a kiss on his cheek and momentarily engulfing him in a cloud of delicious, spicy scent. 'Oh ye of little faith. Goody, you've got the supper.'

She ushered him into the trailer.

'This is a slum,' Giles said.

'Isn't it? But you wait. By this time next year, I'll be living in a perfect recreation of my ancestor's vision.' She swept a clutter of stained paper napkins off the table, and wriggled into the vinyl bench. 'I think of old Joshua sometimes, and what a shame it is that he won't be able to see me.'

Giles, clutching two pungent bags of Indian food, could not help looking round for traces of Johnny. On top of a grubby duvet, far too big for the narrow bed, a grey jersey was curled like a cat. But this might have belonged to either of them. He relaxed.

Melissa said: 'Knives and forks in the sink.'

'Yes, madam. Dear God – ' He fished the cheap cutlery out of the bowl, grimacing as his fingers squashed into floating scraps of food. 'Have you ever actually washed up here?'

'I didn't think you'd be fastidious.'

'Call me a fussy old fart, darling, but there's all the difference in the world between average untidiness and a bacteria culture.'

313

Automatically, he responded to her in the old way; the historical Oxford Giles recalled to life. His sense of urgency receded, and he began to think he might have overreacted. The suspicions that had rotted his soul in the dismal, lonely flat at St Benet's shrank in the reality of Melissa's unmistakable happiness – you could not think of this woman as a helpless victim.

She seemed so genuinely pleased to see him, too. They sat, inches apart, at the cramped table, while he ate and she bubbled on about Quenville. ' – all kinds of toing and froing over one miserable piece of land that isn't really worth a damn. But the last wrinkles were ironed out today, and we can start digging next week.'

'Hang on,' Giles said, his mouth full of nan bread. 'Are you saying you're about to dig for the fabled treasure? Jesus, I thought poor Will had trained you out of that.'

The mention of Will's name tightened the corners of her mouth in a way that was not entirely pleasant. She held out her left hand. 'See that?'

On the fourth finger, where she had once worn Will's wedding ring, was a thick band of chased gold, enclosing a diamond.

'Beautiful. Did Johnny give it to you?'

'No, he didn't,' she flung back airily, 'so there's no need to get that pursed-up, best-friend look. I found it in the field. It means I was right all along, and Will was wrong. The treasure does exist. I'm going to be immensely rich. You'd better be nice to me, because I might be moved to chuck a few bob at your winos.'

'How kind,' Giles said sourly.

'Look, did you come here to lecture me about Will, and the fact that I'm not behaving like a proper widow?'

He laid his fork down in the foil carton of curry, and folded his hands deliberately. Remembering Will had brought him back to his purpose. 'Has it occurred to you to wonder why I did come here?' Being annoyed with her was a great help, he found.

'No.' Her perfect eyebrows arched defiantly. She was haughty. A less beautiful woman would have looked sulky.

'I've got to talk to you.'

'Talk, then.'

He sighed heavily. 'This is serious. Please, don't make it more difficult. Please.'

'If it is about Will – '

'No, it isn't. Not directly, anyway.'

'Hmm. You're obviously going to tell me off. And I do find it most intensely weird – you, of all people, being all churchy and pious. You know I've never quite believed in that dog collar.'

'Mel, I'm here because I love you, I'm worried sick about you – '

'Can't imagine why.' Melissa smiled a teasing smile, and unearthed a jumbo-sized matchbox from the litter on the bed. It was full of ready-rolled joints. She had barely touched her food. 'I've never been happier in my life. I'm about to attain my most cherished dream, I'm about to be stinkingly rich and I'm madly in love.' She lit a joint. 'I don't suppose you want one of these.'

'Bad luck. I do.' Why not? An unfrocked parson could do anything. It was almost necessary for him to behave worse than a man who had never been a priest.

Melissa, her eyes sparking with sudden interest, handed him a joint. Giles inhaled deeply. This was the first cannabis he had tasted since his affair with Johnny, and it was delicious.

'Best rocky,' Melissa said. 'Johnny has contacts.'

'I know. I mean, I can imagine.'

Curiosity had sharpened her dreamy face. 'Giles, what is going on? Have you lost your faith, or something?'

'No. I'd feel better if I had, I think. I came to tell you something, darling. It's horrifically important, and you're going to hate me for it.' Now or never – and he was still hesitating, with a toe above the water. The impact of the cannabis gave each thought five hundred subtexts. 'I'm atoning,' he announced. 'If I was a medieval, I'd paddle off to Joppa in a cockleshell – walk to Santiago with pebbles in my shoes – crawl up the steps at Rocamadour on my knees. And I'd far rather do that than this.'

'Let's go to the house,' Melissa said, standing.

This was one of the best things about her, he remembered: her talent for skimming along with meandering stoned conversations. He had always loved the calm way in which she bypassed convention.

Reality was at arm's-length, and it retreated further when they passed through the porch of Quenville, into the glare of the drawing room. Melissa gazed around her with a purr of satisfaction, taking in the expanse of new parquet.

'They're stage lights,' she said. 'The wiring won't be finished for ages, so we rigged these up to run from the generator.'

Giles felt he was standing in the centre of a proscenium arch, with the dark expanse of Norfolk countryside as his audience. He waited while Melissa made a circuit of the room, watching her reflection in the gleaming floor.

She raised her head, and said: 'Tell me.'

'I came to warn you about Johnny.'

'If you came all this way to tell me about your affair with him, I could have saved you the trouble.'

'Oh. You knew.'

'Giles.' She was amused, but compassionate. 'He treated you rather badly, didn't he? Dumping you in the ditch like that, when you might have been dying.'

This threw him. He felt the frustration of a child who can't make the grown-ups see when something is important. Being laughed at was the last thing he had expected.

'I wish I could assure you,' she said, 'that he's changed since then. But his sort don't.'

'And yet, you stay with him – '

'Oh, darling. Should I be furious with him because he spurned you? Well, I'm sorry.' Her voice hardened, just a fraction. 'He did it all for my sake. He had to be near me.'

'You vain cow.' Giles had often teased her with insults. Now, he meant it. 'You'll forgive him for anything, won't you – as long as he did it all for you. All you care about is your own itchy fanny.'

She choked with laughter. 'Vicar, really!'

'You carried on like that with that common little shit, right in front of Will – and you're so determinedly stupid and self-obsessed, you refuse to see how he's used you. Did he, in this wonderfully honest relationship of yours, tell you exactly how he ended it with me?'

A summer night, the whole world quivering in a miasma of fever. Giles's head was a furnace, singing and buzzing and trying to break its moorings with his neck. Johnny had laughed at him, when he could not keep his shaking hands still enough to snort the line of coke through the straw. Johnny had done mountains of the stuff by then. Giles's cheeks burned. His feet were miles away.

Johnny's face loomed at him. Johnny's voice slashed at him until his heart was in bleeding ribbons. This was not real. A demon had possessed the angel. For some reason, which Giles's swirling brain failed to grasp, the demon had begun his evening by reading aloud from *The Oxford Book of Victorian Verse*, which had been in his pocket on the night of his escape. Tennyson, Arnold and Browning rolled off Johnny's tongue with ghastly fluency, in a savage exaggeration of the West Country accent that had so conquered Giles.

'Aren't you a great teacher, eh?'

Through the scorched rags of his senses, Giles watched his marvellous new world – his dream of fulfilment with the travellers – destroyed without mercy. He learned that he was unloved. A pathetic dupe. A sad, sick fuck who had outlived his usefulness.

'Know what?' Johnny stroked his forehead in a parody of tenderness. 'I think you're really, really sick, Giles. I think you're going to die.'

The woman was already dead. Giles gaped down at her, splayed at the foot of the tree. The memory of where she had come from slipped out of his grasp. She had not been there, and now she was there. Except that somewhere, he could recall – like a jerky, black-and-white silent film – the three of them drinking, smoking, snorting. Johnny and the woman laughing at him. The woman making a grab at Johnny, saying something about you gay blokes knowing how to enjoy yourselves.

Giles had heard, from his own mouth, a silly, braying giggle which had no connection with anything.

The giggle shook through him, though his eyes were wide and immobile, while Johnny fucked the woman in a blind rage. She had been incredibly surprised, and her eyes were still surprised when the heroin stopped her heart.

So this is it, Giles thought. Not such a big deal. A life, and it's gone. They talk about 'taking' a life, as if you got to keep it. It's big, it thinks and feels. And then it vanishes, like blowing out a candle.

One small, abstracted part of himself was filled with sorrow. He tried to feel some pity, and could not get past the inhuman waxwork she had become – a shop-dummy, staring fixedly over the rag Johnny had bunged in her mouth.

He grabbed Johnny's sleeve and croaked: 'I need some water.'

'Your turn,' Johnny said.

The wisps and scraps whirled, then cleared enough for Giles to register that he was sighing and moaning as Johnny's hands writhed inside his clothes. A lapse of time, then he was lying on top of the dead woman, thrusting ineffectually.

Another time lapse. He was spitting out a mouthful of soil, and goggling stupidly at the trail of blood on his head, dripping from his lip.

Johnny said: 'You're no fun, you.'

'No,' Giles begged. 'No, no, no.'

But while his mouth begged, his hand was on the knife. The handle was warm from Johnny's fingers, and slick with blood. He watched the blade plunging into the torso; now squelching into soft tissue, now scraping against bone.

As soon as he realized it was his own arm plunging the blade, Giles screamed and dropped the knife.

'Why did you do it? She hadn't done anything to you – '

'Stop whining,' Johnny said. 'Look at her. She's nothing,

and she always was nothing. Who'll give a shit about her? If they make a fuss, it'll only be because they don't want the same to happen to someone worthy.'

'They'll come looking for you!'

'And you, Giles. And you. You're all over blood.'

Giles held his dripping hands before his eyes and wept.

That was the last he remembered, before he fell into blackness that was all despair, and woke to find his soul destroyed.

'I was stark naked when they found me,' Giles said. 'Every scrap I wore – right down to the earring he gave me – had gone. I never told any of you that.'

There was, he found, a curious kind of relief in putting the nightmare into words after all this time. The tears had finally run dry, and he was left with a hollowed-out feeling of resignation.

Melissa was staring at him. She seemed to have diminished all over, and her face was strained into the lost-child expression. Suddenly, he was acutely aware of her vulnerability. She was tensing, as if ready to recoil from him. But if he wanted to be truly merciful, he had to go on.

'I was to blame, of course I was,' he said. 'It's really not good enough to bleat about being in Johnny's power – though I think I was. I kidded myself that if I worked for people like that woman, it would somehow make her murder all right. And, Melissa, that means I'm the world's leading shit.'

She whispered: 'You were ill. You didn't know what you were doing.'

'I knew that I wasn't resisting something very evil. It's fashionable to say evil doesn't exist, and it's all to do with early deprivation, blah blah blah. But I saw it that night. I nearly died of it.'

'Johnny isn't like other people.' Melissa was rallying. 'You loved him once, Giles, and you must have loved something that was really there.'

'Oh God, don't you see?' he demanded. 'That's his

319

special skill. He reads minds. He plugs straight into fantasies you don't even know you have – or certainly don't admit to. He encourages you to invent him.'

Her soft lips set stubbornly. 'He's never done that with me.'

'Hasn't he? Come on. Do you have the least idea who he really is? What he's really like? No. You decided what you wanted him to be – and he was.'

'I know him. Better than anyone.'

'Okay.' Giles's patience was wearing thin again. 'Where is he now?'

She twitched defensively, but it only lasted for a second. 'In London – he's out scoring.'

'Where in London?'

'Well, obviously I can't give you chapter and verse. I don't care where he gets the stuff.' She let out an impatient sigh. 'Darling, I'm terribly sorry about what you went through. If you did – though do bear in mind, you were practically dead from pneumonia. And I appreciate your concern for me. But Johnny doesn't do things like that any more.'

'God's teeth,' Giles said, 'you make murder sound like any old nasty little habit.'

'You reckoned you deserved a chance afterwards,' she flashed back at him, 'so why doesn't the same apply to him? Oh, you're so full of compassion for the poor and the criminalized and the dispossessed – until you actually meet one!'

'Yes, you've got a point. That's probably one of the things that's kept my mouth shut, all this time. It took me far too long to realize Johnny hasn't changed.'

Melissa whipped another joint out of her box, and lit it with absurd, exaggerated elegance. 'I suppose you're going to tell me about him and Will.'

'So sorry to bore you,' Giles snapped. 'But for some peculiar, unfathomable reason, I still love you, and that means I have to make sure you know it all.'

Melissa said: 'He got involved with poor Will as a way of getting involved with me. And yes, a fair slice of Will's money did go his way – which isn't very nice or refined. You're not what I'd call a genuine poof, but Will was three parts gay as a goose. He acted from his own free will, and probably had a marvellous time.' She blew out an insolent plume of smoke. 'You've fucked him, so you know he's utterly great in the sack.'

'Oh, don't give me that. You know bloody well what he did to Will.'

'That was me,' she said softly. 'I'm the one who hurt Will. You read the note he left.'

'Mel, listen – listen – ' Giles took her face between his hands, forcing her to look at him. 'You love Johnny. Either you're covering up for him, or you simply won't admit to yourself that he murdered your husband.'

'No – '

'Will didn't kill himself. It just wasn't in him.'

As he gazed at her, her expression slowly changed. The anger melted, and her eyes suffused with sweetness. Gently pulling his hands away, she said: 'You loved Will so much.'

'Yes.'

Two tears brimmed, and spilled gracefully down her cheeks. 'Poor Giles. Carrying round all this grief and sorrow, all this time. You can't change the way I feel about Johnny, but you tried, because you're fond of me.'

'Yes,' he said again.

She wiped her eyes with her sleeve. 'I don't deserve it. You shouldn't care about me so much.'

'Can't help it, can I?'

After a spell of silence, she asked: 'So what are you going to do now?'

He laughed shakily. 'Resign my living. Chuck away my collar.'

'Will you – will you go to the police?'

'I don't know. They might think I'm barking mad – one murder without a body, one body without a murder.'

Out in the night, the door of the trailer slammed.

Melissa said: 'God, it's Johnny. He must have parked down the end of the lane, and crept in without us hearing.'

They both turned to look, and saw Johnny's dark figure crossing the trailer window.

She whispered: 'He's seen your car. He knows you're here.'

'So?'

'You loved him once – please don't hurt him.'

Giles said: 'I've thought it over long enough, and I might have to. But you'd forgive me, darling, wouldn't you?'

With a sob, she flung her arms around him, and pressed him against her, stroking his hair. 'You're a wonderful friend, and if I wasn't so utterly gone, I'd jump in your car and beg you to take me away.'

'I'd take you – '

'Oh, I know, but it's too late. I'm so desperately crazy about him.'

'Sweetheart.' He held her. 'Be careful.'

'No,' she said, 'you be careful.'

'I'll be all right.'

'It was tremendous of you to come and see me. Please remember how ghastly I felt about everything – and don't be too hard on me, will you?'

'Oh my darling, as if I could,' Giles said sadly. 'As if anyone could.'

It was her face he had carried in his mind when he dashed back to his car to flee from Johnny. And it was her face before him when the church clock began to toll the twelve strokes of midnight.

The Eve of St Mark, when the shades of the living foresaw their own death.

Slowly, Giles's blood froze in dread. With a hammering heart, he sensed someone – something – opening the lych gate and gliding up the path. The wind died. Not a leaf or blade of grass stirred. Deep in his soul, he heard the noiseless footsteps, moving through the graves towards him.

The figure, carrying the ghostly daylight of another world, moved into the porch.

As he had dreaded, he knew it.

Eight

Frank's college room was a comfortable, if ill-lit, panelled cube. Its mullioned windows looked out on a long, dull wall of weathered grey stone, with sudden slices of baroque bell tower and chimney looming in at peculiar angles — like an elaborate stage set seen from the wings. Despite its lack of a view over the sylvan delights of the college garden, it seemed a perfect fulfilment of all Frank's long-held, Ralph Lauren-ish Oxford fantasies.

Ernestine found him rattling away on his keyboard beside the open lattice, surrounded by Alps of books and papers on the floor. There were more books piled on the desk, the pages bristling with notes. He was working furiously, his lower lip tucked under his front teeth, too absorbed to hear her come in.

She stood in the low doorway for a moment, remembering when the sight of Frank at work had been a familiar part of her everyday life. A single shaft of sunlight, golden as sunlight only is in Oxford, bathed the crisp dark hair on his brow. He had lately taken to wearing horn-rimmed spectacles in front of his screen, and they made him look more like Clark Kent than ever. His sheer handsomeness could still shock her.

'Frank.'

He turned his head quickly, and in the second before he arranged his face into a welcoming smile, she caught an unguarded flash of delight and longing.

'Ernie. My God.' He whipped off the glasses and stood up to kiss her. The ceiling was only inches above his head. 'What are you doing here?'

'I've been giving recipes on Radio Oxford.' Ernestine was

rediscovering her old shyness in the face of his looks. Good grief, how had she ever had the brass neck to pull something as flaringly glossy and expensive? 'How's it going?'

'Too slowly, and I never want to see another Victorian heroine as long as I live.'

'You're cured, are you?' Ernestine was thinking of Melissa.

Frank, for once, was not. 'Yep. Give me a good ole down-home gal, who can bake a pie and chaw terbacky.' He threw his glasses among the drifts of papers. 'Let's get out of here. This place makes me feel like a battery hen.'

'Yes. It's a gorgeous day.'

'Swarming with tourists, unfortunately.'

'I'm a tourist these days.'

He suddenly smiled and swept her into focus, in the old, disarming way. 'Not you. You're in the bones of this place.'

They went down the dank, uneven stone staircase, and emerged into the shimmer of the Main Quad. A party of Japanese, festooned with cameras, were shuffling along the cloister behind their guide. Ahead of them, a dozen sulky, noisy French schoolchildren were being shepherded towards the Chapel.

'I take it,' Ernestine said, 'you haven't heard anything.'

'Not a thing. I spoke to Dan again this morning – he's as mad as hell.'

'Because he's worried. God, just like last time.'

'He thinks Giles has gone back on drugs,' Frank said, 'and done a runner with the money Will left the church.'

Ernestine snorted crossly. 'Really, he should know poor old Giles better than that. Apart from anything else, it was only thirty thousand.'

'What do you think, then?'

They had begun to pace across the Quad, using Frank's right, as a fellow, to walk on the grass. Ernestine frowned. 'To be honest, I don't know. I can't seem to get a handle on anything these days. What about you?'

'I'm getting seriously anxious, Ern. I can understand him avoiding all these ghouls at his church. But he arranged to meet me the day before yesterday, and he never showed.'

'Well, it has been known. He was never exactly the most reliable person on earth.'

'That was in our Bohemian days,' Frank said. After a spell of silence, he added: 'And so was this. Remember?'

He took a large, old-fashioned key out of his pocket, and opened the door of the Rose Garden, which was closed to tourists except for an hour each day in high summer.

The soft breeze fanned Ernestine's cheeks, laden with the scent of countless roses warming in the sun. The garden was at the point of full beauty, before the juiciness of spring turns sere. She felt a wave of deep, pleasurable sadness, recalling the night she had lost her heart there, speared on the exquisite thorns of first love. The Ernestine of that evening, in her tight blue gown, had been a daft little creature – but better, miles better, than the woman she had become.

'So beautiful,' she murmured.

Loving Johnny had saddened her whole world. At this moment, she would have given anything never to have known him.

Frank smiled down at her, momentarily distracted from his anxiety. 'You looked gorgeous that night. I mean, you look gorgeous now – but I kind of miss your curves.'

His blue eyes crinkled in such a friendly, humorous way that Ernestine laughed, and swiped his arm. 'Oh, go on. You miss the meals, I dare say.'

He sighed. 'I miss it all. You, Will, Giles – the whole group. We're older, or wiser. Or deader. When did we all grow up?'

'I was thinking the same thing. I feel about ninety.'

Linking arms, they paced along the gravelled paths between the rose beds.

He asked: 'Do you still have the rose I picked you?'

'Of course. Pressed snugly in the pages of Elizabeth David. A bitter-sweet reminder of my foolish youth.'

'I'm glad I drove you to one bit of sentimentality.' Frank's smile was rueful now. 'Even though I blew it so royally afterwards. Y'know, part of me would love to turn back the clock to that summer.'

'Wouldn't we all?' She was in danger of making a fool of herself, and changed the subject. 'You see more of Giles than I do. Has he been different lately?'

'Tense, stressed out.' He glanced aside at her. 'He's had something on his mind. He won't say what, but I think it's connected with Johnny Ferrars.'

'Oh,' said Ernestine.

'All roads seem to lead to that guy. Are you still friendly with him?'

'Yes. We – we tend to see quite a lot of each other.'

She was trying to sound casual, but it was no use. Frank had always been able to read her, and she knew immediately that he had picked up the deepening of her relationship with Johnny. He was visibly struggling with anger, worry and jealousy, and the miserable knowledge that he had no right to express them.

'Well, the last time I saw Giles, he was dropping hints about unfinished business, and making changes in his life. He promised to tell me everything when we met this week – made quite a drama of it, too. I was all keyed up, then nothing. I rang his churchwarden. I rang Dan, I even rang his bishop.' He paused. 'I rang his local police and reported him missing. I bust my ass making them take it seriously – phone calls every hour, demanding to speak to everyone's boss.'

'Frank!' Ernestine protested. 'He's an adult. He's probably had a typically Giles-ian brainstorm, and God knows what he'll do when he surfaces and Will's not there to pick up the pieces – that's what really worries me.'

'The last time anyone heard from him,' Frank said, 'was Monday night. He left a message on my machine, and he spoke to his stepmother. And the kid – apparently, he told her he had to go out. Then nothing, nothing, nothing. The point is, he is an adult, you're right. And adults, particularly if they're vicars, don't just vanish into thin air without telling a soul. You know how hung up on responsibility he is these days. He can't even go out for an evening without leaving a billion emergency numbers.'

Ernestine was, secretly, far more worried about Giles than she let on. She could sympathize with Frank's gnawing anxiety even as she tried to jolly him out of it, and this was what made her say: 'Darling, I haven't a clue what business Giles thinks he's got with Johnny, but I promise he wasn't with Johnny that night.'

'How do you know?'

It was obvious, but he waited for her to say, in a falsely casual tone: 'He was with me.'

Frank's face betrayed alarm, and a bitter, hard anger. She felt his body turning to stone beside her, and his bicep tensing as he instinctively rolled his hand into a fist.

'Oh, I see.'

'It's not what you think.'

'What do I think?'

Ernestine was humble, hating to hurt him. Why had she imagined he would not be hurt? 'We don't sleep together. It's not that sort of relationship.'

'Relationship?' Frank spat out the word explosively. 'Oh, I get it. He had to have both of you. And you were fool enough to let him do it.'

'That's what you always fancied.' She could not let this past. 'Me and Mel – one for cocoa, one for champagne. Two halves of a perfect woman. Well, for your information, that is not what's going on. It has nothing to do with your tacky, three-in-a-bed fantasies.'

'Shit. You think that's what I wanted? Shit!'

The old wound was still fresh, and the fury rushed out of her mouth before she could stop it. 'I read the notes for your novel, Frank. And when you win the Pulitzer Prize, I'll be just thrilled to be the inspiration for the sensitive hero's brisk, practical girlfriend.'

'It's fiction, for fuck's sake – '

'Oh, sure. Brilliant American poet, madly in love with unattainable angel, and lumbered with Thelma from *Scooby-Doo*!'

'It's a fucking novel! And who gave you permission to read it?'

'I washed your knickers – why couldn't I look at your novel? Highly suitable actually, since it was all about cleaning your smeggy linen!'

They were face to face in the middle of the lawn, and – though they had never been given to hammer and tongs rows – both shouting.

'I didn't force you to wash my clothes, or mend my frigging socks – or squeeze the toothpaste out on my brush.'

'No, you just took it for granted and thought you were doing me a mighty big favour by fucking me occasionally.'

'Jesus, this is a nightmare. You sound just like him.'

'Maybe I like being treated as if I were beautiful, and sexy, and lovable in my own right.'

'What?' Frank roared. 'You think Johnny Ferrars loves you?'

'You can't imagine it, can you? Because why would anyone want me, when they've got Melissa?' For once, her deep anger was flowing out without tears or feebleness. The poison had been building for years. 'Johnny loves me in a way nobody has ever loved me before.'

'And you love him.'

'Yes, I do.'

Frank deflated suddenly. 'God. This is crazy. I mean, where is it going?'

'Don't be so American, Frank. Relationships aren't trains. They don't have to "go" anywhere.'

'Okay, okay. Is he going to leave Melissa?'

'Ha! I might have known you'd ask that.'

'Honey, please – ' He put his hands on her shoulders. 'Are you and Johnny setting up a home together? Getting married? Having kids?'

It was as if he had pressed a button, switching off her rage all at once. She hung her head. 'It isn't like that.'

He groaned. 'Oh, Ern. Of all the situations.'

'I know.'

The shouting match had removed a barrier between them. Frank stroked her face sadly. 'And it doesn't even make you happy.'

'No. The more I love him, the sadder I get. I can't explain, but it's not really like being in love. It makes me feel tremendously old.'

They stared bleakly into each other's eyes, as if from opposite sides of a chasm.

He said: 'You have to be with him.'

'I love him, and it hurts. It hurts.'

His finger went on caressing her cheek. 'This isn't my Ernie. I wonder what's happening to us all?'

She tried to smile. 'Isn't it horrible, being grown-up?'

He took her hand, and they walked, in silence, out of the Rose Garden. When Frank locked the door, it was like the deliberate closing of an era.

PART FOUR

The promise of May has often foretold
Harvests in autumn of crimson and gold,
But the rains of September have washed them away –
And what then of the promise of May?

With inspiration my heart overspilled,
And expectation – never fulfilled.
Though, when we are young, we mean what we say,
It is only the promise of May.

Rose Lamb, 1865

One

'You can't let them dig in the ditch behind the churchyard wall,' Melissa said. 'I'm terribly sorry, but you can't.'

The May afternoon was dying splendidly, in a bloody flush across the towers of Quenville. Johnny and Melissa, with plans and papers and Rose's poems scattered around them, were drinking Bloody Marys on the trailer steps.

Johnny, sure that victory was almost in his grasp, took a moment to redirect his attention to Melissa. For the past few days, he realized, she had been abstracted and odd. They had fucked like animals, but she had been wrapped in melancholy. He had glanced up from Rose's papers to find her staring at him besottedly. She had often stroked his hair, with a kind of brooding protectiveness. Now, she was sorrowful, but businesslike.

He asked: 'Why not?', annoyed to have his plans opposed. 'It's ours now. The locals mightn't like it, but that's tough.'

She sighed and set down her glass. 'I was looking for the right time to tell you. I suppose I hoped I could make it go away. Darling, I'm afraid you're going to be terribly cross.'

'Oh shit,' he said. 'Let's have it, then.'

'There's something you have to clear up.'

Johnny let out a loud groan of irritation. 'Oh, for fuck's sake – I can't let you out of my sight for a minute!'

'I'm so sorry, Johnny.'

'I mean, why didn't you ask me first?'

'There wasn't time. To tell you the truth, I panicked. And then afterwards, I knew you'd be furious.'

'Oh, and my being furious is worse than you being arrested, is it? Jesus Christ! You silly mare. You should have told me.'

'My darling – ' she laid her hand on his hair, and her eyes filled when he jerked his head crossly away. 'I did it for you. I was only thinking of you.'

'Shit, shit, shit.' He drained his glass, and kicked it down the steps, to join the rest of the debris under the trailer. 'Ernie said he'd gone missing. I might have guessed, if I'd had my wits about me.'

'I had to! I couldn't let him get away – it was all I could think of! He was going to the police, and I'm sure he suspected about Will. I did it for you! You'd have done the same.'

'I bet you did it right fucking badly. You've no idea, you.'

'I didn't want to bother you, but it was hard enough rolling him down in the ditch. I couldn't possibly bury him all by myself.'

'Bury him! Thank God you didn't. We'd only have had to dig the bugger up again.'

'Why?'

'Give me strength. Because having a body in your back garden looks a tad obvious – oh gracious, Inspector, however did that get there?'

Melissa hung her head. 'I think you're being rather mean about this. I naturally checked that nobody knew he was coming here.'

Johnny sighed. 'Okay. The light's going, let's take a look.'

Melissa slipped on her Armani sunglasses, and set out towards Shenley as if strolling on the Croisette at Cannes. You have to hand it to her, Johnny thought – another woman would have made a hell of a fuss. In fact, he liked Melissa best when she reminded him what a high-maintenance model she was. Poor bloody Will – no wonder he hadn't been able to handle her.

The field where she had found the ring was irregular in shape, with a ragged edge of brush and bushes which abutted on the most neglected, obscure corner of the churchyard. It was not overlooked by the last, straggling houses of the village. Either she had been lucky, or she had managed the affair pretty well.

She said: 'When did you speak to Ernie?'

'Eh?' His mind was busy on the problem.

'Did she ring you from London?'

'What? Oh, yes. I was in the cottage. She knew one of us would be there.'

'I wonder what she wanted,' Melissa mused.

'She was worried about Giles. With good reason, as it turns out.'

She tucked her hand into his. 'Poor Ernie, she's going to hate this. I'm glad you talked to her before you knew anything – not that I don't trust you to lie.' She smiled to herself. 'Actually, I sometimes think she's got one of her crushes on you. I'd be livid, if it wasn't so pathetic. At least she's got the sense not to try anything.'

She was about to turn into the lane that led to the church-yard, but Johnny held her back. 'Not that way. Someone'll see.'

'But my shoes – oh, all right.'

They ducked into the bushes, where clots of mud and old leaves sloped down towards the ditch. Roofed in by branches, she led Johnny to the deepest place, and pointed.

He stood there for a long time, looking down.

Eventually he said: 'I wondered where that knife had got to.'

It was sticking out of Giles's chest, buried to the hilt in a sticky ooze of black blood. His lips were drawn back over his teeth, in a parody of a smile. His eyes, half-open, were slits of despair. And he was pocked and pebbled and splattered with blood – it had jetted across his face, which had the greyish, bluish tinge of early decomposition, and grotesquely stained the white strip of his roman collar.

Johnny skidded down the steep bank of the ditch for a closer look. Melissa, her dark glasses turned up elegantly in her hair, watched him from above.

'I was awfully fond of him,' she said regretfully. 'I loathed doing it – and you're right, I did it badly. He squirmed about for ages. I ended up begging him to lie still, if you can imagine that.'

With an expert eye, Johnny glanced up the slope to the edge of the churchyard. 'There'll be blood and God knows what,' he said. 'We'd better clear this lot first thing.'

'I was weeping buckets,' Melissa went on, as if she had not heard. 'I kept telling him I didn't want to hurt him. And do you know the worst part? Once I'd got the knife in his chest, I thought that would finish him off – but it didn't. He moaned and groaned, and looked down at it, watching while the blood gushed over his hands. So I thought I'd better have another try, and I grabbed the knife – and, Johnny, I couldn't get it out again! And it hurt him so dreadfully, I couldn't bear it. So I just waited for him to bleed to death.'

'You're all heart,' Johnny said.

'Darling, he was going to tell the police about the night you dumped him! I couldn't let him do that!'

Johnny had seen dead bodies before, and was not afraid of them. But the chill in his veins had nothing to do with Giles. The magnificence of Melissa filled him with awe. Dear God, she was weird on a grand scale. For the first time, it occurred to him that he had made a mistake. She was not his soul mate, his missing half. There was something black and chaotic in Melissa that would be beyond anyone's control.

A picture of Ernestine rose up in his mind's eye. With a supreme effort of will he pushed it away to concentrate on the matter in hand.

'What about your clothes?'

'In a plastic bag, under the bed. Should I have burned them?'

She was deferring to him as an expert in a way that made his mouth taste bad.

'No,' he said. 'We'll have a big bonfire tomorrow, when we start clearing this land. Was there anything left around the church?'

'I don't know. I don't think anything shows. What are you going to do with him?'

He wiped his hands on his jeans. 'First off, we'll wait till it's dark, and bring my car down to the bottom of the lane outside the church. Then you'll get me one of those big sheets of polythene they're using in the library. You'll help me wrap him up. What did you do with his car?'

'I hid it, behind the old kitchens.'

'I need his keys. And some black tape. And a cigarette.'

'What for?'

'To smoke, you daft cow.'

She laughed, and threw him down her cigarettes and lighter. The lighter landed with a dull thud on Giles's stomach. 'Shan't be long,' she said.

Johnny perched on the mulch of rotten leaves and twigs, listening to the silence that followed her hurried rustlings through the bushes. The corpse at his feet mocked the May freshness all around him. Even here, in this rank, forgotten briar patch, the new leaves were fat and green and the hedges jewelled with flowers.

He did not care about dead bodies and he did not care about May, but this had stirred the war inside himself to a frenzy. He found that he was thinking about Rose again, and the poems that he had put aside because they contained no clues. These useless chants filled his head, and he could not help recalling the epitaph she had scribbled for the clergyman who had loved her, all those years ago:

> All sorrows, be they e'er so deep, will end.
> Farewell, my best and truest friend –
> Faithful heart, so vainly plighted,
> May you now love, and be requited.

Ernestine had infected him, and he was suffering an attack of what he supposed he must identify as pity – all the more acute because he had never allowed himself to feel such a thing before. She had, somehow, robbed him of his power to fend off the knowledge of Giles's terrible last moments.

Don't think of it, don't – of Melissa's tearful face, as his life oozed and bubbled away into the earth.

This man, he thought, loved me. Once upon a time, this man used to say he'd die for me. And now he's done it. Well, if there's such a thing as afterwards, I hope you find it better

337

than this, your poor wretched bastard. May you now love, and be requited.

Johnny Ferrars, what the hell has happened to you?

With a shaking hand, he lit one of Melissa's cigarettes. Naturally, his mind fastened upon Ernestine.

She never mentioned it, but he knew she was wondering about their future – to be precise, wondering if they had one. She was deeply, mutely wounded by his failure to consummate his worship with the physical act of love.

It hurt him too, like knives. He was in the ridiculous position of possessing Melissa – the woman who had kept his blood at simmering point since the first moment he saw her – while whacking off over fantasies about her cousin.

But the fact was, fucking Ernestine would mean too much. It would amount to making a choice between the two women. If he had Ernie, he would lose Melissa. And the Johnny who loved Ernestine was knitted into the Johnny who was addicted to Melissa. Love did not come into this one. It was an enslavement, an irresistible pull towards the other half, his worst self. Their minds and bodies operated together in a harmony so seamless, it was almost uncanny.

Yet, at the very moment he should have felt most attuned to Melissa, they had never been further apart. He half wished he could wind the clock back to that first afternoon in the ruins of Quenville, to urge his past self not to pick the wrong girl.

Too late. Staring down at Giles's dead face, Johnny broke into harsh sobs, each one wrenched out of him like a tooth. He was lumbered with Melissa now.

'I'd be livid,' she had said, 'if it wasn't so pathetic.'

Not for his own sake. For Ernie's.

Two

She flung herself against him before he got to the top of the stairs, sobbing with an abandoned passion that made her almost unrecognizable.

Frank, in a peculiar way, immediately felt less frightened. Ernestine's explosive grief was the very thing he needed, to help him control his own. In all the time he had known her, she had never shown herself so abjectly helpless. He wrapped his arms around her, and was shocked to feel her ribs sharp beneath his fingers – when had she wasted away to this? She was in a bad way, and Frank reproached himself for not noticing ages before. This had been building for months, and the latest tragedy had all but broken her – capable, common-sensical Ernie, barely able to hold herself together.

Being Ernestine, she rapidly gathered herself into an approximation of self-control, breaking away from Frank to blow her nose vigorously. Inevitably, she put the kettle on. Frank wrenched it away from her.

'Sit down. Ernie, for God's sake, sit down.'

'No, really, I – '

'I'll make the tea, or the coffee, or whatever.'

He pushed her down into one of the kitchen chairs. Ernestine's flat was crowded with piles of photographs; proofs for her next book. The large cork notice board was covered in beauty shots of hedgerow herbs and wild berries. Beside the smug gloss of these images, Ernestine herself looked terrible. She was barefoot and in her dressing gown, at three in the afternoon. And she had cried herself nearly blind.

Frank sat down opposite her, and pressed her cold hands

between his palms. 'Sweetheart, I only just heard, or I'd have been here earlier.'

'Oh,' she murmured, 'I'm so glad you came.'

He could not resist asking: 'What about Johnny? Have you heard from him?'

'No. I tried, but I can't get a reply. And it had to be you, Frank. Except for you and me and Mel, all the Wild Young Bohemians seem to be gone. I need someone who understands.'

'I know.'

'We're jinxed. We're cursed.'

'Hey, come on. Get a grip.' This was not like Ernestine. Getting tangled with Johnny, he thought, had sent her round the bend. He expected spooks and hobgoblins from Melissa – even found them alluring when coming out of her mouth – but in Ernie it was plain, unvarnished nonsense. 'You need some coffee.' He kissed her hand gently, and laid it down.

She choked an exhausted sob in the wad of tissues clutched to her nose. 'There's some chocolate biscuits in the Country Diary tin.'

In spite of everything, this made Frank laugh. 'Well, that's dandy, but I would have stayed anyway. Jesus, Ern – you don't think much of me, do you?'

'I think the world of you,' she said, with a fresh outburst of sobs, 'and fuck you if you can't see it.'

'Fuck! She said fuck! Oh my lordy, pass the fucking smelling-salts!'

'I'm sorry.'

'Don't apologize. Get it out of your system.' He shovelled ground coffee into the cafetiere, scattering it across the tiled work surface. 'Life is a piece of shit right now.'

'I keep wishing,' she said, 'that I could wake up, and all this past year would be a dream.'

'What, even the discovery of the great love of your life? No, scrub that. What a mean thing to say.'

'Even that,' Ernestine said. 'I told you, it doesn't make me happy. I suppose you think I'm an idiot, still believing in happiness.'

Frank poured coffee, set it down, and joined her again at the table. 'As a matter of fact, I kind of owe Johnny Ferrars an apology. I'd almost persuaded myself that he killed Giles.'

'I know you had.'

'I should have looked nearer home, and guessed that one of his customers would do for him in the end. The priest before him was stabbed too, you know. And I've met the guy they arrested. His name's Ed, and I gave him a fiver once to stop him using Giles as a punchbag.'

'Didn't Giles know he was dangerous?'

Frank shrugged sadly. 'No more so than all the others, I guess. He swore the old drunk was harmless. He reckoned he knew real evil when he saw it.'

'Did they tell you exactly what happened? The police-woman who rang me wouldn't say anything.'

He reached out to stroke her hair. 'Should you be hearing it now? You look just awful.'

'Please. I can't feel any worse.'

'Well, they called me as soon as they found him. Pre-sumably because I was the one who reported him missing.' Automatically, Frank tipped back his chair to reach for the biscuit tin and grab a handful of home-made chocolate cookies. 'He was under a pile of rubbish bags, in an alley behind the church hall,' he went on, with his mouth full. 'He'd been knifed, and the knife was still sticking out of him. Though they took it out, of course, before Dan had to identify him.'

'Poor Dan. Have you spoken to him?'

'Nope, only Nina. He was too upset. Christ, it's been a farce. One of the porters called me out of a lecture: excuse me, Mr Darcy, but a friend of yours seems to have been murdered. Good old Oxford.'

'Why? What made him do it?'

'Drink, drugs, poverty. No point in looking for a motive. Down in the gutter, you obviously don't need one.'

'It's so cruel. Giles loved those people. He was always on about how misunderstood they were. And how we were only scared of them because we realized the basic injustice of their situation.'

'There you are. The old Icarian way.' Frank was looking keenly at Ernestine, taking in the new, careworn hollows in her face and missing the old curves. 'Having such pure ideals means flying too near the sun. And flying too near the sun means getting burned. There's some comfort in knowing what a Giles-ish exit it was – the all or nothing of it. You know he never thought twice about making sacrifices for his dispossessed. They'll make a saint of him at his funeral, I dare say.'

'I don't want to think of him as a saint,' Ernestine said. 'I want the naughty Giles. The one who smoked dope in tutorials and peed out of the window on the tourists.'

She wept again, rasping drily because she had run out of tears.

Frank stood up, plucked her out of her chair, and carried her to the bedroom in his arms, secretly dismayed by how light she was. 'Get some sleep,' he said. 'You're wrecked.'

He dropped her on her unmade bed, and covered her with the duvet.

'Everything nice is over,' she mourned. 'And all the nice people are leaving us.'

'Sleep, Ernie.' He kicked off his shoes, and lay down beside her. It seemed entirely natural to hold her as she fell asleep. Warmed by her body, and feeling her heart beating against his chest, he gazed up at the familiar pattern of light on her bedroom ceiling.

Frank, he told himself sadly, this time you have really cacked up. You miss her, you love her, and now it's too late.

'"The Captain was the last to jump, the first to hit the ground,"' sang Melissa. '"And he ain't going to jump no more! Glory, glory, what a terrible way to die –"'

She was throwing bundles of twigs and branches on to the bonfire, raising a tower of smoke. Since dawn the previous day, she and Johnny had been tearing up the area of the field around the ditch. The guiltiest corner of it was now reduced

to bald soil, from which roots of weeds snaked out like spaghetti. Melissa had proved unexpectedly game about manual
labour. While Johnny struggled with axe and saw, she hefted
and pulled with remarkable energy.

Johnny, on the whole, did not mind. He had intended to
dig up the entire field anyway, starting with this section. He
only felt a little sour when he reflected that he had travelled
a bloody long way to end up covering his hands with common blisters.

' " – what a terrible way to die, and he ain't going to jump
no more!" '

Earlier, Melissa had dealt charmingly with a woman from
Shenley, who had arrived with an angry smile, demanding to
know if they had permission for the fire and how long it was
going to last.

'We're frightfully sorry,' Melissa had said. 'Do forgive us
for not popping round to ask if it would be all right. How
inconsiderate of us.' Afterwards, when the woman had retreated, mollified, she had murmured: 'Cunt.'

Full of surprises, Johnny thought. All those tears for Giles
had turned into a fascinated hunger for the details of his dis-
posal. Now she said: 'How clever you've been. We don't
really need to do all this. They'll have no reason to suspect
he was here.'

'They've made an arrest, according to the bit in the
paper.'

'Yes, wasn't it funny seeing it all in the paper? Funny
peculiar, I mean. Not funny ha-ha.'

'Oh, I dunno,' Johnny said. 'Old Etonian vicar stabbed by
wino. It has its funny side.'

'I'll have to get up the courage to ring Ernie again,'
Melissa said. 'I had to pretend I was too stricken with grief
to talk. Actually, I couldn't bear her howling. God, you'd
think they'd been married or something. She was just as bad
with Will.'

Idly, Johnny amused himself imagining Melissa suffering
real pain – it would have to be physical pain, since she did
not understand any other sort. He hated it when she mocked

Ernestine. And recently it had got worse, which renewed his fear that she had guessed something.

'Thank God,' she said, 'Ernie was away that night. She would have ruined everything, bless her. As it is, there's nothing that can be remotely traced to us.'

'Except that knife,' Johnny said. 'I didn't have time to take it out. It was a posh one, too. Not the sort of thing your average drunk keeps in his kitchen.'

'The Sabatier,' Melissa said. 'Oh, they'd never dream it came from us. It belonged to Ernie.'

'Oh, did it? Well, fancy that.' He struck his spade violently into the soil, mouthing: 'Bitch, bitch, bitch,' with each stroke. His divided self split; one half very much inclined to laugh, and the other dreaming of ramming the blade of the shovel into Melissa's white throat.

Bitch. She would have sold her own cousin into bondage, the person she claimed to love best in all the world. Despite his physical exhaustion, he ached to fuck her.

Three feet down, the spade rang against stone. Johnny froze.

'What's the matter? Oh my God – you've found something.'

He breathed deeply several times, terrified of facing a disappointment like the last. But he could feel the certainty of the treasure running like an electrical current, right to the roots of his hair.

They stared at one another, soul to soul. In tense silence, Johnny worked the spade along the hard ridge under the soil.

'There's something here,' he said. 'A drain? Was there ever a drain here?' He was begging her to contradict him, to comfort him with hope.

Melissa picked up the other spade. 'Don't be ridiculous.'

Impatiently, she stuffed her long hair down the back of her denim jacket, and her eyes blazed when she felt the ridge for herself. She looked so flaringly, incandescently, erotically beautiful that Johnny was shaken by a wave of desire like a punch in the stomach.

Together they worked in silence, white-faced and grimly apprehensive. Occasionally, they glanced up and exchanged tense smiles. In silence, they took a break for a joint, sitting on the earth and staring at the excavation as if it might suddenly vanish.

After an hour or so, Melissa walked over to the cottage, and returned with a Thermos of hot coffee. They drank it from plastic cups, which they stood on the exposed spine of stone. Still silent, they reached out for each other and made love among the heaps of soil. Johnny pulled Melissa's jeans down to her knees, bent her over, and plunged into her from behind, gripping her breasts. His orgasm rocked through them both violently. It was an urgent, ferocious coupling, to be got through as quickly as possible. They began work again while their hearts were still thudding and their loins twitching with the after-pangs.

When the light had begun to fade, Melissa fetched two tins of beer from the trailer, and they drank it while surveying their discovery.

'This ought to be champagne,' Melissa said. They were both too tired for rejoicing, and too sick with anticipation.

'I don't want to stop,' Johnny said. 'But this is going to take days.'

They had uncovered a shallow trough; two narrow stone walls with jagged tops, as if someone had knocked down the bricks in a hurry. There had been a bad spell, when they seemed to have drawn a dreadful blank. Then, pouring sweat, Johnny had attacked the far corner of the trough, and his spade had found the next layer of stone.

Melissa had whispered, in anguish: 'A step!'

'Looks like it.'

Now, sipping her beer, she said: 'This remind me of the stories Tess used to read us. Someone was forever opening a tiny door in a tree, and discovering a flight of steps.'

'Where did it lead?'

'Gnome-land, usually. If there was treasure, it turned out to be a cloak of invisibility, or something equally useless.'

'I dunno. I could do with one of those.'

345

Melissa wrapped her hand around his arm, and leaned her head against his shoulder. 'If this is nothing, I can't bear it.'

'Obviously it's not nothing.'

'What shall we do?'

He frowned. 'Can you remember anything on your plans that might explain this? Anything at all?'

'No. If this had been marked, Rose's son would never have sold the field. And if he'd managed to miss it, my father would have found it. Tess said he walked round every inch of land for miles with a metal-detector.'

'She buried it too deep.'

'Johnny, have you ever tried to imagine what "it" will be?'

'Sometimes. What do you think?'

Dreamily, she considered. 'Well, when I was little, I always assumed it would be pearls, because of the verse in the Bible. And all the poems are about jewels. But it might be money. I only hope she had the sense to change it to gold. I absolutely dread finding some worthless heap of government bonds.'

'Don't!' The bare idea made him wince.

'Part of me wouldn't mind, actually. I've got Will's money, so I'm not exactly poor. And solving the mystery would be wonderful enough.'

Johnny, with a black scowl, shook off her hand. 'Not for me, it wouldn't.'

He knew, in every cell of his body, that he was a hair's-breadth away from the discovery that would give shape and reason to his entire life. Nothing else had any relevance. Nothing else was real, or worth a damn. With his fingers tingling to embrace the ultimate prize, Ernestine and all the pangs she had brought him were blown away to atoms.

Three

The day of Giles's funeral broke in pale May sunshine, with an air of solemn festivity, like a wedding morning. The market outside the church had been closed as a mark of respect, and the traders stood with heads bowed beside their shuttered stalls. Heaps and drifts of early summer flowers lined the gutters. They had been piling up around St Benet's since the day the body had been found.

As Frank had predicted, they were sending him to his long home as a saint and martyr. The remaining Wild Young Bohemians found that all grief for Giles had been taken out of their hands and wrought into a high symbol of sacrifice. Reporters and television crews had come, partly to record the mourning of Giles's famous father, but mainly as a reflection of the intense public interest in the good shepherd of the slums, who had died at the hands of one of his own flock.

The Mayor was there, and the local MP, but the service had been hijacked and orchestrated by the Anglo-Catholic mighty. In robes of gilt and sable they had flocked from all over London, closing ranks around their brother. They had staked their claim upon his body, so that his friends felt almost apologetic for sorrowing for the man himself, instead of the idea. Their invitations were scrutinized at the door, and they were shown into obscure corners of the nave, behind the black wall of priesthood that crowded half the pews.

The Bishop of the diocese, a graven image of tribal burial rites, was enthroned magnificently in his mitre, flanked by six priests from neighbouring parishes, and Giles's successor, who had been appointed in a flurry of publicity and was

347

regarded with sorrowful veneration like a kamikaze pilot. Crowds of acolytes performed a mute ballet around the altar steps, in clouds of incense.

On one side of the chancel, the choir stalls were crammed with a group of singers from Giles's Oxford college. They faced a black gospel choir from a local Pentecostal church; the only splash of colour in their robes of turquoise and crimson.

All that remained of Giles lay on trestles at the top of the nave, in a black coffin, bare except for a biretta perched on the wood above his sightless eyes. The Oxford choir sang Sir John Stainer's 'God So Loved the World', and the lush, Victorian harmonies lent cruel poignancy to the hoarse sobs of poor Dan Ross. Giles's mother was beside him, her black-ringed eyes shocked and tearless beneath inappropriate hennaed hair.

Ernestine and Melissa stood with their arms clasped round each other's shoulders, Johnny and Frank were trying not to look at each other.

Johnny thought: Fuck me, it's like that joke about hell, where you can't see the fire for vicars.

He resisted the temptation to look at his watch, and marvelled over Melissa's grief – genuine without a doubt. The fact that it was genuine frightened him. Had she forgotten watching the poor sod's dying agonies? Had she forgotten wrapping him in polythene, and the hideous time they had had getting the corpse into the boot of his own car? Or the difficulty of abandoning that car in a Poplar back street, without being seen?

What were they doing here, anyway? Quite apart from the fact that the Quenville earthworks were at a crucial stage, their presence was spectacularly ill-advised. They were far too near a pew full of respectful policemen. Besides which, Ernestine was so close, he could smell her. It took all his willpower to stick to his decision, when he longed to wrap his arms around her, and press her against the heart he only knew he had with her.

Frank, a few feet away, was in a crisis of severe emotional

confusion. His chest heaved with the effort of subduing his sobs for Giles. Melissa and Ernestine kept merging and separating in his mind, until he hardly knew where one ended and the other began – let alone which one he really loved. Added to this were the flashes of violent, almost sexual desire to shed Johnny's blood.

From the lectern, someone read: 'Jesus said, Father, forgive them, for they know not what they do.'

Two male singers warbled a duet from Stainer's *Crucifixion*. Johnny saw and heard the spectre of his old headmaster, and for a moment, could have yelped aloud with panic.

> 'Oh! 'twas love, in love's divinest feature,
> Passing o'er that dark and murd'rous blot,
> Finding, e'en for each low-fallen creature,
> Though they slay Thee – one redeeming spot.'

If this terrible, ungovernable yearning for Ernestine is my one redeeming spot, Johnny thought, it burns like acid. I don't want to be redeemed.

The Bishop, a thickset man with jutting grey eyebrows, removed cloak and mitre and climbed the steps of the pulpit. When the rustling and coughing had faded to silence, he said: 'I would like to extend a personal welcome to you all, especially to Father Ross's family and friends. It's hard for you to hear, in the midst of your grief, the word "thanksgiving". But I do want you to leave this church with a feeling of celebration, for a life rich in beauty and fruitfulness.'

Then, in a different voice, dipping down an octave, he intoned: 'Letter of St Paul to the Hebrews, chapter eleven, verse thirteen. "These all die in faith, not having received the promises, but having seen them afar off, and were persuaded of them, and embraced them, and confessed that they were strangers and pilgrims on the earth." In the name of the Father, the Son and the Holy Spirit.'

There was another rustling movement, like wind rippling across a barley field, when the congregation crossed itself.

'"Strangers and pilgrims on the earth,"' the Bishop repeated. 'It's an image full of special meaning for many of us, who remember Giles preaching on the same text at his induction here, only a few short months ago.'

Ernestine realized that she had never heard Giles preach, and that this was a part of his life none of his oldest friends had chosen to share. She turned over her sodden handkerchief, searching vainly for a dry patch. Frank, without looking at her directly, pushed a fresh tissue into her hand.

'Here was a young man following the promise he had seen far off. A man humbled by the constant awareness that he was a stranger and a pilgrim, and driven to include other strangers in his pilgrimage.

'Giles came to me last year, after he had set up his drug rehabilitation programme in Tower Hamlets. It had been a huge success, but he wasn't satisfied. He wanted, he said, to extend the message to all the people who had dropped through the holes in society's net. The poor, the criminalized, the addicted, the homeless, the dispossessed. The travelling people, for whom he had a special affinity.

'Well, it was ambitious, even rather crazy, but those of you who knew Giles will also know how difficult it was to prevent him getting his own way.'

There was a scattering of priestly laughter from the black-clad divines in the front pews.

The Bishop smiled, and leaned on the pulpit almost with jocularity. 'He said, I want your most run-down, needy and desperate parish, and I want to turn it round. You don't want much, I said.'

Another, louder laugh.

'But there was no denying the strength of his ambition.' He was grave again. 'As he was always the first to admit — indeed, it was a cornerstone of his faith — Giles's mission had a deeply personal motivation. Let's consider his history. Here was a young man, blessed with every advantage education and money can bestow. A man who had been to Eton and Oxford, and seemed destined to take his place among rulers and trend-setters.

'Instead, he was called to take a place amongst people society considers the lowest of the low. Now, except in the most general terms, Giles never spoke of his time with the travellers. But we know he emerged from it with a Christian faith that was never to waver again. Like his Master, he suffered rejection and betrayal, yet felt only love for those who had betrayed him.'

Johnny wanted to snarl like a cornered animal. He closed his eyes, to fend off the memory of Giles in the ditch all those years ago, with the rain pelting his naked body. Ernestine's flowery scent was making a knot of queasiness in his stomach, and he could have hit her.

'Love, in the end,' the Bishop went on, 'is what we must take as Giles's standard. Do we want to condemn the man who killed him? Of course. Would Giles have condemned him? Never. This was a man he loved; a man he wanted to help and save. If we allow ourselves to be ruled by anger, we defile his memory.'

Heads turned, as a scuffle broke out at the back of the church. There was a crash as a door was thrown back on its hinges, and angry shouts. A group of about twenty men – filthy, unshaven moving masses of rags – were being pinioned by churchwardens and sidesmen. They had fought their way in, and brought a low, harsh drone of wailing. Many were crying loudly, their tears making river-beds along their grimy cheeks. A few clutched bottles in brown paper bags.

Johnny was near enough to catch the ferocious smell that gusted in with them. He felt as if someone was pressing his temples, and sweat broke out on his back. Jesus, he thought furiously, I'm going to hurl.

In triumph, the Bishop seized the moment. 'Yes, let them stay! Please come in, all of you – you're very welcome – you have more right to be here than any of us. You are Father Ross's own people, and we should thank you for letting us share your mourning.'

Shocked out of their rebelliousness, Giles's ragged customers subsided into a more or less silent huddle at the back of the church – except for one man, who charged along the aisle before he could be stopped, and flung his arms around the coffin with a vinous howl. Two of the priests nearby plucked him off and led him away, and the Bishop continued against the retreating sound of his lamentation. 'This – this is surely the very centre of everything Giles believed. That we should not only help the dispossessed, but lay them a place at our tables.'

Johnny fixed his gaze on the pew in front, pouring every atom of concentration into not throwing up. Of all the places to disagree with his breakfast –

'Because we make all kinds of excuses to ourselves, don't we? We tell ourselves there's a difference between the "deserving" and the "undeserving". We, who are rich in the gifts of human love, cannot understand the lonely outcast who has never known love.'

The varnished wood of the pew suddenly leaped up at Johnny's eyes. He blacked out in the instant before it banged against his forehead.

Ernestine and Melissa, in one voice, hissed: 'Johnny, darling –'

Ernestine scrambled over Melissa to sit on his other side. Both drew his sagging body upright, and both tried to rest his head on their shoulders. Then they stared into each other's wild, anxious faces. A look of outraged astonishment dawned in Melissa's eyes, and was met by Ernestine's look of terrified guilt.

In one blinding moment of recognition, the cousins saw the passionate, unreasonable love they had both saved all their lives, for the same man.

Johnny's eyes opened, and Frank found himself holding his breath, as they moved from one cousin to the other.

He muttered, loud enough for the people behind to hear: 'I'm going to throw up.' Shaking off Melissa and Ernestine, he stumbled into the side aisle, and hared off towards the door.

Melissa and Ernestine immediately ran after him – Frank saw the mutual animosity swallowed in concern for the man they loved. He wanted to crack Johnny's ribs like a walnut shell, and toss his innards to the four winds.

Fortunately, the Bishop had finished, and the congregation were standing for a hymn. Frank, grasping the typed service sheet, followed the words without seeing them. His instinct, he discovered, was to protect Ernestine. Oh God, if that man hurt her . . .

Then he waited for the familiar flash of yearning for Melissa, and did not know which beloved heart he would choose to break.

Once upon a time, everything had been sunny and simple. Sir Bors, Sir Percival and Sir Galahad had sat at the feet of the two girls, taking spiritual nourishment from the beauty of one and physical nourishment from the picnic basket of the other.

But Will was dead, and now Giles. In his bitter loneliness for his friends, Frank could not be comforted by thinking of them in the city of God. Four of the Bohemians had crossed the river into middle-age – Dash, Bella, Cecily and Craig, united in parenthood in another pew. Two of the group were gone for ever. The Reaper was busy with his scythe, and Frank could not help wondering – who would be next?

The street outside was crowded with locals and reporters, a wall of eyes. Ernestine barely noticed them. Johnny dashed into the church hall, and she and Melissa were just in time to catch the stench of the men's lavatory as the door banged in their faces.

Melissa called: 'Johnny darling, are you all right?'

The reply was a gurgle of vomiting, seasoned with moans.

'How revolting,' Melissa said.

Awareness returned to Ernestine, and deep embarrassment with it. Looking through the open doors into the main hall, she saw they had an audience. A dozen churchwomen, with aprons and overalls over their best dresses, were staring at them. Rows of trestle tables, covered with paper cloths, were laden with plates of food, and Ernestine realized they had disturbed a sacred ritual.

353

If the women at the foot of the Cross had been splendid English church ladies, their grief would have found expression in Shippam's paste, extra large tubs of marge and sliced white Wonderloaf. When they met death, they immediately cut sandwiches.

Ernestine found herself wishing she had spent the service being a tower of strength in here, taking trays of sausage rolls out of a borrowed microwave and saying to everyone: 'Don't thank me, dear.' She could have laid out the wine glasses and eased the horrid bought quiches out of their foil cases.

For it would not have done at all to provide a better funeral feast. It was a bishop's duty to drink bad red wine in shabby church halls, and afterwards to put his head into the kitchen to thank everyone for the 'splendid spread'. Ernestine felt a sudden throb of longing to belong to their harmless, righteous world. She smiled timidly. A couple of the women whispered and stared, recognizing her from the television. Then, thankfully, they threw themselves back into their work.

Melissa lit a cigarette. She had not noticed the watchers. For her, any person below a certain social class or level of attractiveness was simply invisible.

She was considering Ernestine, with worrying detachment. 'You didn't need to rush out,' she said.

'I wanted to make sure he was all right.'

'How sweet. But I'm sure he's fine now. You'd better go back.'

Ernestine's scalp prickled. She chose her words carefully, tip-toeing across the dreaded minefield of Melissa's displeasure. 'Oh, I don't want to cause any more disturbance. I just thought Johnny might be ill. I thought I might be able to help.'

Melissa's lips were curved in a calm smile, but Ernestine found herself thinking of the hooded snakes which quiver, trance-like, before they pounce.

This is it, she thought. She braced herself to face the pain of Melissa's anger – the whole battery of coldness, spite and heart-rending reproach she knew so well, and had devoted such energy to deflecting. Suddenly, at this low point in her life, she refused to make the effort. She was not going to launch into her usual routine of grovelling apology. Why, she thought, should I end up begging her to love me when her love has always been so bloody conditional and self-serving?

'Darling,' Melissa said tenderly, 'I'm afraid you made rather an exhibition of yourself just now.'

'Did I?'

'Oh Ernie, come on. You only showed half the world you were nursing one of your pathetic little crushes.'

'I told you, I was worried – '

'Bollocks. You fancy Johnny, don't you?'

'I'm very fond of him,' the turning worm said, with all the dignity she could muster. 'And I know what made him ill.'

'Chips for breakfast.'

'No! If you cared about him at all, you'd know too. It was the Bishop, talking about outcasts. He could have been describing poor Johnny.'

'Poor Johnny!' mewed Melissa, mocking her concern. 'Just be thankful you can't really get inside his head. My God, you'd have kittens.'

'I'm not going to have a row with you outside a lavatory door.'

'Yes, you are. Because if you think I'm going to put up with you mooching around, making sentimental cow's eyes – dear God, I might have known, when you started popping round with little pots of jam.'

'Mel, we're at a funeral – '

'I know you haven't been fucked since the Flood, but I can't believe you'd do this to me.'

'I haven't done anything to you,' Ernestine said. She was sorry now that this was true – you may as well be hanged for a sheep as for a lamb.

'You have! You've dared to fancy the only man I've ever loved in my whole life.' Melissa's eyes suddenly swam in tears. 'You can't care a damn about me, or you wouldn't even dare to think about him.'

355

'Go ahead,' Ernestine said, through gritted teeth. 'Make a scene. Let's seal our relationship with a quarrel over a man, like some photo-story in *Jackie* magazine.'

'It's the nerve of you, apart from anything else – imagining a man like Johnny would touch a woman like you with tongs.'

Ernestine said: 'He never has touched me.'

'I know what this is all about. You've never forgiven me for having Frank that time.'

'What time? Oh, who cares, anyway?'

'You do! Frank's always been stuck on me, and you've dreamed of paying me back ever since – wouldn't it be marvellous if I could steal Mel's man like she stole mine?'

The splendid women were watching again. Ernestine lowered her voice. 'You know I don't think things like that. Bloody hell, you begged me to like Johnny.'

'I didn't expect this. Not from you, of all people.'

'Get this straight, Mel. Johnny has never laid a finger on me. Try to imagine something that goes beyond sex.'

'I've never had to,' Melissa said. 'That's for people who can't get laid.'

Stung directly on her unlaid place, Ernestine reddened, and snapped: 'Actually, there is another kind of communication, between two people who really love each other. I do love Johnny – and he loves me.'

'I dare say. You've made quite a nice thing, haven't you, of providing home comforts for men who love me? A shoulder, a bosom, a nice cup of tea. Well, if what you do is so great, why do they all prefer me?'

The truth of this smote Ernestine to sickened silence.

Melissa sighed, and crushed her cigarette under the heel of her expensive black court shoe. 'I hoped we'd never come to this. I mean, listen to us. I'm sorry for you, darling. But for your own sake, you should drop this silly fantasy about Johnny. Obviously, he doesn't love you. So grow up, and stop playing out of your league.'

Sure of her victory, she opened the Prada handbag slung across her shoulder, and took out a compact. Ernestine watched her dabbing carefully at her damaged mascara.

My league. The B-Team, the eternal understudies. A lifetime of playing second fiddle in the great concerto of Melissa-dom. And people dared to talk about character being more important than beauty – when beauty and character were inextricably bound together. Melissa was a beauty in her bones, and it had shaped her entire personality.

Would I be so different, Ernestine wondered, if I was the one who looked like that?

She had always hoped for 'inner beauty' as compensation. But this was a great deal harder to define than the glaring fact of the outer sort. In the teeth of Melissa's indisputable loveliness, Ernestine had to struggle to remember the particular flavour of her relationship with Johnny.

'He does love me,' she repeated. 'But not in any way that threatens you. I swear, that's the last thing I ever wanted to do.'

'You were nice to him when he had a cold. I expect that's what started it. You know I never can abide a person with a cold.'

In the past, Ernestine would have laughed at this. Now, however, she was in no mood to enjoy the sublime perfection of Melissa's selfishness. 'I listened to him,' she said. 'I allowed him to drop the persona of incurable wickedness you foisted on him.'

'Ernie,' Melissa said, with unbearable kindness, 'this is typical. You know your quest to find good in people leads you up all kinds of garden paths. Look at Joanna Stricker at school, who ended up nicking your purse and your best pencil case.'

'That was years ago!'

'Well, you haven't changed. It's very lovable, darling, but it's very irritating. I told you it was Joanna all along, but you wouldn't listen. You said I was being mean, because she smelled and her eyes were too close together. But which of us was right? Whose locker, in the end, contained your lost Aertex and hockey boots?'

'For God's sake, what a time to bring – '

'I know what Johnny really cares about. My reading of his character isn't as kind as yours, but it's a lot nearer the mark.'

'You make up your mind, and then you'll only see the part that suits you.'

'Oh, I'm completely sick of this. I don't enjoy scrapping with you, Ernie.' As if it were all her fault. 'Let's ask him, shall we?'

She shouted through the door: 'What are you doing in there? Are you ever coming out?'

The door opened. Johnny emerged, wiping his pale, clammy face. He gave Ernestine one glance of shrivelling, dismissive coldness.

Melissa took his arm. 'Ernie was worried about you, darling. Wasn't that sweet of her?'

'Let's get out of here,' Johnny said. 'This was a waste of time.'

'I think you might be politer to her, Johnny. She's just been telling me how much she loves you.'

There was a hair's-breadth pause, in which both cousins waited greedily for vindication.

Johnny scowled, and said: 'Come on, Mel, for crying out loud. We've got work to do at Quenville.'

He charged out of the hall, giving Melissa just enough time to plant a kiss of triumph upon Ernestine's cheek, before rushing after him.

Frank, coming into the hall after the service with Dash and Bella, found her weeping silently in the cramped little kitchen, where she was helping to set teacups on Formica trays. Everyone else assumed she was crying for Giles, but Frank guessed she had suffered the worst, most humiliating kind of rejection.

The man had demanded her love, virtually at gunpoint, and then thrown it back as worthless. Frank saw no limits to his wickedness, yet he was also conscious of relief. When he put his arms round Ernestine, he discovered the first seed of hope for their future. Perhaps they had both been meant to travel round the circle in opposite directions, before coming together again.

Four

'We've found it,' Melissa breathed. She turned eyes that were lamps of exultation towards Johnny. 'This is it, isn't it? And I knew, I always knew I'd be the one.'

They had not risked the rude haste of a jackhammer on something that might be delicate. Instead, they had removed the packed soil from the buried steps with picks and shovels. Melissa said she could happily have torn it out with her bare hands.

There were thirteen steps, each won with rivers of sweat and blistered hands. The night before, they had come up against a thick wooden door, iron-bound and spongy with age. And they had worked all night to unearth it, by the ghostly light of torches, and storm-lanterns borrowed from the cottage. The silver dawn was breaking in the fields above them, as Johnny hefted the last load of clayey soil.

He was haggard and unshaven, burning with feverish energy. His sore, bleeding palms grasped the handle of the pickaxe.

'No – wait,' Melissa begged. 'Now that we're here, I have to think what it will mean.'

He scowled. 'It means we'll be rich. This'll make Will's dosh look like chickenshit.'

'We can turn Quenville into a palace. We'll be the monarchs of the whole county.' She grabbed Johnny's bare, sweat-slimed forearm. 'We can get married. You are going to marry me, aren't you?'

'Course I bloody am.'

'You've never asked.'

He shook her off, snarling softly with impatience. 'You want me to go down on one fucking knee? I'll do it later.'

359

'I'm wearing your ring.' Melissa showed him Rose's diamond, a bulge under a protective sticking-plaster. 'I think of it as yours.'

'Very nice, but hardly necessary. Marrying you is how I get my fair share, nice and legal.'

She smiled, and kissed his cheek. 'You love me a bit, too. We were made for each other, you and I – though in what factory, I shudder to think.'

'Stop pissing about and let me get on.'

'I have to be clear, now that we've reached the final stage. It's going to change so many things. I shall want to have a child. A son.'

'Great. Get the fuck out of my way.'

He swung back the pickaxe. Melissa retreated up the steps. She had begun to pant, as she did when approaching orgasm. 'Yes – yes – I know it's jewels – oh, how shall I bear to sell them?'

'Because I'll make you.' With a shout of triumph, Johnny sunk the pickaxe into the lock. As he did so, he said a mental farewell to the picture of his former self that flashed into his mind; the ragged Ishmael who had staked everything on this moment.

Ernestine? Bugger her. This was all he had ever cared for.

The damp wood around the lock crumbled. When he wrestled out the axe, the iron bonds shivered to dust. The lock broke open in a great, musty exhalation of decay. The barrier was down.

He collapsed against the wall, holding his aching sides. Melissa, white as a spectre under streaks of dirt, crept down to him, holding one of the big torches.

The vault yawned before them, and they stood in the doorway for a moment, staring into the darkness. Both were breathing heavily, and their breath echoed into the unknown. Then Melissa switched on the torch and took Johnny's hand.

For the first time in more than a century, a shaft of light pierced the darkness, revealing an arched brick roof. She gasped as the light snagged a box set into the wall.

'A coffin. Oh God.'

It was wrapped in a grey mantle of cobwebs. Johnny darted forward, tore them off, and exposed a greened brass plate nailed beneath it.

He read: 'Archibald Cameron Menzies Lamb. 1821–1865.'

'Rose's husband,' Melissa said. 'My ancestor.'

The beam of her torch rested on the coffin for a moment, then crept across the vault.

At last, at long last, it fell upon the Quenville treasure. Melissa dropped the torch and screamed.

1865

Dr Arthur Aitcheson took a bite of bread and butter, and threw the rest of his slice down on the rug, where his pet hare was lolloping round his feet. 'I think we may say,' he declared, 'that we have managed our business in a most satisfactory manner. Yes, I think we may congratulate ourselves.'

The three of them were in his study, a large, low-ceilinged room which looked out over the Mulberry trees in his walled garden. There was a smell of ether, chloral and iodine wafting from the rows of bottles in a mahogany cupboard along one wall. Aitcheson was a corpulent bachelor in his fifties, fond of his comforts and happily set in mildly unorthodox ways.

In defiance of any feminine element, his study was crowded with pipes, books, bones, fossils and small animals floating in jars. A stuffed relation of the hare dominated the litter of papers on the chimneypiece. His housekeeper had set the tea table beside the fire, and discreetly left the doctor to the company of the two people he loved most on earth – the Vicar, James Venables, and Rose Lamb.

Venables, tensely perched on the extreme edge of one of the leather chairs, presented the greatest possible contrast to Aitcheson's sleek jauntiness. He was very thin and very pale, and his black clergyman's clothes were rusty at the seams. His lean face was drawn into a permanent grimace of anxiety.

He said: 'I wish you'd be serious. This is hardly the occasion for self-congratulation.'

'Why not? Nobody has found us out. Nor will they, what's more. We are signed and sealed.'

With sudden violence, Venables snapped: 'Dear heaven, as if I cared about being found out! As if that could make the burden on my conscience any heavier!'

'Now, Jim,' soothed Aitcheson, 'who's harmed, eh? That's the way to look at it. We've never seen Rose so happy. That expiates all, in my view.' He filled the bowl of his pipe, and leaned over to light a spill at the fire. 'Don't mind my smoking, do you, Rosie?'

Rose sat in the easiest chair next to the fender, with her feet on a stool and her hands folded protectively over her pregnant belly. She was in heavy widow's mourning, head to toe in black bombazine with a waterfall of black crepe hanging from the crown of her bonnet. Under the deep brim of the bonnet was one glimpse of white – the cumbersome and hideous widow's cap that covered her greying brown hair. The face she turned towards her friends, however, was radiant and almost girlish with contentment.

'Of course I don't mind.'

Both men surveyed her. Aitcheson, who had known her since their childhood, before the raising of Quenville, and Venables, who had loved her since the first stone was laid.

Aitcheson lit his pipe. 'She's our reason and our recompense, Jim. You know I don't have much to do with this God of yours, but even I give the fellow some credit. He wouldn't condemn us for putting her happiness before the letter of the law – a damned unfair law, as I maintain.' He grinned at Rose. 'Have some cake, my dear. Mrs Binner made it for you, and you should be eating. No ladylike appetites now.'

'My appetite is anything but ladylike these days,' she said, laughing, as Venables reverently handed her a slice of cake. 'I'm sure I ought to be worried – the village women shake their heads over me as if I were already marked for the tomb, but I never felt better in my life.'

'You're on the old side,' Aitcheson said briskly, 'but I see no reason why you shouldn't manage just as well as any cottage female. I delivered Meg Streeter's ninth last week, and she's not a day shy of forty-eight. I've been warning Streeter to leave her alone these ten years, but still they keep coming, and she's none the worse.'

An unhealthy flush dyed the Vicar's thin cheeks. 'Arthur!'

'Am I being indelicate again? I beg your pardon. But it's not usually a delicate business.'

'I wish I could make Mrs Lamb's happiness mine,' Venables said. 'I do try. But I've hardly slept since we laid that coffin in the vault.'

Aitcheson gave a shout of laughter, and scooped his pet hare into his lap. 'Our dark secret – eleven and a half stones of Norfolk flint and soil, in the best casket that could be got for money. Even Archie thought it was too good for him.'

Rose smiled, but Venables said, in a low, nervous tone: 'It's not a laughing matter. You don't have to read a Christian burial service over it.'

'Aren't we all dust, Jim, in the end?'

Very quietly, Venables said: 'You didn't have to profane all that you hold sacred.'

Rose's contentment easily flowed into compassion. 'Dear James, I so understand. And I'll be grateful as long as I live. If anyone has sinned, it is I, not you.'

Venables' face plainly showed that he held Rose more sacred than anything. 'Don't be grateful, Mrs Lamb. I would have done more, if I'd had to.'

Aitcheson cheerfully caressed the hare's long ears. 'Well, what have we done, when you get to the bottom of it? The man was a blackguard and a ruffian, who treated Rose abominably.'

'I know, I know – '

'Thank the Lord she came to us first, or he would probably have killed her. Then I would have had to kill him, and he's certainly not worth hanging for.'

'Most certainly not,' said Rose.

'Mind you, I don't think you should have let him rook you for everything, my dear.'

She shrugged dismissively. 'What choice did I have? The money was all he ever wanted from me, or liked about me, and he wasn't going to settle for a penny less than his full due. Legally, of course, it was his anyway. But this way, he could take his mistress away from her husband. I thought it was a fair exchange, for my freedom and my baby. Papa would have hated it – but I paid him when I married Archie.'

'Your father wasn't such a bad man,' pleaded Venables.

Rose's face was instantly flinty. 'How can you say that – you of all people? After he mocked you and accused you, simply for the crime of loving me? He was nothing but a common brewer with a stupid dream about founding a noble family – and he sold me. He handed me over to Archie as a bond-slave, so it serves him right that Archie has his filthy money now.'

'Calm, Rosie, calm,' Aitcheson mumbled through the stem of his pipe. 'Let the dead bury their dead. I still think that black-hearted husband of yours should have left you and your baby with more than a pittance, that's all.'

The anger melted from her face, and the years fell away once more. 'I'm like the man in the Bible, who found a perfect pearl of great price, and sold all he had to buy it. My baby is my pearl. And Ned, of course.'

She was gazing at the fire as she sighed out this last name, and she did not see the reaction it kindled in both men. Aitcheson looked scornful, Venables as if she had stabbed him.

There was a tap at the door, and the housekeeper put her head inside. 'Beg pardon, sir, but Dan Cooper's at the back door. He says the old man's worse, and a-sinking.'

Aitcheson gave a comical groan, and turned the hare off his knee. 'I do wish people wouldn't sink when I'm eating muffins by the fire. All right, Mrs Binner. Tell him I'll be along directly.' He stood up, and plucked off his embroidered smoking cap.

'Yes, sir.' She shut the door.

'I'll make them happy by charging them for one last dose,' Aitcheson said, going to the mahogany cupboard for his black bag, 'then I'll send for you, James. I'm amazed the old fellow has lasted so long. And Rose – you might tell Ned his grandfather's on the way out. If he cares to hear it.'

'I know what you think of him, Arthur. And you are very unjust.'

'Am I?' He threw a couple of bottles into his bag. 'You've spoiled that boy. He was ready enough to make up to old Cooper when he thought he might get some money. Now, he thinks he's above such paltry considerations. The village is talking, my dear, and if you're not careful they'll put two and two together.'

Venables opened his mouth as if to say something, then changed his mind.

Rose said: 'Rest assured, Ned would never do anything to hurt me. One day you'll see.' She rose. 'I must leave, before it is too dark.'

Venables sprang up. 'Allow me to walk with you.'

'Thank you, James.'

When they were outside the house, the doctor kissed her glove. 'Take care, Rose. Remember, I am always here.'

He turned towards the huddle of cottages grouped around Shenley's main street. Rose and Venables, arm-in-arm, took the lane for Quenville. It was autumn, the space before the berries shrivel on the hedgerows. Evening was coming on, and they met several labourers making their way home.

The last of them had tipped his hat. The open country lay before them, with the towers of Quenville looming over the trees.

'Mrs Lamb,' Venables said, 'Rose – '

'Dear James, you only call me Rose when you're about to propose.' She smiled teasingly, so confident of her power over him. 'What can you be thinking of after all these years?'

'Rose, please listen to me. You will think I have lost all reason when you know how I have suffered for my sins already – but I'm ready to commit a graver crime. Far graver. I have buried a man who is not dead. Now, I am asking to marry a widow whose husband I know to be living. No, let me say it!'

Between the high hedges, he halted and took both her hands in his.

'I've loved you for more than twenty years. The day I married you to that brute was the most miserable of my life.'

'And mine,' she said, 'though, God knows, I adored him at the time. How strange, to remember that now.'

'For your sake, dearest Rose, I will turn my back on the laws of heaven, and marry you according to the laws of the earth. And I will love your child as tenderly as I would love my own.'

Tears dripped down his face, which had once been fair and handsome, and was now deeply scored with sorrow and disappointment. Rose caught one of the tears on the tip of her gloved finger, and regarded it curiously.

'Am I worth all this?'

'Will you marry me?'

'No, of course not. You are one of my very dearest friends, but I love someone else. And it's better this way, James, it truly is. I don't deserve a heart like yours.'

'You do – and this heart is so completely yours, I'm prepared to break it once and for all, and make you hate me.'

Rose squeezed his hand affectionately. 'Oh, you can never do that.'

'It's Ned. You must see the truth about him.'

She dropped his hand, and her features froze, as if she was looking at a stranger. 'If you say anything vile about Ned, I shall hate you. Even you.'

Like a man hurling himself over a precipice, Venables gabbled out: 'He doesn't love you. He laughs at you behind your back. When he's drunk, he drops hints about coming into a fortune –'

'You mean, he's after my money like the rest of them?' Rose blazed. 'That's a lie!'

'Have you told him Archie took it all?'

'He won't care.'

'Rose, have you told him the money is all gone?'

'I must go.' She swept her black skirts haughtily in the dust. 'Please don't follow me.'

'Have you told him? No, you haven't!' Wildly, Venables grabbed at her long veil. 'Because you know, in your bones, that he would leave you!'

'How dare you? Let me go at once!' She was trembling with anger.

'Aitcheson forbade me to say anything. He was sure you were perfectly well aware of the young scoundrel's behaviour and turning a blind eye, but I know you better – '

'I won't hear any more slander about the father of my child. If you say another word, I'll hate you for ever.'

'Rose, he's still seeing the girl. The whole world knows, except you. For God's sake, woman – she's bigger with child than you are! And she's the scandal of the village, strutting round calling herself his wife – '

'No, no, no!' Rose screamed, so piercingly that the birds started out of the hedges. 'He loves me! Don't you ever speak to me again. Don't ever – '

And she stumbled away from him, clumsily gathering her yards and yards of black cloth around her.

'This,' said Aitcheson, 'is a glass of brandy. I know you never touch intoxicating liquors, but I'm prescribing. So drink it.' He pushed the glass into Venable's icy fingers. 'You mustn't give way now, man. She needs us more than ever.'

He was whispering. The study was dark, save for the shifting light of the low fire. Rose's inhuman sobs were gradually fading. She lay upon the couch, covered with a rough rug. Both men gazed at her with a kind of awed compassion.

Venables murmured: 'She knelt to me. She begged my forgiveness.' He had been crying quietly, since Rose had thrown herself at his feet in the church porch.

Aitcheson prescribed some brandy for himself, and took a large gulp. 'I'm a fool. I thought she knew. This has all but broken her, poor soul. And she was such a pretty, laughing little creature when I first knew her.' He poured more brandy, and became businesslike. 'It is up to us to save her from being a hanged little creature.'

Venables stifled a high sob of bitterest anguish.

'And I think I see a way,' Aitcheson went on. 'Heaven forgive me for saying so, but I fancy this has happened, if it had to happen, at rather an opportune moment.'

'Opportune!'

'Hear me out, Jim. Consider. The vault Archie built for himself still lies open, and everybody knows she intends to seal the horrid thing. What could be better?'

'You mean – '

'We have a coffin, don't we? Well, now we have a body to place in it.'

Venables goggled at him in horror, but could not help hope dawning in his face. 'So we simply carry him in.'

'It won't be pleasant, old chap. And far from suitable for a clergyman. Perhaps you'd better leave it to me.'

'Absolutely not.' Venables was unexpectedly firm. 'I was in this from the beginning, and this tragedy is probably my fault. I'm damned anyway, so I'll damn myself further.'

'I want James to be there,' Rose's voice floated at them, sharp and clear. Both men jumped guiltily. Rose struggled into a sitting position. Her face was bloated with tears, and her hair wild beneath her widow's cap, but she was no longer hysterical. 'I want you to read the service over him.'

Venables drew in a breath of horror, but Aitcheson signalled to him to be quiet. 'Of course, Rosie,' he said.

'He cannot be laid to rest, without the word of God. And don't we say, he who lives and believes shall never die?'

'Hmm, his own idle, fornicating hide was all he ever believed in,' mumbled Aitcheson.

'He lives – here.' She laid her hand upon her swollen bosom. 'He can never leave me now.'

Venables was alarmed, but the doctor said, imperturbably: 'Rose, go to bed. I'll give you a draught, and wake Mrs Binner to take care of you'

Venables hissed: 'Arthur, are you sure?'

'Binner never asks questions, and never gossips. Now Rosie, tell us where you left him.'

'Asleep. In the meadow where I first saw him, with his head among the flowers.'

'You'll have to be a little clearer. Which meadow?'

'I'll show you.' She heaved herself off the sofa.

'Are you mad?'

'I'm coming, Arthur. I can't leave my darling now.'

The doctor stared at her narrowly, calculating the risk of taking her versus the risk of leaving her behind, and eventually decided it would be safer to take her with them. She seemed strong, but it was a brittle strength. If they crossed her, he did not think he could answer for her mental state. He explained this briefly to Venables, as they collected the dark lantern he took out for night calls, and the gardener's handcart.

'All this has overset her entirely, and I'm all for humouring her. Poor thing, she has a perfect genius for suffering in love. She should have married you years ago.'

'I ought to condemn her,' Venables murmured, 'but I cannot. She laid her purity down in the dirt for his sake. I'd have seen him horsewhipped.

'Thank God, I never fancied marrying her myself,' Aitcheson said grimly, lighting the shuttered lantern and nursing the flame. 'I was never so grateful for my quiet life as I am this minute – though we must be very lucky if it is to remain so. Wait five minutes by the hall clock, then bring Rose through the scullery into the lane.'

The moon was a white sliver, like a nail-paring. It made their progress through the dark lanes slow and hazardous, but reduced the danger of being seen.

Rose insisted upon walking ahead. She did not need the dim light bobbing on the handcart, but strode nimbly over the deep wheel ruts as if it were noon. She did not stop until they were in the shadow of the Quenville gates. Then she picked up the lantern, and beckoned the two men to follow.

Which they did, pressing through a gap in the hedge. Aitcheson swore richly as the branches tore at his clothes, and Venables flinched at the sudden, trundling movement of a cow in the field.

'Here,' she said.

Venables groaned, and began to mumble out a prayer.

Aitcheson said, 'Oh, Rose. Really.'

She sank to her knees in the grass, and tenderly stroked the sleeping shepherd's bloody curls with her hand. His arms were flung out, and his mantle of blood showed black in the feeble glimmer of light. She closed his eyes – those long eyes of arresting, vivid blue, so curiously and seductively shaped.

'Exactly where I found him,' she said, 'like Selene upon Mount Latmos, when she saw Endymion. I couldn't let him leave me. I couldn't let him know corruption. So I made him immortal.'

'Immortal?' echoed the doctor. 'My dear, he is as dead as mutton. Oh, Rose, Rose! What have you done?'

'I have kept him, as the pearl of great price I sold my all to get,' Rose said, with dignity. 'A thing of beauty is a joy forever. Its loveliness increases.'

'Poor Ned's loveliness will not increase, and he will not be a joy. In three days, he'll smell like a rusty cheese.'

'No, you don't understand. This way, he is mine.'

Aitcheson stared down regretfully at the still, handsome face. Rose had learned, belatedly, of passionate love with this man. Archie, before he vanished, had told him what he had often suspected – that he had not slept with his wife for years. Ned, full of sap, had given her the child she longed for, and she had sent her wretch of a husband off to New Zealand with every penny-piece she owned. They had both pined for their freedom, and Archie had easily won the best of the bargain.

If only the beautiful lout had been worth it, the doctor thought. Rose, middle-aged and faded, could not be expected to catch a young man's fancy without money. He was deeply fond of Rose, but in his heart, he was angry. She had used Ned Cooper as a toy, when he might have fulfilled his destiny as a common labourer and married the common village girl he loved.

'Rose,' he declared, 'you're a terrible old fool.'

'Don't speak to her in that way!' hissed Venables.

'And you're another. Help me get him on the cart. What's the bloody woman doing now?'

Rose, huffing under the weight of her pregnancy, was scrabbling in the hedge. 'All the flowers are gone,' she mourned. 'I'll fetch some from the hothouse tomorrow.'

'You'll do nothing of the kind. By this time tomorrow he'll be in that coffin, and my boys from the farm will be sealing the vault and putting it under the plough.'

'No!' She dissolved into tears, and grabbed absurdly at Aitcheson's legs. 'Arthur, let me keep him for a little! Just till my baby comes!'

Venables, with infinite gentleness, raised her up and brushed the dirt from her clothes. To the sound of her sobs, the two men wrestled the dead weight of the murdered man on to the cart.

The bizarre procession moved back down the lane, towards the Egyptian tomb Archie had made for his own bones – he had specified in his will that his detested wife was not to lie beside him.

Rose heaped the improvised bier with weeds, and walked beside it holding Ned's dead hand. She would not allow them to place him in the coffin, but insisted upon laying him out on the stone floor. When Aitcheson tried to take charge of the key, she snatched it from him.

'He's mine. Let me have him.'

She returned the next day, with her arms full of orchids and lilies from her hothouses, and strewed them over her treasure's body. For a month – oblivious to the eye-watering stench – she spent every night sitting beside him, until the first pangs of labour made her double over at the gates of the house, scattering petals.

It was Venables who persuaded her, while she lay with her newborn son at her breast, to let them cover the vault.

'Good man,' the doctor said. 'The village thinks he has run off and taken the shilling – he always was a wild boy. This way they will never know the facts. The minute the plough runs over that monstrosity, Jim my lad, we'll raise a glass to our infernal luck. Rose is safe. Perhaps she'll even marry you, at long last.'

The Vicar, who had grown grey and cadaverous in those few weeks, shook his head. 'Too late,' he said. 'You know how she has changed. When they seal that vault, they'll be sealing Rose's heart inside it.'

Five

The fabled treasure of Quenville gleamed dully as the torch-beam caught it – a grinning skeleton, with rags of leathery skin still clinging here and there to its picked bones. Heaps of mummified flower petals, shuddering into dust, were laid carefully around it.

Melissa picked up the torch, and shone it on the skull, shivering when a spider scuttled out of one of the eye sockets. Slowly, with a face of absolute wonder, she moved the beam down the pathetic, unrecognizable shreds of clothes over the ribcage; the hooked fingers; the lolling feet, bursting through the ghosts of their boots.

'I see,' she murmured, after a long, long pause. 'Of course. Her letters, her poems – it all falls into place. How stupid of us, never to imagine that her pearl might be a person.'

Johnny had been standing like a pillar of stone, as if this outrage had frozen the blood in his heart. Suddenly, with a roar that made the damp bricks overhead vibrate, he swept the pickaxe through the heap of bones.

Melissa screamed: 'No!' and tried to hang on to his arm. He shook her off, so roughly that she cannoned against the wall.

The bones clattered and scuttered across the floor. Johnny hacked at the skeleton in a frenzy of blind fury until he crunched its teeth under his shoes.

'Johnny, wait – '

He hurled himself up the steps. She ran after him, and saw him running through the white early morning sunlight towards the polished shell of Quenville.

'Don't touch it!' she yelled, so loudly that a woman walking her dog on the other side of the church stopped to watch, shading her eyes curiously. 'Johnny!'

He ran past the trailer, where he had spent so many months of acute discomfort, driven by his useless search. Past the cleaned and repointed porch, where he had slept, dizzy with hunger, on the day he first saw Melissa and Ernestine. Past the arched windows, with their scrubbed carvings of heraldic beasts and medieval flowers; so lovingly and expensively restored that they seemed fresh from the mason's chisel.

The stone angel was in the clearing, waiting with outstretched arms to be hoisted back to its pinnacle.

She saw what he was about to do the second before he did it, and implored: 'No – no – no –'

He held the pickaxe above his head like a trophy, then smashed it into the angel's face with all the force he could summon. The stone flew off in lumps and chips, raining down on the bald earth. Blow after blow, until he had reduced the statue to a diseased, shapeless lump, and his first volcanic fury was spent.

He dropped the pickaxe, and folded his blistered, bleeding palms under his arms.

Melissa was weeping. Clumsy with grief, she wiped her eyes on the grimy sleeve of her shirt, and dropped on her knees amid the fragments – the tip of a wing, an ear, a clump of hair, one severed hand.

There was a silence between them, like the shocked aftermath of an explosion.

Johnny, spitting the word out bitterly, pronounced the verdict: 'Fuck.'

'I could see those jewels,' Melissa said, in a wistful voice. 'Diamonds in filigree basket settings. Cabochon rubies and sapphires. Marvellous, tasselled ropes of pearls.'

'Fuck. Fuck. Fuck.'

'And now –' she stared helplessly at her empty hands, 'nothing but the ashes of some Victorian melodrama. I wonder who he was.'

'I'm going to tear down every brick, rip down every last wall.'

'No. I told you before, I'm not going to let you damage my house.'

'I'm going to have it, Mel. If I have to push the whole fucking lot through a hair-sieve. Shit, the time I wasted — what's the point of this heap of rubbish, without the money?'

She shook her head. 'There isn't any money. I have a sort of rounded-off feeling, as if I'd come to the end of a story. Or the closing titles of a film. She wrote about her jewels, and she meant him. That's what she was trying to tell young Joshua, when she lay dying. Do you know,' she added, standing up, with a quickening of interest, 'I believe that bag of bones might have been his real father.'

'Well, isn't that lovely? Perhaps you could write a learned monograph, for the local historical society.'

She forgot the melodrama when she looked properly at Johnny. He was transformed with anger; black-browed and bare-fanged. His sarcasm had a serrated edge of real dislike, which she had never heard from him before.

'We solved the mystery,' she said haughtily. 'It doesn't change anything.'

'No? If we've found your treasure, and it's a load of crap, what am I doing here?'

'Working with me,' she said. 'Rebuilding our house.'

'Why?'

Her voice softened to pleading. 'Can you really not see how beautiful it is? How the discovery of the body makes it even more beautiful, in a way?'

'You're barking. Jesus, when I think what I've been through for you . . .'

'Well, I've suffered too. I made sacrifices.'

'And what for?' Johnny shouted. 'What's left?'

'We've still got Quenville,' Melissa said. 'You've still got me.'

His beautiful striped eyes narrowed, and shrivelled her with scorn. He dug his keys from his pocket, walked over to his Mercedes, got inside, and started the engine revving it furiously.

Stunned, Melissa whispered: 'Johnny?'

He lowered his window, and she took a hopeful step towards him. But he only said: 'I've even ruined my fucking car.'

His foot hit the floor, and his exhaust-pipe bounced and grated sickeningly against the deep ruts in the lane.

Half hoping he would crash, Johnny bombed along the narrow country roads, loudly cursing this ultimate disappointment – the end of the dream that had sustained him for so long. The cruel shattering of the dream he had chosen, above his last hope of what people called happiness. And all for nothing, nothing, nothing.

He was halfway to King's Lynn before he simmered down enough to realize that he was reeling with hunger. On a dismal B-road, he saw a forlorn café, and pulled in to wolf eggs, bacon, chips, beans, fried bread – the eternal breakfast, desired above all else by lorry drivers, advertised as being 'served all day'.

When he went into the Gents to wash his torn hands, he saw in the mirror that he was filthy. He had been labouring all night. His long hair was full of dust; his face marbled with a layer of grime.

I look just like I did at the beginning, he thought.

With some of the dirt splashed off, he returned to his table and hunched moodily over a cup of tea. It was time to assess the magnitude of the disaster.

His commission from the bank and Will's reluctant contributions had amounted to around £250,000. He was now down to £30,000 – bloody Melissa had Hoovered him out to pay for the restoration at Quenville. He had gone along with her, because he had been so sure of finding the treasure.

And he had found it. 'How stupid of us,' she had said, 'never to imagine that her pearl might be a person.'

Johnny laughed savagely to himself at the irony. It had not been stupidity, but raging greed. They had been mad with it, high on it, to the exclusion of everything else. So the moral of the story was ridiculously clear. The real treasure was not money, but love.

He was suddenly terribly tired of himself and his greed. He was sick of Melissa too, though he supposed he had better marry her if he ever wanted to get his money back. Part of him, he suspected – a large and horrible part – would always need her. They were bound together by two murders. Three, if you counted the ancient incident with Giles. It seemed incredible, that she had been willing to bump her off half her friends for the sake of her inheritance, but he was in no position to criticize.

He wished he was. As the crowning irony, he recognized that now he was ready to love properly, he also had to admit that he was not nearly good enough to do so. It would mean deliberately setting out to break the heart he longed for.

Thinking of Ernestine flooded his veins like a painkiller. He climbed back into his car, wincing angrily over the stiffness of his limbs, and turned towards London.

Belsize Park was in the full carnival of a summer noon, crowded with shoppers, lunchers and simple takers of air. Johnny locked his car, thinking what a wild man he must look among the lightly clad idlers.

There was a flower stall outside the tube station. He bought two dozen roses, of a velvety dark red that seemed particularly appropriate for Ernestine.

'White heather, dear – bless you, dear, a nice little sprig of white heather – '

The usual old bag in a balaclava was hopping about like a scaly old pigeon, thrusting dry tufts wrapped in tinfoil at passers-by. Johnny remembered the eternal litany from his childhood. He had sat in a derelict pushchair, eating crisps, while Nan had chanted: 'Lucky face, dear – white heather – just a few pennies for the baby.'

This one did not have the assistance of a baby. When the stallholder gave Johnny his change, he held it out to her, suddenly interested to see what it felt like to commit an act of generosity.

She tottered to a halt in front of him and her doubtful, rheumy eyes seemed to draw him into focus for ages.

'Take it,' he said impatiently. 'What's wrong with it?'

She mumbled: 'It's got blood on it.'

The blisters on his palm were bleeding again, and the engraved indentations of the pound coin he held were faintly threaded with scarlet.

'Why should you care?' Johnny demanded. 'You're hardly in a position to be fussy.'

'No, no – ' she backed away from him. 'Blood all over it. I won't have it.'

'Suit yourself.' Johnny pocketed the money, thinking: That's the last time I try to do something kind. 'Nutter,' he remarked to the flower seller.

But the man looked at him oddly. Or perhaps he imagined it. Bundling the roses in his bloody hands, he hurried to Ernestine's flat.

'Johnny,' he said, into the entryphone at the front door.

'Oh,' her voice quavered. There was a pause. 'Actually, I'd rather not let you in, if you don't mind.'

'I do mind. Let me in, or I'll break in.'

'Go away – please.'

'Ernie, wait.' He took a deep breath in an effort to wipe the aggression from his voice. 'I don't want to scare you, love. I'll only stay a moment.'

Another pause. The entryphone buzzed, and Johnny pounced on the door before she could change her mind. He took the stairs three at a time. She was waiting for him in her hall. A sweet cooking smell billowed from the kitchen behind her, and she wore a striped butcher's apron with an arsenal of pens clipped across the bib.

'Honestly, I don't have any time – '

He kissed her, and thrust the roses into her arms. Ernestine was taken aback. His lips had lingered on hers only a second or two longer than usual, but she felt the quality of his kiss had changed.

'Flowers,' she said. 'Good God. I mean, they're lovely.'

He closed the door, and stood with his arms folded in the

middle of her kitchen, staring at her. The last time he had been here – the night Giles had come to Quenville – he had driven all the way from Norfolk, just to spend a few hours painstakingly de-nobbling Jerusalem artichokes while Ernestine melted a pan of chocolate at the stove. She had been cooking, as a favour, for the baptismal dinner of Dash and Bella's child. They had chatted about babies – how Ernie wanted them and Johnny definitely did not – then he had cleaned the filter on her tumble drier and gone home. Johnny had done some weird things with lovers in his time, but nothing as weird as that. Or as much fun.

And then he had gone and blown it by being such a shit to her at the funeral. Poor thing, there were great black shadows under her wide blue eyes. She was working hard, and still torn with grief for Giles, but he selfishly hoped he had been at least partly responsible. The idea that she had suffered over him filled him with an exquisite tenderness.

With an embarrassed half-smile hovering around her lips, she watched him, hugging the roses. She was beautiful. Images of her special type of beauty crowded into his mind. It was like an apple, which is white and perfect to the core when you cut it open. Or a lump of ivory, smooth and hard and close-grained all the way through; or a glossy brown nut, plumply filling its tight shell with sweetness. She made him think of things whose outsides were good, and their insides better, more satisfying, the nearer you got to the centre.

'Ernie.' He had smashed the false angel. Now he embraced the real one.

She stiffened defensively, but melted against him the moment he put his tongue between her lips. He had never done this before, and it felt shockingly intimate. The inside of her mouth tasted of violets and chocolate.

Pressing his hardening erection into her leg, he ran his hands over her soft buttocks and breasts, marvelling at the healing experience of sex which started off at such a deep level, and could only go deeper.

Faces alight with anticipation, they went into the bedroom. In silence, they peeled off their clothes. Johnny saw and adored Ernestine's gentle curves.

Her bed, when he rolled into it, smelled of her – powdery, faintly spiced, sweet but not cloying. He lay as close to her as he could get, without welding their two bodies into one.

She caught her breath, as he slid the tip of his forefinger into her moist split. Caressing her clitoris, and making her arch and sigh beneath his touch, was a pleasure beyond imagination.

His prick swelled and swelled, in a delicious agony of suspense, until a breath could have made him come. But he wanted to savour the sensation of stroking the wet, secret place. He could have gazed down into her face for ever, watching the scrunching of her eyelids as she climaxed.

The second time, she bucked and convulsed under his fingers, and yelled, in a kind of despair: 'Oh please – please – come inside me, please –'

He pinned her down under his thundering heart, and when he eased himself into her, he had to bite his lip to stop himself coming immediately. It was important – vital – to savour each second. He poured concentration into building a rhythm, sustaining his thrusts as long as he could.

Then, with a long moan of relief, he allowed himself to surrender control. The orgasm took possession of him, and tore out of him in a storm of sobs and shouts. Love made flesh – he had never believed it possible.

Afterwards, they lay clasped in one another's arms, in a torpor of animal contentment. Occasionally, he rubbed his lips in her hair and on her neck, but they did not speak for ages.

Ernestine broke the silence, by asking: 'What made you come?'

'When your fanny went all tight.'

She snorted with laughter. 'I meant – what made you come here?'

This struck him as hilarious, and they both laughed until the mattress shook. Reducing the anguish of that morning to a joke was deeply comforting – and he refused to spoil this moment by telling Ernestine about the treasure. What did treasure matter now?

'I felt terrible,' he said, 'because I behaved like such an arsehole at the funeral. Melissa was being a cow – I could hear her through the bog door – and I didn't say a word.'

'I was hurt,' she admitted. 'I howled all over Frank afterwards, and he knew perfectly well it had nothing to do with Giles. But this changes everything, doesn't it?' She raised herself on one elbow, to gaze down into his face. 'Melissa's suspicions, as it turns out, were extremely well-founded.'

'You hate cheating on her, don't you?'

'Yes,' she said briskly, 'but I'm afraid I do think it slightly serves her right. In her heart of hearts, she can't believe anyone would fuck me when they could have her.'

Johnny said: 'You don't really believe it either.'

'Can you blame me? It's never happened before.'

'Well.' Johnny ran his finger lightly along her spine. 'There are a lot of stupid men in the world.'

She sighed. 'Don't encourage me. It's awfully petty and childish to feel pleased about scoring points off her.'

'It does her no harm.'

'But it harms me.' She was very serious. 'It forces me into such an unattractive role – the jealous, vengeful plain one. If I was ever going to play it, I should have got it over with when we were teenagers, and she kept snogging my boy-friends.'

'Oh, charming. You must have loved that.'

'No, no. You don't understand. When every boy in the world wants to snog you, you can either spend your life screaming for help, or you can snog them right back. It wasn't entirely her fault.'

'You're too good to live, you.'

'I love her. More than love her – she drives me crazy, but she's always been there. She's in my bones. We're so different, but part of her is me, and me her. And when she loves me, when I please her, I'm more myself. I could live without my Mel-part, I suppose. But there wouldn't be any relish in it. She can make the world glorious – so that when she switches off the magic, you crave it, like a drug. Oh God,' she added suddenly. 'What's that?'

From the front door came the rattling sound of a key. It closed, with a confident slam.

'Ernie?'

'Frank!' She sat bolt upright.

Johnny hissed: 'What's he doing here?'

'I gave him back my keys so he could water my plants.' She raised her voice, in a cautious shout. 'Hello?'

'Where are you?'

'Just coming – ' She leaped out of bed and pulled on her dressing gown.

Johnny took grim delight in her appearance. There was no way on earth she could hide what she had just been doing. Her hair was tousled, and her face had an unmistakable glow of sexual repletion. This would teach the arrogant sod a lesson.

Frank was his enemy, a living symbol of everything Johnny had never had. He was not going to miss this supreme opportunity to prove his superiority over the gilded American.

From the kitchen, Frank's embarrassed voice mumbled: 'This is a bad time – right?'

'Right,' Johnny said, appearing in the doorway belting the spare dressing gown – which had evidently, judging from its size, once belonged to his rival.

Frank stood staring from one to the other, absurdly clutching an identical bunch of red roses to Johnny's.

Ernestine pulled her dressing gown around her, looking absolutely stricken. 'Roses – how gorgeous – '

There was a long moment of tension, during which Frank's ridiculously handsome face expressed anger, mortification and sorrow – all balm to Johnny's jealous soul. He was not prepared for the way Frank broke the tension. He saw the other bunch of roses on the table, and exploded in a great bellow of laughter.

'Oh my God, I just slipped into a *Carry On* movie. Ern, I'm so sorry – '

To Johnny's annoyance, Ernestine was laughing too. To his even greater annoyance, Frank held out his hand, and said: 'Hi, Johnny.'

Johnny shook the hand, wincing slightly at its powerful pressure on his lacerated palms. He had been hijacked into a feeling of liking for Frank – or, at least, of toleration. He had been disarmed against his will. The monster had been ousted from his imagination, and replaced with a normal bloke. This was how ladies and gentlemen conducted their affairs, and Johnny smarted, feeling distinctly outclassed. Frank and Ernestine, at close quarters, spoke in a code he did not understand.

'Hi,' he said suspiciously.

'Hope I didn't interrupt. I mean, I obviously did.'

'We'd finished.'

This gave Frank a stab of pain, as intended, but he disarmed Johnny once more, by making a visible effort not to mind. 'I should have called first, but I didn't think you guys – well, the situation's changed.'

'I should have posted a notice on the door,' Ernestine said cheerfully.

'What are you going to do with all these flowers – make a salad?'

'My cakes!' Ernestine shrieked suddenly. She dived to the oven, and dragged out a pan of American blueberry muffins, blackened at the edges. 'Oh, shit! Shit! They were supposed to be starring in a photo-shoot this afternoon.'

Frank was laughing again. 'Great, let's eat them instead.' He flung down his flowers, parked himself at the table, and said: 'Kettle, Ern. Mine's a coffee.'

'Get it yourself,' she said. But she put the kettle on all the same. Why did she find this funny?

'You're honoured, Johnny,' Frank said. 'In all my time with Ernie, I never made her burn anything.'

'You were the one who would never let anything burn. We could have been in the middle of a Roman orgy, and you'd have kept one eye on your dinner.'

'Cruel, cruel woman.'

It did not matter that Johnny knew he was the one responsible for Ernestine's glow of happiness. He felt robbed and excluded – far more than he would have done if Frank had reacted properly, and tried to punch him. Worse, he was conscious of looking like a sullen lout.

If I was a gentleman, he thought, I'd know how to behave.

'Johnny – ' Ernestine grabbed his hand, with automatic intimacy that comforted him a little. 'What have you done to yourself?'

'Blisters, that's all,' Johnny said, whisking the wounds out of sight.

'Of course, you've been digging. How's it going?'

Here was a wound he would never, never show her. 'So-so.'

'You haven't found the treasure yet, I take it?'

'Not yet. Mind if I roll a joint?'

'Go ahead.'

'Wow, have you got some?' Frank exclaimed. 'Could I buy some?'

'I'll give you some.' Johnny would have loved to charge him, but knew he had been asked as a gentlemanly formality. He went back into the bedroom to get dressed, straining to hear their conversation. Instead of the whispered reproaches he had hoped for, however, Frank's voice remained at exactly the same pitch of loud affability.

'I haven't told you the big news, honey – I exchanged yesterday.'

'Frank! That's brilliant. When do you move?'

'Day after tomorrow. You must come and see it.'

Ernestine said: 'So you'll be living somewhere decent, at long last. I knew your father would stump up in the end. You're reverting to type.'

He laughed. 'I guess.'

Johnny returned to the kitchen table to roll his joint.

Ernestine put a cup of coffee down in front of him. 'Will you let me put some Savlon on your hands?'

Johnny realized she had mentioned his hands again purely as a way of including him. And in that moment, he knew

Ernestine was still in love with Frank. Suddenly, he was watching the pair of them from an immense distance; seeing their rightness together. It was more than habit that bound them. With Frank, Ernestine seemed to reveal a fuller self; an entire dimension he had never seen and could never reach.

Nothing could have brought him more forcibly against the change in himself. The old Johnny would have dealt with such a situation by obliterating Frank. The new Johnny saw how futile this would be. Suppose he had found a way of removing Frank? There was no way on earth of removing the man from her heart, without cutting that heart he loved so much to shreds.

It was the hardest, bitterest lesson of his life; harder than the lesson he had learned, too late, when they found the Quenville treasure. If Ernestine did not share his dreams of happiness, they were as worthless as the bones in the vault.

He dropped the lump of rocky he had been paring over his heap of tobacco. 'Listen, you have this, Frank. I'd better be going.'

'Oh, Johnny – ' Ernestine looked sorry, but not surprised. She knew, as well as he did, that he did not belong.

Six

Ernestine swung her car round the bend in the lane and saw Melissa standing in the porch; a living image of still solemnity in a Gothic frame. The light slanted through the fretted stone, making her dress of peacock silk blaze like stained glass.

The peacock silk slightly annoyed Ernestine. People who had worn out the night with sorrow surely did not wear dresses like that on a weekday morning in the depths of the country. A weeping phone call, practically at dawn, had called Ernestine away from urgent work on her book: 'Please come, I need you.'

It was the kind of summons she had always obeyed without question, however, and her guilt about Johnny made it doubly sacred. Will's name had been mentioned, too. The wedding anniversary was approaching, and as she belted up the motorway, Ernestine had shed tears of remorse. Will's ghost reproached her, as nothing else could. If she was in for drama, she was duty-bound to grit her teeth and take it.

Melissa did not move until Ernestine was out of the car, and hurrying towards her with a carrier bag full of milk and croissants. Then, she ran down and pressed her cheek against her cousin's.

'Darling. Thanks so much. I've been so lonely, I didn't know whether I was alive or dead, and you have the most marvellous talent for spreading sanity.'

'Where's Johnny? Wasn't he with you?'

Sadness suited Melissa. It sanctified and adorned her beauty, like a lily in the hands of a figure on a tomb. 'We had another of our spats. He's being a pig at the moment.'

This was salt rubbed into the wounds of Ernestine's lacerated conscience. 'What on earth was all that about the treasure? Don't tell me it exists.'

'Johnny can't see beauty,' Melissa said, 'unless it can be sold. He's turned against my house – which is the same as turning against me.'

Ernestine wanted to reassure, but did not dare to discuss Johnny in any detail. If she had known he was to be top of the agenda, she would not have come at all.

'Not that he's left me, or anything ghastly like that – you know how we go together. Tongue-and-groove, as he says. But he said he'd marry me.' Her voice trembled. 'And now the bastard's changed his mind.'

'Oh, Mel – ' What else could she say?

'I kept seeing Will, and remembering how we were a year ago. He'd never have treated me like that. But Johnny will realize, eventually. Marriage is another thing he doesn't understand.'

'Let's go down to the cottage,' Ernestine said, clutching her bag of eatables. 'I'll cook you breakfast.'

'Very sweet.' Melissa smiled mistily, and stroked her arm. 'And very typical of you, darling. But I need to be here, at the moment. To remind me why I've sacrificed so much. Oh, it's given me a night of agony – you wouldn't have been me last night for anything on earth.'

'Mel, what are you talking about? You know I can never hold my end up in this sort of conversation.'

'That's because you don't listen properly.' For the first time, a little dagger of frost crackled in the gentle voice.

'I know, I know,' Ernestine said grimly. 'Deaf to the horns of elfland. Blind to the light of other worlds. Constitutionally incapable of seeing anything in this bloody place, beyond a house.'

Melissa turned away, and ducked into the chilly shadows of the porch. 'Come inside. Eat your breakfast, if you must, but don't make crumbs on the parquet.'

Ernestine followed her, and was startled afresh by the newness of the hall. The blues and terracottas in the tiles seemed harsh and aggressive. Melissa went into the library, where one huge wall was a blank space, waiting for the first strokes of Seddon's murals.

The climate had subtly changed. Melissa's sadness still scented the atmosphere around her, but there was an edge of rather desperate determination.

'Look, I didn't get you here to snipe at you. I might have laughed at your talent for the prosaic in the past – but only because I know I need it. D'you remember my wedding morning? When I said you reminded me of Will?'

'Of course. You gave me this.' Ernestine showed the single pearl at her neck.

Melissa, facing her in the middle of the floor, went on as if she had not heard. 'I think that's why I kept remembering Will last night.' Her lashes were suddenly wet with tears. 'When you love someone because they're very good, in a way you're not, it makes betrayal worse.'

They were silent. The silence roared in Ernestine's ears, and she felt sick.

Melissa knew. Johnny had told her.

Ernestine had prayed this would never happen. Every cell in her body still sang with the memory of his lovemaking, but it took more than this to stifle her common sense – which kept telling her, no matter how she tried to ignore it, that the love she had for Johnny was not the kind she could live with.

Melissa folded her hands calmly. 'You know what I'm talking about.'

'Yes.'

'Johnny has some stupid idea that he is in love with you. Now, it's partly my fault. I should have seen it coming. It was his first dose of sentimentality, and he simply couldn't cope with it.'

'I – I shouldn't have done it.'

'No, you shouldn't.' Her calm was horrible. 'And you won't again.'

'No, I won't – though I think that's up to me. But I won't.'

'Look at yourself,' Melissa instructed her sternly. 'You have this picture of yourself as Miss Virtuous. You just

388

assume you must be better than me because you're not as pretty. It was the part that was left for you, since I never got the hang of being good. And I believed in you!'

Ernestine felt this was true. It was as if she had looked into a mirror and seen a monster.

'And apparently,' Melissa said, 'you don't even want Johnny, anyway. So Miss Goody-Goody has ended up betraying us both. That's nice, isn't it?'

'For God's sake,' Ernestine protested, 'it wasn't like that!'

'That's what really tore me apart last night. I know what a shit Johnny is – more than you ever will, incidentally. That poor, lost sinner you got all gooey over doesn't exist. My God, you tell me I'm over-dramatic – and you fell for a story that belongs in the pages of some Victorian religious tract. I've got enough on that man to put him behind bars for years.'

'Why don't you, then?'

'We're talking about you, Ernie. He could never break my heart, like you have.'

'Bollocks,' Ernestine said. 'Hearts don't break. Certainly not yours. It's a durable old pudding, if ever I saw one.'

'Well, now we come to it, don't we? What you really think of me. I loved you more than anyone in the world. I trusted you, and you despise me.'

'Oh, don't be ridiculous – '

'That's what made me think of Will. I haven't felt so utterly devastated and alone since he betrayed me.'

Ernestine dropped her carrier bag on the polished floor. 'Will killed himself. Is that what you call betrayal?'

Melissa shook her head. 'He should have killed himself. I thought I'd die when he told me.'

The world was changing around her. Ernestine felt herself sliding into another dimension of reality. 'What is all this? I saw the note he left – '

'No, you only saw part of it. I tore up the rest. It was a horrid letter, all about how he was going to leave me.'

'Leave you?' Ernestine echoed stupidly.

'It always came back to money in the end, you know, with

Will. The moment I realized he was never going to let me have Quenville, I decided he would have to go.'

'What on earth are you talking about?'

Melissa's lips twitched. 'Darling, I'm trying to tell you that I killed Will. How plain do I have to be?'

'Rubbish!' Ernestine snapped. 'Absolute crap – one of your silly fantasies. Well, I'm not playing!'

'I made up my mind to kill him the night we had that massive row about Monksby. All right, I thought. I'll murder him – just like that. It was a revelation. The idea that it was – you know – possible.'

'That's crazy.'

'I don't know. I'm surprised it doesn't happen more often. You must have thought, sometimes, that it would be convenient if someone died. Well, it's a very short step from there to murder.'

The word made Ernestine wince. 'Stop it, please. Look, this whole thing is ludicrous – '

'I know the word sounds awful. And I didn't have a clue how to go about it. I wonder if I ever would have, if I hadn't met Johnny? Everyone thought we were so happy at Monksby. And in a peculiar way, we were. I might have left the murder on ice for years, keeping the idea like a sort of insurance policy.'

Ernestine's mouth was dry. She thought, I'll wake up in a minute, or she'll tell me she's teasing. 'So it was because of Johnny?'

'Indirectly. I wanted Quenville, and I wanted him. And then Will forced my hand rather, by deciding to divorce me. With a generous settlement, I hasten to add – credit where credit's due. Still,' Melissa added briskly. 'A divorce settlement wasn't going to be handsome enough. So I'm afraid I panicked.'

'But I found him. He was on the bed – '

'No, darling. Not exactly. He made it easy, I have to say, by hitting that whisky bottle during the most ghastly scene of self-pity. You know I never could stand that. I came back and caught him at it.'

'At what?'

'Leaving notes all over the house. You found the last one.'

'Thirty pieces of silver.' Ernestine's stomach was in knots. She could hardly breathe.

'So naff. He had terrible taste sometimes. That note was the literary equivalent of Mantovani strings. How we missed it when we were clearing up, I can't imagine.'

'We?' There was something dreadfully plausible about all this.

'I'd been staying with Johnny. And I can't tell you what the place looked like when I got in. Will had puked all over the hall, for one thing. To cut a long story short, I mashed up the pills in his drink. Then I had a bath upstairs. Then I came down and looked at him on the sofa, and knew he was probably dead. So I rang Johnny. He sorted it all out, thank God. He's terribly good at things like that. Moved the body, saved the last page of the letter, and told me to get out.'

'Mel,' Ernestine pleaded, 'I saw you when you came in. I was there. You were out of your mind with grief.'

Melissa's forehead puckered. The tears trembling on her lashes spilled down her cheeks. 'Yes,' she said simply. 'I felt terrible afterwards. His face was so lonely. I'd have given anything not to have done it – but I had to, I had to.' She broke down into terrible, whooping sobs, reaching out blindly.

Ernestine went to her, and wrapped her arms around her. 'All right.' Strength and sanity were returning. 'It's all right, darling. This is nothing but delayed reaction. I told you at the time, you should see a therapist, or a counsellor.'

Melissa's tears oozed warm on Ernestine's shoulder. 'I hated myself so much, I hardly dared to close my eyes, in case the awful part of me would do something else when I was asleep. And when I found out about my mother, it was like some terrible curse – my real inheritance – '

'This is such nonsense! You shouldn't be here, all on your own.'

'I killed Giles, too.'

'No, you didn't.' Ernestine soothed. It was extraordinary,

she thought, how Mel had got her going. Now that the drama-shields were up, the problem was entirely different. The row with Johnny had tipped the poor creature over the edge. Her fragility was a known fact, which Ernestine and her parents had accommodated all her life. Her own selfishness, from this perspective, struck her as even more monstrous.

'I did!' sobbed Melissa. 'He squirmed like mad. I wish I hadn't, but I did!'

'Oh, Mel. Honestly.'

'You don't believe me.'

Ernestine chose the words carefully. 'I believe you're far more upset about Will and Giles than you let on.'

Impatiently, Melissa jerked out of her arms, mopping at her face with her sleeve. 'Of course I'm upset. Stop speaking to me in that condescending way. You'd be upset, if you'd killed two of your best friends.'

Ernestine stifled an unholy desire to giggle, shocked by the impulse. 'You surely don't expect me to – '

'The point is, whether you believe me or whatever, I'm not entirely inhuman. I want you to know, I suffer as much as anyone.'

'Mel, did you call me out here just to give me this cock-and-bull confession?'

Strands of Melissa's long hair were clinging to her sticky, tear-stained face. She pushed it back with one hand. 'I wanted to punish you for carrying on with Johnny behind my back.'

'It's over. I mean, it wasn't ever anything. I couldn't be sorrier, if it's any consolation.'

'I know. I don't want to hurt you any more. The thing is, I can perfectly see why Johnny loves you. For the same reason I do. He and I are so alike, it's eerie.'

Ernestine sighed shakily, allowing herself to relax a fraction. 'You two have the oddest relationship.'

'I used to snigger when people said they couldn't live without other people,' Melissa said. 'My punishment is learning that it's true. When we found the treasure, it made

392

me realize I could stand pretty well anything, except losing him.'

'So you did find something. Are you going to tell me?'

Melissa sniffed. 'Better than that, I'll show you.'

'Have a tissue.' Ernestine dug one out of her handbag.

'Oh, aren't you wonderful?' She took it, laughing softly. 'You always had a pencil-sharpener at school. And a rubber. And the right change for the bus. Choosing between you and Johnny was no easy task, let me tell you. He might be good at clearing up after murders, but he's as hopeless about practicalities as I am.'

'Good thing you've decided not to make the choice, then,' Ernestine said, swallowing an uncomfortable frisson of doubt.

Melissa seemed to have cheered up. Ernestine had to canter to keep up with her, as she hurried out of the house. On the edge of the field, she pointed to the mound of broken soil. 'Don't be squeamish – it's a body, but a terribly old one. And Johnny smashed it, so the bones look as if they could belong to anything now, from a knackered horse to a stegosaurus.'

'A body? You're kidding!'

Briefly, over her shoulder, Melissa described what had happened.

Ernestine asked: 'Shouldn't you have called the police?'

'What for?'

'I don't know. To give the poor thing a proper burial, at least.'

'I'm having it filled in again. I'll respect poor old Rose's wishes, and leave her treasure in peace.'

They stood at the top of the excavated steps for a few minutes, staring down at the door with its splintered lock. It was guarded, grotesquely, by the ravaged stone angel. It leaned against the wall at a perilous angle, and the cousins had to climb over it to get inside the vault.

'What happened to the angel?' asked Ernestine. 'It looks as though someone's deliberately tried to destroy it.'

'They did,' said Melissa. 'Johnny smashed that too.'

With the door standing open, there was just enough light to see the fan-shaped bricks in the ceiling, the coffin on the shelf, and the heap of bones.

Ernestine was, in truth, a little squeamish. She also wanted to cry over the pathetic appearance of the skull, which had a great, jagged hole in it like an Easter Egg. She was startled, when she looked at Melissa in the dim light, to see that she actually was crying again.

'The point is,' she said, frowning down at the bones, 'that he was loved.'

'But you said he was murdered.'

'It's perfectly possible to love someone and kill them. Didn't I just explain?'

Down here, in the rimy damp of this robbed tomb, there was no defence against the worst thoughts. Laughing nervously, and half thinking she must be barmy, Ernestine said: 'It's true. Isn't it?'

'Yes, I told you. Will and Giles. I didn't kill that one – but I expect I would have, if I'd been Rose.'

Ernestine was cold all over, and her pulse throbbed in her throat. Her voice came out, amazingly normal; almost conversational. 'I wonder what he did.'

'He betrayed her,' Melissa said. 'Obviously.'

Ernestine clenched her jaw, to stop her teeth chattering. 'That's what I did. And you don't want to kill me.'

'No,' Melissa said, with a tear-laden sigh. 'Not you. I don't want to at all.'

Far off, as if from another planet, Johnny's voice roared: 'Mel! Ernie! Can you hear me?'

Both cousins jumped, and gaped at each other.

'Shit,' Melissa murmured. 'How did he know you'd be here?'

'No idea – oh, wait, I left a message on my machine.'

'Shit and double shit. Saying what?'

'Just that I'd been called out of London.'

'And, of course, Johnny was trying to reach you as soon as he'd left me. Beloved Ernie, whose exceedingly dowdy laces I am not fit to tie. No – I won't get cross again. I won't do it like this.'

Ernestine felt as if she had slipped off the edge of the world.

'Do what?'

'Don't you dare call to him!' Melissa blurted out. With a palpable struggle for control, she breathed heavily for a few seconds, then said coaxingly: 'Please, darling. He'll ruin everything.'

It was too late. They heard Johnny running down the steps. The light was, momentarily, blotted out, as he squeezed past the angel. He flung himself into the vault, wild-eyed, and gasped: 'Thank fuck!' when he saw Ernestine.

'Well, well.' Melissa was sulky. 'Here's the cavalry, in the last reel.'

Johnny bent over, gasping, to get his breath.

'He thought,' Melissa said icily, 'that he'd be too late. If you can imagine it darling, he thought I'd do a Giles on you.'

'Get out, Ernie,' Johnny said tersely. 'Get out.'

'My God, you two are as barking as each other,' Ernestine snapped, cross because she was so frightened. Looking from one beautiful face to the other, and recognizing neither – barely recognizing herself – was like waking up one morning to find the trees blue and the sky green.

Johnny had his eyes pinned to Melissa. 'I thought I'd made myself clear. Touch one hair of her, and you're meat.'

'Look, she hasn't done anything to me – '

His attention snapped to Ernestine. 'Get out, I said.'

Getting out suddenly seemed an excellent idea. She was pining for fresh air. On shaking legs, she moved towards the door.

'No!' Melissa shrieked furiously. 'You stay right there!' Her fingers sank into Ernestine's forearm.

'You promised,' he said.

'I changed my mind. If you can change your mind about marrying me, I can change mine about killing Ernie.'

'Let her go.'

Melissa's fingers tightened, but her voice was imploring. 'Do you think I like this? Don't make it difficult, darling. You'll forget her, once she's gone.'

395

'She's not going anywhere.'

'Johnny, Johnny, can't you see?' Melissa wailed in frustration. 'This is how much I love you! I'll get rid of her to keep you!'

'It won't make any difference,' he said. 'You've lost me.'

Ernestine's ears were ringing giddily. She saw Melissa's shadowed face, as it slowly crumpled into a rictus of pure fury, and hideous reality exploded into her consciousness at last.

The worst of it was that she was not surprised. Acknowledging the real Melissa was like unlacing a corset, or taking off a pair of spectacles. It was a surrender to something she had driven deeper and deeper underground. The cousin she had loved so slavishly wanted her dead.

No, no – too awful, too devastating to be the truth.

Even now, she scrambled blindly to save her picture of her world. Melissa's fingers were hurting her, but Ernestine pretended they were not. She laid her own hand across them.

'Mel, darling – '

Melissa pushed her roughly away, shrieking like a small, misunderstood child. She had been given to awful tantrums once, and Tess used to shut the little biting, kicking angel into the scullery until the tempest blew over. Ernestine remembered sitting on the kitchen table in Islington, having a bleeding wound on her head sponged by her father, while they all listened to Melissa banging the washing machine behind the door. Ernestine, taking her cue from her parents' dogged calm, had accepted the occasional bumps and contusions as the price of her devotion.

When there was actual bloodshed, Tess had tried reason. 'I want you to tell me what you were thinking,' she would bawl through the scullery door, 'when you bashed the lavatory seat on poor Ernie's head.'

The demonic little voice would shrill: 'I wanted her to die!'

Once, George had murmured: 'Ask a silly question.' And both Tess and George had gone into desperate paroxysms of silent laughter, while Ernestine stared wonderingly into their faces.

In those days, the tantrums had been about the disputed ownership of Barbie dolls or crayons. Now, perhaps inevitably, they were fighting over a man. Except that Ernestine did not want to fight. She wanted everything to be nice and normal again, as it had been when they were children – clinging together on the sofa after the storm, watching *Blue Peter* and sharing a plate of Marmite sandwiches.

Tess might have said: 'Don't be silly, Mel. Ernie knows he belongs to you – she was only borrowing, darling. You must learn to share.'

'Not share!' had been Melissa's earliest complete sentence.

She had hidden the sacrificial knife on the lid of the coffin. For the smallest fraction of a second, time stopped while Ernestine watched it dangling from her hand.

It happened, when it happened, very fast. Ernestine saw the blade slicing the air as it cannoned towards her. Even more quickly, Johnny flung himself in front of her.

Her eyes saw, but her brain would not make the connection. Johnny appeared to embrace Melissa, folding his body over hers. There was a peculiar gurgling sound. Melissa fought him off, and Ernestine watched his shoulder blades writhing underneath his shirt.

Melissa's hand was wet and scarlet. The handle of the knife, which Ernestine had often used to cut vegetables, stuck out of Johnny's sternum. He staggered drunkenly. He dropped to his knees, as if praying. With trembling hands, he held the knife and tried to pull it out.

With a long, despairing, horribly liquid moan of agony, he fell among the bones of the treasure, and was still.

Melissa howled, holding out her reeking hand. 'Look! Look what you made me do!' A demented maenad, she daubed Ernestine's face with the blood. 'Have him then. Keep him.'

She dived out of the vault and slammed the door. Ernestine was suddenly cloaked in total, absolute darkness. She was so frozen with terror, she could not even scream or move.

Muffled behind the thick door, she heard Melissa's sobs changing to purposeful grunts. Like Jacob, she was wrestling with the angel. It crashed against the door with a shattering thud.

Ernestine whimpered: 'Mel! Let me out!' She blinked, trying to make her eyes adjust. There was no light. She was blind. 'Mel, I can't see!'

Silence. She tried to quieten her own breathing, to listen.

Presently, from the shattered keyhole, she heard another sob.

'Mel, please!'

A muted, wretched voice said: 'Oh God. It's all gone wrong. I didn't mean it to be like this. I wanted it to be quick. Please don't scream, darling. Don't, don't – I can't bear it – '

Ernestine had to make a conscious decision not to obey. She sucked the mouldy air into her lungs, and let it out in a roar.

'Don't!' pleaded Melissa's voice. 'Honestly, nobody will hear you when I've gone.'

'Help!' screamed Ernestine. She reached out in the darkness for her mother's arms. 'Help!'

'Please, Ernie. Just lie down beside him, and let it come quietly. If I have to think of you yelling like that, I'll go crazy.'

'Wait – you're not leaving me? You wouldn't – '

'Ernie,' Melissa sobbed, 'don't be afraid. I still love you, and I'll miss you, sweet darling. Kiss Will and Giles for me, when you see them.'

'Don't go! Let me out!'

'I'm kissing the keyhole as if it were your face. Goodbye, Ernie. Goodbye.'

Then the silence went on and on, and Ernestine realized Melissa had gone. She thrashed about wildly, grazing her wrists and knuckles against the brick walls. Her fingernails caught at the door. Ernestine cast herself upon it, but the stone angel was jammed against the step. She was trapped.

This was her tomb. Far away, in the land of the living, Frank would wonder what had become of her. She would be as dead as a pharaoh, before he thought of searching for her here. Perhaps the diggers would come to fill in her grave while she was still alive, but too weak to cry out.

Ernestine drummed on the door with her fists, shedding bitter, bitter tears. She wept and wept, till a kind of dull calm descended. Her sobs had shaken her to exhaustion. She would have liked to sleep – but could not face the horror of waking up.

A hand suddenly gripped her ankle.

Ernestine screamed, then gasped: 'Johnny?'

He moaned.

'I thought you were dead!' She crouched down on the floor, and groped to clasp his hand. It was warm and sticky. Not to be alone was such a relief, she was almost happy.

'You okay?' he rasped, in a ghost of his normal voice.

'Me? I'm fine. But you must be in terrible pain. I wish to God I could do something.'

'Not too bad,' he said.

She managed, trying not to hurt him too much, to cradle his head in her arms. She asked: 'Do you think you're dying?'

'Course I'm fucking dying.'

Strangely peaceful, with his warm weight sagging against her, Ernestine considered this. 'Actually, I think I'm dying too. I wonder how long it takes.'

'No – '

He was so distressed that she quickly added: 'I haven't given up. I'll try screaming again in a minute. Who knows? Someone might hear. You lie still, and save your strength.'

'Ernie,' he sighed out, 'I'm sorry.'

'What for? You saved me. I mean, all right – it might be rather academic now. But you didn't let her hurt me.'

'Never.'

She could smell his sweat and his blood. 'This is so weird,' she said. 'I keep rubbing my eyes, expecting to see better, and nothing happens. When I see daylight again, I'll hardly be able to look at it.' She added, 'If I do.'

'You scared?'

'Yes, but it's not so scary if I can talk to you. Oh, Johnny – don't you leave me too.'

His breathing was becoming more laboured. She could feel him fighting for each breath. But he did not seem too bad, she thought, hope rising. He might be all right. Melissa might come back. Yes, of course she would.

'Pocket,' he panted. 'Matches.'

'Sorry – ?'

'To see you.'

'Oh yes, yes.'

The memory of sex hung between them, as she cautiously felt his body. By mistake, she touched the knife in his chest, and when he cried out, it was an echo of his orgasm. The box of matches was in his trouser pocket. Ernestine held it reverently, absurdly thrilled. It was odd, she thought, how quickly one adapted to circumstances. In such a short time, the striking of a match had become a treat.

She struck one. And nearly dropped it when his face sprang into view, unexpectedly close to hers. His eyelids drooped, as if holding them open was too much effort. She saw the tongue of flame reflected in his eyes, and herself holding it.

Her fingers burned. She dropped the spent match, and watched, bereft, as the spark died on the floor. The darkness swept over them, more profound than before. She lit another match, and another.

'I'll save the rest for a bit,' she said. 'Let's not use them all at once. Johnny – are you listening?'

'Yeah.' But he was floating away, and he clung to her as if he knew it.

A chill settled over her. She was desperate to make him talk. 'Are you frightened?'

'No,' he whispered.

'I wish I knew a prayer. If God exists, he can't possibly love you any less than I do. So don't worry.'

He said, 'I'll just climb inside you. And lie against your nice warm heart.'

*

400

'I still don't see why we have to stop,' Craig Lennox grumbled. 'She won't be pleased to see us. She doesn't like us.'

'She does,' Cecily said. 'She's always telling me to drop in if I'm passing.'

'Huh. How often are you likely to be "just passing" the middle of nowhere?'

'Don't, love. I think she must be very lonely out here. And anyway, the poor thing hasn't seen Jack for ages.' Cecily looked fondly over her shoulder at her baby strapped in his car seat. Like many new parents, she was deeply sorry for the childless, and convinced that showing them a child was an act of kindness. Jack was fifteen months old, and the apple of his mother's eye. 'Poor little love,' she said. 'He needs changing, and he's been so patient. Are you all poohey, treasure-man? Never mind!'

'I don't think Melissa will be too wild about seeing his shitty bum,' said Craig.

Cecily stretched over to thrust a rattle into Jack's fat hand. 'Oh, baby-shit's different. And to tell the truth, I'm dying to get a squint at Quenville. Ernie says it's fabulous.'

'Will that bloke of hers be hanging around?'

'Yes, of course. He lives with her.'

'He gives me the creeps.'

'Ernie says he's rather nice when you get to know him.'

Craig said, 'Ernie thinks the whole world is rather nice. Ouch! Bugger! That was my exhaust.'

'It's rather off the beaten track,' Cecily remarked.

'This is the bloody beaten track.'

Craig's prim, navy-blue Volvo swayed drunkenly along the unmade road. Quenville leaped at them round the bend, stripped and pristine.

Cecily squealed with delight. 'Wow – isn't that fantastic? And there she is! There, by that trailer!'

'I've never understood why you're all so potty about Melissa,' Craig said. 'Five minutes, hello-goodbye, and we're off. Okay?'

'Cooee!' Cecily was already waving eagerly out of the window.

Melissa had come out of the trailer when she heard the car.

She stood on the steps, holding a cup of coffee in one hand and shading her eyes with the other. She looked anything but pleased to see them, but Cecily had, in their Bohemian days, developed a hide like a rhino's where Melissa was concerned.

'You look wonderful, the house is wonderful,' she babbled, jumping up to plant a wet kiss on Melissa's cheek. 'How are you? I got so tired of only seeing you at funerals, I said to Craig, let's pop in.'

'And here you are,' Melissa said. 'What a surprise.'

'You'll be surprised, all right, when you see the size of Jack.'

'Isn't he at university yet? Goodness, babies last for such a long time.'

Craig took Jack out of the car seat, and stood looking gravely at Melissa, with the little boy crowing in his arms.

'Hello, Craig.'

'Hello, Melissa.'

'Still in the Civil Service? No, better not tell me about it. The doctor says I mustn't on any account get excited.'

Cecily asked: 'Are you ill?'

'Joking,' Craig mumbled, out of the corner of his mouth. 'Oh.'

'I'm terribly sorry,' Melissa said. 'If only I'd known you were coming – there's nothing for lunch.'

'We can't stay,' said Craig.

'What a shame.'

'Still, now we're here, we've got to have a look around,' Cecily cut in decisively. 'Do you realize, we haven't seen your house since that summer at the cottage? I can't believe what you've done to it.'

'We haven't finished.' Melissa, unable to speak of Quenville without passion, thawed a fraction. 'Finding the craftsmen has been an utter nightmare.'

'My God, though. Imagine actually living here. It's pure poetry.'

'I'll change Jack's nappy,' Craig said. His spotty, sullen face plainly showed a determination not to be interested in Melissa's house. He remembered, even if Cecily chose not to, the poisoned darts that could spit from that perfect mouth.

When the two women re-emerged in the porch, Melissa was in full flood, pouring the guided tour into enchanted ears.

' – the original golds and blues, which refer to the floor tiles in the hall. When it was first built, of course, they would have choked the windows with draperies and Nottingham lace, but I'll be keeping it as uncluttered as possible. You won't really be able to see the full effect, until the furniture is out of store. Will and I brought a lot of pieces with Quenville in mind.'

'How you must wish,' Cecily said soberly, 'that he could see all this.'

'Well, yes. It's a monument to him, in a way.' Melissa's lashes drooped exquisitely. 'Where's Craig?'

Cecily pointed across the field. Craig was strolling with his hands in his pockets, while Jack climbed the mounds of earth outside the vault. 'Bless him, he's at the mountaineering stage. We've had to take down our bookshelves.'

'Get him off,' Melissa said. 'I don't want him nosing round my garden.' Realizing she had sounded fierce, and that Cecily was staring at her in surprise, she added: 'He'll hurt himself. It's not safe.'

'We should be going, anyway.' Cecily began to make her way purposefully towards her husband and son. Melissa, after a second's consideration, followed.

Jack, by the time they arrived, had found the steps. He was wailing, and straining to fling himself down them. Craig held him by the back of his little jersey.

'Oh my God,' Melissa hissed.

'It's all right, Craig's got him. What is this?'

'Nothing. Must you be so nosy, Cecily? Get that bloody baby out of there!'

Cecily looked uneasy, but gamely explained: 'Mel's scared he'll hurt himself.'

Jack wriggled free, and shinned off down the steps, happily paddling his paws in the mud. At the bottom, he bumped his bottom against the broken angel and grinned up at his father.

Melissa, tense and anguished, clenched her fists.

'You naughty little pixie,' exclaimed Cecily. She picked her way down the steps, and scooped the child into her arms.

'How funny,' she muttered. 'Mel, what did you say was inside this thing?'

'I didn't. Will you come out?'

'The thing is, I could swear there's someone crying in there.'

Melissa, obviously furious, made a great effort to force out a laugh. 'Oh, yes. The wind plays the most extraordinary atmospheric tricks.'

Cecily had been trained to take her cues from Melissa, and laughed too. But there was a doubtful twist to her mouth. Timidly, she ventured: 'I – I don't think wind ever says "help".'

'Cec, your imagination!'

Craig said: 'Up you come. I'll take a look.'

Melissa grabbed his sleeve. 'Gracious, don't waste your time. Come back to the trailer, and we'll have tea.'

He repeated doggedly, with a glint of pleasure at opposing her: 'I'll just take a look.'

The last, diaphanous veil of politeness vanished. Melissa said, between clenched teeth: 'Craig Lennox, you're the most ugly, boring man in the world. How dare you interfere? Get into your nerdy little Volvo estate, and fuck off out of my house.'

Craig, with the veins standing out on his forehead, hefted the stone angel as far as the first step, enough to open the door. Cecily bit down a scream, and pressed her baby's face against her bony bosom.

Blinking owlishly in the light, Ernestine crouched on the brick floor, surrounded by spent matches.

'Help,' she said, as if repeating a magic spell whose meaning she no longer remembered.

She cradled Johnny's body in her arms. He was waxen-white, blanketed in thick, congealing blood around the hilt of a kitchen knife. His dull eyes and lead-coloured lips were wet with tears.

Craig climbed over the fallen angel, and said, in his emotionless voice: 'Get an ambulance. Get the police.'

Cecily turned round to Melissa, still hoping for a reasonable and comfortable explanation.

But Melissa had gone.

Seven

Ernestine had arrived early at the cemetery, hoping to avoid the reporters. She need not have worried. A cabinet minister had been caught having his bottom smacked in a brothel, and the papers had lost interest in the TV Cook, her Crazed Cousin and their Demon Lover.

She paced the cinder paths between the ugly shrubberies, looking at the neat lines of tombstones, and wondering why so many people chose to decorate them with heaps of green pebbles like lumps of nougat. It was ten in the morning, grey and muggy. Ernestine thought: I'm the only person here who's not in a box. Her relief at finding no reporters had collapsed into depression. Nobody waiting, nobody mourning. Nobody expecting more than another number on the production line. At the deserted gatehouse, he was posted on the list of the day's funerals – Ferrars, Number Four.

The chapels dotted the vast body park like squat, red-brick mushrooms. Ernestine had gone to Number Four, and seen the undertaker's men chatting with the sexton among the dripping rhododendrons. The back of the hearse was open, the coffin simply waiting to be unloaded, like a crate of fish.

Unable to bear the loneliness, she had fled, to kill time until the appearance of the priest. Then, at least, there might be some semblance of dignity. Since they had taken him out of her arms, Johnny's body had suffered all kinds of humiliations. He had been photographed by the police, unzipped at the post mortem, then left in a fridge in Norwich until released for burial.

Ernestine did not know who had arranged for its transportation, or paid for the undertaker. Could Melissa have done it, without being discovered? This was a silly thought, but Ernestine still expected to see Melissa round every corner. They had found her car in a field a few miles from Quenville. Somehow, she had got herself to London and removed large sums, in cash, from Will's bank account. And that was the last of her. At the height of public interest, Ernestine had appeared on the television news, tearfully begging Melissa to turn herself in.

Secretly, though she longed and pined for her cousin, she hoped she would not come back. They would shut her away in an institution – an idea so dreadful that Ernestine dreamed of it, and woke up whimpering. Melissa had suffered enough.

Tess, who seemed to blame herself for the whole affair, had not understood Ernestine's concern. 'If you want to be kind to her, darling, you should pray she gets help. Stop imagining she thinks and feels like you do.'

But Ernestine had always known how Melissa felt, and she knew now. She would never get over the loss of Johnny. Somewhere, she was dying of grief – Ernestine felt it, like the ghost of a severed limb. Melissa was never coming back. She had known for certain when she returned to Monksby, to pack the furniture for storage. The drawing room had been carpeted with broken glass, and a pile of empty gilt frames lay in an untidy heap on the sofa. The Seddon drawings, symbol of Melissa's lifelong dream, were gone. Ernestine realized then that the dream, as represented by the drawings, was immortal – more potent, in Melissa's obsessive imagination, than the house itself.

Loneliness was the theme of the day. Ernestine was as solitary as poor Johnny, in his coffin. Once she had despised self-pity. Now she was rotten with it, to the point of sitting up half the night over scummy cups of coffee, telling herself that all love was dead and life was useless. She could not even cry, and this made her sadder than ever. Johnny, who had known so little love in his wretched life, would be sent off without a single tear.

A dirty yellow sun was struggling through the pall of

cloud. Ernestine was hot inside the black linen suit she had bought for Giles's funeral. She turned back towards the chapel, hitching up the waistband. The weight was falling off her again. The producer of her television programme, already infuriated by the scandal, had lectured her about getting too thin.

She halted suddenly on the path. A tall figure in a grey suit was furtively smoking outside the door, whisking up his cuff to look at his watch. He saw her, and tossed away the cigarette.

'Thank God. I was beginning to think you wouldn't show.'

'Frank? What on earth are you doing here?'

'Hell, you know how I love funerals.'

Ernestine said: 'It was you, wasn't it?'

He folded her in his arms. She automatically went rigid, as a reaction to the sudden rush of warmth. She had seen him at the inquest, but she had not answered the daily messages he left on her machine. He was another figure from the distant past.

'I guessed you were too caught up to see to the practicalities,' he said.

'You were right. I felt awful about forgetting him. God, I was relieved to find it had all been dealt with. It's very kind of you.'

Frank stroked her cheek, his big hand incredibly gentle. 'You're disappointed. You hoped it might be Mel.'

'Not hoped, exactly . . . Oh, all right. Yes, I did.'

'Let her go, Ernie. She won't be back – she's not stupid.'

'If I just knew where she was.'

'I know. If only.'

They were silent for a moment. Then Ernestine said: 'I never imagined it might be you. I didn't think you liked Johnny enough to pay for his funeral.'

Frank's eyes were tender, gazing down into her face. 'I owed him. He taught me a lesson I should have swallowed years ago.'

'Did he?'

'He recognized the difference between real love and the paste variety. He was smart enough to choose the right cousin. While I was still hung up on Melissa.'

'You were hung up on her, then,' Ernestine said. 'I never heard you admit it before.'

'I'm a fool, is the long and short of it. I teach literature, and I can't even recognize a decent poem when I see it. Or the real beauty that makes a fit subject for poetry. "To make a happy fireside clime,/ To wean and wife,/ That's the true pathos and sublime/ Of human life."'

'How lovely. Tennyson?'

Frank grinned suddenly. 'Robert Burns. He may be adored by guys in skirts, but he recognized the true sublime. It has nothing to do with women like Melissa.' He took her hand. 'And everything to do with women like you.'

'Oh, Frank – don't, please.'

'Sorry. Let's go inside.'

He kept hold of her hand, and Ernestine was inexpressibly glad to have him beside her. Alone, she could not have faced the coffin, so isolated among the rows of empty pews. An elderly priest was there, poring over a clipboard which he hastily put down when he saw them. She remembered Giles telling her once that retired clergy made a nice few quid out of funerals.

'Er – mourners for John – er – Ferrars?'

Frank put his arm around Ernestine's shoulders. 'Yes.'

'Good-oh. If you'd like to pop into a pew, we can start.'

He took his place at the bare altar, and Ernestine desperately tried to think about Johnny. It was like thinking of a character in fiction – she could not summon a single throb of emotion. She had gone through blame, thinking that Melissa might have been all right if he had never appeared. Then she had pitied his loveless history. Now, she felt nothing.

While the priest rattled out the Roman Catholic service, with his solemn gaze fixed rather obviously on the clock above the door, Frank whispered: 'Nice flowers. Are they yours or mine?'

409

'Aren't they mine? God – did you send the same?'

'It was all I could think of.'

They were dark red roses, tight and velvety. Ernestine had hurriedly chosen them the previous day, in memory of the roses Johnny had brought her on the only occasion they made love. And then as now Frank had had the same thought.

She began to giggle. Immediately, Johnny was in front of her again. She saw his eyes, striped and insolent, smelled his hair and heard his low laugh. She remembered how her arms had ached with holding him, and how she had not known he was dead until she had seen the expression of horror on Craig's impassive face.

He had said he would lie against her heart. She prayed, to whatever force one was meant to pray to, that he had found his warm place, at last. The glacier of indifference inside her melted. She was crying.

Frank's arm was round her again. He held her close to the comforting, solid bulk of his shoulder, letting her sob out all her grief for Johnny, Melissa, Will, Giles – lost loves, lost friends, lost dreams.

Afterwards, when they had moved to the seared grass beside the open grave, she realized why funerals were so important. They forced out the sorrow, instead of allowing it to fester under the skin. The sexton handed them a little shovel, and Ernestine and Frank scattered earth on the lid of Johnny's coffin.

The two identical bunches of roses lay side by side on the newly turned earth.

'The ones on the coffin were yours,' Frank said. 'Well, I'm glad. "All my Love, Ernestine" sounds a hell of a lot better than "Regards, Frank Darcy".'

She laughed. '"Regards?" Frank, honestly.'

'"Best wishes" was like somebody's autograph. And I didn't love the guy. We're both Catholics, don't forget. So I may have to meet him again some day.'

'I bet you're looking forward to that.'

'We had a lot in common. Like I said, we chose the right cousin.'

Ernestine said: 'It took you long enough.'

'Ernie, I'm not joking. I knew I'd made a mistake the minute I let you walk away from me.' Frank took both her hands, and gravely kissed her palms. 'Seriously, why do you think I wanted Johnny Ferrars to have a decent burial? Because he died for you. Never mind what else he did with his life. He did that.' His blue eyes were moist. Softly, he murmured:

> 'If I were loved as I desire to be,
> What is there in the great sphere of the earth,
> And range of evil between death and birth,
> That I should fear, – if I were loved by thee?'

She felt the warm strength of his fingers, clasped around her. 'Well,' she said, 'you've nothing to fear, then. You know you're loved by me, so you don't need the Tennyson.'

'That quote was for Johnny too. This is for you, Ern – come back. Drape my new apartment in tasteful pastels. Put on some weight, before you waste away. Get fat. Better still, get married.'

For a long moment, Ernestine looked up into his face. Out of habit, she was tipping back her head, and he was meeting her halfway by crouching slightly – the disparity in their heights had been a joke once.

'I don't know, Frank. This is hardly the time.'

'But you'll think about it.'

'I might.'

They turned their backs on the heaped soil and the deep red roses, and walked, arm in arm, towards the cemetery gates. Both were peaceful, seeing no point in the future at which their paths would divide again.

Epilogue

'Fellow Bohemians,' Dash pronounced in his rolling, flourishing voice, 'before I fulfil my traditional function of proposing the toast, I would like to take this opportunity to thank Mr and Mrs Darcy for their hospitality. And to complain, ever so slightly, about the underhand way in which they sneaked off to the Oxford registry office without telling any of us.'

'Hear, hear!' Cecily interrupted. 'It was desperately mean of you, Ernie. I'd set my heart on being your matron of honour.'

'On second thoughts,' Dash continued, 'it was a highly sensible decision, which spared us all the pain of seeing poor Cecily decked in flowers, like a cow at a pagan sacrifice.'

There was general laughter, even from Craig. Cecily said crossly: 'Oh, I see. The same old jokes, too.'

The Wild Young Bohemians, reduced to three companionable couples, were grouped around Ernestine's big pine table, now the centrepiece of the Darcys' elegant Boars Hill dining room. For old times' sake, they had eaten watercress soup, roast duck, and Ernestine's legendary chocolate trifle. They were now sagging comfortably on the six Shaker chairs, shipped over by Frank's parents as a wedding present. There was, as yet, no other furniture in the room. The empty claret and champagne bottles were lined up on the bare floorboards, beside the door.

Dash, twirling his glass in one hand, and caressing the pocket of his violet brocade waistcoat with the other, was standing in his place, as if delivering a Shakespearian soliloquy. 'I would also like to ask – does anyone mind if we dispense with the ritual of smashing the glasses?'

'I bought them for breaking,' Frank said.

'My dearest old darling, at the risk of sounding like an old poop, I'm terrified of waking the babies. I don't know about the infant Lennox, but Ms Imogen Dashwood is a dreadfully light sleeper. I swear to you, she wakes if I get an erection in the next room.'

'Wait till you have a brat,' Bella told Ernestine. 'When she finds herself in her travel-cot, her fury will know no bounds.'

'Oh, Jack's never any trouble,' Cecily proudly informed the table. 'You can put him down anywhere, and he's out for hours. Sometimes, we have to wake him up!'

'My God,' Bella muttered, just loud enough for Ernestine to hear, 'they're boring the poor child to death already.'

'Mind you,' Cecily said. 'He was very unsettled after that terrible business at Quenville.'

Ernestine flinched, and there was a sudden, frigid silence. Cecily went on obliviously eating macaroons, until Dash said: 'Darling, does your foot ever leave your mouth?'

'What? What? Are we all supposed to pretend it never happened?'

'Yes!'

'Well, I'm sorry,' Cecily said huffily.

Ernestine had started laughing. 'No, it's fine. Stop teasing her, Dash.'

'Craig saved her life, you know.' Cecily was in full flood. 'We were the last people to speak to Melissa, before she took off. She showed me all round Quenville.'

The word had been spoken.

Frank said: 'Shut up, Cec.' Leaning over, he picked up Ernestine's hand, and kissed her wedding ring.

'I think it's healthy to talk about things openly. It's not natural, just sitting here chatting. And I'm involved, so I think I have a right to ask questions. Like what you're going to do with Quenville now.'

'Nothing to do with me,' Ernestine said. She tried to keep up the smile, but it was stretched thinly over very evident pain. 'Until – until she comes back, I expect it will do what Quenville has always done. Which is fall into ruins. And then, one day, it will vanish altogether.'

Silence had fallen across the table, chilling them all, as if a spectre had suddenly walked into the room.

'Maybe you're right,' Ernestine said, 'and we should be talking about it all.'

'I was going to hint at it in my speech,' said Dash. 'Obliquely, without a welly protruding between my lips. Great heavens, Cecily, will you never learn tact?'

Cecily frowned, and opened her mouth to argue.

The whole table chorused: 'Shut up!' and collapsed into laughter. Even Cecily eventually joined in.

'We ought to be grateful,' Dash said. 'At least she hasn't changed. Unlike the rest of us. I certainly didn't think, the first time I proposed this toast, that I was headed for a career of such devastating inanity. Or that dear old Frankers, who once shared my squalid loft, would be living in a palace that would not disgrace a television commercial. It only needs me, dressed as a gnome and peeping coyly from a paintpot, to make it complete.'

All tension had gone. The other Bohemians howled at this reference to poor Dash's latest career-move. Smiling and nudging each other's feet under the table, they exchanged affectionate glances.

Dash's voice softened and vibrated. 'But the changes are only on the outside. All of us are married, some of us are parents, most of us have mortgages and drive exceedingly dull cars. Scratch us, however, and we are Wild Young Bohemians still. Will you please rise, and charge your glasses for the toast?'

They all stood up. The moment was unexpectedly solemn. Ernestine and Bella caught each other wiping away tears, and smiled self-consciously. Frank moved round the table, to put his arms round Ernestine as if he would never let her go.

Dash raised his glass. 'To youth, hedonism, brilliance and beauty. They never have faded, and they never will.' His voice shook. He cleared his throat, and said, with barely a hint of a flourish: 'Love being stronger than death, ladies and gentlemen, I give you – Absent Friends.'

ALSO AVAILABLE IN ARROW

Lily-Josephine

'I loved *Lily-Josephine*. Kate Saunders is such a
wonderful writer . . .' Jilly Cooper

Lily-Josephine had a talent for love. Wilful, enchanting and
passionate, she was the centre of a charmed universe – until her
foolish, indulgent father married again.

Like Snow-Drop in Grimms' fairy tale, Lily ran from her jealous
stepmother one idyllic summer evening in 1941. She escaped to
find sanctuary but, at Randalls, discovered a love far greater than
any she had ever known . . .

A generation later the events set in train that night begin to unravel
when Sophie Gently falls in love with Octavius Randall and
the bizarre and tragic history linking their families is uncovered.
Not until ancient passions and betrayals have been confronted
can Lily-Josephine – long gone, but never forgotten – truly be
laid to rest.

arrow books

Night Shall Overtake Us

Kate Saunders

'If it is possible to imagine Jeffrey Archer and Jilly Cooper pooling their talents, *Night Shall Overtake Us* is exactly the sort of book they would produce' *Sunday Telegraph*

In Edwardian England a vow of friendship is a thing of innocence. Even when tested by the passionate militancy of the suffragette movement or the rigorous demands of the Season, the bonds between Rory, Eleanor, Jenny and Francesca hold fast. But nothing can withstand the unprecedented onslaught of the First World War – and as the best of an entire generation is extinguished on the battlefields of Europe, a schoolgirl pledge, too, lies broken . . .

'Saunders writes with real pathos . . . a rattling good yarn' Rosie Thomas, *Sunday Times*

'Sex, suspense and rip-roaring romance' *The Times*

'A rich, rollicking novel you don't put down easily' *Independent on Sunday*

'Saunders joins the blockbuster hall of fame with this big splash of a romantic novel' Maureen Owen, *Daily Mail*

arrow books

Trust Me I'm a Vet

Cathy Woodman

City vet Maz Harwood has learned the hard way that love and work don't mix. So when an old friend asks her to look after her Devonshire practice for six months, Maz decides running away from London is her only option.

But country life is trickier than she feared. It's bad enough she has to deal with comatose hamsters, bowel-troubled dogs and precious prize-winning cats, without having to contend with the disgruntled competition and a stubborn neighbour who's threatening to sue over an overzealous fur cut!

Worse still, she discovers Otter House Veterinary Clinic needs mending as much as her broken heart. Thank goodness there's an unsuitable distraction, even if he is the competition's deliciously dashing son . . .

Praise for Cathy Woodman's previous novels:

'Funny, truthful and original . . . I loved this book'
Jill Mansell

'Her style has a lightness of touch that can bring a smile, but also poignant moments that can bring a tear to the eyes'
Writing Magazine

arrow books

Must Be Love

Cathy Woodman

It must be love. What other reason could there be for city vet Maz's contentment with her new country life? The vet's practice where she's a partner with her best friend Emma is thriving, and so is her relationship with the gorgeous Alex Fox-Gifford.

But then circumstances force Emma to take a break from the practice, and Maz's life spirals out of control. What with working all hours trying to keep things going, fending off insults from Alex's parents, keeping one eye on the lusty locum – who's causing havoc amongst the village girls – and dealing with Emma's precarious mental state, it won't take much to upset the apple cart. So when she gets some unwelcome news, only time will tell whether Maz and Alex's love can withstand the fallout.

Praise for Cathy Woodman:

'Funny, truthful and original . . . I loved this book' Jill Mansell

'Woodman's warmth and wit are set to make her the next big thing in rural romance.' *Daily Record*

arrow books

Heiresses

Lulu Taylor

They were born to the scent of success. Now they stand to lose it all . . .

Fame, fashion and scandal, the Trevellyan heiresses are the height of success, glamour and style.

But when it comes to . . .

. . . WEALTH: Jemima's indulgent lifestyle knows no limits; Tara's one purpose in life, no matter the sacrifice, is to be financially independent of her family and husband; and Poppy wants to escape its trappings without losing the comfort their family money brings.

. . . LUST: Jemima's obsession relieves the boredom of her marriage; while Tara's seemingly 'perfect' life doesn't allow for such indulgences; and Poppy, spoiled by attention and love throughout her life, has yet to expose herself to the thrill of really living and loving dangerously.

. . . FAMILY: it's all they've ever known, and now the legacy of their parents, a vast and ailing perfume empire, has been left in their trust. But will they be able to turn their passion into profit? And in making a fresh start, can they face their family's past?

arrow books

ALSO AVAILABLE IN ARROW

Midnight Girls

Lulu Taylor

From the bestselling author of *Heiresses*

From the prestigious dormitories of Westfield to the irresistible socialite scene of present-day London: everywhere Allegra McCorquodale goes, scandal follows her. And in Allegra's shadow are her closest friends since school, the Midnight Girls.

Romily de Lisle: super rich, brilliant and bored. She's as blessed as Allegra when it comes to looks, but she's a force to be reckoned with. And Imogen Heath: pretty, timid and hopelessly drawn to Allegra's reckless charm. She longs to be a part of the glitzy high-society world where her friends move with such ease.

Once free of the cloistered worlds of school and university, greed, tragedy and sinister passions threaten the girls allegiance and each of them stand to lose what they love most . . .

Praise for Lulu Taylor's *Heiresses*

'Addictive, decadent and sexy' *heat*

'This is such great escapism it could work as well as a holiday'
Daily Mail

'Pure indulgence and perfect reading for a dull January evening'
Sun

arrow books